The Girl Who Broke the Rules

MARNIE RICHES

avon.

AVON
A division of HarperCollins*Publishers*
The News Building
1 London Bridge Street
London SE1 9GF

www.harpercollins.co.uk

First published in Great Britain in ebook format by HarperCollins*Publishers* 2015
This paperback edition published by HarperCollins*Publishers* 2018

1

Marnie Riches asserts the moral right to
be identified as the author of this work

A catalogue record for this book
is available from the British Library

ISBN: 9780008271459

This novel is entirely a work of fiction.
The names, characters and incidents portrayed in it are
the work of the author's imagination. Any resemblance to
actual persons, living or dead, events or localities is
entirely coincidental.

Set in Minion by Palimpsest Book Production Limited, Falkirk, Stirlingshire

Printed and bound in Great Britain by CPI Group (UK) Ltd, Croydon CR0 4YY

THE GIRL WHO BROKE THE RULES

MARNIE RICHES grew up on a rough estate in Manchester, aptly within sight of the dreaming spires of Strangeways Prison. Able to speak five different languages, she gained a Master's degree in Modern & Medieval Dutch and German from Cambridge University. She has been a punk, a trainee rock star, a pretend artist, a property developer and professional fundraiser.

Marnie is the author of the bestselling George McKenzie series of eBook thrillers, the first of which, *The Girl Who Wouldn't Die*, won The Patricia Highsmith Award for Most Exotic Location in the Dead Good Reader Awards, 2015. In 2016, the series was shortlisted for The Tess Gerritsen Award for Best Series (Dead Good Reader Awards).

BACKSTAIRS
BILLY

THE GIRL WHO BROKE THE RULES

PROLOGUE

Amsterdam, red light district, 16–17 January

The jagged pain between her shoulder blades was fleeting. Magool flinched. Breathed in sharply at the unpleasant sensation. She loosened her seatbelt. Wriggled in the passenger seat to look behind her.

In the dark, there was nothing to see.

Then, she tried to reach behind to feel the leather. But her hands would not move. She stared down at them, bemused. They felt neither leaden nor numb. It was simply as if they no longer existed. And yet, there they sat, chapped from the cold, bitten nails, primly folded over her wringing-wet, jeans-clad thighs.

Frowning, aware of her accelerated heartbeat, she tried to lift her legs, move her feet, wiggle her toes. Nothing. Why was her body not obeying her brain? She looked askance at the driver.

'I can't move,' she said in Dutch. 'What's going on?'

The driver stared resolutely ahead. Peering through the windscreen of the car as hail rattled onto the glass, accompanied by fat snowflakes. Swept by the wiper-blades into thin white columns on the windscreen's periphery that grew thicker and thicker with every second that passed; white screens closing slowly on the real world.

'Hey! Stop the car! Something's wrong, I'm telling you. I can't

1

feel a thing.' With difficulty, Magool could still turn her head – enough to see the side of her driver's face. 'Did you hear me?'

Silence enveloped her, and she realised her words had not sounded at all except inside her head. Through the windscreen, she could just about make out the white-dusted cobbles of the road. The snow, illuminated by the bright, triangular shafts of the streetlights, came down like yellow-gold icing sugar, falling through a sieve. But where the hell were they going on this beautiful, foul night? Not towards her apartment, she was certain. And what was happening to her?

She started to loll forward, held in her seat only by the belt. The driver reached out and with a large, strong hand, pushed her up against the window.

'Don't want you to hit your head, do we? Try to relax, Noor. It won't hurt.' Her captor had finally spoken in a kindly voice. 'I've given you a very strong spinal block. The syringe was rigged in your seat. But try not to worry. I promise you, I know what I'm doing.'

Magool wanted to scream. Her brain shrieked for help; phantom hands hammered on the window each time they passed a figure on the street, huddled in dark winter clothes, braving the blizzard. Unaware of the young girl who was imprisoned in the same vehicle that had just splattered their work trousers with virgin slush.

With only her mind unfettered, she considered the sequence of events that had brought her to this terrible place.

Standing in her booth, she had watched with fascination when the flakes began to waft down from the heavens. Pink sky over-head, as though the very neon lights of Amsterdam's red light district were reflected in the snow clouds hanging above her in the night sky. It was the first time she remembered ever having seen snow. The mangroves that clung to the coastline like grasping old men's hands; the turquoise splendour of the Indian Ocean; the baking heat of her homeland – they were all half a world away. Now, the hail came down among the snow, making the same musical rattling noise against the glass door of her booth that the tropical rains of the Gu and Dayr wet seasons had made on the corrugated iron roof of her family's shack.

Just hours earlier, watching that snow, Magool had felt something bordering on elation. She was finally safe. On these crimson-lit streets, she was Noor. Different girl. Different continent. Different life. Magool resolved, there and then, as the hail pounded against the glass door to her booth, to look upon her parents' selling her and her infant brother to the al Shabaab militia men as an act driven by desperation, not greed. They had thought, perhaps, that she and little Ashkir would both have a good life in that exotic, far-off place they called Italy. Hadn't the soldiers promised?

When she had arrived in the arid, rubble wasteland of Mogadishu, clutching the squalling infant, her hope had faded quickly. Tears had pricked the backs of her eyes as she remembered Ashkir being plucked from her bosom by those corrupt African Union troops. Burundian men, who had laughed heartily and exchanged easy greetings with her couriers.

She had overheard them saying that her brother was destined for adoption in Milan. But, at thirteen, she had been too old to be adopted.

Magool had cursed the name that marked her out as the early flowering girl. Had cursed her parents, each time the men forced themselves on her. Her own kind, amid the diesel-stink and filth of the ramshackle Somali ship. Then, white men when she reached Rome. There was no distinction to be made between them. By the time she had escaped the cocaine fug of nightly abuse and arrived in Amsterdam on the train, she was already five months pregnant. Not showing yet.

Two full years later, now. Watching the snow and feeling hopeful, just as that charlatan showed up, knocking on her window. She should have known better than to let him in.

He had caressed the jagged, lumpy line of her caesarean scar before putting his hand between her legs.

'You healed well,' he said, kissing her neck.

She bit her tongue. Swallowed the retort. Money was money and he'd paid up front.

He lay down on the narrow bed and pulled her on top. Guiding her onto him. Hands on her small breasts. 'Tell me I'm the best,' he said, closing his eyes. 'Faster.' His voice was high. His breath came short. 'Tell me again how I saved your life.'

As she stared down at his corpulent pink body with its nauseating smattering of fluffy blond chest hair that crawled from one flabby tit to another, she fantasised about strangling him with her bare hands. Her small slender fingers would never stretch around that red bull neck. He was twice her size.

'I saved you, Noor,' he said, thrusting himself upwards into her.

Her words slipped out, unchecked.

'You're a butcher,' she said. 'I have to charge less because of you.'

The fat pig showed no remorse. He did not even open his eyes to look at her. Merely smiled, gripped her tightly by the hips and ground her pelvis harder towards him. 'Nonsense. I'm a master craftsman. Black skin just scars more.'

Afterwards, they had squabbled over the fee. He snatched up the euros he had given her at the start and stuffed them under the bulk of his body.

'Come and get it, little Noor!' he said, starting to laugh. Glee in his eyes.

What was this? Some kind of perverse game? Wasn't it enough that he had cut her baby out of her in that cold, damp back room he called a surgery and stitched her back up like an old sack? Fury flared within her.

'Give me my money back!' she said, trying to roll him over to reach the notes.

He grabbed her by the wrists and pushed her away so that she fell against the wall. Suddenly, fear snuffed out the flames of her anger.

'What made you think I would pay, you dumb bitch?' He pulled the foreskin back down on his flaccid, spent manhood. A sea slug stuck to his thigh. 'You owe me. You'll always owe me.'

She rose to her feet. Backed into the corner, folding her arms over her naked chest. 'I already paid through the nose!' she said, wanting to show this beast that she wouldn't be trifled with. Wanting him to see that she wasn't a defenceless little girl. But she knew her body language betrayed her and she was annoyed by the waver in her voice. 'Give me the cash or I'll report you to the authorities!'

He smiled brightly. 'An underage, illegal Somali immigrant, working as a whore? Report me, a pillar of the community? I don't think I'll be losing any sleep on that front, little Noor. Do you?'

He was already dressed. Stuffing the notes back into his wallet, now. Magool steeled herself to step forward and snatch it from him. But the doctor sensed her intentions, leaned in and punched her hard in the face.

Her cheek stung. Tears sprang from her eyes against her will. She failed to swallow them back.

'Get out, then! Go on! Fuck off and don't come round here again. Ever.'

But as he opened the door, he looked back at her. A pause that perhaps betrayed the flicker of remorse in those bloodshot blue eyes. He reached inside the breast pocket of his overcoat and retrieved the leather wallet. Pulled out a twenty. Threw it at her.

'No hard feelings?' he said.

She picked up the money from the threadbare brown carpet. Pushed it back into his hand.

'Stick your money up your ass, *sharmuutaa ku dhashay*! You

need this more than me,' she said, bundling him out the door and locking it behind him.

Waiting until the clatter on the stairs and the glazed door slamming marked his departure, she crouched in her small room and clutched her knees. Allowed herself to weep, but not for long. Cursed him and vowed she would get even one day. Somehow.

Her thoughts turned to her shared bedsit.

Enough for one night. It was time to shut up shop and go home. Get her shit together so that, tomorrow, she could face a new day. Hell, the weather was terrible anyway.

Outside, the mixture of hail and snow bit into her flesh. Her jeans and even her padded coat seemed to provide no protection from the unforgiving elements. Peering ahead down the street, it was as though she were watching whiteout static on the old black and white TV her parents had in their shack back home. And it had looked so picturesque from inside her booth. It would be an arduous walk back.

At first, she had not noticed the dark Lexus sliding slowly alongside her. She walked ahead of the car, pulling her hood further down over her eyes; following what she saw at her feet as a guide to which direction home lay in. But when the car edged forward and remained at her side, she lifted her hood to see if it was a familiar punter, hoping she might reconsider, retreat and reopen the shop.

The Lexus stopped. The driver's window opened just enough for her to see who was behind the wheel.

'You?' she said. Hard to keep the incredulity out of her voice.

'Get in!' the driver said.

Magool clutched her shoulder bag across her chest defensively. 'I said I never wanted to see you again.'

'Look, it's a storm out there. It's warm in here. I'll drive you home. You're wringing wet.'

'No thanks. I'll walk it.'

'Come on! Don't be ridiculous. I've got heated seats.' Placatory tone. Friendly eyes. The driver's face and body language were benign. 'Get in, for God's sake!'

By now, she was quaking with the cold. Beyond uncomfortable. Despite sensing that the driver's concerned gesture was off key, Magool walked round to the passenger side. Opened the car's heavy door and registered the sting between her shoulder blades, as she sank back into the luxurious, leather heated seat...

The snow had stopped falling by the time Magool Osman returned to the red light district. Her makeshift bed was a bench beneath the windows of the Old Sailor Café Bar at the junction of Oudezijds Achterburgwal and the cobbled alley of Molensteen. Fittingly opposite the Erotic Museum, and ironically within spitting distance of her compatriots in their relatively safe, red-lit booths. But she had been dropped off after her final ordeal in the small hours, when only the water rats and the ghosts of Amsterdam's Golden Age roamed those streets. The darkest hours before an unforgiving, wintry dawn.

Just after 6.30am, Magool's empty eye sockets stared blankly up at Chief Inspector Paul van den Bergen. With a cracking hip, wishing he had had time for breakfast and a coffee before leaving home, he crouched to get a better look at this young woman:

Dark skin. Diminutive stature. Completely naked. Frozen solid, with a dusting of ice that still sparkled like fake diamond dust beneath the harsh light in the makeshift forensic tent.

He thumbed his white stubble in contemplation of her corpse; once a thing of beauty, now defiled and incomplete. It was as though the girl had been unzipped from her throat to her pubic area, revealing all the fragile matter that lay beneath. Chest framed by the white stripes of her ribs, which had been split down the sternum and levered apart. Where once her lungs must have breathed in this sharp, Amsterdam air; where once her stomach might have digested a moreish meal; where once her kidneys and liver might have filtered celebratory wine...now, there were but gaping holes, frozen blood and a mere suggestion of the life and hope that had once inhabited such a young body.

Elvis, one of van den Bergen's two most loyal protégés, moved the flap of the tent aside. He entered the scene, wearing white plastic overshoes.

Van den Bergen rose to his full height. Noticed the alarmed grimace on his subordinate's face.

'Stop gawping, Elvis,' he said. 'Show some fucking respect for the dead.'

'Sorry, boss.' Elvis covered his nose, though the icy conditions meant there was nothing unpleasant to smell. 'What do you want me to do?'

'Is Marianne de Koninck and her team on their way?'

'Yep. Due any minute now.'

Van den Bergen nodded. Sniffed. Acknowledged the black dog lurking inside the tent, outside the tent, in the warmth of his car. Bearing down on him. Casting a long shadow over everything. He swallowed painfully, prodding at the swollen glands beneath his ears. 'My throat's on fire. Think I'm coming down with something. Just my luck, it will be Ebola. Grab me a coffee, will you?'

Van den Bergen withdrew his phone from his coat pocket and brought up his contacts list. Scrolled down to G. There was the number. George McKenzie. He sighed deeply.

CHAPTER 1

Broadmoor Psychiatric Hospital, UK, 17 January

The slight man who sat facing her examined the fingernails at the ends of his slender fingers with an expression of intense concentration. George noted that they were always very clean and manicured. His lank, thinning hair hung sullenly over the shoulders of a faded blue sweatshirt. Dirty dark grey. Starting to recede at the temples. Perhaps his haggard, small-featured face might once have been attractive, given its delicate, perfectly symmetrical bone structure. George shuddered at this thought that had popped, unbidden, into her mind. She averted her gaze from his hands and focussed instead on her pad.

'Cold, Georgina?' Silas Holm asked. A smile playing on his chapped lips, he leaned back in his chair and looked up at the tall, arched windows of the Victorian building. The perfectly white expanse of snow-heavy sky outside was carved up by peeling painted bars that stretched ceiling-wards. 'It's that period of architecture,' he said. 'Terribly draughty because of the lofty proportions, you see. Doesn't matter how much they crank up the heating.'

His gaze found her face and focussed sharply on it, now. George McKenzie knew this much without looking up from her notes. The prison officers said his manner was always one of an attentive vicar, listening with dedicated enthusiasm to the concerns of his adoring flock. It was unclear, therefore, whether Silas Holm was staring at George because he was genuinely engaged by their conversation or whether he was simply fantasising about what he could do to the only woman he was allowed to see on a regular basis, if he still had his liberty. Either way, the fact that he had noticed her shiver – almost imperceptibly, she had thought – made George feel very itchy. She started to arrange her pens in perfectly parallel lines on the desk. Then stopped herself. *Reveal nothing about you as a person or the details of your life,* her Cambridge University supervisor, Dr Sally Wright had told her. Not only was Sally the senior tutor of St John's College – the Big Boss-woman in what was otherwise still a man's world – but she was also the country's foremost criminologist. If she didn't know what she was talking about where handling dangerous psychopaths was concerned, nobody did. *Dress dowdily. Be on your guard. Don't get involved.*

'What's with the tracksuit?' she asked, deliberately steering the focus back onto her study subject. 'Where are your tweeds? What did you do?'

Silas Holm gave a small sigh and a resigned smile. Rapped on his leg with his knuckles. The sound was hollow. 'What could a harmless amputee like me ever do to warrant such a petty punishment? I ask you!'

'Well you must have done something pretty bad to have your normal clothes taken away,' George said. 'It's not like you're in prison.' She shot a questioning sideways glance at Silas' nurse, who was seated at the end of the desk, within reassuring reach of this small but deadly psychopath.

Graham's muscle-bound bulk heaved up and down beneath his T-shirt. Laughing heartily. He smoothed a hand over his shaven head. 'Dr Holm. You are funny,' he said. His Nigerian accent was pronounced. 'You are lucky you weren't transferred back to high dependency. Poor Kenneth! Why don't you tell Ms McKenzie straight about your little set-to with him?'

The small-featured face of Silas Holm appeared suddenly sharp, grey, remorseless. His voice was clipped. Words came fast. 'No. I don't think I will. And I don't think it warranted being singled out this way.' The sneer that turned his mouth into a thin, drooping line and the way that he tugged at the sweatshirt with his finger-tips marked out his disdain for the garment and that place. 'The other men look up to me.' He shuffled in his seat, straightening his posture. But something within him clicked and the friendly smile reappeared. Locked onto George's face with those ice-blue eyes. 'They come to me for wisdom, the men in here,' he told her.

'What sort of wisdom?' George uncapped her pen.

'I know about the world, of course! These oiks know nothing. Most of them are semi-literate at best. I, however, am a man of learning as you know. Before I was subjected to the indignity of coming to this dump, I was celebrated in my field of expertise!' He leaned forward and stretched his fingers out towards George's side of the desk.

'Back up, Dr Holm,' Graham said calmly.

Silas colluded; withdrawing physically but somehow clinging onto the intimacy he had implied was between them by winking and keeping his voice low. 'I won the Evelyn Baker Medal from the Association of Anaesthetists, you know.' Nodding. Matter of fact. Trying to impress.

The session was not progressing as she had hoped. George determined to get her study subject back on track. She tapped the pencil drawing that Silas had brought along to show her. It was the most recent work, contained within a sketch pad that was full of semi-pornographic images.

'Tell me about this, Silas,' she said, pointing to the perfectly executed illustration of a woman in a black gimp mask – only her heavily made-up eyes were visible. Startled, yet alluring. Her mouth was contained behind a brutal-looking zip. Her nose trans-formed into two miserly slits in the black leather. Oddly, she was hanging by her neck from a tree bough. Hanging as though dead,

11

which made the focussed clarity in her eyes all the more alarming. Clad in what appeared to be a black rubber leotard with the breasts and vagina cut out. Two circles. One triangle. 'Why have you drawn her with one leg?'

Her question was met with laughter. 'Oh, come on! You know better than to ask that of me!' Silas said, toying with a strand of his hair almost coquettishly. 'Am I not famed for my specialist taste in erotica?'

His tone was so smug, so arrogant, that George could not stem her response. Neither could she keep the vitriol out of her voice.

'Is she one of your victims, Silas? Is she the prostitute from Middlesbrough that you picked up, strangled, partially dismembered and then masturbated over? Oh no! Silly me. Perhaps she was the prostitute from Nottingham, whose arms were found in your freezer at home? Mother of four. First time on the streets because she owed a loan shark money from Christmas. Last time on the streets because you strung her up from the railings of a local school. Or maybe one of the four others that we know about.'

'Ms McKenzie!' Graham said, raising his eyebrows.

George's red mist cleared and revealed a grinning Dr Silas Holm.

'The trial was a shambles,' Silas said, flicking his tongue over his narrow, discoloured incisors. 'I'm putting together a case that I plan to take to the High Court. It was all circumstantial evidence and I intend to get out of this hellhole.' He examined his fingernails again. Sighed. 'Anyway, if you must know, that is a portrait of a famous Latvian beauty who stars in all the very best erotic horror films. Quality productions. I was quite a fan before coming in here. I think I got her eyes just right.'

Scratching away at her pad, noting down the salient detail of his response, George considered her next question.

'Do you find your own artwork arousing?'

No response.

'What is it about amputation that interests you sexually?'

No response. Silas was peering up at the bars on the windows. He seemed no longer to be listening.

'Silas!' George was careful to keep the impatience out of her voice this time. It was a difficult game of cat and mouse with Silas Holm. On the one hand, she found him repugnant, although he was always perfectly calm and charming when she visited, putting her in mind of a great white shark circling slowly, just beneath the surface of shallow waters. On the other, she needed his responses for her study. She knew how lucky she had been to gain access to this place and to secure the willing participation of men like him. *Keep a lid on it, George. A psycho like him will never stay quiet for long.*

'In your opinion, Silas, did the pornography you used on the outside in any way influence the manner in which you killed your victims? The strangulation. The dismemberment.'

Seemingly bored now, Silas flung his arms behind his head and rolled his eyes. 'Did you see that thing in the news about the eviscerated fishermen? That was *quite* a story. But Kenneth switched the television over to some tawdry soap. Most annoying.'

Dumbfounded. George stopped writing. Stared at him. 'What has that got to do with your violent sexual proclivities and pornography?'

Silas stood and bowed with a flourish. 'Always lovely to see you, Georgina.' He picked up his sketchpad from the desk and nodded to Graham. 'Lunchtime! I'm famished.'

The frustration of not having got what she needed abated incrementally, with each security door that clanged shut behind her, giving way finally to relief that she had completed another session with one of Broadmoor Hospital's most infamous and dangerous residents, without sustaining any personal injury – physical, at least. Only once she had had her mobile phone returned to her at reception did she discover the text from van den Bergen. His words caught her breath.

CHAPTER 2

Amsterdam, the set of a porn film, then, Sloterdijkermeer allotments, later

Watching the actress swig from her bottle of Evian was fascinating. She had such ridiculously full lips from too much collagen filler that merely drinking from a sports-cap looked like an obscene act. Her peroxide blonde hair hung in over-processed clumps down her back. Off camera, the cellulite on her thighs and backside was visible between the straps and buckles of the bondage gear. The inverted 'T' scarring beneath her bare breasts gave the augmentation away, of course, destroying the illusion of perfectly buoyant, round orbs. But despite the actress' flaws, she was striking. Still young. The high cheekbones. The good skin. The bright eyes. Naturally white teeth and an otherwise perfectly worked-out body, with its sculpted obliques and defined triceps. This one was an ideal specimen. Healthy. And these porn actresses were such readily available raw material for a killer, whose job it was to hang out in a professional capacity on the sets of erotic film shoots. Easy pickings. Tarts with hearts of gold.

The actress approached, strutting in those ten-inch platforms. Smiling. Kisses on both cheeks, followed by something on the mouth that was overly familiar and tender.

'Hey! How are you, darling? I didn't see you there. Nice to have you on set.'

Her English was good for an Eastern European of humble origins. Though this woman was humble no longer. She was revered in her circle. Seemed almost a shame, but then, business was business.

'We still going for that drink we talked about?'

Wide-eyes betraying excitement or was it the line of coke the actress had hoovered up as the director had shouted 'Cut' on the previous scene? She reached out with a manicured hand. Her caress was gentle. Flirtatious and promising.

'Why not,' she said. 'When I finish here, right? Just you and me. I'd like that.'

She turned to walk away, poised to resume her position, artfully strung between two posts on some medieval-style wooden contraption that looked like the base of a trebuchet. Where did they get these ridiculous ideas from? The red stripes on her back looked livid.

'Do those hurt?'

The actress looked back and smiled archly. Raised a plucked eyebrow. 'Makeup, sweet thing. You should know that!'

No damage. That was good. And the space was prepared. Perfect.

Van den Bergen sat on a camping stool inside his gloomy cabin, which was situated on a prime plot in Sloterdijkermeer's allotment complex. He had no intention of gardening, of course. Outside, the frozen ground was too unyielding to work, but the afternoon half-light and silence of a freezing cold super-shed was preferable to enduring another afternoon at the station, gawping into the existential void. Listening to that frog-eyed prick, Jaap Hasselblad, pontificate about the girl they had found.

'This is a sex pervert. Mark my words!' Hasselblad had announced. 'Round up the nutters and serial jerk-offs. Bring them all in for questioning. We can't have a dangerous woman-hating psycho on the loose.'

Just because he was the commissioner and had recently been on a criminal psychology refresher course, Hasselblad thought he knew everything. That uniform-clad, industrial strength arse-kisser had not done a day's decent detective work in about fifteen years, van den Bergen mused. Why did he always end up with such utter morons above him?

He cracked open a can of Heineken and swallowed down a tablet for gastric reflux. Thumped himself on the chest as the beer winded him. No, Hasselblad's field of expertise was drinking Kir Royale in Michelin-starred brasseries with slimeball politicians and the other top brass.

'Guy's a wanker,' van den Bergen told the poster of Debbie Harry that was fastened to a damp wooden wall. Curling up in one corner and mottled with mould. 'He's no better than Kamphuis.' He raised his can to the once universally adored singer. 'Just me and you, kiddo. We don't need them.' Then, he turned to the mildewed photo of his father that sat on the table amongst empty pots, seedling trays and a split bag of ericaceous compost. 'Five years.' Made a contemplative clicking noise with his tongue and breathed out heavily. 'Five years, now. Long time.' A fleeting memory of his father, sitting in a chemo chair at the hospital, with the hopeful poison running into his wasted, sinewy arms through a drip. 'Miss you, old man. I hope you're somewhere better. Cheers!'

Van den Bergen drank the freezing lager and was surprised and angered by the tears that seemed to leak from his eyes unbidden. For the second time that day, he thumbed out a text to George, telling her the other dreadful thing that had happened. But as he was about to press send, the phone rang.

'Van den Bergen. Speak!'

'It's Daan Strietman,' a man said.

'Who?'

16

'Marianne's colleague. Forensic Pathology. We met last May at her birthday party. Remember?'

Van den Bergen cast his mind back to a balmy evening, standing on the balcony at Marianne's apartment, wishing he didn't have to make small talk with her inane boyfriend, Jasper, who had brought that sap, Ad Karelse, along because George had been in England and Karelse was 'lonely'. Boo hoo. What a pity. He had no recollection of a Daan Strietman. 'No. Where the hell is Marianne?'

'Norovirus. Listen, come and see me. I've finished the autopsy on your Jane Doe.'

'And?'

'Oh, you'll be interested in this! I've never seen anything like it.'

CHAPTER 3

Soho, London, later

Are u coming back? the text demanded to know.
I miss u. xxx

Ad had only been holed up at Aunty Sharon's for three days, this time, and already he was moaning he was bored. He had British television to watch, for God's sake. In all its multi-channelled, digital and Sky Plus glory. In fact, Aunty Sharon had a dish on top of her garage that was so big and contravened local authority regulations by such an excessive margin, that he could probably pick up broadcasts from outer space, if he used his initiative. How could he possibly be bored? Or he could simply go for a walk. Okay, so maybe a white boy going for a walk down the high street of Aunty Sharon's South East London neighbourhood at dusk was not such a bright idea. But still…

'Stop nagging, man!' she told the phone. Typed out her response:

Missing u 2. Back by 9.x

One kiss. One was enough. The three were getting on her nerves. Always three, sent and expected in return. He was being demanding.

'I've come over here especially,' he had said; hurt visible in those sensitive brown eyes. 'I don't understand why you can't take time off.'

What was there for him to understand? The bills didn't pay themselves. After all, he had just turned up on her doorstep. A surprise wooing that she hadn't solicited, using birthday money from his parents for the flight. Bet they didn't know he was squandering it on his English girlfriend. That sour-faced cow, his mother, certainly wouldn't have given the trip her blessing. Wonder what excuse he'd given them this time? Four years of excuses.

Ad would just have to suck it up.

In the confines of her store cupboard, George squatted on the floor and checked that the thick wad of notes she had taken from her morning meeting with Silas Holm was securely zipped away in the side pocket of her bag.

'Holm's such a perv,' she told the mop.

She donned her polyester overalls and changed into her beat-up old sneakers. Filled the bucket with hot, bleachy water at the crackle-glazed Victorian butler's sink, shoved a range of cleaning products into her deep pockets and emerged into the dimly lit fug of the club. The air was rank with heady, synthetic air fresheners, barely masking the cheap, over-perfumed smell of the girls; the floor sticky with spilled alcohol from the night before.

'*Ciao, bella!*' the manager said, checking his watch. He leaned in for a kiss, which George dodged.

She slammed the heavy bucket onto the floor and started to wring the mop out. Mop, mop, mop by his feet, almost soaking his hand-stitched loafers and brown Farah slacks. 'Wotcha, Derek. Sorry I'm a bit late. I've been rushing around interviewing people. Part of my doctorate, you know?'

Out of earshot of the girls, who were already limbering up on the poles or else in the back, exchanging squealed gossip about the previous night's punters whilst they back-combed their hair,

Derek rounded on her. Grabbed her by the arm. Whispering sharply so that nobody else could hear.

'Not fucking Derek! Giuseppe. I told you.' His grip was sharp – the kind of grip George might have expected from a ratty-looking man who ran a titty bar.

Wanting to knock his ill-fitting toupee from his head but resisting, George pulled her arm free. 'Get off! Just because you're my boss and Aunty Sharon's your barmaid doesn't give you the right to manhandle me,' she said. 'Anyway, you were Derek when you were with Aunty Sharon. What changed?'

He stood poker-straight momentarily and eyed George. A thin-lipped mouth and puffy eyes from too many late nights and vodkas. Aunty Sharon said he had been a royal pain in the arse, but generous with it. Here, beneath the half-light of dusty crystal chandeliers, however, with no other employees within earshot, George didn't like his expression at all.

'Sharon was a long time ago,' he said. 'But me and her are still good mates. Only 'cause of her working here and being something more than a colleague to me that you got this job, right? And I'm running in different circles, now. So, if I say I'm Giuseppe de Falco and not Derek, then it's Uncle Giuseppe to you. Like the other girls. Uncle Fucking Giuseppe. Same as Daddy Fucking Warbucks, but more Italian.'

'Suit yourself, Uncle G,' George said, sucking her teeth and steeling herself to desist from drowning his loafers with mop water.

When she sprayed the brass handrail of the staircase that led down into the club with anti-bacterial spray, she did so with venom. When she wiped the laminate fixtures and PVC uphol-stery, she applied the rough, hot cloth with something bordering on aggression. Polishing mirrors, dappled with greasy fingerprints and, in the VIP area, traces of coke. Wiping semen from the walls of the men's toilet cubicles. Unblocking the women's toilets that choked with stinking discarded tampons and paper towels. It was demeaning, backbreaking work. But the job earned her an honest crust, where her PhD funding wouldn't quite stretch to trips to Amsterdam and the odd night of decadence inside London's better clubs. At least the act of cleaning was therapeutic. Especially after spending a morning with Silas Holm. Especially for someone like George.

As she polished the metal pole on the main stage, she paused to check her phone again. Peered in the gloom at the glowing screen which offered up van den Bergen's alarming, unanswered words.

CHAPTER 4

Amsterdam, mortuary, later

'Paul. Thanks for coming.' The wholly unfamiliar man stood in the spot that Marianne usually graced, by the side of the steel mortuary slab.

Van den Bergen refused to shake his latex-clad hand. 'It's Chief Inspector van den Bergen. And I prefer to deal with Marianne,' he said.

He looked this interloper up and down, though it was difficult to get the full measure of him in his scrubs. He looked young. Fresh face and shiny eyes. Certainly in his early thirties. And small. Though at six feet five, van At home, as the pan of pasta boiled en Bergen could see the top of pretty much everyone's heads as they scrabbled about beneath him. Maybe the guy wasn't small. But he definitely had the upright posture of a cocky little arsehole, van den Bergen decided, and he wasn't the lovely Marianne de Koninck.

Daan Strietman smiled at him. 'I'm her number two. You knew that, right, Paul? She introduced us at the party. Ha! You're such a funny guy. You're pulling my leg, now, aren't you?'

'No.' Van den Bergen scratched at his aching hip. Fingered his scabbed-up knuckles. Hadn't he just told this idiot he was Chief Inspector van den Bergen? Was this guy deaf? And where did this notion of funny come from? 'I want number one. If I want second best, I'll—'

Daan put his clipboard and pen down. Slapped van den Bergen across the back in a chummy style. 'Look, your Jane Doe's in good hands, big feller.'

'But Marianne… She was at the scene this morning.'

'I told you. She's ill. Throwing her guts up. Forget Marianne. Okay?'

Van den Bergen noticed a pause before the okay, which meant Daan Strietman had finally decided that being challenged by a policeman was not okay, even if it was by a senior one. He smiled again. What was with all the smiling? Was this guy simple? The smile disappeared once the idiot noticed his scabbed knuckles.

'Just give me the lowdown on my victim, Strietman. *Okay?*'

Now that she was on the slab, van den Bergen was hoping the girl would look like any other cadaver – a spoiled mannequin, devoid of any remaining trace of vitality; deserted by her humanity, so that only an abstract husk was left; dissected like an oversized scientific experiment. He would find it easy to give a corpse like that the once-over and then listen to the pathologist's report. But she didn't, this Jane Doe. Her elfin face, framed by the wisps of black curly hair that still remained – after her cranium had been removed to allow examination of her brain – was outlandishly at odds with those unseeing eye sockets, staring out at him. Ghoulish. Vulnerable. Her dark skin, which must have been a warm hue when she had breath in her body, was flat grey. But so slight was her build with those spindly little arms and legs, so lost did she look in the aseptic white glare of the mortuary's overhead lights, that van den Bergen had to swallow an unexpected lump in his throat. He almost felt compelled to hug the girl, though she had been utterly disembowelled both by her murderer and by the process of the post mortem. George was slightly built like that. George's skin was dark like that.

Feeling momentarily dizzy, he steadied himself on the steel sink at the dead girl's feet.

Daan Strietman chuckled. 'I wouldn't have put an old hand like you down as squeamish! You want to sit?'

Van den Bergen glared at him. 'I'm not squeamish.' He pointed to his ear. 'I have this balance thing. Sometimes it… Anyway. What did you find?'

'You're not going to believe this.'

CHAPTER 5

Soho, London, later

```
I did a really stupid thing & I can't
tell anyone else. I'm losing my grip.
Call me. Paul.
```

George read the words out loud, as though giving voice to them would reveal the truth behind the cryptic, partial revelation. Should she call? She had been sitting on his text all day. Staring at her phone, as the train had carried her back from Broadmoor. Her heart told her to respond to this wonderful, troubled man. Didn't she spend at least as much time with him during her trips to Amsterdam as she did with her boyfriend? Pottering at the allotment. Talking about music. Life, the universe and everything. Hadn't their bond become the elephant in the room, whenever Ad questioned why she had grown distant and disengaged?

'All right, darling? What you looking so shifty for?' Aunty Sharon asked, grabbing her in a bear hug and planting a lipsticky kiss on her cheek.

'Just a text,' George said.

She made to turn the phone's screen off and slip it into her back jeans pocket beneath her overalls. But surprisingly for a woman of small statue and large volume, Aunty Sharon was agile enough to reach around and snatch the phone right out of her George's hand.

She gazed down at the screen, grinning.

'Aunty Sharon! Gimme the phone, man.'

Her aunt brought the text back up and read the words. 'Paul? Oh, yeah?' Fixed her niece with a knowing look. Nudged her joyfully and a little too energetically, so that her flamboyant head attire wobbled – a sculpture fashioned from a scarf, the colours of the Rasta flag, intertwined with platinum blonde, curly hair extensions that looked incongruous next to her mahogany skin. 'You two-timing that poor Ad with some geez named Paul? Girl, you're harsh!'

George snatched the phone back. Jammed it into her pocket. Relieved that in the dingy light, Aunty Sharon would never suss she was blushing. 'I'm not two-timing anybody. I told you about Paul. It's just van den Bergen.'

'The Dutch cop?'

George nodded. 'He's just a friend, yeah?'

'Oh, really? That why you hiding your phone, then?' For all George's qualifications and finesse and Aunty Sharon's lack of them, this one-time Jamaica Road rose in Betty Boop heels and laddered sparkly tights had the measure of her, all right.

George was searching for a way to change the subject, when three men entered the club. Two of them were tall, burly, wearing outmoded single-breasted leather jackets and cheap shoes. Cropped hair, dark eyes, olive skin. The third was small in stature and somewhat older-looking than the man-mountains that flanked him. Had the beady-eyed look of a coke-head, George swiftly estimated.

'Get out the way and keep your gob shut,' Aunty Sharon said, grabbing the bucket. Thrusting the mop into George's hand. 'Don't attract no attention to yourself. Thems is bad news.'

As she ushered George behind the bar, the men escorted inside four bewildered-looking white girls, who were quickly divested of

26

their fun-furs by a sycophantic, scuttling Derek. Beneath their coats, they wore either string bikinis or lacy lingerie, all covered only by sheer net babydolls, as if they had been provided with uniforms. Heavy makeup. Fluttering eyelashes and bouffant hair. Flawless, tight behinds, which only the really young could boast, George noted. On their feet they wore identical Perspex-soled platform shoes.

'Jesus,' George said, pretending to dust down the vodka and whisky optics that lined the walls when in fact, she was scrutinising the girls. 'They don't look much more than about fourteen.'

Walking uneasily in the vertiginous footwear, they advanced towards the main stage and came to a halt, as if awaiting instruction.

'They're crippled in them bloody stripper shoes, that's for sure!' Aunty Sharon said, wiping a wine glass with a tea towel. 'They're gonna end up with fallen arches.'

The sound system was not yet switched on. George could clearly hear the girls chattering nervously to one another in an Eastern European language. Could have been Russian. Could have been Polish. Who knew? Not George. They blinked fast. Flutter, flutter, butterfly lashes. Taking in their new surrounds, while their escorts spoke to Derek. Clapping him on the shoulder. Nodding. Smiling like old buddies at a reunion.

'Listen that! See how they're chatting in Italian?' Aunty Sharon said, raising an eyebrow. She sucked her teeth long and hard.

'That why he's going round asking everyone to call him Giuseppe?' George spritzed the till with anti-bacterial spray.

Aunty Sharon shook her head. 'He's into something, that scrawny fucking idiot. Well out of his depth. Them geezers been round here three or four weeks running, now. New girls every time. Young foreign girls. They dance for a night or two. Rake it in. Then they're gone. Sometimes it's African girls. Sometimes from the Far East. They don't talk no English. Derek thinks cos his grandfather came from some tin-pot shithole outside Rome that he's fucking mafia or something.'

'Porn king that owns this place know?'

Aunty Sharon shook her head. 'Nah. Don't reckon so. These girls ain't legal. He'd lose his bloody licence. Dermot Robinson ain't that daft. But I'd put money on it that Derek's on some kind of fiddle. Fucking Uncle Giuseppe. Rarseclart.'

The tallest man locked eyes with George. Started to walk towards her.

'You!' he said. Clicked his fingers, as though she were a willing waitress. 'Come here!'

CHAPTER 6

Amsterdam, mortuary, later

'Her vital organs are all but gone. Can you believe it? Kidneys, bladder, pancreas, liver… you name it,' Strietman said. 'Everything except the two biggies – her brain and heart. Hard to tell with so much of her missing what the actual cause of death was. I'd put my money on cardiac arrest. I'll need more time to examine her brain properly.' He gestured towards the girl's groin area with his pen. 'She shows signs of having had rough sexual intercourse either just before death or shortly afterwards. Difficult to tell. No semen, but we lifted a couple of pubic hairs that didn't belong to her. There are some signs of a struggle – thumb prints to her wrists. Bruising to the left side of her face, as though she's been struck, but not trauma like you'd expect from a blunt instrument. Maybe a fist. Beaten, then raped, I guess.'

'Don't guess,' van den Bergen said. 'The sex may have been consensual and the bruising part of rough play.'

Daan Strietman shook his head. 'She's been murdered! It's got to be rape, hasn't it?'

'Has it? That's for me to discern. Continue.'

'Well, I've really never seen anything like it.' The pathologist was smiling again. Almost feverishly. 'I think we've got some kind of ritual sex murder on our hands, here.'

Van den Bergen peered inside the girl's chest cavity where the ribs had been peeled back to reveal black, coagulated blood and a rag-tag confusion of muscle and sinew. 'Have *we*, indeed? Ritual sex murder. Why do you say that?'

'Well, her uterus is gone.'

'Yes, along with pretty much everything else, you're telling me. Any trauma to the genitals other than what you'd normally expect from intercourse?'

The sombre proceedings were interrupted by a woman, knocking at the door.

'Knock, knock! Can I come in?' she asked. A cheerful voice. Searching eyes. Looked over at Strietman and smiled. 'Hello, Daan. They said it would be okay for me to come straight down here.'

'Sabine!' Strietman beckoned the woman inside. 'Perfect timing! Paul, this a good friend of Marianne's – a very well-respected paediatrician.'

Van den Bergen moved away from the slab and was leaned against a tall storage cabinet. Arms folded; long legs entwined around each other. Wasn't sure about this interloper.

Strietman offered the woman a typing chair to sit on. 'I felt I needed a second opinion from someone who knows more about children's physiology than me, since our Jane Doe shows signs of aggravated sexual assault and has given birth underage.'

Sabine perched elegantly, with the perfect posture of a yoga enthusiast on the edge of her chair. Ran a manicured hand through her long, thick chestnut-coloured hair. Van den Bergen assessed she was in her early forties, but she had that youthful glow to her skin that said this was a woman who looked after herself. Expensive-looking clothes. Nothing flashy. Pale grey co-ordinated knitwear. Leggings that emphasised her long, slender legs.

'Anyway. Formal introductions,' Strietman said, clapping his hands together. 'Paul, this is Dr Sabine Schalks. Sabine, this is

Chief Inspector Paul van den Bergen. There. Now we all know one another.'

Sabine examined the Jane Doe. 'Interesting,' she said. 'There are signs of partial female genital mutilation, but the scar tissue is old, indicating that it was performed years ago and not related to this girl's death. Your Jane Doe must come from an Islamic country. Possibly East African.'

Van den Bergen nodded. 'Anything else?'

Sabine Schalks backed away from the body and sighed. 'She's definitely a victim of sexual abuse. She could only have been about thirteen when she was carrying her child. Tragic. Absolutely tragic. Worse still that she's ended up in here.' She turned to Strietman, eyebrows raised. 'What are the other circumstances of her death, in your opinion?'

Strietman thumbed his chin. 'She's suffered what we call a catecholamine "storm".' The pathologist made exclamation marks in the air with his blue, gloved fingers. 'Her body's been flooded by catecholamines – hormones made by the adrenal glands – and that's caused ventricular damage to the heart. It's often related to an overdose of cocaine or psychedelic drugs. There are MAOIs in her blood.' He turned to van den Bergen. 'Know what those are?'

'Monoamine oxidase inhibitors,' van den Bergen offered. 'Used to treat depression.'

'How do you know that?' Strietman's eyebrows shot up. He studied the chief inspector with something bordering on fascination. As though van den Bergen himself was a subject to be dissected, weighed and pronounced upon.

Van den Bergen wasn't giving this over-enthusiastic dipshit anything. He remained silent. Peered down his nose at the younger man. Shot a furtive glance at the paediatrician. 'What the hell have anti-depressants got to do with ritual murder?'

The feverish grinning continued.

Did this asshole think he was putting forward a case for

winning the Nobel Prize? Or did he aspire to swap careers, trading his coroner's stink and the solitude of the morgue for the lingering, heady musk of IT Marie's three-day-old BO when they were pulling overnighters on a big case? Van den Bergen longed for the familiar sparring he enjoyed with the entirely sober Marianne. Wondered if George had read his text. He'd heard nothing. Yet.

Strietman expanded: 'Well, Paul, MAOIs are used by spiritual drug users to increase the bioavailability of the hallucinogenic, DMT. In other words, MAOIs help them get a better psychedelic high. And this girl…guess what else she has in her blood!'

Van den Bergen swallowed down a fireball of gastric discomfort. 'Tomato ketchup? Coriander? Anti-bacterial gel? I don't know. Just tell me.'

'MDMA.' Strietman punched the air triumphantly with his pen. 'Ecstasy.'

Groaning, van den Bergen removed his glasses and cleaned them on the bottom of his shirt. Replaced them and almost glimpsed a younger Elvis in this interloping pathologist. 'The girl lives in Amsterdam, *Daan*. We're at the European epicentre of ecstasy production. It's entirely possible she went out and got bombed the night before this…' he described the girl's remains with a wave of his large hand '…happened to her.'

'Daan might have a point,' Sabine interjected. 'Child abuse victims are often drugged by their attackers.'

'No, Paul,' Strietman went on. 'She's definitely been drugged, and that's ultimately caused her heart to fail. There's a puncture wound from a cannula in her arm.' He lifted a grey/brown arm and displayed a tiny black mark, the top of which was encrusted with a small, dried bead of blood. 'Abrasion up her nostril and the remnants of surgical tape, which suggested a tube has been put down her nose. Think about it! The missing organs. The sexual intercourse. The fact that she's maybe of Eastern African origin, given the presentation of her genitals. Voodoo ritual killing. Ever hear about the torso of the African boy they found in the UK in the River Thames?'

'Please stick to the medical facts and stop trying to play detective. That's my job. What else have you got?' van den Bergen asked, impatient now. Wishing he could somehow turn back time. That Marianne would get better and come back into work with her nice neck and strong runner's physique. Wishing he didn't find this new woman so attractive. This was neither the time nor the place to be checking out women. *Keep your dick under control, you moron.*

'We're waiting for more refined information to come back from the path lab regarding her blood,' Daan continued. 'But initial tests show hypernatraemia. Electrolyte imbalance. Dehydration. Consistent with ecstasy misuse. She's undergone a caesarean delivery within the last twelve to eighteen months,' Daan said. 'The suturing style is unusual. Unidirectional barbed suture instead of bidirectional or traditional knots.'

Studying what was still evident of the scarring to the girl's abdomen, van den Bergen grimaced. 'That means nothing to me. Explain!'

'She's been delivered of a baby and sewn up by someone who clearly knew the *theory* of what they were doing. But I guess they weren't very good with a needle and thread. The lumpy scar tissue's a giveaway. I don't think a qualified surgeon would do a bodge job like that in the Netherlands.'

CHAPTER 7

Amsterdam, private medical surgery, much later

The instructions told him to enter his user name, which he did. His password had been stored. Unsurprising, given how frequently he visited the website. He ordered five sterile suture packs – the budget ones – three blue disposable couch rolls, although he saved money by using a length twice if it hadn't ripped, and a new scalpel. The blade on his other one had snapped off from the handle, despite still being pretty sharp. What a waste. Rummaging through the other supplies on the shelf in his surgery, he ascertained that he still had an adequate supply of syringes and needles. He was good for butterfly cannulas and tourniquets. Ah, but he was on his last speculum, so made a last-minute addition to his basket. Clicking on the checkout icon, he looked at the running total.

'Fucking rip-off merchants!' he told the screen. 'Decimating my bottom line. What am I? A bloody charity?' Took a large swig from the bottle of single malt. Swilled the hot, stinging liquor around his teeth before swallowing with a gasp.

It had been much easier when he could lift these supplies from the hospital in the normal course of duty. Nobody seemed to notice for a long, long time that stocks were depleting. Once they

34

did, he was the last person to come under suspicion. Happy days, long gone.

He sighed. Took another slug of whisky. Pulled a scuffed-up credit card out of his wallet and typed in the details, which the website had not saved. At least business was brisk. The Pole was coming at 5pm. That was more cash, plus she would help him magic away the guilt.

The guilt. Oh, how he struggled beneath its weight. He hadn't meant to do that to the girl. Noor had always been harmless enough. And she was some kind of hot with those narrow hips and big, brown eyes. But he had so little control over the monster within. The beast that had somehow, over time, made it from the shadows under his cursed childhood bed into his head. Just as the dragon, Ladon, had guarded the golden apples of Hesperides, the monster had always been his saviour. His downfall, too. When the monster wanted to take charge, he had no option but to submit.

The doorbell sounded shrilly. He put his wallet away and moved from the cold, damp surgery to the waiting room at the front. Peered briefly into the mottled mirror on the wall. Licked his fingers and smoothed his strawberry-blond hair down. Pulled his trousers over his gut. Undid the three heavy-duty locks and grinned at the leggy Pole, who was primping her fire-engine-red curls.

'Hello, darling,' she said. Pouting. Kissed him on both cheeks. Grabbed his crotch. 'Botox time for Katja! My lips are pruning like an old man's testicles and my forehead's like a road map.'

'You brought the money?' he asked, eyeing her buoyant breasts in the tight top she wore beneath her puffa jacket. He had done an excellent job on those puppies.

She pushed past him and strode inside. With some effort, given the skin-tightness of her jeans and the length of those pink talons she called nails, the Pole levered an envelope out of her back pocket. Waved it under his nose. 'It's all there.'

'You brought the whip?'

She giggled. Actually, it wasn't a giggle. More of a cackle. He could tell she was looking forward to that bit, as a sweetener to take the edge off the pain of having her face poked and prodded with fine needles; filled with botulism until it was shining and tight. From inside her bulky jacket, she produced a black leather cat-o-nine tails. Swung it around her head so that it made a pleasing swishing noise, as it cut through the dank air. Slapped his behind with it playfully, though he was hoping that once her cosmetic surgical needs had been met, it would hurt enough to make his eyes water. Yes, that would be a tremendously rewarding punishment for the terrible, unpredictable way the monster was behaving at the moment.

'A promise is a promise, darling. A fifty-euro reduction for the beating of your life. Seems a bargain.' She set the cat-o-nine tails down on the waiting room coffee table as he locked the door. Removed her coat. Strode into the surgery at the back and sat on the crumpled blue covering on the examination couch. 'Have you been a bad boy, then?' She raised an eyebrow archly.

He snapped on blue latex gloves, took up his prepared syringe and ejected a sprightly fountain of the Botox solution from the end of the fine needle. 'Appalling, my dear. A modern-day Caligula. Truly appalling.'

CHAPTER 8

Amsterdam, police headquarters, 18 January

'Okay. Jane Doe.' Van den Bergen started to affix large photographs of the disembowelled girl to a pinboard: in situ, glittering with frost on the bench at the crime scene; detailed close-up shots, taken whilst on the mortuary slab. His senses were sluggish from taking too many codeine tablets before he'd even had breakfast. Fumbling with the tacks, he managed to impale his thumb on a sharp point. 'Ow. Shitty little things. Give me a hand, somebody!'

Van den Bergen turned to scowl at the members of his team. They had assembled around the large table in meeting room four in order to be debriefed on the previous day's autopsy. The air was heavy with curiosity and the smell of burnt rubber and cabbage.

'Give them here, boss.' Marie was the first to volunteer. Van den Bergen's internet research specialist gave a sharp intake of breath as she levered the photos from his oversized clumsy hands. She started to pin them in a row at the top of the board. 'Jesus. Poor woman. She's been sliced open like a...a...boil in the bag sausage. I've never seen anything like it.'

'Thank you for that analogy,' van den Bergen said.

Kees, one of the detectives who had been drafted in from a

drugs case, nudged Elvis knowingly. Winked and grinned at Marie. 'Squeamish, love?' he asked, patting his stomach. 'Bit too much for a girl like—?'

'Hey, smartarse!' van den Bergen said, mouth downturned with disapprobation. 'You'd better not be trying to bait a senior member of my team, or I'll hand you straight back to that fat prick, Kamphuis. See how much more fun you can have, rifling through piss-ridden crack dens in Bijlmer.'

'You're such a jerk, Kees,' Marie said, miming masturbation. 'I've seen more depravity in an afternoon on my work laptop than you've seen in all your born days, peering up Kamphuis' hairy backside.' She studied the board, wearing an expression that married sympathy with respectful sobriety. Took her seat slowly. Clearly mesmerised by the images. 'Kind of glad I was still redecorating my toilet with that stomach bug when you guys got the call. It's one thing to see photos…another thing entirely to find a body in that state.' Kees was treated to a particularly pointed glare. 'You'd better watch yourself, pal, or I might slip a little something in your sandwich when you're not paying attention. Very contagious, that norovirus.'

Van den Bergen allowed himself an amused snort. 'Pay attention, children!' He clapped his hands together. 'Now, our victim is about fifteen. Sixteen at most.' He sighed involuntarily. Relayed Strietman's findings.

Despite the fact that everyone was now eyeing him, rapt with attention, van den Bergen realised he had clammed up. He was sketching a cactus dahlia in the corner of his pad. Mind wandering elsewhere, thanks to yet another sleepless night. He grabbed at his stomach, still sore from the procedure.

'Boss?' Elvis said. 'You okay?'

'What? Yes. The only thing we can be certain of at this point,' he said, focussing on Elvis' greasy quiff. 'Is that we're looking for someone with surgical training.' He pointed to the girl's unfurled ribs and exposed abdominal cavity with his pen. 'The prat standing in for Marianne de Koninck – Strietman – said she's had...' He grabbed his glasses which hung at the end of a chain around his neck. Perched them on his straight nose and squinted at his notebook. The writing was a blur. His eyesight was deteriorating rapidly. For God's sake! If he'd have known his self-indulgence would have had such annoying after-effects, he would have found a better way of dealing with his demons. '...I can't read a damn thing I've written.' Thrust the book at Elvis. 'Read this out, will you?'

Elvis held the notebook close. His lips moved as he tried to decipher the tight scrawl.

'Well?!' van den Bergen snapped, crossing his long, thin right leg over his left knee. Failing to wedge his sneaker under the table top because there was simply insufficient space for such a large shoe. Uncrossing his legs. Damn it, if he could get comfortable. Visualising his father's feet, near the end. So sinewy and yellow, in carpet slippers that swam around his bony ankles. Five years.

'Had you been drinking when you wrote this, boss?' Elvis asked. He took one look at van den Bergen's face and apologised quietly.

Over the years, Elvis – so nicknamed by van den Bergen because of his propensity for wearing the ridiculous King-like quiff – had gained in confidence. Rightly so. He had earned van den Bergen's respect. But there were some lines the loyal little dipshit should never cross. Van den Bergen maintained his admonishing glare.

Elvis cleared his throat. 'Okay. Says here, "Jane Doe was subject to a midline laparotomy and sternotomy". He pronounced the medical terminology hesitantly, like a child trying to read long words in easy, phonetically distinct chunks. 'What the hell are those? You've written, "Murderer knew exactly how to do it."'

Van den Bergen nodded. Laced his fingers together behind his head. 'The clinical terms refer to the way she has been cut open. Strietman says the technique used is the same sort of thing a surgeon would do when performing abdominal or heart surgery. The murderer has cut around the belly button, instead of through it.' His junior colleagues' faces were blank. 'Apparently, the belly button is full of bacteria and surgeons cut round it to avoid infecting the patient. But I want to know...' he ran his hands back and forth through his thatch of thick, prematurely white hair '... is why would a murderer take so much care, if the only goal was to kill his victim? Why the missing organs? What do we think about the drugging theory? Or ritual killing? Any thoughts?'

'Ritual killing,' Marie said, nodding slowly. 'We haven't had one of those before. Was that your idea, boss?'

Van den Bergen shook his head. 'We have a stand-in pathologist with a very vivid imagination. Still, anything's a possibility at this stage. The paediatrician Strietman brought in for an expert's opinion seemed to think he may be onto something.'

Van den Bergen allowed himself a fleeting moment to savour the memory of Dr Sabine Schalks, as he had escorted her from the mortuary to the lift.

'Sabine,' he had said, stifling the inclination to touch her arm. 'I'd love it if you'd come in and meet my detective, Marie. She does our internet research and has some experience with child pornography and paedophile rings. I think input from you would really help.' He had given her a business card. 'Will you pay us a visit?'

The paediatrician had smiled. It was a wide smile, showing perfect white teeth. He had admitted to himself that this was an attractive woman. Of his own age. No wedding ring. Potentially so easy. And yet, his heart belonged to a woman much younger.

The doors to the lift had slid open and Sabine Schalks had stepped inside. Pressed the button. The doors started to close. Disappointment setting in fast. But then, she had treated him to a glorious grin.

'Nice line, Chief Inspector. If you wanted to go on a date with me, you could have just asked!'

Elvis interrupted the memory of this unexpected flirtation.

'The murderer took her organs as trophies,' he suggested, fiddling with the buttons on his leather jacket. 'That's common, isn't it? Trophies, I mean. Like the Firestarter, with his test tube rack full of frozen fingers.'

The others nodded.

'Maybe this perp wants to keep his victim unspoiled,' Kees offered. 'A clean-freak who can't stand bacteria. That's why he did the belly button thing.'

'If he's a medic or vet, he's used to doing things a certain way,' Marie said, 'So, it stands to reason he'd open her up carefully instead of hacking her apart. Those guys train for years. Old habits, and all that...'

Sagely nodding, van den Bergen filled in the petals of his doodled dahlia with cross-hatching. 'Any feedback yet from the door-to-doors?' he asked. 'Witnesses?'

'Not a sausage,' Elvis said in English.

'Not even a boil-in-the-bag sausage.' Kees winked at Marie, who thrust a middle finger skyward in response.

CHAPTER 9

Soho, London, Skin Flicks Media Group, later

'Yeah. Come up,' the girl said through the intercom. 'Top floor.'

The buzzer sounded. George pushed the heavy green door inwards and started to climb the stone stairs two at a time. The air was heavy with that smell of damp and neglect that you got in Victorian buildings. Peeling magnolia paint and ingrained dirt from who knew when. A musty tang that made her sneeze. She was careful to pull down the sleeve of her sweater and put it between the handrail and the naked skin of her palm.

Rhythmic, dance-music thump issued forth from the music business on the first floor. Stoking up the dust, no doubt. George covered her mouth with her free hand to avoid inhaling it.

Second floor up, two bearded white boys dressed in pastel-coloured jeans and ugly Fair Isle jumpers descended as she climbed. Talking about the tedium of a sweaty editing suite.

Pausing on the landing, struggling to catch her breath, she regretted the two cigarettes she had smoked in quick succession on the way from Piccadilly Circus through the narrow Soho backstreets.

Above her, a woman leaned over the balcony at the staircase's summit. Lines etched deeply into a well-scrubbed face. Welcoming smile. Poorly dyed orange hair and a loose fitting jumper that draped over pendulous breasts. She looked like somebody's mother.

'You Georgina McKenzie?' the woman asked.

'Yes. Sharon Williams-May's niece.'

George shook the woman's hand as she finally reached the top step. Made a mental note to use some anti-bacterial gel on the way out.

'I'm Marge, Dermot's PA. Come in. He'll see you shortly.'

George followed Marge beyond a steel security door which announced, by dint of an engraved brass plaque, that this was the London office of Skin Flicks Media Group, parent company of Skin Magazine, Skinclicks.com, Skin Licks Gentlemen's Clubs and Skin Dicks Adult Toys. Spotlit, framed covers from *Skin Magazine*, hanging in a perfect line along the red crushed velvet walls, guided her down a narrow corridor. The covers featured an array of topless girls sporting disproportionately enormous pneumatic breasts on top of tiny, bony chests. All pouting lips, spidery eyelashes and big hair. The photographic trail opened out onto the reception area. Black carpet. More red velvet on the walls. Black leather sofas.

After some ten minutes, during which time George noted, with a degree of surprise, that the sofa she sat on smelled good and was soft to the touch – not like the hard, cheap crap Aunty Sharon owned, which had the fishy stink of a bad tannery – a white-haired, moustachioed man bordering on elderly leaned out of an office door and waved her into an office.

Smiling benignly. Red-faced. His gut overhung his baggy slacks by some margin. His legendarily large feet were clad in moccasins. George marvelled that this innocuous-looking man, who could be a semi-retired chip-shop owner, judging by his appearance, was one of the most successful creators of multi-platform erotica and related branded merchandise in Europe.

'So, you work for me, do you?' he asked, running an arthritic-looking hand through the thinning white hair.

'Yes, Mr Robinson,' George said. 'I'm one of the cleaners at Skin Licks on Peter Street. My Aunty Sharon has been a barmaid there for ten years.'

Dermot Robinson appraised her through rheumy eyes and rubbed a purpling nose, both of which attested to late nights and too much scotch. 'You could be a dancer with a body like that,' he said, stretching out the vowels with his East End tongue. 'Want a promotion? My girls earn good money.'

George opened her pad and clicked her pen into life. 'That's not what I'm here for, but it's kind of you to offer. I've been keen to interview you for my PhD for over a year, Mr Robinson. Thanks so much for this.'

This unprepossessing Soho porn king crossed his enormous feet on his desk top and leaned back in his chair. Arms behind his head. A man at ease with the world and with women.

But not women like her.

George cleared her throat and read her first question aloud. 'Your harder stuff. The SM magazines and websites that are subsidiary Skin Flicks brands – do you create the content to meet an existing demand, or do you think your content drives consumer tastes in erotica?'

'You think I'm a dirty old man? That Skin Flicks is just my own personal fantasy?' Dermot Robinson leaned over the desk as far as his gut would allow. Stretched his arms wide along the rosewood. Narrowed his eyes at George and tried to see what she had written on her pad. 'You can put in your notes that this is a multi-million-pound business, love. You think it's all budget home movies and readers' wives?'

She shook her head avidly. 'Not at all.' Though she had seen the production values of many a porn film, and a sizeable proportion looked like they might have been recorded on amateur equipment. George had wondered if any of the Skin

Flicks filming was done within the offices to cut costs.

'My last film cost me over a million to make,' Dermot said. 'Think about it. All them staff. Location. Catering crew. Consultants for this. Advisers for that. Editing and post production.' He pointed to a blown-up black and white photograph of him receiving an award in a dark and dingy-looking place. 'See that? That's me, getting a SHAFTA. Know what that is?'

'Soft and Hard Adult Film and Television Awards,' George said.

Dermot closed his eyes and nodded. 'The stuff we do here is art. I got marketing people who market research my films to death before they even see a story board. What the punter wants, the punter gets. That's why my products get picked up by the likes of X Broadcasting network in Canada. My films is seen all over the world, love. Internationally successful.'

'But the violent content in some of them. Women being tortured. Some goes beyond standard BDSM, wouldn't you say? Do men really want to see that?'

The Soho porn king rose and moved to his window, looking down onto Wardour Street below. Lord and master of all he surveyed, rolling up his sweater sleeves as though he were preparing for a fight with the entire West End. 'Listen, darling, ain't nothing been produced under my brand what's not got artistic merit. I got good scriptwriters. Excellent camera men. Even medical people telling the directors what's legit and what's not. Looking after the health of my stars. And my legal team cost me a fucking fortune.' He laughed mirthlessly. 'You wouldn't sleep nights if you seen my legal bills. Now the government's banning all sorts of acts in UK porn. It's gonna put the smaller guys out of business.'

He was side-stepping her questions. George checked her watch. Irritated. Drumming her pen on the pad. For a start, the SHAFTAs picture was hanging too high on the left by at least 5mm. And those feet. Robinson's feet were preposterous. She knew he had starred in porn films himself back in the seventies. His shoe size reflected how well he was endowed in other areas. An erotic legend who was about as sexy as a bucket of cold sick, George reflected. She wanted to go. Her cleaning shift began in less than thirty minutes and she would be glad to exchange the luxurious black carpet of Skin Flicks' head office for the smell of bleach in the store cupboard of Dermot's titty bar.

No. Focus, George, she thought. *You're here to get the other side of the story. Don't leave without it.*

'Do you think your erotica inspires men to commit sexually violent crimes against women, Mr Robinson?'

Dermot turned away from his view and stared at her in silence. 'You understand the true nature of your average red-blooded male, love, you don't need to ask that question.'

The phone rang, preventing George from asking her next questions. Dermot picked it up. Looked grave. Said, 'OK. Jesus. Right. Well get another bloody girl in!' and then hung up.

'I'm going to have to cut our entertaining little tête-à-tête short, love,' he said, scratching his moustache with a Biro. 'Seems one of my actresses has gone AWOL. She was due on set two days ago. Now they're telling me nobody's seen the silly cow.' He shook his head. 'Can't get the staff. You sure you don't want a promotion?'

CHAPTER 10

Amsterdam, Norderkerk, later, then, van den Bergen's apartment

The actress, or what was left of her, was stretched across the rear seat of the Lexus. Having a wide car was very handy under these circumstances. After the bombing of the Bushuis Library, vans were still drawing the attention of the police. You were far more likely to be stopped and searched in one of those. Plenty of room for explosives in the back, if you had aspirations to becoming a terrorist. But a luxury saloon in black, with no changes to the manufacturer's specifications, gliding along, observant of the speed limit and traffic lights…who would pay attention to a car like that? Certainly not the police. It didn't scream, 'drug dealer' or 'master criminal'. It was discreet. Elegant. Moneyed. The tinted rear windows also helped with anonymity. It wouldn't do for a passerby to peer inside, even if the actress' body was covered by a black tarpaulin. Obviously, lining the leather seats with plastic sheeting had been a necessary precaution, although the woman's blood and bodily fluids had long since ceased to flow. No, this was definitely the most comfortable, logistically most effective method of disposal.

The actress had been a surprisingly good conversationalist in the end. A vivacious woman. Talking about her unusual line of work had proven fascinating. Discussing her childhood in her country of origin was an eye-opener too. And she had been an excellent lay, of course. Though she'd had enough practice in her professional life, so it had hardly come as a surprise that she'd known one end of an erogenous zone from another. She had emitted some wonderful sounds from that surgically enhanced mouth. Like a wounded animal. Vulnerable. Pliable. Submissive.

They had shared a fun evening together. Collecting happy memories was important.

It had almost been a shame to destroy that glorious body. Well, not so much destruction, really. More of a surgical deconstruction. But then, a pact was a pact, and those months of scoping the actress out had had to pay off. Obviously, there was a tremendous buzz to be had from the act itself. Getting it just right was an art of sorts. Preparing the correct environment. Actively managing her ventilation, fluid levels and organ functions to keep her in optimum condition for as long as possible, before removing the body parts. Then, finally allowing her to die. It was no small joy to feel like the techniques were being improved upon each time. Definitely better than the preceding efforts. Mastery would come eventually. In the meantime, it had been a job well done.

Now, there was just the disposal to take care of. The arrangement of the body and location in which it was left would be important to the way the police regarded the deaths and the investigative path that they took.

Pulling up outside the church, nobody was in sight. The terrible weather always drove people indoors. For a slightly built woman, the body of the actress was cumbersome. Dead weight flung over the shoulder, still obscured by the tarp. This final stage had to be deftly executed. Quickly now, with a beating heart, praying nobody was watching. It wouldn't do to be interrupted or identified.

Whipping off the tarp at the last moment to reveal the shell that was once inhabited by an actress, famous within tight, specialist erotica circles. Admittedly, the end product didn't look very nice. Empty eye sockets weren't exactly a turn-on. But that was collateral damage, really. An unavoidable side-effect of the… what was it again? Oh, yes. Surgical deconstruction. That was a good one. Witty. Best to remember this woman the way she had been on the film set, and afterwards in bed. Happy memories only. Find the positives.

Of course, there was the hunt for the next subject to look forward to. And it would be imperative to keep an eye on that tall policeman who was heading up the case. The haunted-looking one with the white hair. Perhaps a little trip out to his apartment was in order. The view was astoundingly clear and uninterrupted from the street below…

At home, as the pan of pasta boiled, van den Bergen leaned over the kitchen worktop. Clutched at his stomach.

'Jesus, help me,' he implored a God he had no faith in whatsoever.

The pains were sharp tonight. Presenting near his kidneys. Perhaps he had kidney failure. Was that one of the symptoms? Maybe. He would Google it, although George had told him the internet was not his friend, as far as Googling illness was concerned. Every spasm, every ache, every blemish was cancer. Fast-forward to the apocalypse. He'd been that way for a long time. But now the five-year mark was upon him, it was worse. And, of course, he had something legitimate to worry about, given what he had stupidly done to his body.

He stared down at his phone, as if that had the answers. 'Text back, goddamn it!'

Reflected in the shine of the grey tiled splashback, he considered the fragmented representation of himself that stared back at him. A scowling middle-aged man with sunken cheekbones and dark patches under his eyes. Glasses hanging at the end of a chain around his neck atop an old shirt that had a frayed collar.

All wrapped up in a moth-eaten cardigan he'd had since 1995.

'You're a mess!' he shouted at the grey cubist counterfeit. 'Who would ever find you attractive? Not Andrea, that's for sure.' He conjured an image in his mind's eye of his ex-wife. Happy now, with that balding prick, Groenewalt. Both of them living high off the hog thanks to the maintenance payments he still had to fork out from his modest chief inspector's salary; atoning for a teen romance that outlived its natural best-before-date because of Tamara's arrival. A marriage which had now been defunct for more than a decade. No, that hard-faced cow, Andrea, wouldn't look twice at him any more. 'Tamara thinks her dad's some geriatric joke, too. And George...'

Feeling irritation bite, he dug his long finger inside the frayed hole in the shirt fabric and ripped along the collar's edge. 'Sort yourself out, van den Bergen. Get a fucking haircut!'

When the pasta pan started to spit water all over the hob, he flung it into the sink in temper, fusilli everywhere. Poured himself a glass of orange juice. Downed two codeine and winced.

He was poised to call George when his phone rang shrilly.

'Van den Bergen. Speak!'

It was Elvis. Sounding hyper. As if Elvis sounded anything apart from bloody wired, like a kid on sugar. 'We were just finishing up, boss, when we got a call.'

Involuntarily, he groaned down the phone at his detective. 'Go on,' he said.

'Sorry, boss. I know you're coming down with this stomach thing or something but—'

'Spit it out.'

'There's another body. A woman. Left at the back of the Norderkerk.'

Van den Bergen sighed. Hastily grabbed a fistful of almost-boiled pasta from the bottom of the sink. Poised to down this makeshift dinner to keep the codeine company. 'I'm on my way.'

CHAPTER 11

South East London, very late

'Hey. You're back,' Ad said, sleepily.

He rolled over, putting himself at the edge of the single bed, facing her. Flicked back the duvet, so she could clamber in and nestle into his bare chest. Groggy. He had only half-slept, of course. One ear constantly on alert for the key in the door. It wasn't lost on him that she'd actually returned from work a full hour ago, and had sat downstairs with Sharon, swigging that drink they drank. What was it? Rum n Ting. Conspiratorial giggling about something or other. He only hoped he wasn't the butt of their jokes. But how could he be? He'd been there for more than forty-eight hours and had only seen George for about three of those in a state of wakefulness. 'Good day?'

'Knackering,' she said.

Failing to ask him about his day, which he had spent sprawled on Aunty Sharon's fishy sofa, propped on overstuffed cushions that stank of baking and hairspray, watching some daytime soap on television called *Doctors*. Stuffing his face with fruitcake to stave off boredom.

George disrobed and pulled on a baggy T-shirt that sported some musician's name. One of those English acts he didn't recognise. Dubstep something or other. Maybe that wasn't even a musician. He couldn't keep up with George's likes and dislikes. Deep house. Garage. Old skool. It was an entirely different language for a small-town Groningen boy like him; serving only to estrange, where once it had exerted a strong, magnetic pull. But still. She was a sight for sore eyes, even silhouetted against the landing light.

'Come here, hard working genius. I've missed you.' He had kisses for her, filled with desperation and longing and ardour and not a little disappointment. Here was his erection, pressed into her warm, voluptuous body. 'Oh, I love you so much.' A hand between her legs. He would show her how he had been thinking of her all day long. Surely, she must have given him some thought, in amongst her mysterious schedule of 'research' and 'work', none of which she ever expanded on.

George pushed him away. Treated him to a peck on the cheek. 'Aw, I'm sorry, Ad. Do you mind if we don't?' Turned her back on him and shuffled to the other side. 'I'm proper shattered. I've not stopped all day.'

In such a narrow bed, his knees inside her knees, his erection touching her bottom technically counted as spooning. Didn't it? Spooning was what you did when you were in a comfortable relationship. He could definitely do spoons.

Deflating slowly, he asked, 'How come you're always back so late? Last night. You were even later. I asked and you never answered me.'

There was a pause. A considered intake of breath.

'Sometimes new people turn up. Last night, there was a bit of a set-to between Aunty Sharon and the manager. Then, there was some mess to clean up. I had to work longer, is all. It's one of those jobs. It's complicated. I'll tell you tomorrow.'

In the darkness, breathing in the musty smell of old wallpaper and eavesdropping on the soporific sound of passing cars, at odds with the disconcerting whistles of insomniac youths, roaming the local streets and up to no good (he knew he was beginning to sound like his mother), he decided privately that she was being evasive. He wasn't even entirely sure what 'one of those jobs' constituted. Cleaning something or other, though he didn't know where. He would quiz her about it over breakfast, before he left for the airport.

When her phone buzzed insistently at 2am and she left the bedroom to answer it, he made another mental note to quiz her about that over breakfast too.

CHAPTER 12

Manhattan, New York, 1981

Laughter trilled from somewhere along the hall, carried laterally to the sleeping, dreaming girl along with a rotten perfume of cigarette smoke and alcohol. Though it was ring-fenced beyond several thick walls, the tendrils of this throbbing organism – her mother's own experiment in grafting rare cultivars with exotic pond life and social climbers, fed by hedonism and infamy – crept under her bedroom door nonetheless.

The Police were in attendance, reggae beats syncopating badly with the even rhythm of her dream. Sting's voice ushering her towards wakefulness. De Do Do Do, De Da Da Daddy's home: sitting with his legs crossed in the modest garden of their large Mayfair townhouse, reading a medical journal in summery warmth. Watching him intermittently, revelling in his presence, she frolicked with her mother's beloved terrier, Rudi, beneath the whippy branches of their small maple tree. Helping Gretchen to pour into glasses the cloudy lemonade, which, standing on a chair, she had helped to make and which she and her father would now drink together.

Except Daddy wasn't home. And the thud, thud, thud of Blondie's beating glass heart pushed sleep further and further away from the girl on unforgiving waves of sound, until she realised that this was neither their London house, nor their Berlin residence, nor the villa in Juan les Pins.

More laughter. Men's this time. Deep and throaty. Glasses clinking.

Consciousness had taken a hold of her fully, now. The comforting dream had slipped beyond her recall. Soft Cell were complaining, instead, of having to endure 'Tainted Love'. Staring at the high ceiling of that New York apartment, she considered that she might have liked that music, given half a chance. She was at an age, after all, where she had just started to take an interest in the charts. *Top of the Pops* on their television in London. American Billboard's Hot 100. Full of new, exciting bands. Boys with lipstick, wearing black. Cheap-looking, stubby keyboards sporting mysterious names like Roland and Yamaha, that were a world away from the grand piano in the music room, at which she sat for hours every week, having Mozart drummed into her reluctant fingers by that stern old hag, Frau Bretschneider. Both instrument and teacher had been imported all the way from Berlin, like Mother's favourite dinner service. But Mother and her friends were greedy. They had claimed the youthful synthesised beats as theirs. Though in truth, some of Mother's younger friends *had* created those songs, thereby distorting even the soundtrack to her childhood with her mother's notorious celebrity and her cronies' sycophancy. How she'd like to run away, get away from the pain it drove into the heart of her.

Advancing in her pyjamas and dressing gown down the hall, the music thudded louder. The smells became ever sharper. Those tendrils beckoned her forwards; pulling her in towards the melee. On the other side of the door, beyond which she had been expressly told by Gretchen that she must not under any circumstances venture after lights-out, she beheld the writhing organism. A gathering, at least two-hundred strong, that stretched from one end of the vast, wood-floored drawing room to the other. Semi-naked men. Suited men. Men dressed as women. Women clad in outlandish, futuristic outfits. Some, barely dressed at all, breasts jiggling as they danced. Wearing incongruous hats. Dwarves carrying platters of food on their heads which some guests stuffed lasciviously into each other's mouths. Pyramids of white powder, which most guests were snorting enthusiastically through small tubes. Dancing, smoking, kissing and more. The sort of thing the girl did not want to see and yet, driven by an eleven-year-old's avid curiosity for all things grown-up, a scene she was compelled to gawp at and consign to memory. It was horrible. It was wonderful. She was not sure what it was.

To the left, beneath the apartment's tall windows, with the towers of downtown Manhattan glittering in the background, the old guard sat in their off-the-shoulder dresses, sipping champagne with their stuffy-looking husbands. At odds in this uptown Babylon. She recognised them from the photos of her mother that often appeared within the pages of *Vanity Fair*. Lunching at Le Cirque with other thin, bouffant women.

But her mother was not seated among them. Where was she?

The girl's gaze wandered to a far corner of the room. And there she was! Sporting enormous shoulder pads and a tiny, cinched-in waist, chatting animatedly to a man dressed in black, whose heavy spectacles and bushy white hair marked him out as some famous artist or other.

'Mama!' the girl shouted, advancing past a sweaty, topless man. He almost knocked the teddy bear clean out of her hand, as he danced with abandon with a sequin-encrusted he/she/it guest.

When her mother caught sight of her, her fury was self-evident. Instead of responding in their native tongue, Mama chided her in English; her transatlantic drawl made sluggish and clumsy with alcohol, the girl knew.

'Veronica! You were told to go to bed and stay in bed.'

'But I got woken up.'

'Get back to bed this instant, young lady! You are very diso-bedient.'

Her mother grabbed her with bony, iron fingers. Dug her red nails in. The champagne stink of her rancid breath bore down on her. 'Naughty little girl. What were you told?'

'I miss Papa.' The girl looked up at her mother with imploring eyes. Part of her acknowledged that she would rather be tucked in bythe homely, loving Gretchen. But she had needed to see what lay beyond The Door. And this was Mama. *Her* mother. She could not stem an instinctive, primal craving for maternal reassurance after a disconcerting dream, though she realised it would not be forthcoming. Mama took her parties very seriously. Mama had to look glamorous. Mama had to dedicate herself to her friends. It was expected.

'Papa's at Harvard,' her mother shouted over the music, digging her nails in deeper. 'You know that. He's back next week. Then, we fly home.' Her affected smile turned into something sinister, making the sinews in her thin, dancer's neck seem taut and stringy. Speaking to her daughter through gritted, white teeth that seemed somehow sharper, nastier, reptilian. 'But right now, little miss,' the glossy brown tresses of Mama's hair coiled and squirmed like the snakes on Medusa's head that Veronica had peered at through parted fingers during the premiere of *Clash of the Titans*, 'I am having a very important conversation with Andy, here, about my fundraiser for the Museum of Modern Art.' Mama turned around and beamed warmly at the white-haired man. Gorgon's head gone.

Back to bed, annoying little cunt. Veronica found herself being dragged by the belt of her dressing gown. The long walk of shame across the makeshift dance floor, past the great and the good and the downright rotten of New York high society, was punctuated by several photo opportunities. Red light. Hold the front page. And pose! Whenever a flashbulb popped in their faces, Veronica registered that her mother had instantly rearranged herself into a photogenic shape. Hand on hip. One foot forward. One to the side. Knee slightly bent. Easy smile. Arm draped around Veronica's shoulder, as though she were a novelty prop. It had been the same on the red carpet at the premiere. The blinding glare of flashing bulbs, illuminating bleach-white grins of her mama and papa. Gretchen had shown her the photos in the gossip columns the following day, above a caption that identified their family trio as 'mining heiress and former Broadway star, Heidi Schwartz, with plastic surgeon husband and daughter'. Veronica had recognised herself in one of the photos, trudging behind Perseus, looking downright glum. Too shell-shocked by the press attention to feel excited about being close to the star of the film.

Together, they stumbled away from the party, back down the hall, Veronica being dragged and at the mercy of her mother's unsteady gait. Reeling. Bursting into her room. Harsh light on. Pyjama bottoms yanked down around her ankles.

'Don't…let… me…see…you…come…out…of…this… room…again!' Mama said, slapping the words out onto her thighs with the flat of her hand like the drummer in a military tattoo. Yanked back up, once the skin was livid. 'Horrible girl. Into bed!'

'I'm so sorry, Mama,' Veronica wept, climbing under her blankets and clutching her knees. Making herself as small as possible. Thumb in. Teddy next to her heart, at first.

'You're not sorry. You're never sorry!' Mama screamed. She removed her thick, red leather belt with its deep, jewel-studded buckle. Brought it down on her hard, so that it whistled through the still air and cracked as it made contact with her shoulder. The blankets provided a merciful barrier for its sting, at least. 'Go to sleep! Go to sleep, you fucking pain in the ass!'

Veronica shut her eyes tight, though the tears leached onto her face and coursed freely into her ear. She was careful to hold her teddy protectively over her head, as the belt buckle found its mark again and again. The light of a Manhattan morning seemed a long way off.

CHAPTER 13

Amsterdam, police headquarters, then, a building site, 19 January

'Are the rumours that it's a serial sexual killer true?' asked a woman he recognised as a big ticket reporter for *de Volkskrant*.

Where the hell had she got that? Who had opened their big mouth?

Suddenly the entire meeting room erupted with the probing voices of media representatives. On their feet, all demanding to have their questions answered. Hands in the air. Voice recorders pointed in his direction. The room was full to claustrophobic bursting point as it was, but the clamour made it all the more unbearable. Van den Bergen could feel sweat starting to trickle down his back. All eyes were trained on him. He had to address them. Opened and closed his mouth. But no words would come.

Hasselblad tapped the microphone. Brass buttons clinking on his commissioner's jacket. Frog-eyes bulging. The PA system's feedback whistled around the room, reinstating silence.

'Chief Inspector?' Hasselblad was staring at him expectantly. His best trick. Daring van den Bergen to challenge his authority.

Only moments before they had filed into the room for this press conference, van den Bergen had been trapped inside Hasselblad's office, arguing vociferously about which line to take.

They had been at it, on and off, ever since van den Bergen had come back with Strietman's preliminary report.

'Paul, I *want* them to know we're after a serial killing sex pervert,' Hasselblad had said, strutting up to the ornate mirror that hung next to a sizeable oil-on-canvas portrait, painted of him when he had taken up office and had been a good stone lighter. He checked his tie was straight. Held in his gut. Smoothed his shirt as he viewed himself sideways-on and nodded at his reflection. Satisfied. 'You play down the depravity of these murders, and this department gets sod all kudos when you come to solve them. *I* get sod all kudos.' He was still in socks. He marched back over to his rosewood desk, lifted up one of his already gleaming dress shoes and buffed it uselessly with a cotton handkerchief. 'I don't need to remind you that I'm the commissioner, do I? You tow *my* party line.'

Van den Bergen fingered the frayed collar of the shirt he had not yet had time to change. 'Jaap, you embrace headline-grabbing sensationalism, and you're going to end up with mass hysteria on your hands. We *should* announce there's a murderer at large. Of course, we should! We—'

'Not murderer. Serial killer.' At that moment, Kamphuis was visible through the glazed partition, walking past Hasselblad's office, taking a large bite out of an oversized syrup waffle. Notably, Kamphuis waved merrily to the commissioner. 'On. The. Rampage.'

Kamphuis and Hasselblad. Pair of pricks together, van den Bergen thought. *Not a club I'd ever be invited to join. Not a club I'd want to fucking well join.* 'Look, we need to encourage the public to be vigilant. Yes. But the whole point of the press conference is to identify these women. Missing persons has thrown up zilch.' He stared at the sorry-looking parlour palm on Hasselblad's desk. Fingered the compost, which was utterly dried out. Moron never watered it. 'Not a shred of clothing on either of them, let alone ID. No witnesses so far. How can I investigate murders with nothing to go on but two carved-up cadavers, some dodgy scarring from past surgery? A vague notion of their ages and ethnicities?'

'Stick to the brief, van den Bergen!' was all Hasselblad would say before barrelling out of his office and down the hall to where the nation's media had been assembled.

The reporters were rapt with attention, now. Waiting to hear what the infamous chief inspector had to say – the man who had solved the mystery of the Bushuis library and Utrecht synagogue bombings. A catcher of murderous psychopaths. One of Amsterdam's most celebrated sons, when it suited them to deem him one. An abrasive, white-haired dinosaur who should hand in his badge, when it didn't. Casting an eye over their hungry faces, he could almost see them silently deciding on today's headline. Manipulative sewer rats, the lot of them.

He cleared his throat. Finally, imagining George had placed an encouraging hand on his shoulder, his voice came.

'Er, thank you for coming.'

He started to talk about the victims, being careful to hold back the information that their organs had been removed and that they appeared to have been butchered by an expert. He deliberately omitted to deploy the phrase, 'serial sex killer'. Steadfastly denied they were looking for a crazed pervert, when quizzed about it by a researcher for NPO 1 television.

'We have yet to profile the perpetrator,' he clarified. Watched the research guy's face fall with disappointment. 'At this stage, we have two female victims.' He clicked the mouse button on a laptop Marie had set up for him and two artist's impressions appeared on a large whiteboard behind him. He didn't think much of the artist's efforts. The pictures were guesswork, at best, hastily scribbled onto paper. 'Two murders that share several similarities. But I wouldn't label this as the work of a serial killer. Not yet.'

He could feel Hasselblad's eyes boring a resentful hole in the side of his face. He could almost hear Elvis' and Marie's jaws dropping with disbelief. All hell would break loose once the microphones were switched off and they returned to their offices.

But he was safe for now. Hasselblad wouldn't dare shed light on an internal disagreement in front of scandal-hungry reporters.

'I need to know if anyone knows anything about these two women.' He thought about the slight build of the victims. Their vulnerability. The black girl's obvious youth. The white woman's flawed, augmented breasts. Thought about George and Tamara. Spoke into the microphone in an impassioned way. 'Husbands, family members, lovers, colleagues, friends. Somebody must be missing someone close to them. If there is anybody out there that can help or who thinks they might have witnessed the abduction of or attack on women who resemble these sketches, call the hotline in confidence.'

Iwan watched the live press conference on NPO's breakfast news bulletin, as he sawed open a crusty bun with the sharp bread knife. Into the soft, doughy innards of the cob he stuffed several slices of kielbasa and cheese. But his girl had bought him that cheap shit sausage from Lidl and the cheese was Dutch. It looked right but didn't smell right. Nevertheless, with large unthinking bites, swilled down with strong coffee, he manfully made short shrift of the first disappointing meal of the day. That he got the food to stay down at all with such a stinking hangover was a miracle. It had been a good night – early on, at Stefan's, drinking Tyskie and playing cards. Then, later on…better still.

'The boys are outside,' Krystyna shouted from the kitchen.

The honking horn of the van signified that it was time to get to work. 6.57am. By lunchtime, he should feel fine. He picked his plate and cup up from the scarred pine table and swapped it for the lunch bag that Krystyna gave him. Grabbed her slender frame around the waist and pulled her close for a kiss.

'Get off! You stink!' she said, giggling. 'Go and work the beer off. Go on! You'll be late.'

Engine running, outside.

'Come on, Iwan!' Stefan said, leaning nonchalantly out of the driver's window. 'Get a bloody move on, you pussy.'

He lit a cigarette but was forced to flick it out the window half-smoked because the pitch and roll of the van, with its sagging suspension, made him seasick.

'You're green!' Michal said. 'And you ducked out early! Lightweight!'

Iwan just puffed out his cheeks in response. Wiped away the cold sweat on his face. Stared blankly out of the window, as shabby, 1970s apartment blocks on the poor outskirts of town gave way to grand red- and grey-brick buildings – some converted into elegant apartments, some still four-storey family homes for the very rich. Here, the streets were tree-lined, with chi-chi delis and boutiques on every corner. He was working. He was earning. Life was good. It was just a hangover. He wouldn't vomit. He was a man. Men didn't vomit.

The van pulled up in Valeriusstraat, outside the building site. Scaffolding encased the neglected façade, with its cantilevered bay window on the second storey and the balcony above. At the very top, on the fourth floor, the stepped gable bore down on them. He peered up at it and shuddered. Shook his head.

'You're such a superstitious old woman!' Stefan said, punching his shoulder.

'This place is haunted,' Iwan said. 'I'm telling you.'

The gable window was dark, but his fevered imagination conjured up a ghost from the past eyeing him from above. Perhaps a Jew, sheltering from the Nazis. Maybe a sick or deformed child from Amsterdam's glory days gazed down at him. Some merchant's dirty secret, locked in the attic. Protruding from the gable was a beam with the hook on the end – so useful for hoisting materials up to the top floor. But Iwan imagined it was a witch's finger, beckoning him up to the top, so he might plunge to his death.

He crossed himself and followed his workmates inside.

'We're going to get you plastering out the top floor today,' Stefan said. Laughing raucously.

The others joined in. Iwan might have retorted with something witty, had he not felt like he was dying. All he could manage was a 'Ha ha. Very funny.'

'You think I'm joking?'

'Stefan! Come on, man. No!'

Stefan pointed to the giant sheaf of plasterboards that were stacked in the hallway. 'Top floor. Board and skim by the end of the day. Take Pawel up there with you. He'll fight the ghosts off.'

Iwan groaned. Picked up his drill case from the cupboard under the stairs. Collected the bucket containing his trowel and saw.

'You seen the rest of my tools?' he asked the others.

They replied that they hadn't. He shrugged. They'd be around. Trudged to the top. There was a strange smell on the air. Something more than just dust, damp and rotten wood. The precise nature of the scent eluded him. Never mind. He'd have a cigarette and a coffee from the flask Krystyna had made him, first. Fuck Stefan!

As he passed beneath the threshold that marked the smaller of the attic rooms, he heard Michal shout downstairs.

'Someone's been in! Back door's been jemmied, by the looks.'

'Anything taken?' Stefan shouted between floors.

Iwan backed onto the landing and bellowed down the stairwell, 'My drill is still here. They'd have taken that. You sure you're not still pissed, Michal?'

'Nothing missing here,' Stefan shouted. 'Have a good look round, lads. Then, screw the door shut for now. Can't have cats or squatters getting in.'

Iwan nodded. Sighed. Progressed beyond the threshold, traversing the smaller ante-room that would be divided into a hallway and en suite to a master. Entered the main room. The one with the window. The one he had been dreading entering. He dropped his drill case and bucket. Screamed. Then, he vomited over the steel toecaps of his boots.

CHAPTER 14

Amsterdam, police headquarters, later

Van den Bergen was sitting in the disabled cubicle on the top floor. Clutching at his spasming stomach. Contemplating the frenzy of excitement that had been almost palpable during the press conference. Imagining the dressing-down he was going to get from Hasselblad when he eventually emerged from his hideaway. His throat burned as though he had swallowed razor blades. Maybe he wasn't coming down with a throat infection. Perhaps he was just hoarse from talking to George for ninety minutes or more, in the freezing cold of the small hours. Last night. Seemed a lifetime ago now.

'Paul, you're driving me mad,' she had said. Whispering at almost normal pitch above the noise of what could have been an extractor fan. Her voice sounding tinny, as though she were in a tiled space like the bathroom. 'Just spit it out. What the hell have you done?'

He had sighed. 'I'm struggling. I've been…you know? And I took these…'

'What? What did you take, you silly bastard?'

'Too many codeine.'

There had been a silence that he wasn't entirely sure he'd be able to breach.

'You telling me you OD'd?'

He had nodded, though she couldn't see him, sitting as he was on the end of his bed in his pants and his frayed work shirt. Head in his left hand, staring dolefully at his bare feet.

'You okay? Paul? Speak to me!'

'They pumped my stomach. I'm fine, now,' he had lied.

In the ensuing silence, he had held the phone close against his heart and let out a silent sob. Glad that nobody was watching. Took a deep breath and returned the phone to his ear. 'It's all getting on top of me. I—'

'For God's sake, Paul, get some help. Go to Narcotics Anonymous or something. See a doctor. Anything. But acknowledge you've got a problem.'

'Come over.'

'How can I just drop everything and come running? To Amsterdam! It's not round the corner. And you're not the only one with commitments. I'm in the middle of a PhD. I've got Ad here, for Christ's sakes!'

'Oh?'

It had not been his intention to let that out, and especially not in that piqued tone. An indicator of how he felt about Karelse. Nearly four years on, and his resolve to keep his misgivings about George's boyfriend to himself had morphed into regular, semi-naked scorn.

'Stop! Before you start, just bloody stop!' George had warned him.

So, he had quickly changed the subject and told her about the first dead girl, then the gruesome discovery of the second earlier that evening. An equally troublesome scenario, where a woman's mutilated body had been found naked, dumped in a public place. And yet, nobody had seen a thing. Not yet. She didn't have enough face left to make an ID possible. Strietman had bleated on about ritual sex killings yet again. Worse still, Hasselblad agreed.

'What are the similarities?' George had asked.

Van den Bergen picked at his toenail and recalled the second victim's body on the slab. 'Unzipped from neck to vagina. Disembowelled. Organs removed. Signs of rough sexual intercourse and lacerations on her back commensurate with a whipping. Similar scarring on her breasts that suggest maybe the same guy had given her a breast augmentation as performed the caesarean on the first girl.'

At the other end of the phone, it was easy to detect George's immediate interest. The silence and quickening of her breath said it all. Two unidentified women. Mutilation. Probable sexually motivated murders. After all these years, van den Bergen knew which buttons to push to get her intellectually fired up. He certainly knew better than that loser, Karelse, who wouldn't know finesse if it was a silk-clad fist, punching him in the face. That mamma's-boy had no mastery of the subtle art of manipulation. You needed years of wisdom to really get a feel for that. If he could only get George hooked on the case, perhaps she'd come over. Visit. Stay a while. But her silence continued for a couple of beats beyond what might pass for curiosity.

'You think you can lure me over there with this?' George asked.

Not so subtle. How the hell did she know? Maybe he was losing his touch.

'I'm not trying to lure—'

'I'm hanging up, Paul. Go see your doctor.'

'But George, you could work as a profiler. You always said you'd love to do that. We could be a team.'

'You don't need me to solve this case! You're a pro.'

'It's the perfect opportunity for both of us. Think about it!'

'Tell me you're not going to try any more funky OD bullshit.'

He gave her silence this time. Hated himself for not responding. As manipulation went, he knew this was low.

'Hanging up. Night.'

The line had gone dead and he was left in the oppressive loneliness of his bedroom, clutching the phone to his cheek, as though the smooth warmth of the casing were her face.

Checking the phone's display now, in the privacy of the disabled cubicle, he contemplated sending her an apologetic text. Started to type one out with his thumb. Was just about to send it when the door to the top-floor men's toilet smashed against the wall.

'Boss!' It was Elvis. Could see his brothel-creeper shoes under the door.

Van den Bergen closed his eyes. Saw his father, sitting in the chemo chair, hooked up to the drip, reading a well-thumbed thriller. 'Tell Hasselblad he can bloody well wait.'

'No, boss. You've got to come down quickly. We've had a call. Some Polish builder working in the Museum Quarter reckons he's found a murder scene.'

CHAPTER 15

Amsterdam, Valeriusstraat building site, later

'The blade of the scalpel is broken,' van den Bergen told Elvis. 'Make a note of it. Get a photo, Marie.'

As Elvis scribbled feverishly in his pad, Marie moved closer on van den Bergen's right. Pointed the digital camera at the broken surgical instrument, lying on the floor. With a bleep and a flash of light, it was captured, along with the other oddments in this gruesome montage. A woman's blood-stained thong. A butcher's cleaver. A hammer. A chisel. A cat-o-nine tails.

Van den Bergen squatted, close to the ground. Eyeing the blood-soaked mattress. He touched it tentatively, feeling that the wadding that lay beneath the surface was still damp.

'There must be litres of blood on here,' he said. 'Someone's life's blood.'

'But no body,' Elvis said. 'Could this be where our second victim died?'

Van den Bergen continued studying the mattress in silence. It was one of those heavy, pocket-sprung jobs like his own. Good for a bad back like his. Weighed a tonne. 'Who the hell would have the strength to get a double mattress to the top floor of one of these old houses on their own?' he mused. Shook his head and pursed

69

his lips. Slid a codeine from its blister pack in the inside pocket of his coat and deftly swallowed it using only the spittle in his mouth. It lodged in his throat. His heartbeat sped up. He felt his eyes bulge. Last thing he needed was to choke to death at a bloody crime scene. Heartbeat calming slowly, once he had painfully gulped it down. Sixth one this morning and the medication hadn't even started to take the edge off. Although, he couldn't remember what the doctor had said about codeine reacting badly with his anti-depressants. What had he said? Racked his brains. Nothing.

'Maybe the mattress was here already,' Elvis suggested.

Van den Bergen shook his head. 'No way. Didn't you notice imprints in the dust all the way up the stairs? More than just footprints from the builders. I put my money on drag marks. Dust from downstairs on the sides of the mattress. See?' He used his pen to point out a film of white that had become ingrained in the jacquard fabric of an otherwise filthy, greying mattress. 'This has been brought in from elsewhere, so maybe we're looking for two men. A team.' He turned to Kees. 'Right. We need to dust for fingerprints. Get on it!' He turned to Marie. 'And get forensics to go through the whole place with a fine tooth comb. What's the ETA on Strietman?'

'Any minute now,' Marie said.

'Good.' He gestured towards the video tripod standing tantalisingly at the foot of the mattress. The camera that sat atop it was pointed right where any action would have taken place. 'Can we get the camera running? See what's on it, if anything.'

'It's got to be a recording of the murder,' Elvis said, excitement visible in the high colour that crawled up his neck and into his cheeks.

Van den Bergen stood, hip cracking. Thoughtful. 'Hmn.' He strode to the window and peered down at the builders, all leaning against the side of their transit van, smoking. Pale-faced. The guy who had made the discovery... 'What's the name of the builder who was first on the scene?' he asked Marie.

'Iwan Buczkowski, boss.'

'That's right.' ...Iwan Bucz-whateverhihad thrown his breakfast up all over the floorboards, contaminating the room; not just with his own DNA, but also with the acrid stench of stale alcohol and rancid stomach acid. Van den Bergen hated a contaminated crime scene. He remembered cleaning his father's bathroom, after the chemo had made the old man sick. He hated vomit.

'You're growling, boss,' Elvis said. 'You told me to tell you when you did that.'

Van den Bergen swung around to face the younger detective. 'What do you see of this building from the street?' he asked.

Elvis frowned. Fingered the dyed-black hair that he had artfully sculpted into a quiff, earning him his moniker, together with the oversized red-brown sideburns. 'It's a building site. Empty house, right? Exactly the sort of place you could commit a murder and be left undisturbed.'

'Not really,' Marie interjected. Examining the camera carefully with latex-gloved hands. Blushing. 'Valeriusstraat is quite a busy road.'

'Correct,' van den Bergen said, narrowing his eyes as he peered into the attic room opposite. 'Houses either side with multiple occupancy.' He strode to the wall and knocked on the brick. 'Party wall.' Turned to Elvis. 'Get statements from the neighbours. If someone heard screaming or shouting on the other side of this wall, I want to know about it. There must have been some commotion.'

'Unless the victim was gagged,' Kees said, dusting the chisel on the floor with grey powder, using a fine bristled brush.

Thinking about the two disembowelled women, van den Bergen reflected on the fact that Strietman had found hallucinogenics in their bloodstream. 'Or drugged. Most importantly, though, there are signs on the safety fencing marking this place out as a building site. Men coming in here every day to work. These Polish guys are renowned for their work ethic. They start

71

early. They leave late. Whoever left all this shit lying around was either stupid or had intended for it to be discovered.'

'No body, though,' Marie said. 'Just a blood-soaked mattress and what appear to be murder weapons. How could you get a butchered corpse out without being seen?'

Van den Bergen shrugged. 'If you can get a mattress into a building site unseen, you can get a body out, too. Our perp—'

'Or perps, plural,' Kees said.

'Or perps, if there are two involved, are stealthy and strong. Let's see if another body shows up in the next couple of days. Or maybe this mess *will* be linked to our second Jane Doe, as Elvis has so astutely suggested.'

Kees lifted a print off the chisel, using a strip of clear tape. Held it up to the light. Smiled triumphantly. 'Got one! It's a beauty, too. Clear as a bell.'

Below, the sharp honk of a horn alerted van den Bergen to the forensics van. It pulled in between the builders' vehicle and his own Mercedes. More honking, warning the group of rubber-necking neighbours and passersby to move it.

The scientists started to clamber out. For a fleeting moment, van den Bergen was hopeful that Marianne de Koninck would be leading them. How long could norovirus last after all? Surely she was back on the job.

His hope soon dissipated when he spotted Strietman's head from above. Noticed with some satisfaction that, despite his relative youth, the pathologist's hair was starting to thin. A circle of pink scalp, the size of a one cent coin, had already punctured the thicket of blond, short curls. Van den Bergen ran his hand through his own hair and grunted with approval. One thing he had inherited off the old man that he could be thankful for, at least. Even if his hair had turned snow white by his late thirties, he had plenty of it.

As the forensics team donned their protective jumpsuits over their own clothes on the pavement below, van den Bergen walked away from the window in disgust. Sighed heavily.

'Bloody Strietman. Again,' he said.

But before van den Bergen could go into disgruntled overdrive, Marie looked up. Her eyes seemed to glitter. Her florid face was even more flushed than usual.

'You're not going to believe what's been caught on this camera, boss,' she said, breathless, wearing a crooked smile that was somewhere half way between bemusement and horror.

CHAPTER 16

Stansted Express, East London, later

George gave a half-hearted smile for the camera. One of Ad's arms territorially around her shoulder, one extended. His face pressed up against hers. She could feel his stubble burn against her cheek. He smelled of Aunty Sharon's soap. Ad clicked the button on his phone, capturing the two of them in a selfie on the Stansted Express. Made to kiss her but she had already shuffled squarely into her seat, leaving more space between them than was strictly acceptable for lovers.

'What do you think?' he said, showing her his photographic efforts.

It was a photo that showed only hangdog disappointment in his brown eyes. Boredom in hers. 'Yeah. Nice.'

'Something to remember this trip by.'

In her head were layers of competing voices. Good George apologised profusely for what she knew must have been an utterly soul-destroying trip for her boyfriend, the highlight of which had been Aunty Sharon's rum-laced fruitcake. Bad George just wanted to tell him to sod off. Sod off for turning up unannounced. Get lost for thinking she'd drop everything to play happy housewife. Shove it up his arse, if he thought he could demand sex at a time when she was utterly overworked, overwrought and so overexposed to the sex industry that all she had the inclination to do was masturbate furiously while thinking of someone she definitely shouldn't have been thinking about.

'You going to come over to see me soon?' Ad asked, studying his ticket, as though her answer was written there.

'When I get some money together. Yeah. Course.' Van den Bergen's name was on the tip of her tongue, as usual, but she was careful not to mention him. She eyed the table. It was covered in somebody else's crumbs. Held her breath and counted to ten. There was nothing with which she could wipe the surface. 'Let's move to a clean table,' she said.

'No need,' Ad said, taking a tissue out of his pocket and wiping the crumbs into the aisle. He remained silent for several uncomfortable beats, then asked, 'Who were you speaking to in the middle of the night?' Pushed his glasses up his nose.

It was inevitable. She didn't like lying to Ad. Keeping quiet about the clandestine call would have been what Sally called 'being economical with the truth', but now he'd expressly asked… 'Van den Bergen. He's not well.'

'I don't like you putting so much energy into him,' Ad said, thumping the table. The other passengers looked at the two of them, askance. 'Sorry.'

George sucked her teeth. Shook her head. 'You should be, mate. You telling me you never catch up with the Milkmaid when you're back home? Seriously!'

Ad blushed. Opened his mouth once, twice. 'Don't start. That's not what I meant.'

'That's exactly what you meant,' she retorted. 'You said the words now. Don't act like you can just suck them up. Time travels forwards in the universe, Adrianus. Not back. Face it, you're jealous. And what of? A forty-odd-year-old with a painkiller addiction? Van den Bergen's my friend. I get him. He gets me. That's all. A friend. *My* friend. How many times I have to tell you, for Christ's sake?'

75

George looked out of the window – anger simmering, but just keeping a lid on it. The train to Stansted airport rattled and swayed through East London. Not George's familiar turf but not dissimilar. Same disappointing back gardens, full of broken plastic kids' climbing frames and slides. Washing on the line that had been forgotten. Dog shit lurking in the long grass, no doubt. Bare bulbs glowering out of single-glazed windows. A glimpse of high streets as they chugged through the postcodes, stopping only in Tottenham Hale. Tags spray-painted on the walls by gang members long since grown up or inside; once colourful, now faded and flaking. Cash your gold. Send money worldwide. Southern Fried chicken. Legal services: We speak Urdu, Gujarati and Punjabi – living in grand Victorian buildings that might have once been pubs, by the looks. Women wearing full burka, carrying bulging plastic bags with coriander hanging out the top. Small kids running on ahead in their puffa coats. Chatting shit like they hadn't a care in the world on this dismal, pissy weekday in January.

George noticed it all in a bid to avoid looking at Ad. Every time he clasped her hand, she found a reason to let go. Scratching her nose. Fluffing up her curls. Pretending to wipe the window with her sleeve so she had a better view of the grey urban scene that was unfolding on either side of the train. But this really wasn't the way she wanted his trip to end. In a bid to bridge the yawning chasm that was growing between them, she put her head on his shoulder for the rest of the journey.

The airport, still the most glamorous thing in that drab eastern England locale, was bustling with grey-suited businessmen, wheeling small overnighter suitcases with purpose and very shiny shoes. Kids with backpacks gazed up in awe or perhaps just bewilderment at the branches of the steel structural trees that supported the airy roof canopy. It was an airport George liked and loathed in equal measure. Happy when she was setting off for Amsterdam. Bereft, as she returned, leaving love far behind on the other side of the North Sea.

Beneath the 'Departures' sign that marked where the soulless lounge ended and where the inner sanctum of passport control began – with the promise of duty free Toblerone and a view of the planes beyond – Ad kissed George until his glasses steamed up. A passionate kiss that she couldn't quite return with the same level of enthusiasm, though she tried.

'I love you, you know that, don't you?' he said.

She nodded. Felt like a shit of the highest order. 'I love you too. I really do.' She said the words. They sounded correct. Looked into those eyes that had once all but electrified her.

'You have to come. Seeing you every now and then, like this…' He clutched her hands and kissed her knuckles tenderly. She stroked the stump where his index finger had once been. 'It's not enough. It's tearing us apart. You're here. I'm there.'

George blinked back a tear, though she wasn't sure why it had appeared. Couldn't articulate the grief she felt. 'Ad, I'm in the middle of a bloody PhD. My research project… It's ground-breaking. It's going to make my name. I've got a job, however mundane. This is serious, man. This is my career. I can't just drop it and come running.'

She rubbed an imaginary speck of dirt on his cheek. That beautiful pale olive skin. She had been so hot for it once. Ran her hand gently over his soft, shorn dark hair. He looked deflated. Defeated. But then, suddenly brighter.

'Ask for study leave. Go on. I bet you can do it.'

'Think I haven't already asked Sally a million times? Think I wouldn't be in Amsterdam if I could swing it? Six months here. Six months there.' She shook her head.

Ad grabbed her chin. Lifted her face so that she had no option but to meet his gaze. 'Ask again. For us.'

She looked up at the departures board. 'Your gate's been up for ages. Go on! Else you'll miss your flight. Aunty Sharon said you're costing her a fortune in cake and Sky subscription as it is. Go!' A smile was easy, now he was hoisting his rucksack on his shoulders. Guilt weighed heavily on hers.

He walked towards security. Took one last look at her over his shoulder.

'Ask. For us,' he repeated.

'I'll ask for us,' she said. *And for van den Bergen*, she thought.

CHAPTER 17

Amsterdam, Valeriusstraat building site, later

'Run it again,' van den Bergen said, as Marie clicked the stop button on the camera.

'I don't think I can bear to keep watching this,' Elvis said, leaning forward between the driver's and passenger seats.

'Wimp,' Marie said, digitally spooling back to the beginning, forcing the others to watch the brutal scenes backwards and at four times the speed of live action on the camera's tiny preview screen.

Van den Bergen peered over his shoulder at Kees. 'Don't you throw up in here. Do you hear me?' The young detective's face looked like putty. He had wedged himself right into the corner on the rear passenger side, as though the supportive structure of the vehicle would provide him with an emotional bolster. 'You're a policeman, for God's sake. If you can't control yourself, get out.'

'Need…air. Sorry.' Kees opened the door to the Mercedes and stepped onto the pavement. Icy air whipped into the cabin.

'Close the bloody door!' van den Bergen yelled. With a hefty thunk, just the three of them remained. 'Useless turd.'

He felt suddenly claustrophobic. Though the smell of the leather seats and the wool carpet of the slip-mats was still pleasantly strong – the E class, a perk of being a chief inspector with impractically long legs, was only two months old – it was not strong enough to mask Marie's stale sweat and Elvis' appalling cologne. He would have to valet the interior at the weekend or else go to the allotment and bring the honest scent of earth and pine back home with him. He remembered his father, sitting in a deck chair in the allotment, enjoying the morning glories and the summer sunshine. He had been near the end. The old man's clothes swam around his skeletal frame. *Not now! Not now!*

Marshalling his thoughts, van den Bergen turned to Marie. 'Go on. Play it.'

There was the blonde woman. She was dressed in a PVC catsuit, which clung to her body like a shining, black second skin. Slim and honed like a gymnast but for disproportionately large, orb-like breasts that sat high on her chest. Hair tied severely into a high ponytail. Smiling at the camera with lascivious, crimson-lipped promise. Smoky made-up eyes with black false lashes. She was probably a high-cheekboned natural beauty underneath all the paint. Clutching at a cat-o-nine tails. Swish, swish. Whipping it provocatively between her own legs. The picture was of a high quality, though there was no sound. The setting was a large bedroom that could have been anywhere, its focal point, a brass bedstead framing a mattress that had been wrapped in a red satin sheet. There were no windows to gauge the age of the building in which this took place. The bare walls were painted black. And there was no other star of this movie. Only the blonde woman.

It began with auto-erotic scenes, where the woman played mischievously to the camera. Slowly peeling away the PVC. But with a series of obvious edits, the action degenerated quickly into something that was more akin to a horror film. The woman was on her back. Naked, spread-eagled and strung by her wrists and ankles between the posts of the iron bedstead. Subject to all manner of sadistic acts – all perpetrated by someone just off screen, using the sort of implements one would find in a builder's toolbox – and culminating in dismemberment with a hedge trimmer, which, despite having seen the film four times already, still made Elvis squeak and squeeze his eyes shut.

Marie turned the camera off. Placed it on the dash. Exhaled heavily. Hooked her red hair behind her ear and started to finger a scab on her cheek.

'What do you think, Marie?' van den Bergen asked, turning to his almost perfectly composed passenger. 'You're my internet-nasty expert. Looks very much like a recording of a murder. Snuff porn, maybe? Could the mattress in the footage be the one upstairs in this house, minus the sheet?'

'Whatever it is, it's disgusting,' Elvis said, pulling a box of cigarettes out of his breast pocket. 'Just…just…horrible.'

'Not in here!' van den Bergen said, eyeing the cigarettes venom-ously. 'Let Marie speak.'

Marie blushed. Tugged at the turtle neck of her green jumper. 'Well, it's certainly not a recording of either of the Jane Doe murders we're looking at. Both of those women were at least left their limbs.'

Van den Bergen scrutinised Marie. How the hell did this girl even sleep at night? She had never once taken up the force's offer of counselling, to help her do the job she did. He sighed. It was a damned crummy profession they were in. Briefly, he felt a pang of nostalgia for his time as a fine art student. Ancient history, now.

'I need to see this on my big monitor, boss,' Marie said. She bit her bottom lip; looked through the windscreen at the builders, who were now talking to Kees. 'It's certainly not continuous footage and if it is snuff…' she inclined her head in the direction of the building site '…it definitely hasn't been recorded in that attic with a camera just stuck on top of a tripod. There are close-ups, for a start. From different angles. Someone was walking around the room while they were filming. Maybe there was a second camera man.'

Elvis leaned forward again, blasting van den Bergen with a whiff of peppermint. He chewed gum noisily. Clack, clack, clack. 'What's the bet another body turns up in the next couple of days? I think Hasselblad's right. We've got a serial killer on our hands.'

Van den Bergen grimaced. 'You sound like a Friesian cow chewing hay, do you know that?' But though Elvis irritated him, his focus did not waver from Iwan Buczkowski. Speaking on his phone. Leaning with one arm above his head against the van. 'Somebody was behind the lens. Some depraved bastard wielded those tools and that hedge trimmer. The print Kees lifted belongs to someone.'

Just then, Kees walked around the bonnet of the car and rapped on the glass, driver's side, with the edge of his notebook.

At the push of a button, the window slid down with a satisfying whir. 'You knock on my car like that again, and I'll knock *you* all the way down to traffic detail,' van den Bergen said. 'What do you want?'

Kees leaned in. His putty-pallor was gone now, and had been replaced by flame-cheeked enthusiasm – almost palpably buzzing. 'Been quizzing those builders a bit more. Getting chatty, like.'

'And?'

'I've got a hunch, boss, and you're gonna wanna hear it.'

CHAPTER 18

Cambridge, St John's College, later

'Let me go,' George pleaded, folding the wrapping paper from the jaunty poinsettia plant she had brought her supervisor into tight, ever-shrinking squares.

'Absolutely not,' Sally replied. She carried the gift gingerly, as though it were radioactive material, and plonked it into a ceramic plant pot holder at the side of her computer. Murmured something inaudible that had a sour tone to it. Turned to George, hooking her battleship-grey, bobbed hair behind her ear. 'And don't think you can bribe me so easily! I see through your pot-plant charms, young lady.' Her pointing index finger was nicotine stained, but her fingernails were the same bright red as the plants' leaves. She sat imperiously in her typing chair. Queen on her academic's throne. The large, oak desk wedged a physical barrier between them, leaving George feeling like she had been abruptly banished from court.

George blushed. Bit back her irritation. Crossed and uncrossed her legs. 'Come on, Sally! It's a bona fide request. An Overseas Institutional Visit. You had no problems with me doing the internship in Westminster. You've never taken issue with me divvying my time between here and—'

'That's entirely different. It's London. The two things are not comparable. Especially not in your bloody situation.'

George quietly mused that it was a good job Sally didn't know about her gig as a cleaner in a Soho strip club. The shifty Italian chaperone for those young pole dancers whom Derek had been clucking around had only asked her for a double whisky and a private lap dance. But he had got pretty nasty when she had turned him down. No, her brush with a man who was clearly something far more sinister than just an ageing wide-boy was exactly the sort of thing Sally didn't need to hear.

Sticking her finger defiantly through the rip in her jeans, George searched all the admissible arguments filed away in her brain as to why Sally should sanction overseas travel. She downloaded the sure-fire winners. 'I study the effects of pornography on violent offenders, for Christ's sake! I'd be a visiting scholar in a city that's one of the biggest players in Europe's porn industry. Amsterdam, man! My funding body would agree immediately.'

'No, I said. And don't "man" me!'

'But think how cool it would be, if I could just hop on the overnighter to Prague to do some qualitative research there as well. Porn was totally banned in the Czech Republic under Soviet rule. Now they're going mental with themselves. Imagine how revealing that would be about the effects of pornography on sex crimes. A breakthrough study with *your* department's name on it!' George was willing Sally to relent. For Ad's sake. For van den Bergen's sake.

'Nice try, you persistent little bugger! The phenomenon has already been studied, as you well know. Diamond, Jozifkova and Weiss. I know you've done your homework, so don't pretend to be a fool and don't try to take me for one, either.'

George threw her hands up in the air. Stood and walked over to the mullioned window that looked onto the frosty courtyard below. Her breath steamed on the air. 'Jeeesus! I'm a boring PhD student doing dry academic research. What the hell could happen to—'

Behind her, Dr Sally Wright slammed her hand down on the

desk top. 'I will *not* authorise it. Do you hear me? Because I *cannot* authorise it. You've been told to stay put. After last time. Your track record for staying out of trouble is not exactly unimpeachable, is it, Ms McKenzie?' She looked over the top of her winged glasses, fixing George with a gaze so unyielding that she felt silenced like a rebuked child. 'That is my final word on the matter.'

George folded her arms, flung herself back onto the chaise longue and dug her short nails deeply into the plush velvet covering. Stared into the glowing embers of the fire that heated only two feet directly in front of it, leaving the rest of that cavernous old room feeling like a morgue. 'But if anyone can swing it, *you* can.' She kept her voice small. Flattery was the only weapon left in her arsenal, though she knew it would not work.

Sally lit a cigarette and coughed wheezily. Her throaty, rasping voice was punctuated by bouts of choking. 'I know I could swing it. Theoretically. Not for nothing am I the senior tutor of St John's College, Cambridge. I got MI5 to agree to you visiting for weekends, didn't I? Study leave for half a year is, however, an entirely different kettle of fish.' She started to type on her keyboard, cigarette hanging out the corner of her pruned mouth as she spoke. Studied indifference, George knew. Then, pausing dramatically, her eyes sought out her protégée once more. 'But I do not *wish* to swing it. *Capisce?*' Sally inhaled deeply. The hacking cough started up anew. She thumped herself in the chest. 'Because the last time you went gallivanting off to Amsterdam for the year, you nearly wound up dead and could have taken half of Trinity Street with you. Stay put, young lady! My rules. Good reasons.'

George took the sucker punch.

Dragging herself over the hump of the narrow stone corridor that was the Bridge of Sighs, traversing the sluggish, inky, almost frozen River Cam and negotiating the frost-dusted backs, she acknowledged that she had lost this bout with Sally. Trudging up towards the monolithic brick phallus that was the University

Library tower, George resolved that she would come back fighting in round two. *I will not go down and stay down. Got to get the hell out of this beautiful prison. Got to help Paul.*

'Stop torturing yourself, you donkey,' she said under her breath, as she cleared the library's security and climbed the stairs to the silent, gloomy stacks, where under the timed lights, she would find what she was looking for.

CHAPTER 19

Amsterdam, police headquarters, later

'No. Sorry. Didn't see a thing.'

One by one, the doors had all slammed in van den Bergen's face. Same lines, almost verbatim, from neighbours who differed in age, gender and ethnicity but who all had that upper-middle-class Museum Quarter/Old South thing in common. Nobody seemed to be neighbourly. Everyone kept themselves to themselves. Unfortunately, the woman, whose Koninginneweg house faced onto the back of the building site, was away on business, according the cleaner.

Van den Bergen slammed his pad onto the meeting room desk. 'What have we got?' he asked Elvis, Marie and Kees.

'*Nada*,' Elvis said. 'Absolutely zilch. Not a single eyeball on our man. Nobody heard the back door being forced. I mean, Christ! Nobody saw someone dragging a double mattress over a fence. I can't even see how it's possible to get a mattress from the street into the back of that house. Our guy must be a damned magician.'

'Unless I was wrong, and the mattress was already in situ,' van den Bergen said.

Kees shuffled out of his bright red anorak and draped it over his chair. Ruffled his mousy, thinning mop. Rolled his white shirt sleeves above his brown jumper, as though he were about to reveal something breathtaking. 'About my hunch…'

Van den Bergen sighed. Rubbed the tiny remnants of scabbing on his knuckles, which had given way to new skin beneath. 'Go on. Let's hear it.'

'I think the builder's our man.' Kees smiled triumphantly, treating the team to an eyeful of his jutting tombstone teeth. 'Well, one of our men. Old Iwan.'

It was all the chief inspector could do to stifle a groan. 'Do tell us, Mr Leeuwenhoek! Why is, "Old Iwan" our man?'

Kees folded his arms; his smile gone, now. Clearly not the reception he had been expecting. 'He's got access to the building,' he began, counting the facts off on his fingers. 'He pukes all over the crime scene, meaning his DNA is everywhere anyway. So chances are, if we find his DNA on the mattress, it's inadmissible in court. The perp uses builders' tools in the film. His mate's got a van. And there was something about the guy. I dunno. He's got one of those tattooed sleeves down his arm. Pentangles and skulls and shit. My detective's intuition is just screaming that we should look into him.'

'Bollocks!' Elvis said, rocking back on his chair. 'Poor guy was shaking like a leaf. He was genuine.'

'Kees, you're such a dick,' Marie said, shaking her head. 'We're looking for someone who can wield a scalpel, not a pickaxe.'

Van den Bergen pushed his chair out from the table. Drummed his pad with his Biro and bounced his right foot on his left knee. 'No. Kees has got a point. It's far-fetched, but we do need to check into the Poles' alibis. That building site is simply not accessible from the back. You've got two parallel rows of terraces with no alleyway between. The gardens are all fenced off and overlooked. How did that mattress get in there? One of the builders might be covering for someone. Kees, it's your hunch. You get on it.'

Van den Bergen caught sight of Marie rolling her eyes, but opted not to challenge her. 'Marie. Footage?'

She jumped. A flush of red crawling up her neck. 'I've examined it in detail, boss,' she said, toying with her pearls. 'It's not a film of a murder.'

'What absolute crap!' Elvis said.

Holding up his hand, van den Bergen silenced his scoffing sidekick. 'What do you mean?'

'It's a porno flick,' Marie said. 'Shot on a quality camera. Professionally edited. Only thing that's missing is the bum-chicka-wow-wow soundtrack. All that gore you can see...' She smiled wryly and sipped from her plastic cup of coffee, as though she were savouring the undivided attention of the men. 'It's special effects. The footage on the camera's memory disc is basically a kinky slasher movie.'

'You certain?' van den Bergen asked, recalling the horrific scenes that had appeared so convincing.

'Yep,' Marie said. 'If anyone knows the difference between genuine snuff and horror CGI, it's me. I love horror films.'

Though it was done surreptitiously, van den Bergen noticed Kees nudge Elvis.

'The blonde's an actress,' Marie clarified. 'She's probably walking round the supermarket right now, doing her shopping. Fit and healthy with a fat wad of cash in her back pocket, while old perverts all over Europe are tugging themselves senseless over her on-screen demise.' She turned to Kees. 'I saw that! I have got the gift of sight, you know.'

Kees said nothing. Pulled the wide-eyed face of the innocent.

Van den Bergen nodded. Clicked his tongue against the roof of his mouth repeatedly, while he absorbed this revelation. 'Do you know who she is? The actress.'

Marie shrugged. 'Never seen her before. Never seen porn this violent before that wasn't actual snuff.' She handed a small disc to him. 'I made copies and filed the original with the other evidence.'

Opening his laptop, van den Bergen loaded the film up.

Watched with utter absorption as the blonde filled the much larger screen. Paused it, once the actress was spread-eagled and naked on the bed. Pointed to the undersides of her ample breasts with the chewed bottom of his Biro. 'See that?'

The others leaned in closer, their breath on the back of his head.

'What?' Elvis asked.

'I saw this scarring on the mortuary slab with my own eyes. It's not like the scarring you normally see from shoddy boob jobs. It's too distinctive not to be from the same surgeon's hand. I'd put money on it that this actress is our second Jane Doe.'

CHAPTER 20

Amsterdam, 20 January

'I'm ill, Paul,' she said through the half-open letterbox. 'Just leave me be!'

Van den Bergen took a step backwards on the landing and examined Marianne de Koninck's eyes through the rectangular gap. They were red and puffy.

'Please open the door. We need to talk.' He thrust the tulips closer to the door, so that she could inspect his gift. As though this were some kind of entry code to her apartment.

The flap of the head pathologist's letterbox clattered shut. He heard her sigh behind the door. A chain being removed and a bolt being drawn back. The door opened about six inches. He could see she was wearing a fleecy all-in-one with a dressing gown on top. Furry slippers on her feet. He had imagined she would wear elegant lace-trimmed silk to bed. Perhaps that was wishful thinking.

'I'm contagious,' she said. Her short hair was dishevelled. Split on one side, as though she had slept in the same position for several days without washing it.

'I'll be the judge of that,' van den Bergen said, pressing the tulips into her hands and stepping inside.

At the breakfast bar of her expansive kitchen island, he warmed his hands on a cup of espresso that she had fixed him using a shining steel coffee machine. It was a sleek place, all right. Aubergine gloss cupboard fronts; the worktops, some sort of glittering man-made composite. He ran his fingertips along the edge, as though a grand piano's keys were embedded into it. A dining area with Perspex table and chairs to seat eight flowed into the adjacent austere and fashionable living area. This was the sort of pad a man like him should own. Uncluttered. Full of gadgetry. Somewhere to entertain. But then, van den Bergen liked his vintage thrift-market tat and bookshelves full of old vinyl. And, he realised, that not only was Marianne full of surprises, but she didn't have to pay maintenance to an ex. What he had noticed on entry, however, was that only women's shoes sat in a rack on the polished parquet.

'Nice place,' he said.

'Cake?'

She offered him a slice of apple cake that had been all but eaten. There was an empty plate on the kitchen island, bearing telltale crumbs. A used fork next to it. Comfort eating, van den Bergen assessed.

'Where's your boyfriend?' The dimpling in Marianne's chin told him everything he needed to know. 'You and Jasper split up? That what all this is about?'

The pathologist nodded and sighed, wiping away the threat of a tear. 'Bastard upped and left me for some nurse his own age.'

Making sure he did not betray the satisfaction that lurked just beneath the surface of his empathic expression, he patted her hand. Moved around the island and enveloped her in a stiff hug, which he immediately regretted. All those years, he had wondered if their professional rapport would translate to a physical one. It didn't. There was no chemistry between them, whatsoever. And it was clear from the backwards step that she took that she thought so too.

'I'm sorry to hear that,' he said, retreating to his bar stool.

Baffled that disappointment did not stir within him.

Marianne looked up to the spotlit ceiling with sorrowful, watery eyes and sniffed. 'Do yourself a favour, Paul. Never fall for a younger woman. You'll spend your life wondering how the hell she could fancy you, with your deteriorating eyesight and decaying body. Then one day, she'll just up and leave for someone firmer. Honestly, they just eat you up and spit you out.' She started to cry. Angry sobs with tears soaking the collar of her dressing gown. 'He took my bloody stereo!' Her words started to break into hiccoughs of sound, as though she were speaking down a phone line with intermittently poor reception. 'I wouldn't...mind but...it was m—my...birthday...present...a—and I...gave him the god—goddamned...money to...pay for it.'

Van den Bergen's coffee had long gone cold before he could turn the subject to the case. 'Look, Marianne,' he said, spreading his fingers wide. He related what he knew so far about the murders.

'So, what has all this got to do with me?' Marianne asked. Her tone was sour. 'Aren't I allowed to take some sick leave? I've got a perfectly capable—'

'I don't trust Strietman,' van den Bergen said. 'Sorry. The guy's just not you. He comes over like a crap crime noir film, full of theories and gum-shoe fucking interpretations.'

Marianne rubbed her face and groaned. 'Daan Strietman is highly qualified, Paul. Yes, he loves his job—'

'I don't need Dick bloody Tracy or...' He struggled to think of an illustration that would suit his purposes, but in truth, he hadn't seen more than a handful of films since Tamara was at that age where the cinema had seemed a suitable activity for a father who saw his daughter every second weekend. '...I don't know. Just Dick bloody Tracy. I need a pathologist who gives me straight facts.' He withdrew a sheaf of paper from the inside pocket of his raincoat. It made a hefty thwack as he slammed it down emphatically on the worktop. Pulled his reading glasses up from their resting place on his stomach, at the end of their chain, and pushed them up his nose. Started to read the reports from the autopsy, giving extra emphasis to the hyperbole and melodrama with which Strietman had studded his otherwise dry medical observations.

'Give me those sodding print-outs, you annoying old bugger!' Marianne leaned over the island and snatched the sheaf up. The suggestion of a half-smile playing on her lips. Eyes darting from side to side as she skimmed the pages.

'Intrigued?' van den Bergen asked, staring at her from over the top of his half-moon glasses. 'We should get the forensics back from the building site any time now. I'd prefer it was you who delivered the results to me.'

'Look, I'll come in tomorrow. We'll see what we see.'

CHAPTER 21

Cambridge, Mill Road, later

George saw nothing but a green and grey blur as she rattled across Parker's Piece. Teeth juddering. Eyes streaming. Cycling on her rusting sit-up-and-beg diagonally across, from the University Arms towards Mill Road with aching legs that were out of practice. Every time she hit a bump in the giant criss-cross of tarmac that cut through the huge green square, her Sainsbury's bags, full of tins that she vowed she would cook with, as Ad had shown her, bashed painfully against her shins.

'Fucking man!' she complained aloud, garnering a bewildered look from the pimple-faced boy (a fresher, by the looks) who approached from the opposite direction, only feet away from her now. 'Not you, tit!'

The boy continued on his way, leaving George to ruminate over what a liability van den Bergen was, and how Ad was not much better. She had been back in Cambridge less than twenty-four hours. It had been her intention to do a little quiet reading, although she had admittedly gone off piste by selecting a criminology book that dealt with trafficked women, working as slaves in Britain's sex industry. But she did, at least, have noble intentions of typing up her notes from her interviews with Silas Holm and Dermot Robinson. Van den Bergen had ruined all that with the email.

From: Paul van den Bergen06.27
To: George_McKenzie@hotmail.com
Subject: Victim ID

I'm attaching a video we pulled from a camera found in a crime scene. Marie says it is horror porno, but nobody can ID the film or the actress. You might know. Let me know a.s.a.p. if you've got ideas.

Come back to Amsterdam. It's almost time to pot up the dahlias.
Paul.
PS: There's something else I need to tell you.

She had deliberately not switched on her phone until she was in the supermarket and it had gone nine. Ad-avoidance. Ad had already left four messages, sent six texts and attempted a further three calls – all missed. Wanting to discuss the trip and her behaviour. Insisting he had to tell her what was on his mind and how they could sort things out and how he *really* didn't speak to Astrid any more, despite George's misgivings, *and* how he could come to terms with her hygiene obsession *and* that van den Bergen was absolutely not the only one who understood psychological problems. Being assailed by a defensive Ad was bad enough. But here, van den Bergen had sent her a video she did not have the credit to download. Her phone's monthly contract was almost at its limit. Plus, it had been accompanied by a message that was both tantalising and tugged at her already compromised heart. What did he need to tell her, exactly?

'Incorrigible arsehole!' she said, as she cycled the length of Mill Road.

It felt like a five-mile hike. She would have liked a cigarette at the end of it with the fresh, ground coffee she had just bought.

But she had sworn to both Ad and van den Bergen that she would stick with the e-cigarettes. They weren't the same.

She turned into Devonshire Road. Opened the door to the terraced house she shared with another PhD called Lucy. Lucy was a tall, long-limbed rich girl who spent most of the time at her undergrad boyfriend's place, four or five miles away, up in Girton College. Given the frequency with which George shuttled back and forth from London and Amsterdam, she and Lucy had met only a handful of times in a term. Probably just as well, since Lucy was a slovenly little shit, who didn't know one end of a toilet cleaner bottle from another. Lucy had left a scum ring around the bath on three occasions, early on in the tenancy, rendering George apoplectic with rage. But Lucy had left a mess in the toilet only once. George smiled at the memory of threatening leggy, entitled Lucy with a beating, using the toilet brush as a weapon. No. Lucy didn't come home very often, now. Though a note on the kitchen table said she planned to return tomorrow evening, and could George please leave the heating and hot water on? No. Fuck her. George didn't have the money to subsidise Lucy's preferred twenty-six degrees of tropical in winter. It wasn't the Costa del Salcombe. She could put another sodding ten-ply cashmere jumper on.

Coffee on, and George picked up van den Bergen's email on her laptop. Watched the video nasty, whilst chugging on her e-cigarette. Peered through her fingers as she reached the climax.

'Jesus, man. That's some fucked-up shit, right there,' she told the screen.

The film was high resolution. Perhaps owing to the fact that the close-ups were all of body parts and implements, rather than focussing on her face, and that the lighting was sharply directional, George found she was struggling to place the actress. Certainly, despite having notched up some serious hours watching hardcore violent pornography until revulsion and outrage had turned to numb indifference, she did not even recognise the tasteless niche genre.

She captured the woman in a freeze-frame. Leaned in close. There was something about the woman's eyes that seemed startlingly familiar, though she could not articulate why.

'She looks like Katja with a wig on,' she said aloud, swigging coffee from her special Amsterdam mug. 'Is it Katja?' Scroll back. Freeze. Scroll forward. Freeze. The woman flickered in slo-mo through her erotic cabaret. 'Fucking looks like her, as well.'

How long ago had her erstwhile neighbour, Katja, gone into porn flicks – boosted from prostitution, where she had rented a humble room above the Cracked Pot Coffee Shop, directly beneath George's attic bedsit, to the small screen? A step up the erotic career ladder, because giving a blow job to that prick the Firestarter had catapulted her from being a fifty-euro-a-trick nobody to being a sex-industry celebrity.

Sweat beaded instantaneously on George's forehead. She pulled out her phone and dialled Katja.

Ringing. Ringing. Ringing. No answer. Then…

'George, darling!' Her voice was sluggish, as though George had woken her.

'You alive?' George asked, breathing deeply to slow her heart-beat.

'Yes. Last time I looked, honey.'

'Good. Listen, I'm going to send you a still of a porn actress. Do you think you could tell me who she is? It's pretty important.' Van den Bergen had told George that he had released limited information about the murders to the media. Should she tell Katja that there was a possible serial killer of women on the loose in Amsterdam? Did Katja already know? But George did not have time to get sucked into the melodramatic upwards-spiral of panic that would surely ensue if she levelled with her friend. 'It's for my course. I need to know straight away.'

Silence crackled along the line. 'I'm very tired, darling. I only went to bed two hours ago.'

'Sorry. Look, text me yes or no when you get the picture. And stay safe, you big tart. I'll see you soon.'

George hung up. She saved a screen grab from early on in the film and texted it as a JPEG. Within five minutes, Katja's answer came back as:

```
No idea.xxx
```

Feeling hopeful, she then emailed the picture to Dermot Robinson's PA, Marge. She might know. Surely she would help. An hour passed. The response came back as negative.

Then, it occurred to her. The eyes. The niche interest. There was one person who would definitely be able to identify both actress and film.

CHAPTER 22

Amsterdam, police headquarters, later

'Where were you on the night of the eighteenth, Iwan?' Kees asked in English.

As they faced one another across the table in the interview room back at the station, Kees tried to get the measure of this Polish builder who spoke such bloody good English. There was something about the man that he instinctively did not trust. Not in the slightest. For a start, Iwan Buczkowski was pig ugly. His unshaven face was swollen; his complexion grey. Blue eyes were red-rimmed; the blond lashes crusty, giving him a demonic appearance. Baggy lower lids bore a purple tinge in the corners, as though he were recovering from black eyes. Had he been fighting? Kees' scrutiny turned to Iwan's knuckles. No cuts. No scabs. Perhaps he'd *been* punched. With a broken nose like that and the black remnants of a laceration visible beneath his fair buzz-cut, Kees felt certain he was on the money. This guy was a brute. A fighter. Bad news. And he, Kees Leeuwenhoek, had undoubtedly inherited his father's sleuthing instincts – a man who had received so many commendations for bravery and excellence, that his reputation throughout Limburg was the stuff of legend. Kees Leeuwenhoek senior: lion by name. Lion by nature.

'Can I smoke?' Iwan asked, pulling a pack of Marlboro from

the breast pocket of his red and black lumberjack shirt.

'No. Tell me where you were two nights ago. I want your movements from the time you left the building site to the time you returned, the following morning. I want you to give me names of the people you were with.'

Though the man was a good three or four inches taller than he was, Kees had been careful to seat him on a lower chair – a trick Kamphuis had taught him – so that they were now equal in height. He deliberately sat bolt upright, where the builder slouched. Even better. Kees was careful to speak in a commanding voice, projecting from the bottom of his diaphragm – a trick the speech therapist had taught him as a child, to counteract his naturally soft voice; something his father agreed to only after he had received four beatings from the other boys at school. Perhaps, in a moment, he would stand up and lean over the table, arms spread wide, like he had seen US detectives do in thrillers on TV. Bear down on this thug a bit. Then, his having the upper hand would be unquestionable.

'I already told you,' the builder said. 'I went straight home for my dinner. My girl, Krystyna, will confirm what I say. I left for Stefan's after I'd had a shower.' He rolled the unlit cigarette between his fingers. Failed to make eye contact with Kees. 'Drove over to his place in my van. We all played cards and drank beer. Me, Stefan, Pawel and Michal. I got very drunk. Pawel wasn't drinking, so he dropped me back at my place about three am. Then I crashed out and got picked up for work just before seven am.' Raising his head slowly, he locked eyes with Kees. 'When can I have my drill and my toolbox back? I need them for work.'

Despite his best intentions, Kees found himself wriggling free of the clutches of this Pole's malevolent stare. Unable to settle on anything and feeling downright uncomfortable, his gaze eventually rested on the man's tattoo, which was just peeping beneath the cuff of the lumberjack shirt.

'What are you hiding under that shirt sleeve?' he asked.

'Hiding?'

'The tattoo. Show it me.'

Iwan Buczkowski shrugged and rolled his sleeve up to reveal a beefy, muscled arm, tattooed with an elaborate black design from shoulder to wrist. The peripheral markings were detailed and delicate representations of tree branches in full leaf. But the focal points – a naked woman nailed to an inverted cross, a skull and several pentagrams – were nothing short of ghoulish. The design made Kees shudder. His father had always abhorred tattoos, and they had been outlawed in his house as something only the dregs of the barrel subjected themselves to.

'Explain the design to me!' Kees could feel adrenalin starting to course through his tired, disappointingly average body. It was a wonderful feeling. One of the things he loved about being a detective.

'This?' Iwan said, rolling his sleeve back down. 'A friend did it for me back in Poland. I just let him do what he wanted. He's one of the best tattoo artists around.'

Kees snorted with derision. 'You don't just let a friend tattoo you with upside-down crosses and all that devil-worshipping shit.'

Iwan frowned. He stood abruptly, towering above Kees. The scraping noise of the chair on linoleum felt like violence. 'What the fuck do you know?' He was shouting. His previously impassive expression had given way to open hostility, scowling as he was. 'And what's it to you, anyway? I gave you the information you needed. So, unless you're planning on arresting me for throwing up on a building site, I suggest you open that door, give me back my bloody tools and leave me the fuck alone.' He stuck the unlit cigarette in his mouth.

At this stage, there was nothing to be gained by Kees standing as well. He had ceded any physical advantage that his higher chair had briefly given him. But his father said a good detective never gives up, and he was not ready to let this belligerent Pole go. *Remember, you are a detective on your home turf,* he counselled himself. *Iwan Buczkowski is a lowly Eastern European manual worker inside a Dutch police station. Your police station. Strietman said ritual murders. Follow your nose. Van den Bergen has given you a green light to follow the line of inquiry. Kamphuis personally promised you promotion if you can crack this case. Fuck that ponce, Elvis. Fuck Marie. Fuck van den Bergen. Fuck teamwork. Kamphuis is your sensei. Show this Pole no mercy.*

Kees allowed himself an inward smile, reasoning that he definitely had the upper hand, psychologically. This man would surely submit to his authority.

He steeled himself to push one more time. 'Are you a Satanist, Iwan?'

'Fuck you!'

CHAPTER 23

Broadmoor Psychiatric Hospital, later

The sight of the Victorian sprawl that was Broadmoor Psychiatric Hospital made George's heart sink. The gateway to hell. Twice now, inside a week. A large, black, arched entrance, presided over by orange-brick Italianate towers that stood like stout sentinels either side of an ornate clock face. Guarding time itself – entire lifetimes for some of the men who dwelled behind those thick walls, including the Firestarter, twisted Firestarter. If it weren't for the bars at the windows and the high fencing, if she screwed her eyes up very tightly until everything became blurred around the edges, a stranger might mistake the place for a grand spa hotel. George sighed. It was not a grand spa hotel. And even if visitors could bring fluffy towelling robes in with them, they would almost certainly not be allowed to keep the belts, so easily used as ligatures with which a patient might hang himself or one of his fellow residents. In fact, with more than six sheets of paper on her person, George knew she might get into trouble just for that.

Now, she produced her documentation yet again for security to see. Walked through the metal detectors. Checked in her phone, which she could retrieve only on exit.

'Back so soon, love?' the security officer said. She arranged her face into something resembling a warm smile. Started to frisk George. Her smile faltered.

George had stupidly left a chain hanging round her neck featuring her name in gold lettering. She didn't like the adornment, but it had been a present from Ad. She might as well have been planning to board a flight to JFK from Gatwick with contraband liquids in her handbag.

'Take it off, please,' the officer instructed her. 'You know the rules about jewellery.'

'Sorry. I forgot. This is an impromptu vi—'

'In here!' The woman's tone was now castigating. She pointed to the container, that already held George's phone.

'Fine.' *Frosty-faced cow.*

The gates clanged open. Despite conducting research inside this infamous psychiatric hospital for a year now, George still felt jittery. She was on the inside; less than ten years since she had worn a standard issue tracksuit. Not inside these walls, but inside others like it. She willed her hands to keep from shaking. Clenched her fists tight. Keeping her clammy hands to herself, George was escorted across the deserted grounds to Silas Holm's lair.

It was neat in that wing where the sex offenders lived. Quiet. Orderly. Utterly eerie. As usual.

'You couldn't bear to be apart from me, could you, my love?' Silas Holm said. Smiling. Arms outstretched. His nurse, Graham, was sitting at his side. Alert. Poised, by the looks.

'Come on, now. Sit down, Dr Holm,' Graham said. 'Show Ms McKenzie some respect, please.'

George took several screen grabs from the film out of her leather courier's bag. Laid them on the table. 'Silas, it would be very helpful if you could tell me the name of this actress.' She pointed to the anodyne still she had texted to Katja without success. 'This woman has very similar eyes to the woman in that drawing you showed me.' She pushed the more violent images closer to Holm.

Silas Holm snatched up the pictures and started to grin.

CHAPTER 24

Amsterdam, police headquarters, later

'For God's sake, give her some eyes, will you?' van den Bergen said, watching with awe as, with a series of clicks, Marie started to transform the photo of the first victim from a sorrowful shot of an enucleated cadaver to something that resembled a portrait of a living girl. At her side, Sabine Schalks watched, also clearly rapt by Marie's digital artistry.

'Do you think her skin should be darker?' Marie asked.

Van den Bergen peered over the rims of his glasses and stared blankly into the middle distance. 'Yes. Yes, definitely.'

'And perhaps you could sort out her facial proportions so she looks like she's sitting up,' Sabine said. 'She must have been lying down when rigor mortis set in. See how her face sags?' The paediatrician pointed at the screen with a long, slender index finger.

'Yep. No problem.' Marie cut dark brown eyes from a model in a fashion shoot close-up, and pasted them into the composition. With a tweak here and there, she was done inside twenty minutes. 'What do you think?'

'Fantastic!' Sabine exclaimed, clasping her hands together. 'You're a genius!'

Van den Bergen nodded. 'Better than the sketch artist.

Hasselblad would never have forked out for forensic facial reconstruction, the tight bastard.' He clapped Marie on the shoulder. 'This is our girl. We'll get this in all the newspapers. See if anyone knows her. I want you and Elvis to show this picture round organisations that shelter refugees and trafficked women.'

He turned to Sabine, affording her an awkward smile. Thought better of it, when he realised Marie was watching him.

'Right. I'll leave you two to discuss paedophile rings. Can I make you coffee?'

'Are you being funny, boss?' Marie asked. 'You? Make coffee? Since when?'

Sabine toyed with her pearl earrings and crossed her legs. The hint of a blush in her cheeks. 'Am I getting special treatment, Chief Inspector?' She looked up at him. Flicker, flickering eyelashes.

He swallowed hard. 'Absolutely not. I always pamper my staff.'

'What a fibber!' Marie said. She rose from her chair. Beckoned Sabine to come with her. 'I'll make us both a drink, shall I? Best not to tempt fate. Last time the boss made coffee, he gave Elvis legionnaires' disease.'

'Slander!' van den Bergen shouted after them. Marie and Sabine left him staring at the photoshopped girl. They could not have known that he was thinking of George. Remembering last time she had visited and stayed over in his spare room. They had shared burnt pepperoni pizza and a bottle of shiraz. Discussed the peculiarities of aggressive, under-educated young men in Britain's Category A prisons. Spoke at length about van den Bergen's descent from the pinnacle of culture as an art-school golden boy into a job as a uniform in the Netherlands police, booking drunks and responding to concerned neighbours, reporting wayward burglar alarms in Amstel. Reminisced about the time when George was chasing down ghetto back alleys to get away from a mother who had encased herself over time in a hard, unloveable veneer; lacquered with the colours of the

107

Jamaican flag on a Saturday night. Laughed at the fact that neither he nor George could cook for toffee. He had sketched her afterwards, sitting on his sofa, while they talked about Charlemagne, the library in ancient Baghdad under Abbasid rule and the Silk Road. It was a good sketch. It was a great evening. He could not think of one other person he could spend six hours talking to and still feel there were too many things left unsaid by bedtime.

Was there someone out there who felt that way about these dead girls? One thing he knew for certain: if he didn't succeed in identifying them, he didn't have a hope in hell of finding their killer.

CHAPTER 25

Broadmoor Psychiatric Hospital, later

'How did you get them to agree to show me these?' Silas asked.

His eyes sparkled with mischief. He reached down beneath the table and adjusted the crotch of his flannel trousers – back in his tweeds now, but not for long, judging by the look of horrified consternation on Graham's face.

'I cannot believe they allowed you to bring these in,' Graham said. He grabbed Silas' arm. 'Hands on the table, Dr Holm.'

George looked apologetically at Graham. 'It's not just for my own curiosity, I promise you. These are tied to a crime scene. I can't say more.' She turned to Holm, whose cheeks were pink.

He licked his lips. That tongue flickering and reptilian emerging from his small mouth. Those ice-blue eyes, one-way mirrors revealing no soul behind them, staring down at the still taken from the point in the film where the hedge trimmer had just come into shot.

'Who is she, Silas? Come on. Amputee erotica. It's your thing, isn't it?'

But he was transfixed and did not look up. George grew irritated. Gathered the stills up and shuffled them into a neat pile.

Silas Holm looked crestfallen. Cocked his head to one side and tutted. 'You are cruel, Ms McKenzie. Denying an old man like me a little light entertainment.'

'Tell me her name. Please.' She was poised to write down whatever he said.

'Let me keep the pictures.' The directness of his stare had a manic quality to it.

There seemed to be no space between them. George touched the place on her collar bone where the gold chain normally lay. She looked over at Graham questioningly. It was no skin off her nose, to let him keep the images. And if it meant he would play ball…

Graham shook his head.

'No,' George said. 'Sorry.'

Silas sighed dramatically and looked up at the tall ceiling. Pulled his lank hair behind him in a ponytail. Though his skin stretched tight over the sinews in his neck and over his prominent Adam's apple, George could see it was beginning to crepe a little with age. He had the papery complexion of northern Europeans. Too pale. Almost translucent, betraying the network of thin, blue veins that ran just beneath the surface. Giving its owner the appearance of vulnerability. But the fallibility of the man's skin bore no relation to the condition of the flesh beneath. Silas Holm must have had the strength of a man twice his size to have dismembered those women. George glanced over at Graham's reassuring bulk and felt thankful for his presence.

'You know, one of my favourite postings was with Médecins Sans Frontières,' Silas said. 'An anaesthetist can do such good work out there, in the kill zones of Africa.'

'Why won't you help me, Silas?' George asked.

'We had to leave the medical facility of course, when it was bombed. I spent a while at Dadaab refugee camp over the Kenyan border. Helping out, you know? I think that's why they gave me the medal.'

She had one shot at this, goddamn it. Van den Bergen was relying on her. She could tell that Holm did know the actress.

She had seen the recognition register in his face, as it lit up like a hopeful flare.

'I know you're an intelligent man, Silas. And I can tell that you're playing me. But two women have been murdered and I think you can help.'

Those ice-blue eyes locked onto hers. He was studying her face. Her inclination was to look down at her blank sheet of notepaper but George girded herself to hold his gaze for as long as was necessary. To show him she was not intimidated.

'Murdered? How?'

'I'm not at liberty to say.'

Staring at the ceiling again, he rocked back on his chair. 'Of course, the tour of Afghanistan was also very satisfying,' he said. 'It's amazing how many soldiers lose an arm or a leg in a skirmish. That's active service for you. I'm not a surgeon, but assisting those doctors as they operated on limbs that had been blown to smithereens was *very* informative.'

Barely able to suppress the urge to punch this self-aggrandising animal, George unfurled her fist and clicked her fingers instead. Snap, snap, ricocheting around the sparsely furnished room. Regained his attention.

'You want some nice juicy details about some new psychopath on the block who's doing the stuff you can only dream of now?' she asked. 'Is that the way this rolls? If I tell you, will you give me the actress' fucking name? Right?'

Running a fingertip along those thin lips, Silas Holm nodded. Van den Bergen didn't need to know, did he?

George relayed as much information as she had been given and watched with disgust as Holm's expression transformed from one of polite indifference to incontrovertible relish. His grin revealed those incisors. Described by a thick outline of yellow scum, they put George in mind of the teeth of a cartoon villain and made her want to set about him with a stiff toothbrush and scouring powder.

Holm sighed. Looked wistful. 'Masterful,' he said. Raised an eyebrow. 'Unzipped? I like your metaphor. Although obviously, I can't condone that sort of thing, because, as I said, *I'm* innocent.' He held his slender hand aloft and spread his fingers, as though studying the empty space between them. 'My trial was pure conjecture and defamation.'

'Name,' George said, thumping the table.

CHAPTER 26

Amsterdam, police headquarters, later

'Linda Lepiks,' George said on the other end of the phone. 'Latvian porn actress. That's the name of the woman in the horror porn flick.'

'You're amazing!' van den Bergen said, smiling for the first time that day. 'You know I need you here, don't you?' On a fresh page in his notebook, he sketched the outline of George's face. Got her left eye too high up. Struck a line through the lot but still found himself smiling.

'Paul, I asked. Sally said no.'

'Is she the boss of you, George?'

'Yes. No. Oh, come on! Don't try child psychology on me, you manipulative—'

Van den Bergen set his pen down. Squeezed the bridge of his nose between his fingers. Conjured an image in his mind's eye of the second victim on Strietman's slab. 'Look. I'm putting money on it that Linda Lepiks is our second victim. Dental records should prove me right or wrong. Marianne's back in the lab tomorrow. Thank God.'

'And?'

'Well, if one of our victims is a porn actress, that adds credence to a theory that's being pushed that these murders are sexually motivated killings.'

'You know my involvement with this case could make my PhD research sing, don't you?' George chuckled. 'You're so fucking crafty, old man!'

'Less of the old, thank you. I can still show the likes of Elvis a thing or two about stamina and flexibility.' He was flirting. He knew he was flirting. It was inappropriate, given the circumstances. He needed to stop right there. Allowing himself only the flicker of a wry smile, he said, 'Why don't you go back to Sally, and ask again? I'm going to email her right now and tell her if she doesn't let you come over here, I'm going to clap her into handcuffs and put her behind bars for obstruction of justice.'

'Kinky,' George said.

Balls. *She* knew he was flirting. He had been too obvious. Stupid old fart. George had Karelse. She would never look twice at someone twenty years her senior. And yet. And yet…

'Will you come, George?'

'If I thwart Sally—'

'Please. I need your insight.'

George went quiet, as though she were pondering something. Then, she said, 'Fuck it. I'll need you to give me a job though. I'm totally skint, man. Filing. Making coffee. I'm not bothered, so long as I can cover my overheads.'

Van den Bergen leaned back in his desk chair and crossed his legs. Bounced his right foot triumphantly up and down on his left knee. Hoped his team wouldn't catch sight of their boss, grinning like a fool in the confines of his office.

'How soon can you get over here?' he asked.

CHAPTER 27

Amsterdam, mortuary, 21 January

Four bodies lay on their respective slabs, spotlit by the bright theatre lights that hung above them. The first cadaver was an old man. With his mouth open and his eyes closed, he could almost have been sleeping, were it not for the fact that his lips, earlobes and fingertips were bordering on violet and the rest of his skin was yellow. The second, already in the process of being dismantled and weighed by Strietman, was an obese woman. It was difficult for van den Bergen to tell how old she was because of the bulk that stretched her now-grey facial skin taut. Strietman's cranial saw buzzed merrily. There was an unpleasant sucking sound as he removed the top of her head. Two others were covered by sheets.

'You can see we're snowed under,' Marianne de Koninck said. 'I'm off for a matter of days, God forgive me!' She rolled her eyes. That, coupled with the undisguised sarcasm, gave her an uncharactedramatic air. 'And I come back in to find this.' She waved a clipboard animatedly in the direction of the bodies. 'It's winter. Half of Amsterdam is dropping like flies from flu complications, pneumonia and dehydration due to norovirus. These people don't realise how inconsiderate they're being. They don't tell anyone they're ill. Nobody sees them for days. Next minute, a neighbour notices the stink and rings them in as dead. Coroner wants to know if foul play's involved. Maybe a lot of people bump off their relatives just after Christmas.'

'Can you blame them?' Strietman chimed in. 'They're probably murdering for kicks. The television's terrible this time of year.' He laughed at his own joke as he logged the weight of the woman's brain on a computer.

'Where's my scalpel gone?' Marianne asked. She slapped her clipboard against van den Bergen's chest. 'Hold this. I've lost my bloody scalpel. And where have you put the formalin, Daan? You've moved it!'

Strietman looked apologetic. 'We're out. Sorry. I forgot to reorder.'

De Koninck stopped rummaging through a glass-fronted cabinet and turned to face her junior colleague. Stony-faced. 'You *what*?'

Strietman laughed heartily. 'Gotcha!'

'Ha ha.' She didn't sound as though she had found the practical joke funny in the slightest. She still looked like she might turn him to ice with her stare alone.

Van den Bergen leaned against the white tiled wall and appraised Marianne. He had never seen her so agitated before. Ordinarily, with her athletic form and her neat, short hair, she exuded an air of quiet self-discipline.

'Look,' he said. 'I don't want to get under your feet, but I have to get the results from that mattress and the weapons we found on Valeriusstraat. I need to know about Jane Doe two's dental records. I've got a double murder on my hands.'

'Voodoo ladykiller on the loose,' Strietman told Marianne, wide-eyed. Miming strangulation with blue gloved hands. He sat heavily on a wheeled typing chair by the steel worktop and whizzed himself backwards, half way across the mortuary to a computer terminal.

'We don't know that, actually,' van den Bergen said.

'Dr Schalks agreed with me.'

'You met Sabine?' Marianne asked van den Bergen, her mouth curling upwards into a half-smile. 'Oh, I knew you'd like her. Me and her go back a long way, you know.'

'I didn't say I liked her,' van den Bergen said. 'But, yes. She's very nice. Although that does *not* necessarily mean we're after a "voodoo ladykiller"!'

With a few clicks on his mouse, Strietman brought a screen full of results up. 'Here you go. The blood on the mattress does *not* match that of either victims. It's universal type "O" – the stuff you're given in a blood transfusion. There was so much DNA on that filthy old mattress, though. Hairs. Semen. Stale vomit. I think half of Amsterdam's down-and-outs must have slept on that thing at some point. See what your perp database throws up, but there's no match to either of your victims.'

Van den Bergen thumbed his stubble. Took several steps towards the glowing computer screen. Pushed his glasses onto the end of his nose and stared at the baffling numbers, medical terms and statistics. 'We lifted prints off the hammer and chisel that matched the builder who was first on the Valeriusstraat scene,' he said. 'Any DNA? What about the scalpel and the cleaver? The other bits: the thong. The whip.'

Strietman smiled, as he read through the results. '*Cow* DNA found on the scalpel and cleaver! Ha. Ever heard the English phrase for a vagina: *beef curtains*?' He snorted with laughter. 'Maybe your murderer took that too literally. Nothing on the thong.' Clicked open several more tabs. 'But, oh! Looks like the dental records you asked for came in quickly.' He brought up two x-rays of teeth side-by-side. 'The name you gave me last night…'

'Linda Lepiks.'

'You bet, kemosabe.' He turned around to face van den Bergen, seemingly oblivious to the chief inspector's withering look of disapproval, and winked. 'Looks like you've got yourself a perfect match.'

'Strietman, did you seriously just call me kemosabe?' van den Bergen asked.

Strietman's smile was sunny and seemingly guileless. 'Lighten up, pal. We're both on the same side here. We're both in the stiffs business.'

Van den Bergen took his glasses off. 'Marianne, can I talk to you in private for a moment, please?'

In the flickering fluorescent strip lighting of the corridor, Marianne looked harried and tired.

'You read the case notes?' van den Bergen asked. 'His report?'

She nodded. Looked sickly, where the green of her mortuary scrubs reflected on her skin. Her eyelids were still swollen and red. She held her hands up in a gesture of surrender. 'I know Strietman's a pain in the arse,' she said. She chuckled and looked down at her rubber clogs. 'God knows, you don't need a sparkling personality to work with the dead.'

'Well, he's certainly not got one of those. That guy's got no respect. He called me "kemosabe"! He said I was *funny*. What a prick.'

Marianne clasped the chief inspector's arm and walked him to the coffee machine, as if they were long-standing elderly friends out for a stroll. She kicked the machine in a sweet spot, which caused it to malfunction – red flashing lights and a string of digital gobbledegook on the display. Presently it provided her with a scalding cup of something she hadn't chosen for free.

'Daan's conclusions are sound,' she said. 'Logical and well-founded. He knows his onions, Paul. The shoddy barbed sutures on both victims puts me in mind of something.' She held a sinewy, veined hand over her forehead, as if she were trying to tease some enlightening piece of information from her memory. 'Something I heard on the grapevine a while ago. I don't know. I'll have a think. Reading the report, though...I'd agree with Daan that you're looking for a vet or a medically trained person who actually did the cutting. You mustn't judge his scientific nous by his witty repartee.'

Van den Bergen tried to convey his scepticism with sighing alone. 'I can't come up with a motive to save my life apart from sex-pervert medic going on the rampage! This thing's a mess. Can't *you* give the women the once-over for me? Outside hours. Please! I'll take you to dinner now the amazing idiot toyboy has cut you loose.'

Marianne de Koninck looked at van den Bergen sideways on. Shook her head. 'No. This is winter. Crazy time. I can't let the bodies stack up to duplicate work that's already been done. I haven't got the resources or the energy. When I finish my shift this evening, I'm going home. Okay? I'm going to open a bottle of wine, eat potato salad from the tub and play "me and Jasper's song" over and over until I've drowned in my own sorrow.'

'Since when was it okay for people like us to feel sorry for ourselves?' van den Bergen said. 'This is not like you at all.'

The pathologist pushed past him, though there was ample room in that basement corridor. She glanced back over her shoulder. Tears stood in her eyes but did not fall. Her lips trembled, as though she were about to cry. But her voice was strong and even and full of cold anger.

'You get yourself a broken heart and see how "not like you at all" you suddenly feel.'

CHAPTER 28

Amsterdam, red light district, later

Sitting in the Cracked Pot Coffee Shop, he dragged hard on the ready-made joint and held the smoke in his lungs for the requisite amount of time. The sensation of the blood draining from his cheeks was almost instant. His brain felt sluggish. Good. It had been a while since he had smoked dope, but he knew it would give him the numbing sensation he needed.

'Here's your coffee, feller,' the old hippy who owned the place said. He slammed down onto the table a chipped mug containing some oily-looking liquid. Seated himself on the opposite side of the booth, as though they were old friends. 'Not seen you around here in a long time.' The hippy took off his round spectacles and started to clean them on the bottom of his batik-print T-shirt. 'Short term memory's a joke, but my long term… I never forget a face. You're the doctor. Right? How's tricks?'

Taking his hip flask out of his coat pocket, he poured some whisky into the coffee. 'You don't mind, do you?' he asked the hippy.

A shake of the head said he didn't. 'Booze and dope don't mix, man. But it's a free country.' He took a drag from his own funnel-shaped joint. Switched to American-style English. 'As long as no feds come in. I haven't got a liquor licence.' Back to Dutch. 'You understand?'

He nodded. Of course he bloody understood. 'Do you mind? I've had a rough morning. I just want to get stoned in peace.'

'You do look like somebody took a piss in your vla, man. Inneke's upstairs. What a lovely woman that is.'

Perhaps silence would make him go away.

'She's got special hands, like a reiki healer for your dick. You should treat yourself, if you're feeling low.'

Perhaps not.

He was just about to tell the hippy to leave him the hell alone, when the doorbell to the shop tinkled. Some young black woman walked in. Put him briefly in mind of poor little Noor, with her dark skin and wild hair. Although the one who had just come in had the fully-formed hourglass shape of a grown adult.

The hippy leaped to his feet and yelled. The woman shrieked and they started to hug one another and gabble in English. Good. At least that got the 60s-throwback idiot off his back.

What a fiasco, before the day had even got started. Before breakfast, for Christ's sake. He dragged on the joint and recalled with some distaste how the man had burst into his surgery under the pretext of making an outstanding payment. All, my-daughter's-in-hospital-fighting-MRSA-and-poisoned-tubes-because-of-you. All, we're-going-to-get-deported-because-of-you. For a slightly-built Chinese, he had been damned strong too. Stroking his jaw gently, he could feel that it had already swollen up like a balloon where the Chink had punched him.

He let his ash droop mournfully into the ashtray. At least now the slant-eyed fucker could legitimately join his daughter in the emergency room. The cracking noise had told him he had definitely broken Concerned Daddy's arm with the baseball bat. Served him right. Although now, of course, there was a risk he'd have the cops on his back. The Chink had nothing left to lose by ratting out his little backstreet business. Shit.

He was so absorbed by the conundrum he found himself in that he hadn't noticed the coffee shop's doorbell sound a second time.

Had failed to notice the eye-catching, fire-engine red of the Pole's hair. He caught her eye immediately.

'Ruud, darling! Are you waiting for me?'

Upstairs, George stood in her old room with Jan. Same gabled ceiling. Same old furniture. Same scuff marks on the magnolia walls. Nothing had changed, except the place now stank of stale frying and the carpet had been replaced by something cheap and nasty in medium beige. A colour that betrayed too well all manner of spillages and soiled outdoor shoes being worn indoors. Reflexively, she scratched her scalp at the thought. Was torn between wanting to slip her own shoes off but feeling the carpet was too dirty to risk sullying her clean socks. She felt tears prick at the backs of her eyes.

'I first got a grip of Ad on that chaise longue,' she said quietly.

She had written political blogposts on her laptop in that lumpy old 1930s bed. Had loved to gaze out at the red light district's rooftops through that window. But then, she remembered the frightening spectacle of discovering somebody had intruded on her territory – marking it by leaving their stain on her pillowcase; their used match on the floor. Now, she fingered the gold chain Ad had bought her. It hung around her neck like some dog tag. She was his, because he had named her in nine-carat gold. Her very body had become his territory. Silently, she took the necklace off and slid it into her jeans pocket.

'The place isn't tenanted at the moment. You can stay here for a couple of nights,' Jan said, pulling clean bed linen from the larder unit in the kitchen.

The door was hanging off its hinges now, George noted, but at least the pile of linen he threw onto the bare mattress looked clean.

Her old landlord patted her hand and smiled at her benignly, his eyes crinkling up merrily behind the smudged lenses of his glasses. 'Just like old times.'

'I bloody hope not!' George said, forcing herself to smile.

But sure enough, from downstairs, she could hear squeaking bed springs and the rhythmic grunting of a man, as Inneke entertained a punter.

The clatter of high-heeled boots on the stairs heralded Katja's arrival. She strode into the room. Even if her hair had been an anonymous shade of brown rather than bright red, in her skin-tight, diamanté-studded jeans and sequinned pink top, she would have made the place seem even drabber. She looked around. Rearranged her fat red lips with some apparent difficulty into a shape that conveyed disgust.

'You're such a cheap bastard, Jan, darling. I can't believe your tenants don't charge *you* for this shithole.'

Jan started to wheeze with the somewhat inexplicable laughter of the very stoned. 'Too good for the Cracked Pot now you're a film star, are you?'

'Yes.' She turned to George, hands on hips. Her face appearing slightly startled even though George could see there was an intended smile behind it. 'How come you're not staying with loverboy?'

George groaned. 'Oh, I will. I just need a couple of days. To myself, you know? I only just put him on the flight back here. He turned up unannounced in London.'

Both Jan and Katja inhaled sharply.

'Trouble in paradise,' Jan said. Nodding sagely. 'Shame.'

'No!' George protested. 'It's fine. It's—'

'She's come for the detective!' Katja said, grabbing George's chin between her fingers. Almost scratching her with those hot pink talons. Reminiscent of Letitia the Dragon, but only just. 'Tell Katja, darling. Is the pretty boy no good in bed?'

George wriggled free. Searched for the words. Felt her cheeks warm up as if there were a heating element just beneath her skin which Katja had plugged in and switched on.

A knock at her door salvaged her from ridicule and honesty. There was a portly strawberry-blond man standing in the doorway, combing his hair across his forehead with a meaty pink hand. His face was swollen on one side.

'You coming then, Katja?' he said.

Katja sashayed towards him and slapped the unbecoming man on his behind. Planted a lipstick kiss on his cheek. 'Ruud, honey. Didn't I tell you to wait for me downstairs? You're a bad, bad boy!' She turned to George. 'I'm standing you up, darling. I'll make it up to you.'

'No need to stand your friend up,' the blond man said. 'She can come with us.' He looked at George and smiled. Made a grab for her hand and kissed the back of it. 'Dr Ruud Ahlers. Pleasure to meet you. Come for lunch at mine. I'm quite the cook. And I've got a couple of bottles of champagne sitting in my fridge, unopened.'

Frantically wiping her hand, but before she could respond to the offer, George's phone started to ring. She glanced down at her display. It was van den Bergen.

'Hadn't you better answer that?' Katja asked.

Her thumb hovered over the button. She had wanted to surprise him by showing up later at the station, bearing a packet of convolvulus seeds and the new indestructible Thermos flask she had brought all the way from England for him. But she couldn't resist.

'Hello, Paul.'

'Hey. I got a domestic ringtone,' he said. 'Where are you?'

'Closer than you think.' She was unable to keep the smile out of her voice.

'Really? You're already on Dutch soil?' There was a gruff confidence to his voice, as usual, though she knew different. 'I'm on the road, but I can pick you up if you're in town. Me and Marie are on our way to—'

'I'll come and find you this evening,' she interjected. Though she was yearning to see the cantankerous old sod, it wouldn't hurt to keep him on his toes. 'I'm going for lunch with Katja and her doctor friend, Ruud.' She hung up. Allowed herself a satisfied grin. She couldn't wait for this evening.

CHAPTER 29

Amsterdam, van den Bergen's car, later

'Come on, then,' van den Bergen said. He shot a glance towards Marie, who was sitting in his passenger seat. 'Tell me about Linda Lepiks.' Her normally florid complexion was peaky, bordering on green. 'You OK?'

Marie opened her window slightly, holding her hand over her mouth as van den Bergen's Mercedes lurched out of the way of a tram and sped along Sarphatipark, only to come to an abrupt standstill ten metres further down.

'Bloody roadworks,' the chief inspector said, honking his horn at an old drunk who stumbled into his path. 'They spring up overnight like magic mushrooms.'

He had hoped to reach the porn actress' canalside home on Jacob van Lennepkade inside fifteen minutes, but workmen were digging up asphalt with noisy pneumatic drills that seemed to be knocking on the door to hell itself. Cones studding the road, promising forward momentum, but delivering only irritating stasis and the resulting belch of diesel fumes from a steam roller and other vehicles.

'Damn this traffic!' he said, hitting the dash. 'I've got a doctor's appointment to make after this.'

'Are *you* okay?' Marie said, some of the colour returning to her face as the car's engine cut out, motionless behind a Heineken truck.

Van den Bergen looked at her appraisingly. Felt that it might be cathartic to unburden himself to her. Hers was a sympathetic face – soft-featured beneath the terrible complexion, hinting at a gentle soul. But he was Marie's boss, and she was not George. 'Lepiks. Details!'

Marie hooked her greasy red hair behind her ear and read from her notes on a small tablet.

'Twenty-four. Latvian. Came over here six years ago and has been in gainful employment from day one. Strictly legit, by all accounts.'

'Her apartment. It's not in the cheapest area,' van den Bergen said, restarting his engine and edging forwards by a couple of metres towards some temporary traffic lights.

'She's always been registered self-employed,' Marie said. 'She paid her tax. Her main source of income seems to have come from a company called Scream Screen Productions.'

'Earnings?' Van den Bergen quietly belched stomach acid and made a mental note to tell the doctor that he was certain he had an ulcer.

'She earned a lot,' Marie whistled low. She tutted. 'I'm in the wrong game, boss. Last year, Linda Lepiks took home just over a hundred and seventy-six thousand euros. My God!'

Narrowing his eyes, van den Bergen processed the figures in his head. 'Seriously? That much for pretending to lose her limbs?'

Marie nodded. 'Yes.'

'Jesus. The English have got a saying, "I'd give my right arm…" As in, I'd give my right arm for that kind of money. Now I know why. They clearly watched Linda's films.'

'You're funny,' Marie said.

Van den Bergen scowled. 'I am *not* funny. Continue. Anything in her tax records about payment to a cosmetic surgeon?' He visualised the scarring under her breasts.

'Yes,' Marie said, scrolling down. 'There's a clinic sounds like it could be what we're looking for. "New You Medical Practice". Fancy address near the Museum Quarter.' She frowned. 'Hey, I've heard some really famous celebrities go there. Doesn't sound like the kind of place that would botch a boob job.'

The traffic lights turned to green. Van den Bergen stepped on the gas. His heartbeat started to calm as the car roared away, leaving the congestion and the insistent hammering of the road drills behind.

'No police record,' Marie said. 'Nothing in the gossip pages about Lepiks. She didn't even have her own Wikipedia page. If you Google her, hardly anything comes up, except an official website that has just a front page with a photo of her in a leather basque. Contact details given are for a Viper Management.'

'Any address? Phone number?'

'A generic "info@" email address. All very anonymous.'

'Considering how much money she was making,' van den Bergen said, negotiating the bewildering urban tangle comprised of tramlines, overhead cables and zebra crossings that was the junction between Museumplein and de Lairessestraat, 'I can't believe she was so low profile.' There was a word that George had used to describe the actress' oeuvre. What was it? He wracked his brains, but the codeine blunted the possibility of sharp recall. He almost didn't see the woman trying to cross the road, pushing a pram. Swerved just in time. Damn. He needed to drink more coffee to counter this terrible blurring around the edges.

Slicing through the green of Vondelpark, he remembered. 'Niche,' he said aloud.

'What is?'

'The porno she starred in. An area that appeals to few. Which hopefully means we're fishing in a very small pool of really screwed-up perverts.'

Finally, they turned into Jacob van Lennepkade. The sun was poking meekly out from behind oppressive dark grey rain clouds, transforming the canal that bisected the street full of attractive period conversions from an inky black slug into a glittering strip of blue. Home to boxy houseboats on both sides, the water was wide, here. Wide enough and deep enough to swallow a young porn actress' innermost secrets and carry them to the North Sea. Did the water guard the identity of Linda Lepiks' murderer? Had he been here, to her home? Had it reflected his face on its surface, perhaps in the moonlight of her last night on earth?

Van den Bergen reversed into a parking space. Checked his own reflection in the rear view mirror with a degree of disappointment. Bared his teeth and was at least pleased to see there were no remnants of lunch in them.

'What are Elvis and Kees doing again this afternoon?' he asked.

'Checking the records for surgeons who have been struck off for malpractice,' Marie said, gathering her handbag from the passenger-side foot well.

'Good.' He locked the car and climbed the stairs to Lepiks' apartment. 'That should keep them out of mischief.'

CHAPTER 30

Amsterdam, later

Kees stepped out of the pub and belched loudly. He pulled his collar up against the bitter wind, eyeing the young tourists. Brash and moneyed Americans, by the sounds and looks. They loped in small backpacked, baseball-capped groups along the canals, seeking out the best-looking coffee shops where they might indulge cannabis-fuelled fantasies, enabling them to regale frat buddies back home with tales of their tour of decadent Europe; Amsterdam's red light district and perhaps the seedier parts of Paris being top of the heap.

'Peasants!' Kees barked at a young man who could not have been much older than seventeen, judging by his spots and bum-fluff that heralded the beginnings of facial hair.

Elvis followed behind him. 'If van den Bergen finds out, he'll cut our balls off with his trowel.' He shivered visibly in his leather jacket. 'You know, I've heard he calls that bloody thing "Excalibur".'

'What thing?'

'The trowel! He sharpens it in his office with a gadget, like a bloody hunting knife.'

'Stop being a pussy,' Kees said, feeling buoyed by the alcohol and the promise of a little light subterfuge. 'It was only a couple of beers. He buggers off to his allotment and gets away with it, doesn't he?'

'I didn't mean that,' Elvis said, lighting a cigarette. 'I meant going to the builder's without a warrant.'

Kees checked his phone for messages, then switched it off. 'We're following up a line of enquiry. I'm not waiting for a warrant to come through and I'm sure as hell not spending hours trawling through the database, looking for some quack that can't sew. Leave that to Marie. It's women's work.'

The apartment block they sought loomed before them. Everything about it spelled depressing. Drab, dark brown brick. Here, the windows were unusually small, as though the construction company that had built them in the 1970s had had to pay a premium for letting daylight in. Kees thought it ironic that the predominantly Eastern European inhabitants who lived round here should have opted to begin their new lives squashed into soulless blocks that were not dissimilar to the spartan concrete shitholes that had constituted accommodation under Soviet rule.

Several presses of the buzzer being met with zero response told Kees that nobody was home.

'Leave it, man,' Elvis said. 'Let's just go.'

Kees looked blankly at his colleague and understood why Kamphuis was so disdainful of both van den Bergen and his lackey.

'I thought you were a player,' Kees said, pulling skeleton keys from his anorak pocket. 'Like me. I'm disappointed in you, *Dirk*. Or is it Elvis? Which do you prefer? Your real name, or that disrespectful bullshit label van den Bergen slaps you with?'

Elvis stroked his sideburns and looked down at his shoes. 'Just get the door open and let's get on with it.'

Iwan Buczkowski's apartment was on the second floor. It was tidy, clean and poorly furnished with battered old crap from Ikea that Kees had seen in other downmarket rentals. Same all over the city. Not dissimilar to his own pad. He made straight for the bedroom, where the bed had been made. Opened the drawers to the bedside cabinet. Took out a pair of handcuffs lined with pink feathers and a black rubber dildo. Threw them on the bed for Elvis to see.

'Kinked. I told you,' he said, grinning.

'Put them back, man,' Elvis said, staring at a framed photo on the cabinet. 'That means nothing.'

Kees picked up the photo. It showed an attractive young woman with her arms wrapped around Buczkowski. They were dressed in their best, standing outside a church. Smiling. Lucky Buczkowski. How did a bowling-ball headed, broken-nosed ugly son of a bitch like that get such a hot girl? Kees felt a pang of jealousy. He moved over to a scuffed, white chest of drawers and rifled through the girl's underwear. Pulled out a pale blue bra and sniffed it. It smelled good, of washing powder, but the cups were small.

'Get a load of this,' he said, waving the bra at Elvis. 'Tiny tits.'

Elvis shook his head. 'You're out of line.' He left the room.

What was wrong with him? Kees wondered. He had thought he had an ally in Elvis. Two young bucks, making their way. Showing the old guard how it was done. But Elvis played by the rules. He was pigheaded and unadventurous; preferring to adhere to the chain of command and protocol, rather than to be his own man.

Never mind. Screw him.

If Kees Leeuwenhoek made a collar on the back of his investigation, he resolved not to share the kudos. He felt certain this intrusion would throw up something significant. *Follow your gut instincts, boy.* That is what his father had always told him. That there were cops who were so attuned to the world that they could solve a crime simply by following their hunches. And Kees' hunch said Buczkowski had—

'Jesus,' Elvis said. 'Get in here!'

Kees tracked the sound of his voice to its source in the living room. Elvis stood, holding his leather jacket tightly shut. Open-mouthed at the discovery. He turned to Kees, red in the face.

'Get a load of this!'

CHAPTER 31

Amsterdam, mortuary, later

With Strietman gone for lunch, Marianne fetched herself a cup of coffee and sat in silence in her mortuary. Peered thoughtfully at the fat woman's feet. The corns and hard skin said they had carried a heavy load for most of that woman's life. And now Marianne carried her own. Suffocating beneath the weight of having been rejected by a man she had loved. A divorcée's dream that had turned nightmarish. Shouldering the burden of responsibility to van den Bergen.

'Feeling sorry for myself,' she told the fat woman's big toe. 'He's got a cheek!'

But the chief inspector had been right. She was wallowing in self-pity. The place was a mess. Everything Strietman got out, every implement, every piece of equipment, he failed to put away. This was her domain and she needed to take it back. And Jasper wouldn't break her reputation as well as her heart. She put the fat woman's organs into a plastic bag and inserted the bag inside her ribcage. Sewed her up with large stitches and called for her cadaver to be taken back to the chiller.

After she had tidied to her satisfaction, Marianne located the drawers inside the giant mortuary chiller that contained the remains of van den Bergen's two female victims. Opened the steel doors and slid the bodies out for a preliminary inspection. The peculiar, lumpy scarring that was common to both women caught her eye and brought to the surface a memory long forgotten: a student at med school who had always been hopeless with a needle and thread. A shy, sort-of-blond boy in his first few years with an obsession for Greek mythology, but a real pest by the time he had graduated. Always following girls around, despite their studied disinterest in him.

'What was his name?' Marianne asked the dismantled girls. She slid the bodies back into their cold storage. This was definitely the anomaly van den Bergen needed for his investigation. You just didn't see stitching like that often, unless an unlicensed, under-qualified backstreet butcher was involved.

She padded back through to access the computerised records. Remembered having the body of a woman come in some years ago. She had undergone a hysterectomy that had turned septic. The internal stitching had borne similar evidence of sloppy suturing.

'Where are you?' Marianne said, scrolling impatiently through the records listed. But there were too many and perhaps the woman in question had died before everything had been computerised.

She took a Tupperware container out of the mortuary fridge and withdrew from it a pitta filled with falafel and salad that had long gone stiff and dry. Ate it nevertheless, staring blankly at the stick-thin ankles of the old man on whom she had been working. She remembered the police had been unable to bring a case against the gynaecologist. Their evidence to demonstrate medical negligence had only been circumstantial. But there had followed backlash in the medical community, and it transpired that not only had the gynaecologist probably killed his patient, but he had been accused of trying to sexually molest some of his younger and more vulnerable patients during examinations. It had been quite a scandal.

'Hang on a bloody minute,' Marianne said, spitting falafel inadvertently onto the floor. She sat back at the computer and Googled 'Gynae-sex pest', as she vaguely remembered reading the sensationalist headline of that ilk in the tabloids.

And there was the story.

Some eight years earlier. The disgraced gynaecologist peered out at her from a photo. Leaving a casino. Bleary-eyed and on the arm of a large-breasted woman wearing a micro-miniskirt and stiletto heels. Though the man's face was now bloated and middle-aged, all at once the bell that his name rang chimed inside her head at deafening volume and with shuddering resonance. It was the boy from med school. The stalker-type who couldn't sew to save his life and clearly couldn't sew to save anybody else's either. And yes, now she remembered that he had gone on to major in gynaecology and obstetrics.

Barely able to dial his number for her shaking hands, Marianne called van den Bergen.

'Marianne! How did you know I was going to call?' he said. 'I'm at Linda Lepiks' apartment. I need you to get a team here to go over her place. The murderer's been here. I'd put money on it.'

'I know who it is,' Marianne said. 'His name's Ruud Ahlers.'

Van den Bergen went silent momentarily. 'A doctor? *Dr* Ruud Ahlers?'

'Yes.'

'Shit.'

135

CHAPTER 32

Amsterdam, Ruud Ahlers' apartment, later

As van den Bergen sped away from Lepiks' apartment amidst a cacophony of screeching, smoking tyres, the urgency of the situation heralded by blue flashing lights and the wail of the car's siren, George sipped champagne in Ruud Ahlers' living room. It was decadently early for alcohol, but she was feeling both defiant and celebratory. Irate messages from Sally regarding her absconsion were already stacking up on her phone. She was studiously ignoring them.

Though she scanned the Greek mythology books and Latin texts on Ahlers' book shelves, the wide smile that played on her full lips was not for the dog-eared copy of Tacitus' *Nero et Agrippina* – a name she hadn't heard since high school. Nor was it for the fact that this friend of Katja's had arranged his books alphabetically, despite their being unacceptably dusty. Her smile was one of relief and triumph. Being back in Amsterdam for more than a fleeting visit felt like a sort of homecoming.

Katja came out of Ahlers' kitchen, all clacking heels and jangling bangles. She slid an arm around George's shoulder.

'You look like the cat that got the cream, darling,' she said. Batting her lashes. Pouting theatrically.

George noticed a brown stain on the collar of her friend's pink top and subtly slid out of her embrace. 'I needed a change of scenery. I don't like being told what to do, where to go...you know? The things I've got on the go in England. They'll keep for a few months.'

The smell of frying garlic coming from this strange man's kitchen was good. George's stomach rumbled. With a murdered porn starlet on her mind, she'd taken the first available flight to Schiphol. Meagre funds had prevented her from buying breakfast at the airport. The flight had been a no-frills affair that had not included an airline snack.

'So, who's your friend?' George asked.

Katja threw herself onto a sagging burgundy sofa, that looked as though it had once been expensive but which was now dog-eared and covered in white cat hairs. She sipped her champagne, leaving a greasy lipstick slick on the rim of the simple flute. George perched on the sofa's arm, unwilling to commit to the cat hairs.

'I've known Ruud for years,' she said. 'See these beauties?' She pointed to the fat red pillows that constituted her mouth. Kissed the air as if to demonstrate how they should work. Giggled, though her stiff face did not yield entirely to a grin that encompassed teeth. 'We're not all born with luscious lips like you, darling. Ruud's my cosmetic surgeon. Everyone I know goes to him! Collagen implants. Botox. Nip and tuck.' She poked a nail into George's hip. 'You look like you've been eating too many chips, honey. He could do you some lipo—'

George bellowed with laughter, though inside, she acknowledged a twinge of hurt. 'Cheeky cow! I don't need lipo. The junk in this trunk was all part of mother nature's plan.'

Tossing her red hair over her shoulder, Katja closed her eyes dismissively. 'Suit yourself,' she said. 'I have to keep in shape for the cameras, these days. And I bet Ruud would want more than just a fee off you!' She lowered her voice to a whisper. 'He's got a dick like a button mushroom.'

Wondering fleetingly if van den Bergen's penis was in proportion to his height, George advanced to the threshold of the kitchen. Observed Ruud Ahlers from behind, as he pan-fried something. He wore a navy and white butcher's apron tied tight, so that it dug into his fleshy back. Turned round to face her. She could barely conceal her look of distaste at the sight of the apron, stretched tight over his belly. The white stripes were browny-orange with old blood stains. Worse still, his teeth were yellow. Reminiscent of Silas Holm. But the food smelled nice. She gave the pan a once-over. Looked like steak. Or was it liver?

'I hope that's not offal,' George said. 'I don't eat offal.'

'Let food be thy medicine and medicine be thy food,' Ahlers said, waving his spatula. 'Hippocrates!' He moved to the bank of drawers and opened the top one. It rattled, betraying the cutlery inside. Took out a long, thin boning knife and pointed it at her chest. 'Your Dutch is excellent. I think we're in for an entertaining afternoon.'

CHAPTER 33

Amsterdam, van den Bergen's car, then Ahlers' apartment, moments later

Van den Bergen floored the growling Mercedes along Leidseplein. Travelling down tram tracks. Couldn't get snarled up in queuing traffic. Skirted the length of a tram heading back towards Vondelpark. Maybe six inches between his wing mirror and the body of the blue and white beast. Had to get to George. Had to reach her in time.

At his side, Marie yelped. 'Jesus!'

'Boss?' Elvis' voice coming through on the hands-free. Awaiting instructions.

Past the MINI showrooms on his right. Couldn't remember where he was going. Shit! Hung a sharp left into Marnixstraat. There was the city theatre. Not far now. Flinched the muscles in his upper arm to make doubly sure his service weapon was still strapped beneath his left armpit. Honked his horn at the oncoming cars. Why were there oncoming cars?

'You're driving the wrong way up a one-way street!' Marie shouted. She clung onto her seatbelt with both hands, one eye squeezed shut. White knuckles. Green face. Her tablet had slid to the floor.

But van den Bergen had no time. George was in danger. *Katja's doctor friend. Ruud.* An image of George, staring at morgue lights with unseeing eye sockets, flashed into his head. He blinked it away.

'This is quicker,' he said. 'Get out of my way, you bastards!' Horn honking.

The city road map in his head was codeine-blurred. The right side of the river now, at least. His only thought was to get to Ahlers' address.

'Elvis!' he barked down the car's hands-free. 'You still there?'

'Yes, boss.' Elvis' voice, tinny at the other end of the phone.

'Get uniformed backup to Bloemstraat. Suspect is dangerous and possibly armed.'

'Will do, boss.'

'And Elvis.'

'Yes boss.'

'If you get there before us, don't fuck this up. Georgina McKenzie is there. If she gets hurt, I *will* kill you.'

'It looks nice,' George said, staring down at the plate and thinking that it definitely didn't look nice. The delicious aroma in its cooking had belied the unsavoury mash of suspect meat and burnt potatoes. It could have been something she'd cooked herself, and that was no recommendation. 'Are you sure this is steak?'

'You're a whizz in the kitchen, Ruud,' Katja said, spooning pickled cabbage from a bowl onto her plate.

'Dig in,' Ahlers said, topping their glasses up with more champagne.

He had laid a crisp tablecloth on the table for four. Put some tight ranunculus buds in a small glass vase in the middle. George examined her cutlery for signs of dried-in food remnants or fingerprints. The fork passed muster. She gave it an extra wipe on her napkin, to be on the safe side. The knife...

'Ow!' she said, slicing into the skin on her index finger. 'Jesus, these are sharp. What are they? Bloody scalpels or something?'

Ahlers snorted with laughter. 'Something like that,' he said. 'I don't know about you, but I can't stand to eat steak with a blunt knife.'

It had occurred to George that accepting an invitation to an impromptu lunch with her porn actress, ex-working-girl-friend by a man whom she had never met before in her life had possibly been a rash decision, but she was so heartily sick of doing what was expected of her – by Ad, by Sally, by Derek at the club, even by van den Bergen – that she embraced the opportunity to do something spontaneous. Especially now she was back in Amsterdam. Besides, she was drunk. Champagne on an empty stomach meant the bubbles had gone straight to her head.

Katja raised her glass. 'Here's to George!' she said. 'Welcome back, sweetie!'

They clinked glasses, but Katja leaned over and planted a wet kiss on George's cheek.

'Katja, man!' George said, setting her glass down and wiping at her skin with her napkin. 'Boundaries!' Now the napkin was covered in greasy, bright red stains, which made George's eye start to twitch. She stood abruptly. 'Where's your bathroom?' she asked Ahlers.

He ushered her down the hall. Deftly pulled his bedroom door closed en route. 'This way!'

'Thanks,' George said, wishing she had just grabbed some buns and cheese from the supermarket and then gone straight over to the station to surprise van den Bergen. 'I'm sure I can find it on my own.'

Her host paid her no heed. He marched ahead of her into the murk of the hallway. Stood on the threshold to a windowless room that was in total darkness.

'Be my guest.'

Reaching out, he pressed his hand to the small of her back in a proprietorial manner. Clicked on the light and extractor fan with his other hand. The room smelled strange, as the food had looked strange. Perhaps it was the champagne, George thought. She limboed away from his touch. But, having edged past Ahlers' belly to enter the small, tidy bathroom, she then found that he wouldn't leave. He just stood there, watching her.

'I don't need a chaperone,' she said, closing the door.

The door wouldn't shut. Something barred its progress. She looked down. Spotted his foot, wedged deliberately in the way. His hand dipped into the pocket of his butcher's apron.

An insistent knock at the front door drew his attention away from her.

'Police! Open up!'

Van den Bergen's voice? No. It could not be. George wondered if Ahlers had slipped a little something extra into her drink. But then, something hit the front door with the force of a battering ram. A cracking, splintering sound as the hinges gave way and suddenly van den Bergen was standing in the hallway, pointing his pistol straight at her.

CHAPTER 34

London, 1985

'Sit there and don't speak to anyone,' Mama said, pushing Veronica into an uncomfortable moulded plastic chair in an empty corner by the fire extinguisher. Mama's bared teeth translated into a rough approximation of a smile, but her tone of voice could have stripped the paint off the canvases and boards that hung on the gallery walls.

Rudi wriggled in Mama's arms. His diamanté collar caught the spotlights, transforming him from an ordinary white terrier to a glittering ball of fluff in ironic hot-pink satin dog jacket. 'Canine-drag-queen-meets-Material Girl', as one of Veronica's unsanctioned friends had labelled the look. Mama would not have appreciated that turn of phrase. Particularly not from the new housekeeper's sixteen-year-old daughter, who had light-fingers and a terrible thirst when it came to Papa's drinks cabinet. Mama insisted Rudi was flamboyant and very *now*.

'Why don't you give him to me?' Veronica held her arms outstretched to receive the little dog. 'Come here, puppy!' She searched for vulnerability and understanding in her mother's expression. 'Please, Mama. It's so boring.'

But her mother swung the dog upwards, out of reach and started to talk to it in that ridiculous baby voice. 'Rudi-wudi's coming with me, aren't you, my darling?' The dog yapped and strained to be free. Her mother clutched its body tighter, closer to her chest. It pawed at the jewels that studded her Christian Lacroix bolero, revealing more of her bony ribcage than perhaps she had intended. Mama was too thin, these days. Hind legs scampering up her green silk puffball skirt. 'Yes, Rudi-wudi! Mama's taking you to meet all her gorgeous friends.'

'Why couldn't I have just stayed at home?' Veronica asked, folding her arms across her chest in the hope of conveying some of her dissatisfaction, even if she dare not say she felt sidelined. 'I could have hung out with—'

'You could not have *hung out* with anyone, young lady!' Her mother rounded on her, setting Rudi down on the gallery floor, who scampered off into a fray of Doc Martens and winkle-picker shoes. Dug her fingernails into Veronica's upper arms so that the girl yelped. 'You know how Mama's parties work. I've got a photographer here from *The Face*. When he shoves his camera in my direction, you stay away. But I've also got people here from *Harper*'s. In *The Face*, I'm flying solo. In *Harper*'s, you, me and Papa – we're the Schwartz family. Right? Berlin's best. Got it? So, when *Harper*'s man wants a pretty smile for the birdie, what do you do?'

'Jesus! Can't I even go and get an autograph from—'

'I'll Jesus you when we get home, madam. You fucking stay put until I tell you.' Mama crouched at her side, outwardly smiling as though she were sharing a tender motherly moment with her debutante daughter. But the balled fist next to Veronica's kidneys told her that Mama was interested only in a public display of affection.

'Heidi, darling!' somebody shouted over the hubbub. The voice belonged to a giant of a man, almost as wide as he was tall. He wore a flowery, full-skirted dress, belted at the waist, that reached to the floor. His round face, bull neck and bald head had been painted a ghostly white, but for the black clownish smile that curved upwards from ear to ear. A German WWII helmet on his head. Eyes, obscured by black Ray-Ban Wayfarers over-painted with childish cartoon eyes that looked as though they had been applied to the lenses with white correction fluid. Glaring at her. Terrifying. Angry black stripes for eyebrows. Veronica shrank back into her chair a little at the sight of him, though she was used to Mama's friends. In his arms, he held Rudi like a trophy. 'You didn't tell me Madonna was coming!'

Gales of laughter from the clique of Mama's champagne-swilling cronies standing nearby said this was hilarious. Said, they were all having a fabulous time. Said, Mama was the best hostess of the most glamorous parties in town – the launch of this art exhibition being nothing short of superlative.

'Rudi-wudi, come to Mama before the naughty man eats you all up!'

Veronica watched her mother work the crowd, glass in one hand, Rudi in another. Mwah, mwah sycophancy with the great and the good of London's art, fashion and music scenes. Dead or Alive spinning everyone round like a record, baby through the overhead speakers. There was Mama, puckering up for the camera next to a dark-haired female fashion designer who wore a red T-shirt adorned with black writing, telling everyone she was staying alive in 85. A pretty pop band front-man who regularly adorned the covers of Veronica's copies of *Smash Hits* proclaimed on his black and white T that Frankie said relax.

On the other side of the lofty white space, standing beneath a canvas of some drab, unidentifiable shit or other, she spotted Papa. The polar opposite of her flamboyant mother, wearing a discreet double-breasted suit in dark grey. Jermyn Street, she had once heard him say. Sober silk tie. Appearances reflecting a reality where Papa was a Harvard med school alumnus and expert in his field. Anyone would think *he* was the old money and Mama was just a flashy wannabe who had married well, although Veronica knew the opposite was true. But Papa was publicly proud that he had climbed his way up from humble origins. What an impressive man to have as your father! And now, here he was, chatting up some ageing minor royal from a European backwater. No doubt persuading the old trout that he should rearrange her crumbling face until she looked like a younger Joan Collins. That old woman had spent more time engaging in conversation with her father on a summer's evening in a gallery by the Thames than Veronica had spent in an entire month. Papa's so clever. Papa's so sought after, these days. Papa's never there.

Mama and Papa. She was blessed. At fifteen, she was old enough to realise they had enough money. At fifteen, she recognised they gave her everything: skiing in St Moritz; shopping in New York; a bitch of a private tutor who used to teach at Bedales; ferried around the West End in a Bentley that cocooned her from a lesser world she could only longingly glimpse from behind bullet-proof glass. At fifteen, she would still have liked nothing more than for parents to hold her; to tell her it was okay and that they forgave her for being a disappointing child. Mama and Papa. She was cursed.

Listlessly, Veronica eyed the trays of canapés circling the gallery, carried by liveried waitresses. Acknowledged that her stomach was growling but in truth, Veronica was inured to the hunger that these events occasioned. Mama never let her eat with the grown-ups. Mama had always forbidden her to mingle. Until…

'Veronica, darling, come and have your photo taken!'

Mama calling. She knew the drill. Smile coyly for the upmarket society glossies. Yes, she believed her mother had dressed her in Yves Saint Laurent. Yes, she really enjoyed meeting the interesting people at her mother's shindigs. No, she didn't have a boyfriend! Cue embarrassed giggling. Already tall, Veronica had read in their pages that she 'showed promise', though as what, she had no idea. But, she was not so naive as to fail to understand, that it was only because she had not yet reached the full flush of early womanhood, Mama did not worry that she would risk having her beauty upstaged. Yet.

There they stood. A happy family under the glare of the gallery lights, amplified by the ice white walls and the limelight cast by the glitterati in attendance. Say, 'Fromage!' Beneath Papa's fingers that entwined around her upper arm, old bruises left by her mother were still sore. Rudi, of course, took centre stage. Adorable Rudi! Who could fail to love such an innocent, fluffy soul in his pink jacket?

She was glad when she was sent home with the driver at around 8pm. Pizza cooked by the housekeeper, Tricia. A sneaky half bottle of Papa's vodka with Tricia's daughter, Sharon, while they listened to Depeche Mode in the games room. *Super Mario Bros.* on the games console. Mama and Tricia didn't need to know, right? Veronica would never ever tell. She was good at keeping secrets, and Sharon was her one true friend.

Veronica was woken by her mother's return at 2am, stumbling through the front door with someone who sounded nothing like her father. She crept down to make sure. Peered through the spindles of the grand staircase. No, Papa had not returned. As usual. Mama and the strange man retired to the games room, giggling as they descended the basement stairs. While the cat's away…

At least Rudi came and kept her company, warm and eternally accepting at the foot of her single bed. Together, they passed a slumberous couple of hours, until Mama noticed her precious fur ball was missing.

'Where the fuck is Rudi-wudi?' Mama screamed, smashing Veronica's bedroom door against the wall. She still wore last night's makeup, smudged now, and had a Japanese silk robe tied loosely over her naked, skeletal frame.

Veronica glanced at the clock. 4.30am. Rudi yapped at the foot of the bed. Scampered over to her mistress and leaped into her arms.

'You stole him!' Mama said.

'No. He just wanted to sleep in my room.'

'Thieving bitch of a girl! Naughty Rudi!'

'You weren't here, Mama.'

The slap wasn't so bad. What stung was the fact that she had really disappointed her mother, this time. She just couldn't win.

Mama and her young companion slept deeply and late together in a guest room. The French doors to the garden were open. Tricia had baked muffins. The summer morning air was refreshing. Inviting. With a muffin in her mouth, Veronica pulled on her slippers and took a glass of orange juice and a throw onto the small lawn, so that she might sit and enjoy the sunshine.

When she found poor little Rudi under the holly tree, his severed head lying next to his tragic, blood-flecked body, she screamed loud enough for the neighbours' security guard to leap the fence to see why there was such a commotion.

'O-our dog!' she wept, burying her face, wet with tears, in the guard's shoulder. 'My-my little Rudi. Who would d-do such a t-thing?'

Her vocal grief at the sight of the dead terrier was evidently enough to rouse her mother. When Mama saw the harrowing tableau, she collapsed onto the grass, clutching at her stomach and sobbing silently.

For the first time that Veronica could remember, her mama reached out for her and gathered her up in her scrawny arms. Rocking her like a baby. Weeping hot tears down her neck.

She reciprocated as any bereft fifteen-year-old would. She hugged her mother back.

Poor Mama.

CHAPTER 35

Amsterdam, police headquarters, 22 January

'Did you know the women in these photos, yes or no?' van den Bergen shouted. Poking insistently at a photograph of Linda Lepiks and the image that Marie had put together of the first victim. Bolt upright in his chair. Dwarfing a whey-faced Ahlers, who slouched forwards, toying with his own fingernails and blinking too fast at the table's surface, some six inches to the right of the images.

'Can I have a drink?'

'Look at the damned pictures!'

Elvis stood in a corner of the room. Leaning against the wall nonchalantly. Hands stuffed inside the pockets of his leather jacket. Casual. Doing studied indifference, George could see.

'You really want to play ball with him while you can,' Elvis told Ahlers, gesticulating with his quiff towards the grimacing chief inspector. 'He's a big man, right? Look at the size of those hands. I've seen what he does with guys who piss him around. Honestly, it can get quite messy.'

Ruud Ahlers tugged at the collar on his shirt. Ran a quivering index finger over the swollen side of his face. 'I want my solicitor present. You so much as touch a hair on my head, I'll have you for assault.'

Van den Bergen's mouth curled down at the edges. 'We find a match between nice blond pubic hairs our pathologist found on the black girl and the hair on your *groin*, you'll need more than a solicitor to save you, Dr Ahlers. You'll be wishing Jesus Christ was your legal representation.' He bore down on his interviewee, placing his fingers on the photographs in a custodial manner. The tip of his nose could not have been more than ten inches from Ahlers' face. 'You were struck off the medical register seven years ago for negligence and interfering with your female patients. Both my victims have been scarred by someone who darned them back together like mail bags. Did you perform surgery on them?'

Ahlers was silent. An indolent interviewee, rendering the cross-examination nothing more than a monologue, delivered by a clearly increasingly frustrated van den Bergen.

'Where were you on the nights of sixteenth of January and eighteenth of January? Hello! Are you listening to me?' He waved his hand in front of Ahlers' bloated face.

George's strange and seemingly murderous lunch companion finally shifted in his seat. Examined his nails. Spoke quietly. 'Well, for a start, I can tell you I was at the Holland Casino on the eighteenth of January. People saw me there. I won some money.'

'Did you drive? Walk? Take public transport?'

'Walk.'

'What car do you drive?'

'I don't have a car.'

'What time did you return to your place of residence?' Van den Bergen sounded every consonant clearly.

He opened and closed his mouth several times. George realised she didn't like Ahlers' mean lips or the flabby breasts and large gut that lay beneath his dowdy top. Pregnant with ill intentions; corpulent flesh marbled with sleaze and moral decay like a rotten cheese. What the hell had Katja been doing, hanging out with this chump?

'It was late,' he said. 'I don't remember. But they'll have everything on CCTV at the casino, if you think I'm lying.'

'Anyone able to corroborate what time you got back to your place? You got a woman at home?'

Silence ensued.

'I *said*. What. Time. Did you. Get. Back. To your. Place?'

George peered into the interview room through the one-way glass. Watching van den Bergen's hooded, grey eyes grow colder and colder as though a dark cloud had cast a chill shadow over him. Drumming his fingers on the table, now. Clearly impatient. Something about him had changed since they had seen one another some months earlier. Though he had always been lean, his clothes looked loose on him. His face, thoroughly drawn. Sunken cheekbones under the harsh interview room light gave him the haunted, desolate look of a man stalking along the outer periphery of his own sanity. His complexion appeared jaundiced, rather than tanned or simply wind-burnt from spending hours in the outdoors. She was glad she had come.

'Here. I thought you could use a coffee,' Marie said, pushing a cup of black coffee into George's hand.

George nodded. Smiled uncertainly, as she eyed the thick band of grease that rendered the red-head's hair almost brown. 'Thanks.' She singed her lips on the boiling liquid. Settled for just warming her hands on the plastic. 'I honestly thought he was going to shoot me.' She conjured the memory of van den Bergen, holding the gun with arms outstretched. His expression had had a maniacal quality to it, as though he had been looking at her but had not seen her. Though Ahlers had pushed her to the bathroom floor to make his blundering attempt at escape, it was seeing van den Bergen's wild eyes that had really shaken her up. 'He's not the sort of man you want to get on the wrong side of, is he? Van den Bergen, I mean. I've never really seen that in him before. He normally seems so cool. So in control.'

'He's not himself at the moment,' Marie said. 'He did something totally mental a couple of weeks ago. He was lucky he didn't get suspended. God knows what's eating him.' She sighed. Didn't expand on what it was her boss had done that had been so out of character. 'Whatever it is, he won't talk about it to any of us. Maybe you'll have better luck.'

Turning back towards the interview room, George wrinkled her nose at the memory of the suspicious-looking lunch Ahlers had presented her with the previous afternoon. 'You think that meat was really meat?'

'We've sent it to the lab for analysis.'

She clutched her stomach. Two dead women. Missing organs. The potential ingredients of that lunch had a flavour of tabloid hysteria about them. But George read the broadsheets. She quelled her nausea with a gulp of coffee. 'I step foot off the plane straight into a pile of steaming shit. What were the odds of me being lured to that pervert's flat?'

'Amsterdam's a small place,' Marie said, thoughtfully twirling her pearl earrings around in their holes. 'You mix in vice circles, you're sure to run into trouble at some point.'

George shot her a venomous glance. Slammed the coffee down on the sill of the one-way window, so that the hot liquid splashed over her fingers. Wiped her hand angrily on her jeans. Head bobbing aggressively from side to side as she spoke. Pointing. Realising the heady effervescence of the champagne had given way to sharp-tempered hangover words, but unable to stop herself. 'You making assumptions about me? You judging my mate, Katja? Because I know there's no way she's tied up in this mess. She's going to go fucking ballistic when you question her.'

Marie held her hands up in a gesture of surrender. 'I wasn't—'

'No. You better not be.' George jabbed an accusatory finger towards her hair. 'You get a shower before you come to me with your squeaky clean bullshit. Okay?'

'Jesus! There's no need to be personal.' Marie took a step

backwards and hastily tied her hair with an elasticated grip into a ponytail. Deepened furrows on her forehead and raised eyebrows etched a show of hurt above watery eyes. 'Is this how it's going to be? We've got to work together for the next six months, the boss said.'

George sighed heavily. Reached out to Marie and, defying her inner voice which screamed that touching the woman would mean she would have to wash her hands immediately in very hot water, rubbed Marie's thin arm in a show of contrition. 'Take no notice of me. I was up at six yesterday and nearly got myself killed. Twice. Couldn't sleep a wink last night. Haven't exactly got off to a good start, have I?'

Marie nodded, though the tightly folded arms said everything. 'It's fine.'

'You think you've got your man?' George asked, wishing she had an override button on the smart mouth she had inherited from her mother.

Marie turned to the view through the one-way glass. Watching as van den Bergen thumped the table.

'I can *prove* you've performed surgery on both women,' he shouted. Brandished a sheet of paper in front of Ahlers. Read from it through glasses theatrically held high. A half-smile toying on his lips. 'As fate would have it, there's an assault report just come in about you from a Chinese man. Says you almost killed his daughter with your unlicensed backstreet butchery.' He pointed to Ahlers' swollen cheek. 'Was it him that rearranged your face?' He turned to Elvis. 'I'd say it's an improvement, wouldn't you?'

Elvis nodded. 'Good job. I hope he sends you an invoice.'

Van den Bergen turned back to the report. 'Shall we take a look at the stitching on this Chinese girl?'

Ahlers stared at him. Silent, though it was hard to tell if it was fear or defiance that had a grip of his tongue.

'Stop wasting my time! I can *prove* you had sex with the black girl. What was her name?!' Even with glass separating them, the ferocity of van den Bergen's voice was undimmed.

Finally, Ahlers cracked. First, a startled expression hinted at the fissure underlying his composure. Then, he started to weep. Leaking from those bloodshot eyes turned to torrents. Jerking shoulders. Gripping the table top with chubby hands. Snot descending to his top lip in a glistening rivulet. 'Noor. Her name was Noor.'

'Oh yes,' Marie said, a flicker of a smile warming her face. 'I think we've got our man.'

CHAPTER 36

South East London, Aunty Sharon's house, later

'I didn't know where else to come, Shaz,' Derek said, tilting his head back whilst Sharon dabbed at his bloody nose.

She sighed. Dipped the tea towel into the boiled water and poked him in the eye with it.

'Ow!' he cried. 'Why you do that for? Ain't I suffered enough?'

Sharon dropped the towel on the kitchen table and sat down heavily on one of the pine chairs. She sipped from her mug of strong tea, considering the man before her, whose face looked like tenderised meat.

'You're some kind of fucking idiot, Derek de Falco. What unmentionable shit you got yourself wrapped up in, eh? Which particular brand of fucking nightmare you brought to my house this time?'

Her former lover reached out to grab her hand. She was quick to shake him loose. No point giving that tosser false hope. Bad enough he was Tinesha's baby-father. Twat.

'It was them fellers from the club. Italian geezers, you know?' He shifted his position on his seat and winced. 'Can I have a cuppa tea?'

'Nah. This ain't no caf for waifs and fucking strays. Talk!'

155

Derek pointlessly licked his fingers and dabbed at the large, bloody spatter down the front of his primrose-yellow evening shirt. Sharon reflected that he looked like he had gone to a fancy dress party as a representation of cat sick, but she kept that to herself.

'So, I gets invited to this party out at some farmhouse in the middle of Kent, right? Them geezers is all friendly, cos I let them bring girls to the club.'

'The porn king know?'

He shook his head and groaned. 'Dermot Robinson? You must be joking. He'd string me up by the balls. No, these Italians came to me, right, cos of my family connections? Why you smirking like that, Shaz? That's very cold.'

'Shut it, you fool.'

'Anyway, they make money from the girls. I take a nice cut and don't ask no questions, right? I'm glad of the cash.'

Sharon stood and slapped Derek upside the head. 'You greedy bastard.'

Melodramatically, he jerked backwards as though she had taken a baseball bat to him. 'You hurt me, Sharon.' He thumped his chest where his heart may or may not have been. Sharon wasn't sure. 'Right to the core, babe. And I don't see you moaning when I bung our Tinesha a few quid towards her student digs.'

Sucking her teeth, she soaked the towel in the hot water in its entirety. Wrung it out and flung it on top of Derek's head. 'Thems is underage girls, you morally derelict bastard,' she said, ignoring his complaints. Advancing to the cake tin and cutting herself a slice of swiss roll. She could see Derek's eyes on the cake. Hear his stomach growling. 'You looking at my cake?' Her mouth was full as she spoke. Brushing crumbs off her pink fluffy dressing gown. Licking buttercream off her fingers. 'This my cake, not your fucking cake.'

'You got a big slab there, darling. Give us a piece. Go on!'

Slapping her own ample behind, she waved her finger in

admonition; shook her head. 'You fellers don't get to take that much delicious out unless I put this much delicious in. *My* cake. Eyes forward, little man. Talk. And don't mention *my* Tinesha in this conversation again. Right?'

Bloodied head in his bruised hands, Derek began his tale.

'So, I'm thinking, I'm well in here with the correct people, right?' he said. 'They picks me up in some fancy Range Rover. Man, you ain't never seen such a big fucking car in your life. Real drug dealer bling in all white with black wheels et cetera, et cetera. And we drives to this farmhouse out Canterbury way. Big gaff, like Carnegie bloody Hall. Well,' he grinned. Then thought better of it with a sharp intake of breath. 'It was a fucking orgy. Serious. I mean drugs coming out of me arsehole. Birds, but not like the sort of birds I normally mix with.'

'Thanks a fucking bundle.'

Derek tutted. 'Jeez, Shaz. Don't be like that. I mean, the birds at the club. Some of these was posh. You know? Professional types. Toffs.'

'Rich, white women looking for a thrill,' Sharon offered, one eye on her phone.

'Yeah. Exactly. They're all in the nip or in bondage gear and getting it on with fellers there, in full view, et cetera. I thought – no offence, like – I'm having a bit of that. Right?'

Through the swelling in his eyelids she could see pleading brown eyes, begging forgiveness. Sharon had acquired immunity to that hangdog expression. Derek de Falco wasn't really her problem any longer. She ate her cake in silence.

'Anyway, so, I'm going at it with some bird, trousers round my ankles, like. Out the corner of my eye, I notice this geez holding court on the sofa. He's got all his clobber on. Looks money. And I'm all ears, right? And he's chatting to the short Italian – the one who looks like Al Pacino in *Serpico*.'

Sharon scratched at her scalp under her hair net. 'It's *Scarface*, dickhead. Wrong film.'

'Yeah, whatever. And some posh bird, built like a brick shithouse. Horsey Helen.'

'What's the money one look like?'

Derek rolled some toilet paper into tight bungs and shoved one up each nostril. Tilted his head back. His voice was comically nasal. 'Well, he was white. Hard to tell how tall he was. He was sitting down. Balding geez with a buzz cut. Diamond in his tooth. Bit of stubble. Slim build. In his fifties, I'd say. Sounded proper upper crust. I ain't never seen him before. And the three of them's talking. I can hear something about donors.'

'Donuts?' Sharon was growing bored. Uncle fucking Giuseppe could naff off back to his own place in a minute. She had washing to do before Patrice came home from school. And dinner to make before her shift at the club started. Nice goat curry. Lovely. And the floor needed mopping. Plus, that bathroom didn't clean itself. Wandering over to the kitchen window, she started to water the spider plants on the sill with water in an old milk bottle. Adjusted the tie-backs on her gingham curtains. She could quite fancy a donut.

'Nah. I think maybe the bird was a politician or charity type et cetera. Maybe a banker. I don't frigging know. Cos they was talking about markets and money and pricing and that. Anyway, never mind what they was fucking chatting about. Next minute, Scarface clocks me earwigging. I'm out on my arse, getting beaten to a pulp by the other two on a heated bloody driveway, no less! And them lads can swing a punch, I can tell you.'

In her mind's eye, Sharon caught sight of the two large henchmen who had accompanied the smaller Italian to the club on several occasions. One of them had asked George for a dance, hadn't he? Got nasty and smashed his glass when she'd turned him down. Sharon exhaled slowly. Bit her lip.

'You going to the police?'

Derek scoffed. 'What do you think? Since when have I been a grass?'

'Then you ain't got nothing to worry about, have you? Keep your gob shut. Lay low. It'll blow over.'

Suddenly, beneath the signs of the beating he had received, beneath all Derek's bluff that had at one time attracted her to him but had in recent years grated – like a bad joke, repeated too often – fear was apparent. Sharon could almost smell it on the air. She had always had a good sixth sense for that kind of thing. When he said, 'It'll never blow over. I'm fucked, Shaz,' she knew he wasn't exaggerating.

CHAPTER 37

Amsterdam, the Quick Bite Café, later

Looking at George was difficult. Though they had spoken regularly on the phone and briefly, by email, van den Bergen hadn't seen her in the flesh for months. And that flesh looked amazing – what he could see, at any rate. Fresh faced. Bright eyed. Even in her self-imposed uniform of black jeans and a plain black hooded top, every inch of her was beautiful. Somebody else's beautiful.

'You're staying at Karelse's?' he asked, taking a bite out of his sandwich, though he had no real inclination to eat. The café was mercifully empty. Just a waitress staring up at a small TV, suspended on a wall bracket. He had been careful to select a place several streets away from the station, where he knew his colleagues did not go.

George shook her head. Toyed with one of those amazing curls that sprouted from her scalp like a gravity-defying firework, whizzing skywards in a corkscrew. He loved the challenge of sketching those. Perhaps she would let him paint her this time.

'The Cracked Pot,' she said. 'Just for a couple of nights. Then… I'll see.'

Not staying at Karelse's. This was a turn up. 'How come?'

Slurping her soup noisily, she shrugged. 'Space.' She was eyeing the pink of the new skin on his knuckles. 'You wanna tell me about that, then?'

If he told her, he would reveal too much and risk scaring her off. Damn. Why hadn't he kept his mouth shut about that? 'What are your first impressions of Ahlers?' he asked, pushing a codeine tablet out of the blister pack.

George leaned across the table. Grabbed his hand. 'Hey! You can pack that in, for a start. I didn't come over here to watch you poison yourself slowly.'

He was reluctant. The blurring had worn off during the interview with Ahlers, leaving him exposed to feeling the pain. 'Let me take this one. I can't get through the afternoon without it. The headaches are—'

'Jesus, Paul! You're a fucking mess! What's going on with you?'

She let go of his hand, allowing him to swallow the tablet down with a mouthful of strong coffee. It quelled the anxiety that had been building within him. But he wished she had not let go. Her skin was so soft and warm. It was so long since he had felt a woman's touch. Another man's woman, though. That idiot Karelse's woman. Ha! It was a joke. What did that spineless prick have that was so alluring? He was no better than Numb-nuts – Tamara's buffoon of a fiancé.

Smoothing down the front of his sweater, he was relieved that the musculature beneath it was at least still paunch-free, if a little on the bony side at the moment. She had come all the way to Amsterdam at his request, hadn't she? *Feel the fear and do it anyway, van den Bergen.*

'Let's talk about that tonight,' he said. 'Come round to mine. I'll order in take-out. We'll open a nice bottle of wine. You can sleep in the spare room. It's clean. How does that sound?'

She smiled, and it was as though the sun shone through the café window, warming everything; lighting up the dark places within him. 'Yeah. Okay. Too many bad memories in that old room, anyway.' She pushed her bowl of soup away, half drunk.

'I've been feeling a bit rough since that loon tried to feed me God-knows-what.'

Raised an eyebrow and fixed him with those big brown eyes. Hadn't Marie spoken about some article or other she had read online, that said if you stare into somebody's eyes for long enough, they fall in love with you? He determined to hold her gaze for as long as possible but only managed twenty or so seconds. Damn.

'You're normally a good judge of character,' he said. 'What went wrong?'

'Ahlers seemed all right, I guess,' she said. 'If he hadn't, and if Katja hadn't have vouched for him, I'd certainly never have gone to his place.' She rubbed her face. Rolled her eyes. 'Christ knows. You rang and expected me to come running. But I've been feeling so trapped, lately. So controlled. I was being spontaneous, I guess. Rebellious.'

She started to position the condiments in a perfectly straight line that bisected the table, leading from her to him. Connect the dots. Connect that mesmerising woman and this ageing, crumbling man.

'Was there anything off about him once you got to his place?'

Nodding thoughtfully. 'Definitely. I think he was about to try something on when you burst through the door like Al Capone. He's a creepy bastard. No doubt.' She leaned across the table. Stroked the pink of his knuckles. It was all he could do to stifle a sigh. Then, she withdrew her hand, seemingly thinking better of it. 'What I want to know, is where the hell is that Noor's baby? I mean, if he delivered her child, was it dead? Alive? Is there a toddler at home somewhere and a babysitter wondering where the fuck the mother's got to?'

'Will you do some digging on Noor, then?' he asked, checking his watch. Time to go back.

She grinned mischievously. 'I thought I was supposed to be your clerical assistant. Filing shit in a short skirt, like secretaries do. Keeping you in hot drinks. That's the way this rolls, isn't it?'

Was she flirting? He was sure she was flirting. But maybe she was just being playful.

'You are my new administrator,' he said. 'I bent over backwards to get Hasselblad to agree to it.'

Polishing the tines of her unused fork on a serviette, she was still smiling. Head inclined downwards. Chewing on her lip. But eyes on him. 'He didn't bend you over forwards?' Another raised eyebrow.

He withdrew his wallet from his inside pocket. Pulled out enough money to cover the clandestine lunch. 'I want your input on this case, George. You'll have an insight into Ahlers that the rest of us won't.'

'Don't get me wrong,' she said, putting the fork down carefully. 'I want to interview him. I've still got my PhD to research and write, you know. But you've got your own team of experienced detectives and qualified criminologists.'

'They're not like you.'

'You taking advantage of me, Chief Inspector?' She winked.

He grabbed his serviette, pretending to wipe crumbs away from his mouth. Hiding the blush and the smile.

As they walked back to the station, George linked arms with him. Patted him through his overcoat. He had to curb the pace at which he walked to keep in step with her.

'It's lovely to see you, you know, you big, soft sod,' she said, peering up at him. Her expression was one of thoughtful contemplation.

The huge, 1940s brick box on Elandsgracht that was the police headquarters loomed before them. He spied Elvis and Kees walking ahead, under the cantilevered portico. There was something about their hesitant gait and closeness that made his bullshit-ometer spring to life. What were they discussing? Reluctantly, he pulled his arm free from George. 'You can't talk like that in front of the others,' he said. 'I need them to see me as the boss, not a friend. Is that okay?'

George squeezed his hand surreptitiously. Saluted. Marched ahead without him. Greeted Elvis in English with a merry, 'All right, the King? You ditched Marie and got yourself a feller to love you tender instead?' She laughed at her own joke and disappeared through the glazed doors.

'Hey, you two!' van den Bergen said, catching up with the detectives. Placing territorial hands on their shoulders. Feeling them shrink beneath his grip. 'You've still not told me why you weren't at the raid on Ahlers' apartment and where the bloody hell you've been all morning. You'd better have a fucking good excuse.'

Kees smiled at him. It was a smug smile. The kind he had seen on that obsequious fat turd, Kamphuis', face.

'Oh, we do, boss. As excuses go, you can't get much better.'

Van den Bergen observed Elvis – fingering his sideburns with a slightly quivering index finger; failing to look him in the eye – to see if Kees' enthusiasm was matched by his. Clearly, it wasn't.

CHAPTER 38

Amsterdam, police headquarters, later

Kees removed his anorak with deliberate care. Hung the coat on the back of the chair and took a seat opposite van den Bergen. There was something about the chief inspector's hooded eyes and sharp-featured face that he didn't like. He always seemed to be looking down his nose at life. An austere old bastard, who judged everything around him, constantly. Those unusual, grey irises put him in mind of the North Sea on a foul winter's day. Desolate and devoid of warmth. A man could get sucked into van den Bergen's vortex and drown in his cynicism and disappointment. Kamphuis had said he was a whining hypochondriac, whose skinny frame bore all the hallmarks of a skinny, mean-spirited disposition. What was it Elvis used to call van den Bergen before he turned into a fully qualified, arse-kissing disciple? Evil Yoda. He sniggered.

'What's so funny?' van den Bergen asked.

Kees shook his head. 'Nothing.'

Elvis was perched in the corner of the office on a second chair, looking like somebody had rammed a pool cue up his backside. Had he deliberately distanced himself, or had the chair already been that far from the desk?

Van den Bergen started to sketch some shit or other in his pad. 'This had better be fucking impressive.'

Sensing the need for a little drama, Kees paused. Tutted. Took a deep breath. 'Oh, it is. You know my...' He looked round at Elvis, remembering that the centre stage was not solely his to take. Safety in numbers, after all. '...That's to say, *our* hunch about Buczkowski being suspicious?'

The chief inspector's mouth curved downwards into a grimace. 'Yes. And?'

'Well, he's definitely involved.' He withdrew his phone from his trouser pocket and brought up the gallery. Showed van den Bergen the photographs. 'See? Books on Satanic ritual. Books about the blood libel of the Jews. You know what that is?'

'A load of shocking anti-Semitic crap,' van den Bergen said. 'What the hell does that have to do with two murdered women?'

It was difficult for Kees to conceal his irritation at the wilful nay-saying of the old bastard. Here he was, handing him a second suspect on a plate, and this was the reception he was getting. 'Look!' He pointed to some of the titles on the bookshelves that he had snapped from up close. 'Loads of true crimes books about voodoo killings.'

Turning round to seek Elvis' complicit corroboration, he found nothing beyond his colleague sitting in silence, hunched in his chair. Resigned. Elbows on knees; head in hands.

'That's how come the mattress was in the Valeriusstraat house,' he went on. 'Buczkowski put it there. Stands to reason. His finger prints were on the tools, for God's sake! He's into all this mutila-tion stuff because he's a devil-worshipping son of a bitch. Ahlers' accomplice.'

Van den Bergen put his glasses on and peered down his nose at the phone. 'The evidence linking Buczkowski to the building site is piss-water thin. His tools were at his place of work. Big deal! If they were lying around, the perp could have just taken them. Opportunism. True: Valeriusstraat is somehow connected to Lepiks' murder, but there's no match between the blood on the mattress and Lepiks' blood. If there's been a third victim, we don't even have a body! And, more to the point, I *didn't* realise we had a warrant to search Buczkowski's apartment.'

'Er—'

The chief inspector looked over at Elvis, disapprobation and disappointment etched into the lines in that craggy old sod's face. 'I told Leeuwenhoek to look into the builder, but breaking and entering? Harassing a witness? Maybe that kind of shitty, slipshod police work cuts the mustard on Kamphuis' side of the building but it doesn't on mine.' He pointed at Elvis. A long, accusatory finger that trembled until he laid his hand flat on the desk. 'You, of all people, know better than to enter a suspect's home without a warrant or a more compelling reason than Leeuwenhoek's hunch, *Dirk*. What have you got to say for yourself?'

Elvis slapped his knees. 'Sorry, boss. If it's any consolation, I think Kees is onto something. Didn't Strietman say we were looking at some ritual sex killing thing? He mentioned voodoo, right?'

Polishing his glasses on his shirt tails, van den Bergen frowned. Was silent for almost a full minute. Kees could feel the sweat beading on his forehead. Every second felt like torture. Would he be disciplined for the unsanctioned trip?

Finally, the old pain in the arse looked at him and said, 'Fine. I'll let this breach of protocol slide this one time. Let's pray you weren't seen breaking in, you dick. Get Buczkowski back in for questioning. I'll have another read through the forensic report on Valeriusstraat. See if I can make sense of it.' He turned to Elvis. 'You, me and Georgina are going to Ahlers' surgery now, so don't get comfortable in that chair.'

Kees noticed van den Bergen looking through the glazed door to his office at the new English girl who had started working there on some short term contract or other. She walked past, carrying a file box. Dressed like some student junkie or down-and-out. Though it was hard to see exactly what lay beneath her baggy hooded top, he suspected she had a pleasing curvaceous figure. Nice round arse, in any case. But dark meat wasn't normally his thing. And his father said the English were a backwards race. Hardly surprising, then, that this girl had been mixing with a whore and a murder suspect. But there must have been some reason for van den Bergen getting her over here to work. And, as she glanced inside the office, meeting the chief inspector's gaze, he could see something had passed between them. What exactly was it?

CHAPTER 39

Amsterdam, Ahlers' private surgery, later

'This place stinks,' George said, holding her nose. 'It's damp as hell, for a start.'

She looked around at the waiting-area-cum-reception of Ahlers' surgery: a dingy little ante-room, with eight ugly thread-bare dining chairs that were the sort of thing people left on the street, in the hope that students, idiots or the destitute would magic them away overnight. A 1960s battered coffee table with curling magazines strewn messily on top. Golfing magazines. Celebrity gossip rags. Car journals that were once glossies but the covers of which were now tattered and barely legible. She looked at the publication dates on the spines. June 2008. Last decade. Imagined the germs that must cling to those pages and had to look away abruptly.

The floor was covered with cracked linoleum, framed by decades of black grime that had accumulated around the edges. Overhead, a fluorescent strip flickered on and off. Strobe-lighting with intermittent incandescence the cobwebs that hung in the corners of the ceilings, made thick like dangling grey dreadlocks by years of undisturbed dust. Peeling pistachio paint on the walls. Black, powdery mildew creeping from the dusty skirting towards the old, once-grand cornicing.

The only attractive feature in the waiting room was an ornate, centuries-old marble fireplace, that had been boarded with ply across the aperture where a fire once blazed. Even that was blighted by a red-brown handprint smeared across the mantel. George imagined some poor desperate soul coming into the surgery, bleeding from a failed hysterectomy or lost pregnancy, clinging to whatever support that fireplace offered, since she imagined zero sympathy would have been forthcoming from that quack, Ahlers.

'What a shithole,' she said to Elvis, who was dusting the reception desk for fingerprints.

He nodded. 'Gives me the creeps. Trouble is, I can't see us being able to place the murdered women in here,' he said. 'There must have been scores of patients coming and going in the last few months. Prints everywhere, and it's pretty clear it's never been cleaned. Was his apartment this bad?'

George shook her head. 'It was fine, actually. Not too bad at all. I'd put money on it that Ahlers has a cleaner, but he sure as hell didn't expend any effort on keeping this place sanitary.'

Van den Bergen's tall frame filled the doorway that led to the surgery at the back. He beckoned George. 'Come and see where the action happens. Tell me what you think.'

Taking in the shabby surrounds, George could smell yet more neglect on the air, coupled with stale alcohol and cigarette smoke. Her eyes sought out and found a whisky bottle – half empty – and a cracked crystal tumbler sitting on a sideboard at the back of the room. A full ashtray next to it. Red lipstick, the kind Katja wore, on the end of some of the cigarette butts. There was something else on the air. Stale bodily fluids.

'He's been using this place to party,' she said. 'I'd put money on it that Katja's been here recently.' Pointed to the ashtray. 'We already know he does her Botox, stupid cow.'

Stooping to examine a smashed mug and surgical instruments scattered about, van den Bergen fingered the white stubble on his chin. 'Signs of a struggle. But then we know Ahlers got into a fight with the Chinese guy over the bodge-job on his daughter. Judging by the bruising on our suspect's face, and the fact this puddle of cold coffee hasn't quite dried out, it's obvious something kicked off in here recently. That corroborates the Chinese man's statement.'

George looked at a scalpel on the floor. The blade had come away from the handle. 'Cheap instruments?' she said. Noticed the crumpled paper sheeting that barely covered the split, plastic covering on the couch. 'Hardly surprising.'

She walked to the fridge and, using the sleeve of her hooded top, opened the door. It was dirty inside. Mouldering sweet buns next to two bags of blood. Type 'O'. Vaccination serum on the shelving in the door next to cheese and butter that were past their use-by date by two years.

'He's an animal,' she said, holding her nose at the rancid smell. Something occurred to her. 'Hey, didn't it say in the report you sent me that the mattress in Valeriusstraat was covered with type "O", and that you couldn't work out—'

'Whose blood it was,' van den Bergen finished. 'Yes. That's right.'

He crouched next to her and peered inside the fridge. Glasses on, to examine the label on one of the bags of blood. She could smell sport deodorant on him but noticed his collar was frayed at the corners. His skin was dry. Hair needed cutting, though she wanted to touch it. To know if it was soft like Ad's or coarse, like thick, straight hair often was. Resisted the temptation.

'It's a mystery,' he said. 'Enough blood to have caused death but no body, and what we presume are murder weapons, contaminated with traces of cow flesh.'

The thrill of discovery really sparked inside George, now. Warming her from her toes to her scalp. She fluffed her hair in triumph. 'I think you've been played,' she said.

Van den Bergen put the bag of blood carefully back onto the shelving. 'What do you mean?'

George placed a latex-gloved hand on his shoulder and levered herself back onto her feet. 'What's the bet the blood on that mattress came from bags like this? Type O. If that blacklisted arsehole, Ahlers, is your murderer, he can get hold of fresh blood like you and I can buy milk from the supermarket.'

Van den Bergen closed the fridge door and stood, so he towered above George. Her neck ached to look up at him.

'Right. Go on!'

'So, the Valeriusstraat thing has been doctored to look like a crime scene, but isn't. Neither of the dead women were killed with a hammer and chisel, were they? Or showed signs of having been whipped with a cat-o-nine tails.'

'No. They were cut open and some of their organs had been removed.'

'So, Ahlers is feeding the police misinformation to hide the true circumstances around the murders. I'd say that putting the Linda Lepiks horror porn where you can find it is a ploy to make the killings look sexually motivated.'

The chief inspector frowned. 'You think they're not sexual in nature?'

George shrugged. 'Who knows? If Ahlers is your man, maybe he'll talk in time, but I'd say this runs a bit deeper than some twisted fucker just wanting to hurt women and then get off on it.'

'What do you think of Satanism?'

'Dunno.' She snapped off her gloves and jammed her hands into the pockets of her hooded top. Smiled. 'Not my first choice of a Saturday night out.'

'I've got a detective on my team bleating on about Satanism.' The creases in his brow deepened. His dark eyebrows arched above steely eyes, beyond which she glimpsed a storm. 'If you take away a hatred of women and fetishism, I can't find a bloody sensible motive in all this.'

George put her arm around him, fleetingly. 'You're a pro. You'll get it out of Ahlers.'

172

Van den Bergen blushed. 'The pathologist, Daan Strietman, mentioned voodoo.'

The doorbell tinkled more merrily than befitted such a depressing place. Several people walked in, wearing white protective jumpsuits and carrying cases of equipment. At the head of the group was a man, the sight of whom turned van den Bergen's half-smile into a sneer.

'Speak of the devil...'

CHAPTER 40

Amsterdam, the Cracked Pot Coffee Shop, red light district, later

It had been a long forty-eight hours. Staring out at the rooftops through the window of the attic room that had once been her home, George thought about her return to Amsterdam: a picture perfect city to the untrained eye. But scratch the surface and the quirky, steep-roofed architecture, the flower-filled houseboats, the haphazard beauty of it all soon gave way to something altogether more sinister. A decadent old dame, fed by the rotten arteries of the canal network – rank with diesel slick, abandoned, decaying Christmas trees and the odd up-ended supermarket trolley. Even London's Soho only felt like a shabby cousin next to this multi-faceted city. There was no place like it. How she had longed to be back, and not just for a visit.

Finally, after smoking e-cigarettes all day, she allowed herself to light up a proper one. Felt only a shred of remorse at having broken her promise to Ad. Checked her phone. Her text inbox was bursting with:

```
Where are you? Love you, Ad xxx
Have I done something wrong? Love you,
Ad xxx
```

```
Can we talk about when I was in London?
Love you so so much, Ad xxx
Are you going off me? Love forever, Ad
xxx
Aunty Sharon says you're in Amsterdam.
Call me!
```

Always multiple kisses, apart from the one where her abscansion had been rumbled. His texts had stopped after that.

'Oh, Ad. You sweet, nagging bastard,' George said, breathing her smoke out into the early evening sky, as if her dreams and aspirations were buoyed all the way to God's ears on those noxious blue curls.

Switching to email, she spied one of five missives from Sally Wright. The last one, in actual fact, before Sally had finally gone quiet.

From: Sally.Wright@cam.ac.uk14.05
To: George_McKenzie@hotmail.com
Subject: Unauthorised study leave.

Georgina,

Why are you not answering my emails? Why did I have to find out by dint of your absenting yourself from our planned supervision and from a curt email, sent by that Dutch detective who almost got you killed, that you have gone AWOL? I expressly forbade you to go to Amsterdam for more than a long weekend to spend time with your boyfriend. Phone me immediately or face the consequences!

Sally

Dr Sally Wright, Senior Tutor
St John's College, Cambridge Tel...01223 775 6574
Dept. of Criminology Tel...01223 773 8023

'Fuck off, you frosty old bag,' George told the email.

With a swipe, the disappointed email had vanished and was replaced by her disappointing wallpaper – the photo of her and Ad on the Stansted Express. She felt hounded and surrounded.

'Fuck 'em. Right, van den Bergen. I'm coming to get you, you miserable git.'

With her suitcase repacked, she called a cab from the Cracked Pot below.

'Leaving so soon?' Jan asked, offering her a toke on his giant joint.

George sighed. Looked longingly at the carrot-shaped gift of Moroccan hash and shook her head. 'Last time I stayed here, a nutter tried to rape me and blow me to smithereens,' she said. Chuckled without mirth. 'This time, I almost get cut into bits by the new serial killer on the block. Messages from the universe, Jan.'

'Messages from the universe.' Jan seemed to roll her words around his tongue, savouring their flavour. He nodded slowly, absorbing the profundity. 'I taught you well!' Hooking his stiff, long grey hair behind his ears and pushing his round Trotsky glasses up his nose, he seemed to be considering his next move. Evidently made a decision when he locked George in a bone-crunching embrace which she had not asked for.

Initially, the contact rendered her rigid. Forgetting to breathe. Then she remembered Jan was a friend of old and relaxed into what was, after all, just a hug. Had she not eaten from this man's table? Lived under his roof for a year.

'You're a grotty sod, Jan, but you're the best,' she said. 'Thanks. I know you meant well. Letting me have the room, and all.'

Jan wheezed with stoned laughter. 'You get that obsessive

176

compulsive shit sorted out, Georgina. You never used to turn into an ice-pop when I hugged you.' He added in heavily accented Americanised English. 'It's most uncool, man.'

She arrived at van den Bergen's just a little after seven.

He opened the door, wearing a flowery apron over a pair of baggy jeans and a black turtleneck sweater that made him look even thinner than ever. She smiled and pressed a good barolo into his hands. She had worked the best part of an evening at the club to be able to afford that. Leaned forwards to kiss him on the cheek. Realised his startled expression was not one of a man who was about to serve a relaxing meal.

'What's wrong?' she asked.

'It's possible there's been another,' he said.

'In Amsterdam? Could it be the Valeriusstraat—'

Shook his head vociferously. Checked the landing, as if anyone could have been lurking or eavesdropping in that small space. Pulled her inside and shut the door. 'Rotterdam.'

CHAPTER 41

Over the North Sea, 23 January

Buffeted by a brisk wind; tugged forwards across the North Sea by the droning blur of the propellers, the private six-seater was now some distance from Manston airport in Kent. Homeward bound.

The trip had been a resounding success in many ways. First, a convention with contemporaries in the UK's National Health Service to discuss best practice. Admittedly, meetings like that with those stuffy British bastards had been as dull as the billowing rain clouds that caressed the plane's nose.

The convention had been billed as a cultural and clinical exchange between Europe's finest medical practitioners, blah blah blah. Advanced techniques, some tedious woman had waxed lyrical about. Everyday surgical procedures under the influence of ground-breaking research done by Cambridge's finest at Addenbrooke's, a science nerd had boasted, barely pausing for breath. Excuse me while I just sleep with my eyes open. Reflecting on the opportunity Rotterdam had yielded had provided a useful distraction during the most tedious presentations.

The real reason for attending – apart from an excellent alibi, of course – had been the post-convention conversation, during a deep-fried, carbohydrate-heavy buffet lunch, with the consultant from London. How easily this consultant had coughed up golden nuggets of wisdom, thinking he was merely chatting over golden nuggets of chicken. Yes, my favoured technique is such and such. The primary concerns when maintaining the patient's levels are this, this and this. Spill your guts, Dr Whatever-it-is-your-name-badge-says-you're-called. Like the girls in Amsterdam. Like the little scrubber in Soho. And the others.

The turbo-prop aircraft was lurching from side to side on an unhappy, turbulent bed of cumulonimbus. No need to worry, just yet. Eat some peanuts.

'Would you like a glass of champagne?' the air hostess asked. Smart in a navy blue and green livery. Formal, yet attentive. Too attractive to be the sort of workaday flying waitress who ploughed up and down the aisles of commercial airliners, serving dried-out meals to hordes of complaining British holiday makers all day long. This was a beauty. And today, they were alone in the cabin of a private aircraft. Just the two of them.

'No, I'll leave it for now, thanks. I'm fine with my peanuts and the coffee.'

Under normal circumstances, with her comely, trim figure and encouraging smile, the air hostess might have offered a temptation, but those parties could be very draining.

The farmhouse in Kent had been a pleasant way to spend an evening. Funny how the architecture in that part of Britain was so similar to the gabled Dutch houses over the water. *Op het platteland* – in the country. Not exactly flat, but still a bucolic scene with pastures green and the lopsided cones of the oast house nearby. All it had lacked was a windmill.

'Come in,' the party hostess had said. Madame Whiplash with a crepey orange neck and tonged hair that befitted a younger woman. 'Indulge yourself. The Duke is meeting business partners on the sofa.'

Inside, the farmhouse had been furnished in the artless non-style of the nouveau riche. A grand staircase in Perspex and wood.

Tripping the blue LED light-fantastic up to the galleried landing of the first floor. Supermodern. Supertacky. Marble this and mirrored that. Chandeliers hanging from every ceiling, whether it was vaulted and appropriate or beamed and far too low. Like dangling earrings on a burnt-out strip-club whore.

'You can get changed in here,' the hostess had said, smiling with difficulty through an over-enthusiastically executed face uplift; opening a secret door amid smoked glass mirrored panels to reveal an office of sorts. Filled with piles of discarded clothing.

With newcomers left to find their way to the fun, the way was signposted by condoms in bowls, incongruously placed next to wholesome family photos on this sideboard and flower arrangements on that cabinet. Ushered into the living room by naked girls bearing trays of champagne. More in the living room, where people were already busy indulging themselves. This party was like the others during which The Duke conducted business. Same sex. Opposite sex. Strange formations made from multiple participants, like an erotic game of Twister with added sound effects. Some were body-beautiful types, in amazing shape. Others were ageing, overweight, scarred – looking almost as if they were wearing grotesque body suits that resembled humans or perhaps were a failed human cloning experiment that had produced only ugly counterfeits. Wealth had obviously been their ticket into this party. Most people wore masks.

But The Duke had been seated and fully clothed. Wearing a sharp suit. Holding court on a fuchsia velvet sofa, that diamond in his tooth, glinting. Lines of coke on the table for him to ingest at regular intervals, he was unaware that his left nostril was caked in powder. Sniffing, glassy-eyed. His accent was the finest cut crystal. But his arrogance like overwhelming, cheap cologne. This was a man who had climbed to the top of a slag heap for kicks. Treading on the putrefying corpses of those he had vanquished. Almost certainly to defy family. Public school dropout, though there was a sharp entrepreneurial mind behind those coked-up eyes.

'I'm pleased with the way you've been delivering,' he'd said. Talking just that bit too fast.

'I want more money.'

'Isn't it enough I ship you here on my private jet? Don't I look after you? Show you a good time? Don't you like my parties?'

'I do.'

'Is the coke not good enough?'

The coke had been good, actually. 'It's fine. But I still want more money. You think you can get cheaper elsewhere, we can go our separate ways, if you like. This is difficult and technically demanding work.'

Renegotiating and agreeing terms had been easier than expected. The Duke had handed over a list.

'These are my needs and these are the timescales,' he said, sniffing, sniffing and never managing to stop the dew drop of snot from dropping onto the crotch of his trousers. Wiping his nose. Shaking his head like a dog that shakes rain from its drenched coat. 'There's a freight liner due to dock in Dover about three am. Coming straight from the Congo. What you need's on board that ship but you can pick it up from Ramsgate. Easier to transfer the cargo and have it dock in Ramsgate on a fishing trawler. You can do what you need to do nearby. I've made provision for your requirements, as agreed.'

The party had been less of a buzz than anticipated in the end, because of the need to keep a clear head and steady hand. The list was the list. Business was business. Seeing some loser in a custard-yellow shirt getting the living daylights beaten out of him on the driveway of that farmhouse served only as a reminder that, once an agreement had been entered into with The Duke, it had to be adhered to. He was not a man to be trifled with.

At least the Ramsgate mission had been easy enough. In fact, it was fair to say that the procedures had been refined even further. So, the drab medical convention had truly served its purpose.

Now, as the private aircraft wobbled down perilously on the

insistent south-westerly wind towards Rotterdam The Hague airport, there was a certain comfort in knowing that another job had been satisfactorily completed, the money had been transferred successfully, a glorious professional reputation remained intact and a good night's sleep with a clear conscience beckoned. Because of Ramsgate, some good would be done in a rotten, festering world. The victims racked up but the maths stacked up. And the police didn't have the slightest inkling of what the hell was going on.

The air hostess was about to fasten her seatbelt in preparation for landing. She made eye contact.

'Do you need help?'

'Actually, if it's not too late, I will have that glass of champagne.'

CHAPTER 42

Amsterdam, police headquarters, later

'How has this happened?' Hasselblad asked.

He was pacing, as usual, like a fat cockerel strutting in a farmyard. Hands behind his back. Eyes bulging, boggling, ogling George in the corner surreptitiously. Except it was not his space he was territorially marking out.

Van den Bergen sat behind his desk, feeling like a visitor in his own office. He put his hands behind his head and closed his eyes, blocking off the view of the framed photo of Tamara and the simple white potted orchid that sat by his computer. 'What do you mean, "How has this happened?" Have I got personal jurisdiction over the entire country?'

Hasselblad stopped pacing. Leaned over the desk, so that his paunch rested on the table top. A tic flickering in his left lower eyelid. 'You've got a known pervert and all-round scumbag under lock and key. You *solved* the murders of the year in record time! Those are headlines the chief of police would have been happy to read. But now?' He stood, raising himself to his full height of five feet and eight inches. Pointed with a chubby finger at van den Bergen, as though he were aiming a gun at his head. 'How am I supposed to enjoy my dinner, when there's some hack on the phone from *de Telegraaf*, telling me they've just found another body? In Rotterdam! *Freshly* butchered, "like a side of beef", he said. 'In an opened cargo container.'

'I know. I got the call last night.' Van den Bergen pinched the bridge of his nose and remembered how the news had ruined his own potentially wonderful evening. A bottle of red, airing. A table for two, perfectly laid. A blueprint for romance laid out along with the Thai take-out menu.

But these were not Hasselblad's concerns. 'And is the victim a prostitute or a porno starlet?' He thumped the desk. 'I should be so fucking lucky! Because that would at least make us look like we knew one end of a motive from another.'

Van den Bergen felt like somebody had plugged his head with the soiled wadding from the Valeriusstraat mattress. Wished he was anywhere but in this office, being bawled out by his superior in front of George, of all people.

Only half-listening to Hasselblad, now, he took a blister pack of tablets out of his desk drawer and pushed a codeine capsule into the palm of his hand.

'Are you even paying attention to me, van den Bergen?' Hasselblad's face was bright red, as though he had run a marathon.

Van den Bergen swallowed the codeine with a gulp of cold coffee. Anxiety abating a little. 'You know, Jaap, I think you might suffer from high blood pressure? You want to get that checked out.' Looked over at George. 'The pathologist in Rotterdam puts money on it that the victim's Filipino – the contents of his stomach were largely undigested ingredients specific to some Filipino dish or other. What do you make of that?' he asked her.

Hasselblad jerked his thumb towards George. 'Who's *she*?'

'This is Georgina McKenzie,' van den Bergen said. 'She's my new administrative assistant but is also a very talented criminology student from Cambridge University. Studying for her doctorate.'

George did not rise to greet the commissioner. She merely

stretched out in her chair and crossed her legs at the ankle. One raised eyebrow.

Hasselblad fingered the dimple in his chin. He looked somewhat nonplussed by her body language. Studied her face. 'Aren't you the girl who was caught up in the case of the Bushuis bomber? The Firestarter kid?' He turned to van den Bergen. 'Why the hell is *she* working in my headquarters?'

Finally, George spoke. 'Are you not listening to what your own chief inspector is telling you? Like the man said, I am *very* talented.' She spoke at volume and rather slowly, as if he were a simpleton.

Hasselblad blinked, one two three, like a chugging computer straining to understand the information that had just been input into it. 'Make me a coffee,' he said.

'No. I make *his* coffee...' she pointed to van den Bergen '... and *my* coffee. You want coffee, get your own assistant to make it.'

Van den Bergen felt a flicker of pride warm him from within. He stood, hip clicking, and approached George's chair. Put his hand on her shoulder, claiming her as his charge. His responsibility, though he knew she might not appreciate what she sometimes dubbed his 'alpha male bullshit'.

'Tell the commissioner your theory, George,' he said.

George leaned back in her chair. Chewed intermittently on the end of her dormant e-cigarette. 'Well, I've seen the photos from the crime scene that were emailed over.'

'Who are you speaking to there?' Hasselblad asked van den Bergen.

'Wouter Dreyer from the Rotterdam Port Authority police,' van den Bergen said.

George continued. 'You've got a body, split open. Organs removed. The modus operandi of the murderer is exactly the same. So, unless Ruud Ahlers did the Amsterdam women and this Rotterdam murder is the work of an accomplice with an identical surgical skillset, you've got the wrong man under lock and key.'

'Is that all you've got, Miss Criminologist?' Hasselblad asked.

George stared at the palms of her hands. Pink and criss-crossed with a network of fine brown lines. 'All three are immigrants,' she continued. 'An illegal, underage Somali, a porn-star Latvian and a Filipino, though we don't know anything much about him, yet. Could be a race hate crime or an extreme political statement by anti-trafficking activists.'

Shaking his head like a stubborn toddler who refuses to eat the meal he has been given, Hasselblad emitted a snort of derision. He poked himself defiantly in the chest. 'I'm top brass here, little criminology student. I'm the one with decades of detective work under my belt. You mark my words, Ahlers is our Amsterdam man. We've got evidence says he is. And I think he has got an accomplice. They're a serial killing team of lunatics, keeping those organs as trophies.' He marched back over to van den Bergen's desk and pulled a fat bud off the orchid. 'Get every nut-job who has a criminal record in for questioning.'

'Define nut-job.'

'The mentally ill, of course. There must be a register of the freaks somewhere.'

'Freaks?' van den Bergen said, scowling. Thinking about the anti-depressants in his overstuffed medicine cabinet at home. Insensitive, ignorant bastard.

'Find it!' Hasselblad said, unaware of the animosity encroaching on him in that room. 'Pull them in! And get over to Rotterdam and have a look round.' He tapped the desk insistently, unaware that his chief inspector was wishing norovirus on him for having manhandled his precious orchid. 'Bring me a psychopath, Paul. Bring me one and fast, or you're out. For good.'

CHAPTER 43

Amsterdam, van den Bergen's car, en route to Rotterdam, later

'About last night,' George ventured, as van den Bergen manoeuvred his car slickly out of the car park.

The tyres squeaked noisily as he pulled away. The force of acceleration pressed George back into the leather seat.

'What about it?' he asked.

He honked his horn angrily at a van driver who had carved him up. Jabbed at the car's satnav buttons, which served only to cause a computerised voice to bark a string of disjointed instructions at him. 'Piss off, satnav. Jesus! There's bloody roadworks everywhere at the moment. Why is nothing ever straightforward? Pass me the thing.' He clicked his fingers in the direction of his glovebox and George withdrew a well-thumbed, spiral-bound road map.

'This thing?'

He growled. Snatched it from her. Balanced it on his steering wheel and started to turn the pages. One eye on the road. One eye on the map. 'We need to get out to the E19.'

She covered her eyes. 'Please don't do that. You'll crash the fucking car.'

'I never crash the car.'

Exasperating. That's what van den Bergen was, she reflected, spying his perfectly straight nose and prominent forehead. An angular-looking man with clean, sharp edges to his personality on the surface. Unyielding. Seemingly self-assured and completely lacking nuance. But she knew better.

'You dodged a bullet last night,' she said. 'We were going to talk, but this Rotterdam thing happened. Then you drag me into work at the crack of dawn, and I know you've been up all night. It's a strange bed. I woke up for a pee at three am and could see your light was on. You still haven't told me what's going on with you.' Momentarily, she put her hand on his outstretched right arm that gripped the steering wheel. He looked down at it. 'Paul, watch the road, for Christ's sakes!'

His Adam's apple bobbed up and down inside a sinewy neck. 'It's nothing,' he said, staring through the windscreen as the historical centre gave way to ugly industrial outskirts. The canals got wider here. Grey buildings, grey, bare trees, grey skies reflected grey on the water.

He sighed deeply.

'You're lying,' she said. 'Don't send me cryptic texts and then expect me not to ask when I get over here, you attention-seeking tosspot.'

A smile just about breached the severe expression that was gateway to all that lurked inside this complex man. It dissipated too quickly.

'The anniversary of my dad's death is coming up,' he finally said, turning onto the motorway. The countryside rapidly flattened out to green polders, the canals looking like mercury crawling through the landscape in a grid-like formation. 'I didn't get on with him. He used to call me a pansy when I was at art school. When I knocked Andrea up, I was just a reckless failure. I could never win with the old man. But it still hurt like hell when he got sick.'

'Cancer, right?'

He nodded. Puffed air out of his mouth noisily. 'I've not been sleeping well.'

'You're depressed?'

Glanced at her. His normally steely eyes looked heavy and dull. His upper eyelids, lax and more low-hanging than usual. Medicated. Dolorous. 'What do *you* think? And Tamara's getting married to that utter loser, Numb-nuts.' He shook his head. Exhaled too long and too hard.

But though George wanted to sympathise, a memory presented itself as an unbidden distraction. She held her hand over her mouth to obscure the giggle that was brewing. 'Didn't you tell me you planted a GPS tracker on him, when they first started living together? You were determined to prove he was up to no good, but then he found it in his guitar case or something, and she totally lost it with you.'

Van den Bergen pursed his lips. There was that suggestion of a smile again.

'Oh, stop being so grim-faced, Paul!'

'Are you going to tell me to cheer up?' he said. Was that hurt strangling his voice; making his usual deep, rich rumble seem strained and thin? 'You, of all people?'

'No!' This wasn't going the way she had intended. She wanted to comfort, not castigate. 'I just think…' She sought the correct words from the green fields and the giant, slow-turning wind turbines that studded the view. '…Sometimes you won't allow yourself even the slightest shred of happiness. You begrudge yourself a smile, for God's sake. And who gives a shit if Tamara marries Numb-nuts, as long as she's happy?'

Van den Bergen flung the road map into her lap. Mouth arced downwards in a sneer. 'You'll have children one day. Then you'll understand.'

Was he being patronising? It felt like it. She quelled the temptation to come back with a smart-arsed remark. Turned on the stereo. The angry buzz of distorted guitars blasted from the speakers.

'Jesus. Aren't you supposed to, like, get better taste in music when you have a mid-life crisis, man? What is this shit?'

He poked a long, slender finger at the on/off switch and the car's cabin was silent once more. 'Why are we arguing?' he asked.

'Are we arguing?' she said.

'I've been waiting for you to come over. And now you're here. Can we save the psychoanalytic therapy session for a nice meal and a bottle of wine? That was what I was planning for last night. Right now, I feel like dredging up my innermost anguish like a hole in the bloody head.'

George held her hands up. Sensed she had trespassed on uncomfortable territory. Slapped his thigh. 'You know you're my favourite copper, don't you, you big old lanky sod?'

'Did you really just slap my thigh?' he said. The smile broke through like reluctant sun shining on a storm-ravaged coastline. It seemed to plant a hopeful flag in the stern promontory of his face. 'That's sexual harassment in the workplace, young lady.'

She gasped in faux horror. Placed a melodramatic hand on her chest. '*Moi?*'

He briefly turned to her. Those heavy eyes seemed to have cleared. When he winked, she felt certain the van den Bergen she knew and loved was still present beneath this dry husk. All he needed to do was shed his sorrow like a reptile jettisons dead skin, and she felt optimistic that her friend could return from the shadows. Couldn't he?

'Hey!' he said, almost smiling as he stared at the road ahead. 'There's this paediatrician I want to introduce you to. Sabine. She's offering Marie some advice on signs of child abuse. Paedophilia. That sort of thing. And she's…well, you'll like her. A friend of Marianne's.'

She? George didn't like the sound of 'she'. Perhaps her friend had already returned from the shadows with somebody else's assistance.

'But never mind that. Tell me about Karelse,' he said, unexpectedly changing tack.

Then, it was George's turn to feel the sluggish, draining weight of expectation bearing down on her.

CHAPTER 44

Amsterdam, Ad's apartment, later

The walk down to the postbox in the communal entrance hall felt like an arduous trek. Ad was still wearing his slippers. T-shirt and boxers beneath the navy velour dressing gown that George had bought him their first Christmas together. The novelty of it being from the English store, Marks & Spencer, had long worn off. It felt heavy on him and had discoloured in parts, hanging in the sunshine on the bathroom door for over three years, now.

The front door to the apartment block was open. Two bags of shopping on the coir mat. Syrup waffles. Eggs. Washing powder. Frozen spinach. Out in front, that nosey, well-meaning old twit, Mrs de Klerk, was locking up her bike. Ad groaned. Turned to go back upstairs.

'Adrianus!' Mrs de Klerk said.

He was forced to look round. There she was, waving, as though she were flagging down a bus. Taking laboured long strides with those short, varicose veined legs of hers, mercifully hidden today by green waterproof walking trousers. Summer was a nightmare when she insisted on wearing shorts. He felt certain the first words out of her mouth would be, 'I've been meaning to ask about...' Same every time.

'I've been meaning to ask about that noise,' she said, toying with the silver cross that hung around her neck. 'A terrible racket, it was, coming from your apartment.'

Cornered now, there was no opportunity for escape. Ad withdrew the key from his dressing gown pocket and opened the box that was labelled 'Karelse/Meerdinck'. Took out a sheaf of post, mainly bills and junk. A pink envelope with Astrid's sloping hand on the front. A white envelope from England with a Crowthorne date stamp on it. Written by hand in block capitals that were so neat, they looked almost as though they had been word-processed. Sent two days ago, by the looks. Addressed to George.

'The noise, Adrianus! It was ungodly. I mean, you know I have heart problems.'

She sounded flustered and out of breath. Perhaps it was all those waffles and eggs. He silently rebuked himself for being so intolerant.

'I'm sorry, Mrs de Kl—'

'I think you had a party, didn't you? And you know you're to get the written consent of all the other occupants in this block if you have a party.'

Ad tried to focus on his disgruntled neighbour but his glance was inexorably drawn to the white envelope by the strangely neat handwriting and by George's name. Why had someone written to her at his address?

'Party?' he asked, vaguely aware that he was being taken to task for a transgression he hadn't committed.

'People, coming and going. Doors slamming. Thumping music until four am! You're lucky I'm a Christian, else I would have called the police.'

Finally, he focussed on her. 'I've been away. It must have been Jasper. He's moved back in full time.'

Mrs de Klerk picked up her shopping bags and plunged them into Ad's hands, so that he almost dropped his post. Forced to wedge the mail in his mouth. He carried the bags up to her front door.

'Are you ill, dear?' she asked, sticking her key in the lock. 'Only you're normally quite clean-looking for a student. I like that about you. I said to the ladies at church, I like this young man who lives next door. He's very respectable, even though he's dating an English nigger.'

Ad plonked her bags heavily on the floor – heavily enough that he was fairly certain at least one or two of her eggs must have broken. Took the dribble-drenched mail out of his mouth and thoughtfully stroked the two days' worth of stubble that had sprouted on his face and neck. 'I'm fine, thank you. And I'd appreciate it if you didn't use the N-word when you're talking about my girlfriend. It's racist.'

Mrs de Klerk looked startled. 'Cheeky boy!' Whipped her shopping bags inside and slammed the door, leaving him alone on the landing.

The strange letter had a certain magnetism to it. With the rest of the mail stuffed under his arm, his fingers hovered over the sealed flap. Should he open it? It wasn't addressed to him. But if it had been sent to his flat, that meant he could open it, right? And George, should she ever answer his calls ever again, would want him to open it and read it out to her, wouldn't she? Much quicker than forwarding.

'Screw you, George!' he muttered under his breath as he ripped a line down the fold of the envelope. Pulled out the letter. Shivered when he read the name of the sender at the bottom of a page of inhumanly neat, handwritten prose.

Charging back inside his flat, he bolted the door and put the mortise lock on. Felt cold sweat prickle forth from pores that seemed to know things were amiss before his brain had time to think such a thing. Where was his phone? Where was the damned thing? There! On the kitchen table next to Jasper's cycle helmet and the empty cans of lager from last night. Found George's number and pressed dial. Her face on the wallpaper. A photo from the Stansted Express. Smiling, though he knew the smile hadn't reached her eyes. Ringing. Ringing, now.

'For Christ's sake, George. Please pick up!'

CHAPTER 45

Rotterdam Port, later

Clanging, clashing. Whirring of heavy machinery moving from this grid reference to that stack. The throaty, guttural sound of horns from vessels approaching their birth. Wind, gusting between the towers of multicoloured blocks, like a whistle from the pursed lips of steel giants. Dockside is a very noisy place. Unsurprisingly, since the hundred or so square kilometres that constitute the Port of Rotterdam house everything from the unassuming, picturesque historic harbour, Delfshaven, to the vast tracts of land and water dedicated to processing cargo shipments from all over the world. Shipped in from afar. Sorted into stacks on Dutch soil. Transported by train to the hinterlands of the Netherlands and Germany. George was surprised to see how few people were actually on the ground. A stevedore here, a stevedore there, but mainly, it was a place where those steel containers in an array of different weather-beaten colours were swung around in an almost graceful dance by robotic cranes, driven by automated vehicles, choreographed by computer programs that were manipulated from a distance inside the port's administration buildings.

Small wonder, given the din, that George could not, at first, be sure that her phone was ringing. But after a few seconds, as the specially designated Aretha ringtone got louder, George realised it was Ad. Again. Given she and van den Bergen were being led by a behemoth of a stevedore in a high-viz jacket to the container where the body had been discovered, Ad could think again if he thought she was going to talk to him now.

'Wouter!' van den Bergen shouted, waving to the detective that was heading up the Rotterdam port police investigation.

His long strides seemed to lengthen. She had to jog to keep up with him.

'Wait for me, Paul!'

But he was not listening. Clapping the back of his former colleague instead. Chummy bromance handshakes, like they were besties of old, though he had never mentioned this man once in conversation. Van den Bergen had twenty years on her. How many more people had he got to know during his working life alone than she had met over the course of her entire twenty-four years, simply because he was that much older? It was a bewildering thought.

Wouter Dreyer had a head like a large potato, George thought, with raisins for eyes, a broken carrot for a nose and the most terrible cauliflower ears she had ever seen. She blinked hard, looked again and saw an ageing jock instead of Mr Potatohead. Couldn't remember whether the Dutch played rugby. He certainly looked as though he did.

'George, this is my old buddy from cop school.' Finally her friend was not just smiling but grinning. Why had Mr Potatohead succeeded in eliciting a grin where she had failed?

She eyed Wouter's ears suspiciously. They were the wrongest ears she had ever seen. The retro-stylish brown sheepskin coat that he wore was his only redeeming feature and not dissimilar to hers. How had she ended up hanging out with a bunch of older men – either cops, perverts or psychopaths – who had all the sartorial elegance of septuagenarian refugees from the ice-clad mountains of central Asia? Aunty Sharon had warned her that she was becoming reclusive and odd. That she should have more friends her own age.

'Come and take a look,' Wouter said. He held the police tape up for them to walk under. Nodded at George and called her ma'am – at least, the Dutch equivalent. All very formal and pleasantly respectful. Perhaps cauliflower ears were not an indication of poor character. 'The body's at the morgue. We've arranged for it to be transported to your head of forensics this afternoon. Let your guy—'

'Woman,' van den Bergen said, prising his glasses from their resting place on his chest and pushing them onto his nose. He peered down at Wouter through the thick lenses. His eyes, suddenly far larger than usual. 'It's Marianne de Koninck. Remember her?'

Wouter sniggered in a way George did not entirely like. 'She still—'

'Oh, yes. Very much so.' More grinning, for God's sake. A knowing look passed between them.

An elbow in the ribs from his Rotterdam compatriot suggested van den Bergen might have something to hide, but he merely blushed in answer and shook his head. 'No. Nothing like that.'

George hadn't realised men did telepathy. Their levity in the midst of death was almost unbearable, but only because she didn't feel part of it.

The uniformed officers guarding the site parted to let them through. The shape of the victim had been outlined in white on the base of the giant metal box. Arms raised above the head. Legs splayed slightly. George was struck by the diminutive stature of the Filipino. It was a relief that the body had been removed, although she had a nasty feeling she would accompany van den Bergen to the morgue once they were back in Amsterdam. Seeing photographs and film clips of violent porn was one thing. Being in the same room as the dead, another entirely.

Van den Bergen looked around, clearly surveying the scene.

Stacks of containers all around. Mechanised movement. Off the ship. Into the stack. One by one, driven away during a designated slot by the designated haulage company. 'Not many people around,' he said.

Wouter nodded. Hands stuffed deeply inside his pockets as a foil to the bitter North Sea wind. 'Easy to operate unseen, especially after dark, which we think this was.'

'Problem is getting inside the compound,' van den Bergen said, removing his glasses and appearing suddenly ten years younger. 'You'd need to drive a body to this point. It's too far from the periphery. Too dangerous to walk, even if you had the strength to carry dead weight. Have you interviewed the port staff?'

'Yep. I know all these guys,' Wouter said. 'Working men. An endangered species, now this place is all run by robots and computer nerds. They're pretty damned straight. And even if they weren't, they're pretty damned tight. So, none of them would blab if there were crooks among them!' He laughed heartily. Gave a knowing look to the behemoth stevedore in his high-viz jacket. Winked. Didn't get so much as a nod in response.

Van den Bergen snapped on a latex glove. Fingered the lock. 'I thought this had been broken into,' he said.

'It had.'

Shook his head. 'Looks more like it's been deliberately dented, if you ask me, to give the impression of a break-in. I don't think this has been forced at all. And I think you'd better check the CCTV to see any unregistered vehicles that may have come and gone last night.'

'We're in the process of doing that now,' Wouter said, looking at his shoes, as if he had been chastised by a teacher. The rapport between them seemed to have changed subtly; an icy down-draught of implicit criticism that had sucked the warmth out of the spot. Brotherly levity all but gone, George noted.

'One thing's for sure,' van den Bergen said, 'if the Filipino victim met a sticky end at the hands of our killer, then it's possible he was picked up off one of these ships.' He gesticulated with his glasses towards the enormous cargo ship that was being unloaded at the quayside. 'Did you manage to get on board the ship that was docked around the time of discovery?'

His Rotterdam colleague nodded. 'They didn't speak Dutch, obviously. Most of them didn't speak a word of English. The crew was mainly West African guys. Couple of Asians. Spoke French, native dialects, God knows what else. The one who did speak English really well – the Congolese captain – claimed he'd never seen the victim before in his life. Like he could tell from a naked, butchered corpse!'

'Where is that ship now?'

'Sailed. We couldn't hold it. Their paperwork was all above board. The Port needed the mooring spot for MS *Berge Stahl*, the iron ore freighter. This is only one of two places in the world deep enough for a ship of its size to dock and the tidal window is tighter than a mouse's fanny.'

Appraising his colleague, with his still-dark eyebrows sitting heavy above those hooded grey eyes, it was clear that van den Bergen was disappointed by his friend. And his friend knew it.

'It's just one of those things, Paul,' Wouter said. Looking down at his loafers. Apologising tacitly, though an apology was probably not owed to a chief inspector of Amsterdam's force. 'We never even had time to get a translator down to interview the crew. We did what we could.'

Van den Bergen looked away. Stroked his stubble and contemplated the white outline on the floor of the steel container. 'So, our victim was presumably taken from a ship, though we can't be certain of it. He was murdered elsewhere – it's a process that seems to demand time and privacy, by all accounts – and put here for you to find. Not an easy mission for our killer. So, he's almost certainly getting help and cover from someone who works in the Port.'

Wouter raised his hands defensively. 'It's early days. No

eyewitness statements. All we can do is trawl through CCTV footage and hope we find a rogue vehicle with its number plate clearly visible. Pray for a modern-day bloody miracle.'

'Let's see what Marianne de Koninck finds,' van den Bergen said. 'Maybe if this third body is conclusively linked, it will cast new light on the investigation.'

Finally, he turned to George, as though he had only just remembered she was there. Making her feel like an afterthought, though she doubted he had intended the slight. 'What do you think?'

George hugged her coat closed against the bitter dockland wind and narrowed her eyes. Watched the grey-brown soup of the sea heaving up and down, throwing spurts of white foam into the air as it fought against the land.

'This is about vulnerable immigrants in some way,' she said. 'It's the common denominator between the three cases.'

CHAPTER 46

Amsterdam, police headquarters, 24 January

'Can I at least get a coffee and something from the vending machine?' he asked.

The lumpy-faced detective looked glassy-eyed and hyper. 'No. State your name for the recording.' Pointed to some outdated-looking recording equipment at one end of the table, next to the wall. Short, fat index finger with a bitten nail, though his hands were generally clean and soft-looking like a woman's. You could tell a lot from a man's hands. These said this arrogant son of a bitch had never done a day's proper graft in his life. A pot-bellied Dutch pig-boy, sitting drinking coffee while his interviewee's stomach rumbled.

The discovery of the mattress had been the beginning of this waking nightmare. Leaving his tools out had been a bad idea.

His stomach growled audibly. 'I didn't even get chance to eat my lunch. You've already had me—'

'Name!'

'You already know my name is Iwan Buczkowski.' It was difficult to be pleasant when his blood sugar was so low. He had to eat and fast. Perhaps worse than the hunger and thirst was that the sweat from his morning's labour had pretty much dried on his body but left his damp clothes freezing cold. He folded his arms tight across his chest but still couldn't get the blood to his fingers. 'I must make a phone call. I have to let my girl know I'm here. She'll worry.'

The Dutchman did not answer. Started scratching at a stain on his navy jumper with a non-existent thumb nail. 'How long have you been here?'

Iwan checked his battered watch that was pinned by its strap to the inside pocket of his work trousers. 'Three hours.'

'I mean in this country, smart arse.' The detective had opened a notebook and was poised to write in it. The pages were blank but for 'Iwan Buczkowski' written at the top and underlined three times.

'What's that got to do with anything? I'm an EU citizen. I pay tax. I pay my rent. I'm law-abiding. What do you want with me?' In his head, he tried to say a rosary but the words wouldn't come. He had a feeling he should ask for a solicitor – one who spoke Polish as well as Dutch or English. But he didn't even know if such a person existed. And he hadn't actually been charged with anything. Should he just get up and walk out of this place, as he had done last time? Could they lock him up for uncooperative behaviour? Stefan might know. He'd help. He had already said yes to bending the truth about his alibi. 'I've got to call my boss. Give me my phone back. You're not arresting me for anything, right?'

The chubby blond leaned forward. Kees Leeuwenhoek. That was his name. Dressed like a fifty-year-old man but couldn't be more than thirty. He remembered their conversation when he had been leaning against the van outside Valeriusstraat, having a smoke. The guy had been so chummy, then. But like a dog turned nasty, now.

'You've got mental health issues, haven't you, Iwan?' He drummed his pen against the pad in an irritating manner. Produced a sheet of paper with a photocopied likeness of himself as a youth at the top. 'I pulled your record, thanks to our police colleagues in Poland.' Started to read from the sheet. 'A former drug user, it says here.' He raised his eyebrows. 'Seems you've got quite an interesting story, Mr Buczkowski. Breaking and entering. Car theft. Aggravated assault. Becoming a nuisance and a threat because of psychotic episodes. They locked you up for a while, didn't they, Iwan? Your folks had you sectioned.'

'It was a long time ago.'

'And oh, looky here! Involved in a motorcycle gang with a "known interest in Satanism". Seems your local police were keeping an eye on you. So, I was right, wasn't I?' Pointed to his tattooed arm. 'About the pentangles and upturned crucifix shit.'

Iwan shrugged. He had been to confession. Unburdened himself to the priest. That was the way Catholicism worked. Why should he discuss in intimate detail the things he had sought sanctuary from within the walls of the Catholic Church? With a Dutch detective, of all people. After years of formal repentance, he owed no more explanations. You sinned. You confessed. You prayed for forgiveness. It was a perfect system for a flawed man like him and allowed him to indulge some of his residual weaknesses. What he didn't confess to the priest remained between him and God.

The porky Dutchman leaned forward and cocked his head to the side, as though he were about to confide in him. 'I'm having your place turned over as we speak, you know. You're my favourite suspect. And a little bird tells me, you might be a little bit obsessed by ritual murders. I wonder what we'll find.'

Iwan decided to roll his eyes. Let this Leeuwenhoek bastard think he hadn't a care in the world. But inside his chest, his tainted heart was beating at a thunderous pace. He was treading uncomfortable ground. It was definitely time he called Stefan again.

CHAPTER 47

Amsterdam, mortuary, later

'How do you feel?' van den Bergen asked.

He placed a hand on George's shoulder. She knew it should feel comforting, but she was too tense to appreciate the physical contact. Shied away from it.

'Dreading this,' she said, as they walked along the windowless, institutional corridor to the mortuary. Visualised a gore-fest beyond her imagination behind those doors. 'Will they all be laid out? You know. Ribs akimbo.'

She looked up at van den Bergen's thin face. His eyes crinkled and a deep groove etched its way along the side of his mouth. A half-smile, but a smile nonetheless. 'It's not going to be as bad as you think,' he said. 'Just remember it's police work, not violence.'

He pushed open the double doors, and they made their way to the principal examination room. More like the operating theatres she had seen on television, George thought, squinting at the glaring overhead lights. Except this place was silent; without the beeping life support or myriad surgical staff bustling about the patient that one would expect to attend the sick and still-living. And here were three steel slabs with their own in-built drainage. And there were three…

'Aw, man. Ribs a-fucking-kimbo,' she said, pinching her nose against the formalin stink and other smells – what they were, she simply couldn't articulate. They toyed with her gag-reflex in a worrying way. At first she averted her gaze from the objects on the slabs. Mindful of the fact that 'objects' seemed a harsh label to bestow on the victims of brutal murder. But these spoiled, semi-preserved cadavers were so unlike anything she had seen before, it was difficult to attribute any qualities of the living to them, including language. *Focus, bitch. Show some respect.* George steeled herself to look at them. This mess of flesh was the only body of evidence left that bore witness to the one-time existence of three humans. It was a pitiful sight.

'You okay?' van den Bergen asked, wheeling a typing chair up behind her. Bidding her to sit, which she did.

'I'm fine.' She patted his arm.

A man she had not hitherto noticed, dressed in scrubs with the beginnings of a bald patch, approached her and offered to shake her hand, which she declined. He looked unpleasantly moist, with a shining domed forehead. His ears were red; the lobes too fleshy.

'Strietman,' van den Bergen said. Disdain hung in jagged tracts off those two syllables. 'Where's Marianne? I was told she would be doing this secondary examination.'

Strietman grinned and chuckled, as if van den Bergen had told a mildly amusing joke. 'She's writing up reports on the norovirus gang,' he jerked his thumb in the direction of a door. 'Doesn't feel too clever. I think she's going home in a bit.'

The muscles in van den Bergen's jaw were flinching. Up, down. Up, down. Small yet significant movements, like the flicker of a transmission switch on an early warning system. George saw he had balled his fists and realised suddenly that the pink skin on his knuckles must have been caused by punching somebody. Hard. But that could wait for later. His irritation was obvious. If van den Bergen didn't trust this pathologist, neither did she.

George rose out of her chair, marched to the closed door Strietman had gesticulated towards and walked in.

Marianne de Koninck was sitting at her desk, dabbing watery, bloodshot eyes with a screwed-up tissue that had long passed its best. Sniffing. 'What are you doing in here?' she asked, standing abruptly.

George appraised the situation. Considered what van den Bergen had told her in the car of de Koninck's break-up with Ad's occasional flatmate.

'Jasper has bad breath,' she said. 'You can do better. Now, get out there and help us solve these goddamn murders!'

With Strietman sent home, de Koninck circled the three bodies. But for the Filipino's genitalia marking him as the odd one out, even George's untrained eye could see that all three had been defiled in an apparently identical manner. In silence, de Koninck examined them. Read the reports on the composition of their blood. Disappeared off for a while, leaving George to gawp and grimace undisturbed at the victims' remains. Returned, bearing a cup of coffee and a clipboard under her arm.

'I've just had a chat with an endocrinologist friend of mine,' de Koninck finally said. Sat at the central workstation that held a computer terminal. Put her plastic cup down in a studied manner. Turned to van den Bergen with red-rimmed eyes. 'You were right, Paul. I owe you an apology. I should have performed a secondary examination as soon as I got back in. I've been letting my personal problems interfere with work.'

Shunting his own chair towards her, so that the three of them described an almost intimate triangle, van den Bergen leaned in. Balanced his elbows on his knees. Pressed his palms together. 'Go on.'

'Strietman's misinterpreted the results.' She ran a rugged hand through her hair and sighed heavily. Shook her head. 'It was easy to do. This third victim makes his mistake clearer. In fairness, Strietman wouldn't have—'

'Just bloody tell it, Marianne,' George said. 'Stop making excuses for men.'

The pathologist looked at her askance, as if contemplating a sharp retort for this opinionated, much younger woman. She clearly thought better of it. George was surprised.

'Strietman interpreted the catecholamine storm – that's the flood of hormones causing the heart to fail in the first victim – as being connected to ecstasy overdose. What he's missed, is that raised intercranial pressure can cause the same phenomenon.'

'Come on, Marianne,' van den Bergen said. 'Explain it to the normal folks in simple words.'

She leaned back in her chair. Rubbed her muscular, veined athlete's arms. 'In the first victim, the heart is still in situ. Right? In subsequent victims, the heart is missing. There is a massive black market in organ donation. I mean, the demand for organs outstrips supply by something like seven to one. People are literally dying for transplants.'

'What's that got to do with these three?' George asked, although she already felt that a huge piece of this jigsaw was already being levered into place.

'My endocrinologist friend says you can get this hormone flooding problem when surgeons harvest organs from braindead donors.' The pathologist's eyes widened. The puffiness of her lids was subsiding. George could see she was as enthused by the dawning of this realisation as the rest of them. 'It's really, really hard to take organs in prime condition. You remove this many organs from a living person,' she said, pointing to the cadavers, 'even if you're trying to keep your donor alive for as long as possible by artificial, resuscitative means, it's inevitable your donor is going to die. The onset of brain death brings with it this pressure inside the skull.' She clutched at her own head, as if to illustrate her explanation. 'Once a donor is technically braindead, everything starts to go to hell, then. They suffer hypothermia. Diabetes insipidus – there's sign of that come back in the bloods with these three. Pulmonary oedema. You get this flood of hormones: dopamine, vasopressin – that's the catecholamine storm I'm talking about. Like the brain's anti-inflammatory, protective mechanism, except it can cause the heart to fail unless it's brought under control. So, organ donors need intensive care, basically. Every step of the way. It's a very specialised field.'

Marianne stood and beckoned George to the slabs. 'You haven't seen the women, have you?'

George was reluctant. 'I had a look while you were on the phone, thanks.'

But Marianne grabbed her arm and pulled her slab-side. 'You make me face my uncomfortable truth. I'm making you face yours. They're just people. Dead people. You're going to be a doctor yourself, right?'

Nodding, George looked inside the ribcage and empty abdomen of Linda Lepiks. 'Criminologist. It's different.' Felt grief enter her headspace as an unwelcome visitor, threatening to take her composure hostage. Was this actress so different to her friend, Katja? She stole a glance over at the petite Somali called Noor. Had that poor working girl differed from her in any significant way? There was a mother out there somewhere, wondering what fate might have befallen her daughter. And she, in turn, had been a mother to a baby. Where was that child now? So much loss. So much tragedy. And who was this painfully thin Filipino, covered in bruises, with cuts to his hands and filth beneath his fingernails? Did somebody on the other side of the world pine for him nightly?

She looked up to find the pathologist eyeing her critically. Hard blue eyes. 'Criminology is still a science, Georgina,' she said. 'If you want to take yourself seriously in your line of work, you must learn even the most unpalatable facets of it thoroughly. Like Paul, here.'

George blinked back a tear before it could make a formal appearance. 'You finished patronising me?' she asked. Hand on hip. Tired, now, after an absurdly long day. But realising this was not a time for attitude and sparring with Jasper's ex. *Focus, George.*

De Koninck seemed unperturbed. She ran her Biro along the

line of Lepiks' torso, careful not to make contact with the blackened, coagulated blood or the white dashes of the severed ribs that ran along the edges like cats' eyes on a motorway. 'Only a surgeon would have opened the victims up in this way. It's textbook stuff, and now that I see it for myself, nothing like that backstreet butcher Ahlers could have done.' She pointed to the nostril on the Filipino man to her right. 'They've all had intubation for ventilation and…' moved her pen down to the mark on the crook of his arm '…cannulas inserted into their veins. There are signs of invasive arterial monitoring in the veins of Lepiks and our Filipino. But not in Noor. In other words, the murderer failed to harvest the heart at first but had refined his techniques in these subsequent victims. He knew to expect cardiovascular collapse and avoided it.' She smiled, with something that looked like relief. 'These are all the scars you would expect from a person who has been in intensive care, not bloody drugged for fun, like Strietman said!'

Van den Bergen cleared his throat at the back of them, though it sounded more of a growl. George turned to see a satisfied expression on his face that belied the disapproving noises.

'Here it is!' he said. A wry smile playing at the corners of his mouth. '*This* is the bit I've been waiting for. Ha! I'm not one for enjoying saying told you so, but that guy's a prick, Marianne. A sensationalist idiot who's watched too many two-bit crime dramas on TV.' He bounced his left foot on his right knee triumphantly. Wiped his glasses on the tails of his shirt.

'His conclusions were valid, based on the evidence he had,' de Koninck said. 'But he has ignored the obvious, maybe because it's mundane and logical, not what you'd expect from a serial killer.'

'So, what does this mean about our victims?' George asked. 'The women's uteruses are missing, but you can't transplant a uterus, can you?'

The pathologist stepped back from the slab and drained what

was left of her cold coffee. 'I think your killer has deliberately done that to make the first two murders look sexual in nature. Strietman fell into that trap.'

'That makes sense if Valeriusstraat was rigged to look like a kinky crime scene,' van den Bergen said, pinching his nose. Nodding.

George appraised the three victims beneath the white-out glare of the mortuary lights. The empty vessels of their corpses making the only noise; their voices stolen from them along with the breath in their bodies, leaving only van den Bergen, Marianne de Koninck and her to speak on their behalf. 'So, the murderer is running a human organ factory,' she said. 'With vulnerable immigrants providing his raw materials. And there's a black market out there says the sum of their parts is greater than the whole.' She closed her eyes. 'Oh, Jesus. This is beyond grim.'

CHAPTER 48

Amsterdam, van den Bergen's apartment, 25 January

'Why did I have to track you down like this to speak to you, George?' Ad asked. Hurt in those sensitive brown eyes. Not nearly well disguised enough behind the petrol-coloured coating on his glasses. An all too familiar look, recently.

George opened and closed her mouth, hoping sensible, placatory words would come out. None did. On Ad's left brow was suspended a lump of sleep from his eye. Eye-snot, they called it at Aunty Sharon's. Great. Now, she couldn't tear her gaze away from the eye-snot. She wanted to point, but couldn't.

He had pinioned her hands together inside his, though it strained her arms to reach him on the other side of van den Bergen's kitchen table. She wished he would let go. Tried to prise her fingers free.

'Well?' he asked. 'Why are you staying here and not at mine? Are you not my girlfriend? Why have you been ignoring me, when all the time you were in town? Staying with another man!'

'Let go, Ad! You're hurting me!' George shouted, wrenching her hands free. Finally standing with a teeth-jarring scrap of the chair on the tiled floor. 'I've been staying with van den Bergen, for God's sake! He's not *another* man. Not in the bloody way you mean.'

'But I live in Amsterdam, damn it! Why wouldn't you tell me

you were coming? If I hadn't got this letter...' He pulled the crumpled envelope out of his reefer jacket pocket. '...And if Sally Wright hadn't had—'

George snatched it from him. Stared down at the meticulous handwriting, which she would recognise anywhere. 'Silas Holm?' Felt the blood drain from her face. Suddenly slightly nauseous. Had to sit back down quickly. 'How did that monster get your home address?' She scanned the text inside. It was a long letter. She did not have time to read it in its entirety with Ad sitting there, waiting to hear why she had snubbed him. Snippets of writing registered with her.

Of course, I was young at the time, but I still remember my father, sitting in our living room, playing cards. He and his friends would drink and drink until they swayed in their chairs, and I, only twelve at the time, would watch, thinking this was how men behaved, Georgina. A proper hero, he regaled them with tales of how he had lost his leg in the war, when his Messerschmitt crashed during a bombing raid over London. An air raid warden found him in the ruins of a street of terraced housing that had been lain to waste by his fellow airmen. His internment in the prisoner of war camp was...

...beat me senseless once they had retired with their winnings. He used to remove his prosthetic limb and...

...my mother, both an angel and a hurtful witch, depending on how the mood took her. Worse when she was drinking, naturally.

'What the hell is this?' George said, trying to fathom why Silas Holm, of all people, had chosen to track her down, with such urgency and against such tremendous odds, to her boyfriend's flat in Amsterdam. He had known she was coming before Ad had. 'I went to Broadmoor just before I left. I must have let something slip without realising. He's a wily bastard, if ever there was one. He must have someone smuggling letters out for him.'

'George!' Ad said. 'Why have you been avoiding me?'

She looked blankly at him, only vaguely aware that he had come to confront her; that van den Bergen had left her behind and gone into the station without her, with the express intention that she should remain behind and sort things out with Ad.

'Why's Holm giving me all this reminiscing shit? He's trying to tell me something, maybe?'

Ad's fist made contact with the kitchen table. 'For God's sake, George! Are you coming to my place or what? Are we going to talk about this? About us?'

All at once, George remembered that her boyfriend was standing in front of her, demanding to clear the air. But she had better things to do than kiss and make up or dredge through the prickly tangle of her feelings. She wanted to get to the police station to listen to the debriefing van den Bergen would be giving Elvis, Marie and Kees, based on everything the two of them had discussed – combing over and over the details of the three murders until the small hours of the morning. How long could they keep Ahlers, if he wasn't their man? He would make a perfect research subject for her PhD and right now, he was sitting in a cell with nothing better to do than talk.

'Yeah, yeah. Whatever. I'll bring a bag round.'

She kissed Ad on the cheek absently. Mind abuzz – not with their relationship but with Silas Holm. Clearly, her dangerous study subject had researched not just her, but the people around her too. He had somebody on the outside, doing his bidding. A murderous psychopath with a willing disciple was never a good thing. How had the trail led to Ad? She knew Aunty Sharon was safe and well. Knew she would never blab about her niece's where-abouts – not even to Ad. In which case, had Silas discovered her Cambridge address first? Spoken to someone who unwittingly passed on personal information?

She turned to Ad as something began to niggle at the back of her mind. 'When you tried to get me on my landline at my Cambridge place, did you manage to speak to Lucy?'

'No,' he said. 'Nobody picked up.'

CHAPTER 49

Amsterdam, police headquarters, later

'Our murderer is geographically transient,' the criminal profiler said, pointing to the three murder sites on the map with an index finger that had a rich, brown patina of nicotine, as though it was a nub of French polished wood. 'Two in Amsterdam. One in Rotterdam.'

What's his name again? van den Bergen wondered. In his notepad, he was sketching Tamara from memory, around the age when she had started to walk. It was a good sketch. He hadn't really been listening. Glanced up at Hasselblad's puppet in a pretence of engagement. An old guy in an Arran-knit jumper and navy cords, with a yellowing beard and shining bald pate. Spitting when he spoke. Standing so close to van den Bergen that he could see green algae growth on the nose-clips of the man's old-fashioned steel spectacles. He smelled of cigars and moth-balled furniture. Shipped in from the crappy psychology course the commissioner had been on before Christmas. Bert or Gert or fucking Bart. Yes. Bart. That was it. Van den Bergen slid his own glasses onto the end of his nose and looked at Bart's business card. He had an impressive collection of letters at the end of his name. Bert. Not Bart. Professor of criminal psychology at an institute van den Bergen had never heard of. Still, he was revered in his field, according to Hasselblad. Old Bert, with a face like a shipwrecked mariner and the waterlogged aroma to match. George would need to sit at the back. Especially given the man's propensity to shower everything in spittle.

'What I ask myself, as a criminal psychologist,' Professor Bert said to Elvis, 'is why is our murderer harvesting organs?'

'To sell on the black market,' van den Bergen said, enhancing the toddler Tamara's chubby legs with bold cross-hatching from his Biro.

Bert lurched forward and held his amber finger aloft. 'No, sir! No! This is paraphilia for our murderer. Fetishism. Organs as sexualised objects of desire. Disorganised serial killers like this position the dead body in a certain way. They leave weapons at the scene. Depersonalise the bodies of their victims, as is demonstrated...here!' He smacked the pinboard that held photos of the victims with force, causing a photograph of the interior of Linda Lepiks' gaudy, expensive apartment to fall to the floor.

Marie tutted loudly. Retrieved the photo from the floor and pinned it back up. 'Can you not hit my board, please?' she said. 'It took me ages to get everything up there so neatly.'

'Your murderer preys on the vulnerable,' Bert shouted at the side of Marie's head.

Marie jumped. Blushed. Sat back down rapidly between Kees and Elvis.

Van den Bergen sighed. This guy was like an American evangelical preacher. Any minute now, he half expected him to tell them all to put their hands on the screen and ask for fifty dollars to be sent in to Jesus. 'Can we dial down the drama, please, Professor?' he asked, making eye contact with the man.

Bert looked apologetically at his belly. 'Of course.' Cleared his throat. Began again. 'He's sexually sadistic. Collects violent pornography, as demonstrated by the film of Linda Lepiks. You can bet he's collecting news clippings about his crimes. People like this often have an interest in Nazism, torture, monsters.' His eyes widened. He splayed the fingers on both hands, as though he had performed a magic trick. 'The occult.'

'I knew it!' Kees shouted across the board table. 'Like Buczkowski. He's mad about all that. We finally got into his apartment last night and got hold of all these crazy books on child-eating Jews and devil worshipping. He's an accessory. I'm telling you!' He started to count Buczkowski's personality deficits off on his fingers. 'He's violent. He's got a record. He's an ex-druggie. He's a known head case. The lot.'

Kees looked to his colleagues for appreciation. Marie remained inscrutable, examining her dirty fingernails. Elvis treated his new compatriot to a nervous smile, checking, van den Bergen noted, with his chief inspector first.

'I bet the Pole does all the heavy lifting,' Kees continued, 'and then he's got a partner who does the surgical stuff. I'm looking into Buczkowski's tax records.'

Slowly, deliberately, van den Bergen swivelled around in his chair so that his body was angled towards his borrowed detective. Studied the young man's flushed face. His glistening brow – beads of sweat shining in his hairline. Clenched chubby fists and a buck-toothed grin. If what the criminal profiler was saying was true, could Kamphuis' padawan be onto something? Was it possible that they were looking for a beauty and the beast duo? One, wielding brute force. One, brandishing the surgeon's scalpel. Two sadistic murderers, satisfied by violence and paid well for their enterprise by traffickers?

Dulled by the effects of codeine, his pen slid gently from his fingers, marking the perfectly executed drawing of Tamara. A poor man's Rubens, on lined A4, run through by a rogue Biro. Scanning the row of figures sitting at the table in the boardroom, he realised George had slipped into the room, unnoticed until now.

He raised his eyebrows in greeting. Managed a smile with his eyes only, though he wondered if she and Karelse had kissed and

216

made up in his kitchen. Damned streak of piss had shown up at 7am, ringing his bell and banging on the door. He had been making coffee and burning toast in the kitchen for the two of them. George had been in the shower. A surprisingly strong sun had streamed through the patio doors in the living room that opened onto his balcony, flooding the apartment with spring-like warmth and light. Making everything smell right; George's coconut shower-gel-scent wafting through from the bathroom; the beeswax fragrance of the wooden flooring he'd allowed her to polish; the fresh smell of linen coming from the guest room which she had designated a truly clean space that she could sleep in. All serving to paint his drab bachelor's pad in a warmer palette, where a woman was finally present and correct.

Until Karelse had shown up.

Three was a crowd. He had made a rapid exit to work, leaving them to settle their differences. It was the gentlemanly thing to do, though he hadn't wanted to do it at all. Where had he got this notion of gentlemanly behaviour from? Certainly not his father.

He could see no trace of a feverish lover's bloom in George's cheeks. In fact, she looked downright miserable. She shook her head and put her finger to her lips, indicating he should keep her arrival to himself.

Bert continued for a further fifteen minutes, pronouncing like a convincing clairvoyant that the murderer or murderers were probably well mannered and reserved in the course of their day-to-day dealings. To the outside world, they might seem to be religious, studious, hypochondriacs. But beneath the façade, there would lurk a monster. More victims would follow, butchered in increasingly bizarre ways.

Kees sat through the lecture, nodding vociferously, as though the professor was performing with the skill of a seasoned thespian a script he had personally penned and given him beforehand. Elvis played with his hair. Marie scribbled notes avidly. But van den Bergen listened to the sort of textbook analysis he had heard many times before, concentrating in the main on looking into George's eyes. Darkest brown, ringed with curling black lashes that made them look even larger. Milky white sclera that did not betray the fact she had been awake until the small hours, talking over the autopsy, swigging his Courvoisier from the bottle and smoking her e-cigarettes; Googling organ trafficking on his computer. He had wanted to kiss her. Her full lips had looked so accessible at 2am. There had been no space between them. He had wanted to tell her how he felt. The nights, after all, were mainly made for saying things that he would never say the following day. But he had resisted the temptation. And today there was all the space in the world between them. Worse than that. There was Karelse.

Now, she was silent and brooding in the corner. Casual in jogging bottoms and trainers. A denim jacket on top. Still beautiful, though she was dressed for the laundrette. The others, still unaware of her presence. He had those eyes to himself. Until Bert departed. Then…

'Well. What did you think of the professor's profile, children?' he asked his team.

'Excellent,' Kees said.

'Interesting,' Marie said.

'Can I go get a coffee?' Elvis asked.

'George?' It was her opinion that van den Bergen really sought.

George pulled her chair to the board table. Pursed her lips. 'Pile of shit,' she said.

'Why do you say that?' Marie asked.

'For a start, I think the murderer is *just* dealing in trafficked organs. There's no paraphilia in this instance. No sexy trophies. Nothing kinky.'

'Bullshit!' Elvis said.

'Not bullshit. Admittedly, there is a crazy statistic of something like eighty-one percent of serial killers in prisons rating porn as their highest ranking sexual interest. True, Noor and Lepiks had had sexual intercourse before death. *But* they were in the sex industry, so it's hardly surprising. And the Filipino showed *no* signs of having been sexually active recently. I can see why the professor drew the conclusions he did, but if you ask me, sex as a sole motive doesn't follow on. I was at that autopsy last night with Pau— the chief inspector.'

She exchanged a knowing glance with van den Bergen. Would the others think they were sleeping together, he wondered? The idea that they might gave him an unexpected lift. The realisation that their conjecture would be but a mirage brought him back down immediately.

'Go on,' he said.

'De Koninck is sure we're after a surgeon. I think the killer is organised, not disorganised. They plan the murders. They're not roving at all, but take the victims to the same spot to undergo organ harvesting, basically.'

Marie rubbed her forehead. 'Seriously? Is that all this is all about? There's nothing underlying?'

George and van den Bergen nodded simultaneously.

'The Valeriusstraat scene,' van den Bergen began.

'Was a hoax,' George finished. She took out her e-cigarette and toyed with the chewed end. 'We've got three well-planned abductions. Not a single bloody witness. So, our man has a vehicle – another aspect you'd expect from an organised killer. Our victims have been restrained, drugged, rigged for surgery. The killer has the ultimate control over life or death.'

'What the fuck does she know?' Kees asked, jerking his thumb towards George. Looking for a reaction from Elvis. Scowling at her. 'Fucking English girl that makes the coffee.' He turned to her. Looked her up and down as though she were a substandard side of beef, hanging in a downmarket butcher's window. 'Go and make yourself useful, love. Get me a latte, so me and these police officers can get on with some detective work.'

219

'Shut your trap, Leeuwenhoek!' van den Bergen snapped, crumpling up the drawing of Tamara and throwing the balled-up paper at his subordinate's head. It bounced off and scudded across the table top, coming to a stop by his pad. He was reminded of his father throwing a carpet slipper at his head as a teenager, for mouthing off at the old man about the merits of fine art as a career. Made a note not to throw things at his staff again. A sharp word would suffice. He could not become his father. 'Georgina is a criminologist from Cambridge University, you dim-witted prick. Show her some respect or go back to sucking on Kamphuis' titty.'

George leaned forward. Narrowed her eyes at her critic. Sucked her teeth with slow venom but did not rise to Leeuwenhoek's bait. 'Our killer is trying to make these murders look like the acts of a deranged lunatic. But they're not. We're dealing with a very cunning individual, who's not going to be easy to catch.'

'But Ahlers has got to be involved, right?' Elvis said.

Van den Bergen leaned back and rocked on the hind legs of his chair. He pointed to George and Marie. 'I want you two to track down Noor and her baby. See where she lived. Find out her story. Maybe someone knows where the baby's gone. Ahlers can stay in clink until the hole in his arse seals up, for all I care. I've checked with the prosecutor. The match on the pube is enough to keep him a while. He still doesn't have an alibi for the night of Noor's murder, although he's in the clear for Lepiks' because of his little jaunt to the casino.'

Marie nodded and checked the notes on her electronic notebook. 'The CCTV footage has him playing blackjack at the time Lepiks was being murdered, going by the pathologist's estimated time of death.'

'Find out what you can anyway.' He turned to Elvis. 'You and I are going to look into the Filipino again. I want to track down the vessels that docked in Rotterdam in the course of that day. We're going to re-interview the dockers with Wouter.' Turned to

Leeuwenhoek. 'You get to type up the paperwork for Hasselblad's witch hunt for the mentally ill.'

Kees grimaced and sighed heavily, like a child being told to go and tidy his room.

'And you can straighten your bloody face! Every policeman over the age of forty knows your father was a legend on the force, Leeuwenhoek. Legends don't shy away from doing their paperwork. If it's good enough for him, it's good enough for you.'

Van den Bergen clapped his hands together enthusiastically, though all he wanted to do was crawl back home to bed. The time was coming when he would have to give into the darkness. He could feel it, especially now Karelse had reclaimed George's light. Best not to show his team, though.

'The more we find out about our victims, the closer we'll get to the murderer. The people were chosen, tracked and hunted down. Our man is out there watching and waiting for his next victim.'

CHAPTER 50

Hamburg, Germany, 26 January

'Put your clothes back on and I'll take you for an ice-cream,' the man said, grinning at her over the footboard of the bedstead.

'I don't want a fucking ice-cream,' Ewa said, dimly aware she was slurring.

The man shrugged. Squatted bedside her, low enough to be below her eye-level. She could see his scalp through his greasy ginger hair. Dandruff. 'Suit yourself,' he said in a Bavarian dialect she could barely understand. 'I thought all kids your age liked ice-cream. I was just trying to be nice.'

'Fuck off, pervert.' She took another gulp from the vodka bottle they had given her. Just like Mum, now. She understood, finally. The stinging liquid made you numb. Made this nightmare doable. She was going to get through this. Mum and Günther would come for her when they realised she was missing and hadn't just run off again.

The pervert started to dismantle his camera, unscrewing the long lens and putting it with care back into the foam-lined case on the floor. Next, he switched off the bright lights that had beat down on her like fake suns, making her squint the whole time. The Italian man – at least, she thought he was either Italian or Spanish, judging by his heavy accent when he spoke German

– had threatened to slap her when her eyes had started to water because of the glare. Ugly old bastard with his big fat neck and giant shoulders. He was the worst. He was a giant freak.

She swung her legs off the bed. Clasped her hands over her chest and pubic area, though that hardly mattered now. Stumbled drunkenly in the semi-darkness to the stool where her clothes were stacked in a crumpled heap. Pulled her knickers and jeans gingerly over the places where it was sore. The beginnings of bruises on the insides of her thighs from the sheer weight of that pig they had filmed her with. Sweat rolling off him onto her under those lights.

'I'm going to be sick,' she said, pressing her hand to her mouth.

'Not over the equipment,' the pervert said.

Ewa could not stem the tide. The contents of her stomach splattered everywhere. Her socks were wet. Then, she realised her face was wet. She was crying. 'I want Mutti. I want to go home. Please. Take me home. I won't tell.'

There was laughter to her left in the shadows. A man's laughter. The Italian. 'Your mummy doesn't give a shit about you, *cara bella*. That alcoholic bitch will not come for you! It's better this way.' He stepped out of the murk and offered her a towel. Started to wipe her hands, though she grabbed it from him.

'I can do it myself.' Staggered with the booze still inside her. Fell over, despite her best intentions.

The Italian pulled her up. 'I bought you a gift.' He handed her a childish frilled sundress in pink cotton. 'You can put this on instead, *cara*. You will look like a princess.'

She pushed it away. 'Don't want your fucking dress. Give me my jeans. Let me out of here, or I'll scream.'

Fingers like steel rods bit into her shoulder. That was the Italian, all right. Evil bastard with his beady eyes and mean mouth. He released her shoulder and encased her throat in his hot, clammy hand. His fingers went all the way round. She felt the breath starting to leave her. Her eyes popping. If only this was all a bad dream. If only she was in school; sitting in class with Frau Reichmann at the front, droning on about Pythagoras' theorem. She would listen this time. Honest to God, she would. She wouldn't smart-mouth the old cow. She wouldn't even walk out and slink off to the mall with Alia. Anything but this.

'You scream and I'll squeeze the life out of your little scrawny neck, cheeky whore,' he said. He smelled of cigars and beer. 'You're nothing! Understand? Nowhere, without me. I look after you. Think of me as your uncle. You do as you're told like a good girl. Those are the rules. Put the fucking dress on.'

She nodded. He released her from his grip. Her vomit-covered socks were cold and wet. She started to tremble, stripping them off to reveal scabbed, blackened feet.

Suddenly, it was too bright again. Making her blink. Shielding her eyes with her stinking socks until the novelty of light subsided. The pervert had switched on the apartment's normal lights. Even through the fog of vodka, she saw exactly how things were:

She was alone with these monsters in a filthy two-roomed shithole, not dissimilar from home. But not her home, this time. Ewa knew now, there were worse things than Mum being blotto on the sofa at 10am and Günther scratching himself in front of the TV, smoking dope. Put being bullied by the other kids at school into the shade.

Here were empty glasses on every surface, stinking of stale alcohol. Overflowing ashtrays. Paraphernalia from the drugs they had injected into her ankle. A filthy teaspoon. A lighter. A used syringe with a solitary bead of brown shit mixed with her blood, clinging to the inside, just as she clung to the hope that Mum and Günther would come to save her. A vague memory of the needle stinging her ankle. The Italian said it wouldn't make as much mess if they injected her there. She hadn't remembered what had happened after that but had woken up stiff and sore. Bleeding. There had been a party and she had provided the entertainment. That much, she realised.

The pervert had arrived after lunch with his camera. Told her she was going to be a star, like Katy Perry or Taylor Swift. The part of her that was still a child wanted to believe him. Had enjoyed the shawarma kebab the Italian had brought for her to eat. *Keep your strength up,* cara mia. *He only takes your picture because you are so lovely.* The rest of her knew better.

'Hurry up,' the Italian said, peering between the grimy slats of the Venetian blinds to whatever lay below. Checking his watch. 'We've got to go. The Duke wants to see you.'

'Go?' she asked. 'Leave here, you mean?'

In truth, she had no idea where the apartment was. Had she been there days? Weeks? Longer? She remembered getting into a really nice car, thinking she had been offered a lift into town, to the station. All friendly enough. Felt safe. Next minute, she had woken up on the bed in the apartment with the Italian on top of her.

Outside, there was the hammer and holler of builders. Loud dance music thumping from somewhere close by. Same music day and night. Shouting from drunk men. She had an inkling that they were in Hamburg. It was the nearest big city, after all. She had heard Günther telling Mum about a stag party he had been to that ended up in a brothel in a place called the Reeperbahn. The two of them had laughed hard about it. At the time, she had wondered what a brothel was and what stags did at a party. Had Ewa got herself caught up in that kind of thing?

A knock on the door. The Italian retreated down the hall to answer it. There was an exchange of words in another language. He came back. Smiled like he meant it. Something like pity in those beady fucking eyes. Held his arm out. 'Change of plan. Come, Ewa. There's a nice doctor wants to meet you.'

CHAPTER 51

Katwijk asylum seekers' centre, Netherlands, later

'We take our jobs very seriously, here!' The woman snatched the file back. Held it to her blousy, polyester-wrapped body, as though it were a floatation device and she was all at sea. Her tone of voice, which had started out so friendly, was rapidly turning hostile and cold.

'Then how come you let an asylum-seeking minor slip under your radar?' Marie asked.

It was the fourth place they had visited. The first couple, battered women's refuges in the city itself. Then, homeless shelters. George had had the idea to speak to representatives of African community groups. But nobody recognised the photo of Noor in the young arts organisation, Stichting GAM, which, it transpired, was for young people of *West* African origin, anyway. Blank expressions from the imam at the mosque. Finally, some careful internet research in the unprepossessing café of her favourite shop-full-of-shit, Hema, had allowed George to pinpoint the Asylum Seekers' Centre in Katwijk. Three-quarters of an hour south of Amsterdam in a car. Just northwest of Leiden.

The drive down had been uncomfortable in a standard issue detective's car – a Ford Focus. It was dirty inside – empty chocolate bar wrappers, grit on the slip mats from people's shoes, bits of paper, receipts, a product-laden comb that looked as though it could have belonged to Elvis. The cabin stank of body odour and sour breath, masked badly by one of those cheap air-fresheners in the shape of a tree that hung from the dash. No Merc, with its heated leather seats and comforting thrum. No van den Bergen, smelling of sport deodorant and oranges.

Marie proved a tedious chauffeuse and had said nothing. Ignoring the funk of her infrequently washed body, George had taken the time to study Ahlers' statement about Noor. Somali, probably. Young – under sixteen. Worked out of the red light district on Monnikenstraat, just by the canal of Oudezijds Achterburgwal, where her body was eventually discovered one block down. No known fixed address that he knew of. Ahlers was refusing to breathe a word about the ultimate fate of her baby.

'If I was a Somali girl, new to the country, chances are I wouldn't have made it here under my own steam,' George mused, as they trundled along the dual carriageway of the A44. Passing a BP garage on their left. Flat green expanses to her right. Nothing of note in this unprepossessing, drab part of the country, beyond the dramatic grey and yellow rain clouds that ravaged the insipid winter-blue sky. At her side, Marie sniffed but said nothing. 'Either my parents would have paid every penny they had to get me over here, stowed away on a cargo ship and then in a truck. Or I'd have come a more circuitous route, maybe. Noor was a working girl who knew the ropes, right? So—'

'She'd have been brought here as a sex worker,' Marie said, smiling ever so slightly. Flicking the indicator to turn onto the remote and desolate N206.

How like the fenlands of East Anglia this place was, George thought. She was poised to share that observation with Marie and then thought better of it. It was the sort of thing she could say to van den Bergen. She didn't yet know Marie well enough.

'Which is why I think she'd have sought a roof at this place,' George said. 'Noor – if that's actually her name, which I doubt – would have qualified for asylum, right? Especially if she'd been a victim of sex trafficking and was young. Pregnant.'

Overcome with a fierce conviction that, somehow, they would avenge Noor's terrible end by tracking down her murderer and bringing him to book; find her lost baby and perhaps even place it successfully with a nice Somali family, she squeezed Marie's arm. Marie looked down at her hand long enough for her to realise she was not happy with the arrangement.

'Sorry,' George said. 'It's just, I've got a good feeling about this.'

Marie scoffed. 'You've obviously not been doing proper police work long enough.'

The Asylum Seekers' Centre loomed into view. An institutional red-brick building behind a barrier, that looked rather like the entrance to a hospital campus or high school. George's heart fell.

'Fucking soulless, man,' she said in English.

As they drove through the complex, the larger building gave way to fixed cabins that looked like the prefabs one sometimes still sees in England. Hastily erected bungalows made from prefabricated panels. Flat roofs. Draughty. Damp. Cold. Women, wearing full burka, walked along the pathways between houses, carrying shopping. Men in salwaar kameez; their heads covered by mosque hats. It was a strange theatre. The cast had all the vivacity and diversity of the high streets of London. The backdrop was post-war hell on a disused airfield.

Had this place been the setting for a scene from Noor's story?

In the administrative office, the grey-faced woman, wearing an ID lanyard around her neck that labelled her as Mrs de Witte, sat behind her battered desk. She wore a grim expression that said she did not care for the authorities. Pruned mouth. Cheap gold jewellery. The ill-considered haircut of a social worker.

Mrs de Witte poked at the computer-generated photo of Noor that Marie had put together. 'I recognise this face. It's Magool

Osman,' she said. 'And she didn't slip under our radar. This is not a prison, you know.'

'She was a vulnerable girl,' Marie said. 'Underaged. No parents. Did she say how she'd come to be in the country?'

Shaking her head, Mrs de Witte said, 'She wouldn't tell us anything. All I know was she came from Mogadishu, but I couldn't tell you what clan she was in – Somalis are all from different clans. It's a bit like the Indians' caste system. She kept herself to herself, as far as I know or remember. Only time she really bothered with others was during her Dutch classes. She picked the lingo up very quickly. Not like some of the others. Most of the women in here are illiterate unfortunately. It's a cultural thing not to educate girls.'

'Should she not have been in a young person's unit, where she could be properly protected?' Marie asked. 'Isn't there some government stipulation, says these kids are to be watched, because they're susceptible to traffickers?'

Mrs de Witte gazed out of the window at two small boys kicking a ball to one another. 'She was pregnant and wouldn't let on who the father was. Said she didn't know. What do you do with a teenaged girl who's pregnant? You can't put her with the other juvenile asylum seekers, can you? So, we put her in with the families.'

George had arranged some notepaper into a fan shape with almost exactly a centimetre between each sheet. She switched her attentions to the woman's haggard face. 'Let me guess. There's little or no security for families.'

'Asylum seekers don't have to stay here at all,' Mrs de Witte said, sighing as she spoke. 'The government has what's called a "self care arrangement". While they're going through the asylum-seeking process, people can find their own accommodation with friends and relatives, if they like. As long as they check in at one of the centres every week.'

'Please show us her old room,' Marie said.

'I don't know which was her room. It's not on file.'

'Find it, then.'

Hands in the air, as though she was about to break into inter-pretative dance, Mrs de Witte laughed too hard. 'Oh, wait a minute. I've nothing better to do than dig out a record from over a year ago and see what room Ms Osman occupied. What do you expect to find there, exactly?'

Marie slammed her police ID down on the desk. 'I am a detective in the Dutch police.'

De Witte checked her watch. A cheap bin-lid of a thing in yellow gold, encrusted with cubic zirconia. 'I have got several new arrivals turning up any minute now. They're my priority. I haven't got the time.'

'Make time!'

At her side, Marie's colour started to change from pale pink to an angry shade of homicidal red, but George wasn't interested in point-scoring with a pen-pusher. 'Mrs de Witte,' she said, wondering if reaching out to touch the woman on the arm would forge some kind of connection, but deciding that the chances of succeeding in winning her over with physical closeness did not warrant the risk of touching such slimy-looking fabric and suffering the resulting nausea. Words would have to do. 'Little Magool was butchered and left naked, to freeze like a piece of meat on a bench in the red light district. We need to find out how she got from here to there. You can help us.'

Mrs de Witte's hard-featured face softened almost impercep-tibly. She stood up. Keys jangling at her waist. 'Come on. There's not much to see.'

The room was grey. Just about big enough to fit a single bed. One small window. It looked rather like a sports hall that had been divided up by cheap partitions. No carpet. No home comforts. Literally just a roof. George was reminded of her time in a cell, except hers had had bars at the window and her door had been locked for most of the day. Sent a shiver down her spine, though she was more than used to being inside prisons now.

'As you can see, it's basic,' de Witte said, standing by the door, as if she couldn't wait to make safe her getaway.

George imagined Magool cooped up in here. Pregnant. Thousands of miles from her family. Possibly suffering post traumatic stress disorder from an undoubtedly hellish journey from the boiling, roiling cauldron of an African warzone to the strange, still waters of a cold European land. No real money to speak of. No idea of whether she would be allowed to stay in the Netherlands. The possibility of being deported hanging over her.

'So, Magool slipped out one day and never came back,' George said.

Mrs de Witte nodded. 'Didn't wait to see what happened with her application, the silly girl. She must have been about six months pregnant when she left.'

Outside the room, two young black women were chatting in a language George did not recognise. One wore a sequinned pink hijab, tight jeans and a long sleeved floral top. The other wore an austere black hijab and shapeless floor-length black dress.

'Where would a young woman like Magool go when she leaves here?' she asked.

De Witte ushered them out of the room and started to lock the door. Jangling keys like rows of teeth. A bigger bite in this dog-eat-dog world. Setting too much store by her own authority, George assessed.

'If you're refused asylum, you get deported or end up on the street,' she said. 'There's a place in Amsterdam called the Vluchtgevangenis. An old, disused prison where destitute asylum seekers go to find shelter. She may have gone there.'

'Wouldn't that be mainly men?' Marie asked. 'What about Somali women's groups?'

Together, the three of them walked back to the car. Shivering in the chill afternoon air; wanting to kick against the depressing atmosphere that hung over this drab, purgatorial location, where refugees waited in limbo for a new life.

'There's bound to be a group in Amsterdam,' Mrs de Witte said, checking her watch. 'Now, if you don't mind, I've got some very vulnerable new arrivals to make preparations for. You're the police. Do some detective work!' She offered Marie her hand to shake, which Marie ignored. 'Shame about Magool. Real shame. But you can only try your best for people...' She tutted. 'Bye, then.'

George climbed into the car next to Marie and slammed the door. Waved to the woman. 'Bit of a turd,' she said, the smile slipping abruptly from her face. 'How do you cope?'

Marie turned to her briefly as she pulled onto the main road. 'You'll get used to it.'

CHAPTER 52

Rotterdam, Port Authority, later

'What do you mean, you never saw anyone?' van den Bergen asked the stevedore, who was taking large bites out of a fat ham sandwich.

'Listen,' the man said, grinding his way through the thick pink and white layers. Pausing to swallow. Pieces of masticated pink food visible between his incisors as though his gums had started to grow down over his teeth. 'I operate the computer program that takes containers off the ships and plonks them in stacks.' He took another bite. Chewed thoughtfully, or perhaps, without any thought whatsoever. 'Piet, over there...' he pointed to a colleague who was hunched over a flickering computer terminal '...he sorts the stacks so the right box comes out for the right haulage company to pick up.' Swigged messily from a bottle of cola and belched. 'We don't get a view of the ground below. It's all computerised, see?' Pointed to his screen. 'What you want to do, is talk to security or customs or your mate, Wouter. Port Authority police have got more of a clue who comes and goes on the ground than us. Seriously, mate.'

Van den Bergen allowed a low growl to escape him but clutched his stomach to make it seem like indigestion. Mate, indeed.

'Did you hear any rumours of strange goings on the day that

the Filipino man was found? Any of your colleagues mention something untoward?'

The stevedore shook his head. 'I came in. Did a long shift. Nothing out of the ordinary happened. Ships came in. Ships went out. You've seen the records of what I unloaded. Went home, ate a nice steak and chips. Drank a few beers. Kids were both out, so I boned my wife on the sofa in front of the telly. That was it. A great day.'

In his peripheral vision, van den Bergen was aware of Elvis approaching. He turned around, wishing he was anywhere but inside this chilly, over-air-conditioned office with this man who stank of cigarettes and sweat. His fingers were like blocks of ice. Perhaps he was developing Raynaud's disease.

'Any joy with the CCTV footage?' he asked.

Elvis was walking with a certain swagger. This boded well, he knew. 'You got a minute, boss?'

He followed his detective to the office that housed the security function. With a view through ceiling-to-floor windows of the silvery-grey inlet, Het Scheur, along which a giant freighter was slowly chugging towards the cargo terminal, a small, balding man sat, surrounded by screens. Large screens seemed to float above him. A bank of smaller screens lined his desk, each containing a view of different parts of the Port of Rotterdam campus.

'This is Erik,' Elvis told van den Bergen.

Erik offered the chief inspector his hand. It was a weak, damp handshake which made van den Bergen flinch, but the man had an honest, open face, at least. A network of lines were etched in the skin around his eyes. His uneven jawline had perhaps softened with age. Van den Bergen estimated that he was close to retirement.

'Tell my boss what you told me,' Elvis instructed him.

Erik clicked a mouse several times and brought a screen up which made little sense to van den Bergen. He had no option but to sit in a typing chair which was too low and too small for him. Felt like a tarantula squeezed into a match box. Yanked his glasses free of their chain that had caught on the button of his overcoat and set them on his nose.

'What am I looking at, Erik?'

'The CCTV footage from the day the body was found,' Erik said. 'At first, it seemed the recording from between one pm and five pm was missing. Wiped.'

'And? Who could have wiped it? Who has access to your computer terminals?'

Erik clicked his tongue against the roof of his mouth thought-fully. Laced his fingers together over his uniform. Didn't take his eyes off the screen. 'Chances are, someone's hacked the system. I suppose in theory, it could have been one of the IT guys. I wouldn't like to hazard a guess, because the fellers here, well, they're all good men.' He leaned forward and clicked through several screens. Turned to van den Bergen with shining eyes. 'But anyway, we back the system up, so I found a copy of the footage. Look. Here you go.'

Van den Bergen's heartbeat remained steady while he watched the grainy footage. For a while, even at four times the normal speed, the only things to see of any note were the automated cranes, levering cargo containers off a ship called *The Mighty Horn of Africa*. Rain slanted hard onto the dock, though the camera's resolution was only high enough to show the water bouncing up off the asphalt and the steel containers as mist, rather than as the fat beans one would have expected from such a downpour. Dark grey clouds swallowed up the light almost entirely, making it seem more like dusk than just after lunch. Twenty minutes in, however, a dark saloon car slid into view between the stacks. Not far from the ship. Van den Bergen's heartbeat sped up, now. Thudding in his chest, as he just glimpsed a tall figure getting out of the driver's side. Clad in dark clothing. Wearing a hood. Impossible to see if he was black or white, young or old.

When he held his hand up, Erik paused the footage.

'Can you zoom in?' he asked him.

Erik shook his head. 'Not enough to get any fine detail. Your lad, Dirk, already asked me. It was a very overcast day, as you can see. Pissed it down. And there's gull shit on the camera or something, if I'm not mistaken. Same later on, except it's dark by then, so the visibility's even worse.'

Erik spooled forward, as he was bidden. For almost four hours, the saloon car was absent. Then it reappeared. Not in frame enough to allow van den Bergen to ascertain what make of car it was, let alone to see a number plate. It disappeared behind a stack of containers, in the direction of where they had found the Filipino.

'Wouter Dreyer seen this?' he asked.

Erik nodded. 'Showed it him this morning.'

Van den Bergen took his leave from the security man. Strode downstairs to the parking lot. Unlocked his car. With the doors closed, he was cocooned in near silence; the din from the clanking metal containers and the wail of the seagulls sounding as though it was muffled by cotton wool. He switched on his engine. Dialled Wouter's number. Ringing through the hands-free speakers.

'Wouter Dreyer,' on the other end.

'It's Paul van den Bergen.' He ran his long finger round and around the leather steering wheel, feeling he was on the brink of a breakthrough. A smile creeping over his tired face. 'I've just been watching the footage of that car in the security office. I'll bet a year's rent on my allotment that you've got a record of this guy entering the Port. I think we've got our murderer.'

'Ah,' Wouter said, sounding hesitant. 'About that...'

CHAPTER 53

Amsterdam, Ad's apartment, later still

'About what?' George asked.

She was avoiding making eye contact with Ad. It was late. She was tired. Marie's body odour had permeated her own clothing; her hair; her nostrils. A shower and a meal was all she wanted. The last thing she needed after flogging up and down the country all day, chasing after elusive African community groups in ramshackle, crumbling buildings, was to be cross-examined like this.

Ad stood next to the cooker. Apron on, over his jeans and top. Spoon in hand. The lenses of his glasses were fogged slightly with steam from the noodles he was boiling. Pad thai, he said he would make. She had failed to share pad thai with van den Bergen only days ago.

'You know what!' Ad said. 'I want to know about how you came to arrange work over here. One minute, you're doing some seedy job or other in London that you won't tell me anything about. Next minute, you're working for that bloody miserable bastard van den Bergen. Staying at his flat without telling me.' He gasped when she did not respond. 'You've still not so much as apologised.'

'Apologise?' George said. 'What the fuck for?' She was out of her chair, though she rose without any purpose, other than to express her indignation. This was Ad's domain. Not hers. 'You turn up in London, uninvited, right?' Pointing. Pointing. Waving her hands around, though there was barely the space in that small, galley kitchen. 'Expecting me to drop everything.'

'What's that got to do with you being at van den Bergen's without telling me?'

George could feel the red mist descending. 'Since when was I answerable to you? You're my boyfriend, not my keeper. Don't you understand that I need my space?'

Ad threw the spoon into the wok with something bordering on aggression. It bounced straight out and fell between the side of the cooker and the kitchen cabinetry. 'Jesus! See what you've made me do?'

Hands in the air, now. His back was turned to her. She flipped him the bird and balled her fist at him. 'Did I throw your fucking spoon in the pan like a twat, Adrianus? Did I? Or did you? Like a big spoiled kid.'

He was facing her again now. His handsome face devoid of warmth. Bitterness had set his soft mouth into a hard, thin line. But here, his chin was crumpling up. His eyes reddening.

'Don't you dare bloody cry!' George shouted. 'Act like a man, for God's sake. I'm sick of being the only one with a pair of balls in this relationship. Okay?'

Now, she was torn. The burden of guilt weighed heavily on her, though she felt certain that *he* was in the wrong. Four years in a long distance relationship didn't give him the right to own her and have her qualify how she spent every waking moment, did it? Or was she just being a selfish cow; sabotaging her relationship with this caring, loving man? She hardly knew any more.

Ad sat down heavily on one of his kitchen chairs. Tear-splattered glasses on the table. Hands obscuring his face. 'Why has it ended up like this, George?' he asked. His voice was tremulous and small. 'Don't you love me? I love you.' He laid his hands flat on the peeling placemat, now, revealing the sadness in his eyes and a red nose. 'You're the love of my life.'

George had taken a seat opposite and faced him. Put her hands on top of his. His skin was warm. She wanted to say something soothing to him but couldn't find the words. Listened instead to the bubbling, boiling water on the stove top. Watched the steam from the pan rise to the ceiling, sometimes finding its way to the window, where it turned the reflective glass opaque. It was dark outside. It was dark inside. How could she bring the light back in?

'Love you too.' She said the words quickly. Begrudgingly. No longer certain if she meant them. Sure enough, they elicited the beginnings of a smile from her lovelorn boyfriend.

'Good,' Ad said, kissing her fingers. 'There's nothing we can't sort out, as long as we talk. You know that, don't you?'

He stretched out to stroke her chin. Leaned in for a kiss across the small table. But inside, George felt compelled to shrink away from this inoffensive man she had loved so entirely at the start. She offered him her cheek instead.

Subtle movements in Ad's facial muscles; a certain dull quality to his eyes and the downward droop of his mouth. Here was an expression of abject disappointment on her lover's face. Crestfallen at being relegated to a humble kiss on the cheek. Intimacy between them all but gone, perhaps *because* he demanded it constantly.

George groaned.

'What?' Ad asked.

'Nothing.'

Was she just being difficult, she wondered? Her overdeveloped conscience whispered to her that *she* was at fault. She was a heartless bitch. Poor Ad. Poor boring Ad. Trying so hard and getting nothing but a cold shoulder and mouthful of abuse in return. And yet...and yet. Her instincts told her *he* was in the wrong; the root cause of this irritation. She tried to articulate the elements of his unacceptable behaviour – emotional blackmail? control? possessiveness? – but the nature of it eluded her like a wriggling vein that refused to be pinned and punctured.

Fatigue enshrouded her anger; an acid-resistant membrane, tamping it down temporarily, though neither neutralising nor snuffing it out entirely. Too tired. Now was not the time to have A Conversation about how their relationship had slid from the passionate flush of first love to this suffocating torpor. That could wait. Pour oil on troubled water. Take the water off the boil. George resolved to find soothing words.

'Look,' she said, releasing him gladly so he could drain the noodles and heat the wok. 'You know what I'm like, Ad. I'm impulsive and I need my space and...'

'Do you want it spicy?' Ad asked, less interested in the sticking plaster of her words than she had hoped. 'Or not spicy?'

'Spicy.' She tugged at her hair. Wanting to reach him but feeling she was failing. 'And honestly, van den Bergen's just a friend. You know that by now, for Christ's sake! I just got so wrapped up in the fact there were girls from the sex industry getting killed. Someone Silas knew, in fact! So, I—'

Ad banged the spoon on the side of the wok. Heat on full. Sizzling, prematurely drowning out her repentant monologue. Bastard was closing her down. It felt like punishment.

'Are you listening to me?' She stood. Touched his shoulder. 'You asked and now you're just frying fucking noodles like I'm not in the room.'

His back remained steadfastly turned to her. Jabbing at the frying chicken with his spoon. 'Tell me about your unsavoury friend, Silas Holm, George,' he said. 'Can I expect a visit from some axe-wielding psycho?' Glanced at her over his shoulder and held his right hand aloft, so that she could see the stump that was all that remained of his index finger. 'The Firestarter already took my bloody index finger to add to his crazy little collection, and now I have to do everything left-handed. What's it to be, George? Another finger? Or maybe a leg, this time.'

But now it was George's turn to close Ad down. The light on

240

her phone was flashing. An email. From Sally Wright, whom she had finally made contact with, although it had not been to excuse her abrupt and unsanctioned departure but to warn Sally that her serial-killing study subject might have had a minion pay an unscheduled visit to her Cambridge house.

'Shush a minute, yeah?' She scanned the text.

From: Sally.Wright@cam.ac.uk17.24
To: George_McKenzie@hotmail.com
Subject: Silas Holm.

Dear Georgina,

Thank you for alerting me to the problem of Silas Holm writing to you at your boyfriend's home address. This shocking breach of security is being looked into, although I have recommended that you no longer be granted clearance to interview Dr Holm or any other inpatients at Broadmoor, since there has obviously been some kind of failure to follow protocol on your part. I am also writing to your funding body to ask that approval of your Overseas Institutional Visit be rescinded.

I really preferred not to resort to aggressive tactics to bring you into line, George, but you give me no option.

As for your housemate, Lucy, one of our porters kindly dropped by and reported that she is safe and sound. The locks have been changed in light of the letter, and Lucy is temporarily staying up at Girton, so your conscience is clear on that front, at least.

I will keep you posted on the funding body's response.

Sally
Dr Sally Wright, Senior Tutor
St John's College, Cambridge Tel...01223 775 6574
Dept. of Criminology Tel...01223 773 8023

'Bitch! Bitch! Bitch! Bitch! Total shit-stirring bitch!' George shouted. 'Making my life a fucking nightmare for no bloody reason.' She slammed the phone onto her placemat, unconcerned as to whether Ad was paying attention to her or not. White hot anger back, now, its flames licking unfettered up her throat. 'Bring me into line, will you? You crabby old bag! Oh, my days, what a frigging cheek. Who the fuck does Sally Wright think she is?'

The screensaver had kicked in, rendering the message just a black, shining reflection of George's own face. Angry, twitching nostrils and a grimace that could melt magnesium. There was something of her mother, Letitia the Dragon, in her, all right. She prodded the screen to bring the message back up. Scrolled down to discover a PS: which she hadn't hitherto noticed.

PS: Here is a link to a report in *The Times*. I thought it might have some bearing on your 'case'.

Only dimly aware that Ad was offering her a pile of steaming noodles on a plate, she followed the link to an article – only hours old – where the headline announced:

**MAN BRUTALLY SLAIN: NO WITNESS.
NO MOTIVE. NO CLUES.**
HAS THE PORT-SIDE POLTERGEIST
CLAIMED A THIRD?

Unable to smell the tamarind and garlic aroma of Ad's cooking, George was utterly absorbed in the four paragraphs of writing that reported that an African man, as yet unidentified, had been found in Ramsgate harbour, in a mysteriously bloodless but grue-some scene. He was described as having been 'eviscerated'.

Eviscerated.

'Where have I heard that?' she muttered. It was not a word used in everyday parlance, and yet she felt certain it had been spoken by someone in the course of her day to day dealings only very recently. She rifled through the flotsam and jetsam of her short term memory. Nothing.

'George! I've been standing here for a good minute, holding your plate like an idiot,' Ad said.

Finally, she looked up to find him glowering over her. Still wearing his apron. Her old, grubby Margate tea towel over his shoulder. The lenses of his glasses tear-streaked. Brandishing two full plates. Steam rising in fragrant coils from the heaps of food.

Her senses started to return incrementally. Ad was annoyed at her. She could hear Jasper singing in the living room to a pop song on the television. Her stomach was growling loudly.

With the pursed-lipped expression of an underappreciated cook, Ad set his own dinner down and lowered her plate towards her – encroaching on her personal space with this culinary threat. 'Will you move your phone off the placemat so I can put this down?' He spoke between gritted teeth. 'It might be quite nice to eat before it goes stone cold.'

Eviscerated. The Port-side Poltergeist claiming a third. All at once, George realised. Their killer had crossed the North Sea.

'Eat without me!' she said, leaping up from the table. Bundling her phone and the spare keys to van den Bergen's place into her bag. 'I've got to ring van den Bergen. I've got to go.'

CHAPTER 54

Berlin, Germany, 1989

'How do you think I feel, you inane fucking lump? I feel like shit,' Mama said.

She pulled the covers over her shoulders, shivering. All that was visible above the satin throw was Mama's head. It was a small head. Like a child's, without the outlandish hairstyle or makeup. Bald, but for wisps of remaining hair that needed to be clippered off. Her skin, the colour of strong urine. Mama was a canary down the mineshaft of her own health.

Veronica jerked the gold brocade curtains open with a degree of optimism.

'Come on, Mama,' she said. 'You've been in the dark too long. It's not good for you.' She approached the bed and sat on the edge. Took her mother's thin hand into hers, knowing she was too weak to eschew the physical contact; knowing it would undoubtedly make Mama almost as uncomfortable as the side effects of the chemotherapy. 'They say fresh air and sunlight are powerful medicines.'

'I've got fucking leukaemia, not a cold, silly bitch.'

Veronica stared into her mother's eyes. The clarity had gone. Her irises seemed smudged and muddy. The yellow tinge to the corners spelled liver failure, as did this turmeric hue to her skin

– a strange litmus test, demonstrating the extent to which the disease had got a hold of her.

'I'll help you get dressed. You're seeing the oncologist today,' she said, tugging the covers from her quaking charge.

Even in her loose red satin pyjamas, she could see there was little left to her mother. Always petite, the illness had carved away her meagre flesh to reveal the bony nubs and hollows of a small, near-skeleton. Trying on death for size. Whereas Veronica, who took after her father physically, had grown in inverse proportion like a robust sapling. When she started university in September, she dreaded the prospect of having to stoop in the company of the boys. Still, despite what Mama said about her being a big lump, boys liked long limbs, didn't they?

'I don't want to go to see that know-all prick,' Mama said, clutching her lower legs. 'The morphine doesn't help. I'm in agony. What's the point? I'm dying, aren't I?'

Lifting her mother carefully, Veronica plumped the cushions and made her sit. Proffered her a cup of mint tea. 'Drink, Mama.'

No surprise when her mother batted the china cup out of her hand. A spray of hot liquid scalding Veronica's hand, as she tried to grab the cup before it fell to the ground.

The wry smile on her mother's lips told her that Mama was pleased she still had a little control, even if it were only over how much food and drink she put into her failing body.

'Who's been in touch?' she asked, clutching her knees.

'Nobody,' Veronica lied. 'Sorry.'

When they had first received the news that Mama had leukaemia, the incredible floral displays, cards and gifts had started to arrive immediately. Naturally, Mama had made sure everybody knew. The PR company was engaged immediately before treatment had even started. Papa had colluded, too, feeling that if Mama were to stage a production within the theatre of the unwell, it had better be lavish. The gossip columns gorged on the news. Heidi Schwartz hadn't just been diagnosed with the disease, she had been struck down by it. She was not merely receiving treatment. She was waging her own personal war on cancer. Fundraisers and awareness campaigns and tribute exhibitions in galleries of world cities had ensued. Darling Heidi will not fight alone. There was Heidi in the pages of fashion magazines after her first bout of chemo, looking frail but fabulous, head to toe in Hermès silk. There was Heidi in the celebrity pages of Europe's newspapers, on the arm of the supermodels of the day, bravely getting out of bed for charity functions, even when there were no five-figure sums of money on offer.

But now? Now that Mama was too sick to make it downstairs, and since Papa had been away again, nipping and tucking Hollywood royalty until their faces had been entirely expunged of any character whatsoever, Veronica was in charge.

'But Frau Schwartz wants the flowers brought to her room,' the Turkish housekeeper had said, starting to ascend the grand staircase in their Charlottenburg villa. The arrangement of yellow roses she carried was so large, it almost dwarfed the diminutive, matronly woman.

Veronica had snatched the roses away. 'No, Hilal,' she had said. 'No more flowers. Mama has developed allergies because of the chemotherapy. She's vulnerable to infection. You are not to take anything up to her, do you understand? I'll look after her now. Only me. Understand? If you contaminate her room, she could catch something and die and it will be all your fault. Do you want that to happen?'

The housekeeper's expression, sceptical and almost mocking at first, soon transformed to one of dismay. 'Oh, no, Fräulein Schwartz. What would you like me to do with the gifts?'

'Send them to an old people's home. Anywhere. I don't care. The cards can go in the bin. Really, even the slightest germ could kill Mama and you'll be one more *Gastarbeiter* out of a job. You don't want to go back to Turkey, do you?'

Hilal had shaken her head vociferously.

'Well, then.'

Over the weeks, she had watched her mama become more and more disillusioned at having been dropped by her illustrious friends. Disillusionment turned to despondency, turned to despair. Nobody could contradict the view of the world that Veronica presented to her mother. Papa was absent, as usual – busy with his various mistresses and business. Now, in the claustrophobic Renaissance glitz of the bedroom, her once vivacious, social butterfly of a mother was solely dependent on her daughter for company and care. It felt like a triumph, of sorts. Particularly since Veronica would travel to London in September to begin her degree. Mama would have nobody at all.

'Wear the comfortable tracksuit,' Veronica said, laying a cheap, synthetic outfit on the bed that looked like it had been made for a child.

'I'm not wearing that,' Mama said. 'It's hideous.'

'It's comfortable. You'll wear it.'

'You're punishing me. You're a big, spotty bitch. If I had the energy—'

'You'd what?' Veronica treated her mother to a look of bemusement and pity. 'You'd hit me? Really? When I'm taking such good care of you?!'

All Mama had left in her arsenal was disgruntled silence. She maintained that silence during the drive through town. Stuck in traffic several lanes deep for a while because of some demonstration or other – the way ahead up towards the Brandenburg Gate blocked almost entirely. The silence was soon broken, then.

'Gustav, what's going on here?' she asked the driver. 'Why aren't we moving?'

Gustav did not even turn around. All that was visible of him was his chauffeur's hat and that horrible, creased, red neck of his. Dandruff on his shoulders. Hard, narrowed eyes observing her through the rear view mirror said driving for Mama was not the best job he had ever had. 'Seems there are people on The Wall itself, Frau Schwartz. Some kind of a to-do. I know a good cut-through. Don't worry.'

'I'm not worried. That's what I fucking pay you for.' Her voice was shaky. She lolled against Veronica for support.

Veronica, meanwhile, wondered what it was people were protesting about. To the left of the Brandenburg Gate, in the distance, the shining, winking silver orb of the TV tower in East Berlin had a view of everyone and everything, she always imagined. The world at its base. Wisdom in that all-seeing orb. It would know the truth of what was going on way up ahead; why there were police everywhere and people apparently allowed to clamber onto The Wall without being gunned down.

On either side of the car, banners – fashioned from bedsheets and sticks, by the looks, carried up the Strasse des 17 Juni by young people in amongst those droves of ordinary Berliners – talked of togetherness. Reunification. Freedom. The very things Veronica dreamed of for herself, though she was concerned with a reunification of sorts with her parents. The same people from whom she longed for freedom. Equally bound to and repelled by Mama and Papa, whose genes she carried within her and would gladly have stripped from the very fabric of her being had scientists invented such a novel and thorough cleansing technique.

September. She would be free in September. For now, she anticipated that they would arrive at the oncologist's private practice and be told that Mama only had weeks to live. She and Mama would spend those weeks alone at home, being reunited. Discovering a mother/daughter bond that may never have been there from the start, but which would blossom now, for a gloriously short time.

They arrived at the oncologist's private practice, whereupon the oncologist reported with some enthusiasm that Veronica was a perfect match as a bone marrow donor for her mother.

'Fantastic news, isn't it?' he told Mama, beaming. 'The blood sample we took from your daughter last time shows she will be able to donate with a high likelihood of success, Frau Schwartz.'

At her side, looking like a tracksuit-clad coat hanger in a Gucci headscarf, her mother started to weep loudly. 'Oh, thank you, God! Thank you. Thank you. I'm going to live.' She turned to Veronica and grabbed at her arm, though the strength of old was no longer in her fingers. 'You look so much like your father, but you've got your mother's blood in your veins.'

The heat leached out of Veronica's body as the enormity of what the oncologist suggested registered with her. 'Will it hurt?' she asked, clutching the hem of her miniskirt.

'I'm afraid it's a very painful procedure,' the doctor said. 'But on the bright side, you get to be a hero!'

She glanced at her mother. It was as if all of her own vitality had poured back into this invalid, leaving her feeling drained, and in turn, injecting Mama with some of her old vivacity and spunk. Had she somehow transformed into the Georg Bendemann of Kafka's *Judgment*? Doomed to be usurped by an ailing parent; the proper course of nature inverted by her mother's triumph and her own downfall and death? Perhaps. Perhaps.

'When I'm better, I'll throw a party to celebrate like Berlin has never seen,' Mama said, closing her eyes. A solitary tear trickling down her cheek. 'Then, I'll throw more in New York and London. If this isn't worth celebrating, then I don't know what is!'

At home, Papa was waiting.

'I don't want to do it,' Veronica told him, as he sat stiffly in his study, sipping brandy whilst scanning a medical journal. 'They said it would be agony, Papa. He said they had another match, in case I didn't work out.' She approached her father, hoping to appeal to whatever paternal instinct this distant man might have towards her. Touched the sleeve of his cashmere sweater. Finally, he met her pleading gaze. 'Please, Papa. I'm only eighteen. I've got university to look forward to.'

But Papa merely stared at her blankly over his round spectacles. Fingering his Rolex. Pulling his arm from her reach.

'You think we want some filthy proletarian bone marrow inside your mother's body?' he said, sipping the liquor. 'We'd never know the donor. It could be anyone. It could be a bloody foreigner. The register is confidential. No way.' He shook his head, as if to emphasise how little he thought of the idea. Swivelled his leather armchair around so that he was facing a large Bang & Olufsen television screen, partially concealed inside a limed oak built-in TV cabinet. Slid a tape into the Betamax and pressed play. Golf appeared on the screen.

'Papa.'

'You'll donate the marrow, you spoiled little shit,' he said. 'Don't you want to save your mother's life?'

As promised, the surgery had proven excruciating. When Veronica stood by her mother's graveside, amongst the great and the good of the international jet-set, she was still sore and sobbing, more from pain than loss.

Clad in black Chanel, concealing her agony behind a pair of Wayfarers and a wide-brimmed hat, it took more than an hour for the mourners, sycophants and voyeurs to file past her and her father to pay their respects to them and to say a final farewell to this doyenne of high society; this beloved patron of the arts. The cemetery was splashed bright, like an impressionist's painting, with colour from the incredible floral tributes. Mama would have loved it. Simply everyone was there. Including the paparazzi.

Some European minor-royal, whom Veronica did not really recognise, patted her hand. Spoke Americanised English, as they mainly did.

'My dear, it must be so hard for you. You've been so, so brave.'

A grimace for the cameras. Flash. Flash. Hand on hip. Knee slightly tilted. Still fabulous in YSL.

Next, some medical man whom her father knew from the golf course. An anaesthetist with a strange old-fashioned first name that she remembered from a George Eliot novel. *Silas Marner: The Weaver of Raveloe.*

He kissed her hand. Years older than her but attractive, with a small-featured, symmetrical face. Spoke words she recognised from Shakespeare's *Romeo and Juliet* in a rich voice with deferential, lowered gaze, still holding her hand:

> *Death, that hath suck'd the honey of thy breath*
> *Hath had no power yet upon thy beauty;*
> *Thou art not conquer'd; beauty's ensign yet*
> *Is crimson in thy lip, and in thy cheeks,*
> *And death's pale flag is not advanced there.*

She was smitten.

CHAPTER 55

Over the North Sea, then, Ramsgate, England, 27 January

The light came on overhead, telling them to fasten their seatbelts. It preceded a stomach-turning jolt only by moments. The dense cloud enveloping the plane, which scudded over the wings in long grey wisps like wizards' beards, gave no indication of their altitude. But they were descending. In the seat beside her, van den Bergen fidgeted.

'I hate turbulence,' he said. Yanking at his belt. 'The fat bastard next to me is sitting on the buckle. I can't—' Yank. Yank. His brows knocking together in consternation or irritation or both.

George leaned across and tugged the buckle free.

'Ow! What are you doing?'

'You were sitting on your own buckle, you berk!' She fastened the seatbelt for him, as though he were a large child. Gave him a disapproving look but winked. 'Remember the last time we flew together?'

He rested his head back and looked at the panels and air con above them. His Adam's apple pinged up and down in his sinewy throat. Rough red skin that said he'd shaved in haste. But he smelled good, permeating the aircraft funk of stale vomit and industrial cleaning fluid with citrus scent, or was it something like bergamot?

He turned to her, looking rather like a man who hadn't slept for days, judging by the dark circles beneath despondent grey eyes.

'Last time we flew, we were coming back from Cambridge after you'd been abducted by that psychopath,' he said, the corners of his mouth turning upwards; laughter lines deepening, making those sunken cheekbones even more pronounced. 'I made you drink gin.'

Impulsively, she grabbed the back of his head, pulled him down towards her and kissed him squarely on the cheek. Memories of the many inappropriate scenarios she had imagined herself in with this middle-aged policeman grappling for prominence in her mind's eye.

'What's that for?' he asked, touching his face.

She was surprised that he looked more amused than startled, as he would have been in the beginning. He hadn't shuffled up towards the fat man seated on his other side, next to the aisle.

'You,' she said. 'You're a curmudgeonly old sod.' Pointed to his curling shirt collar. 'You need to go bloody shopping and get yourself some new threads, man. And you need to sort your fucked-up head out. But you're my hero. You saved my life back then.'

Colour crept into his face. He blinked hard, cleared his throat and pointed to the green quilt of England's countryside that spread out below them, now that they had dropped beneath the clouds, passing the jagged white line of the UK's coastline.

'Ready for some detective work, Cagney?' he said.

'I thought I was Lacey and Ad was Cagney,' she said, grinning furtively out of the window.

'Don't spoil it by saying that prick's name,' her travel companion said. 'He gives me indigestion.'

She turned back to him. Stared at his thick white hair. Would it be dry like hers? Soft like Ad's? Coarser? Did it stand up that way because he had product in it or was it just too thick to flop?

'Ad went mental when I said you'd booked us into the same hotel. Where the hell did he think I was going to stay?'

Spied a degree of mischief in his tired eyes, now. Another flicker of a smile.

'Good job I didn't tell you we're in adjoining rooms, then.'

Before she could respond, she was taken aback by their little KLM Fokker 70 bouncing onto the runway at Kent International airport.

'Jesus.' She grabbed van den Bergen's arm. Peered out in disbelief at the flat landscape and terminal building scudding past at speed. 'That was quick!'

He patted her hand but only momentarily, in favour of switching on his phone. Within seconds, it pinged. He frowned.

'Anything interesting?' she asked.

'Shit,' he said, nodding. 'There's been a development with the Polish builder. Leeuwenhoek has stumbled onto something you won't believe!'

The biting north sea wind whipped George's unruly curls this way and that. Her eyes streamed, barely able to glimpse the silver clouds that threatened the Kentish coastline with sleet, hail or possibly snow. Even in her sheepskin coat and a thick jumper, she was shivering almost to the point where her teeth clacked together. At her side, van den Bergen was grey-faced but for a red nose, his head bent against the wind, his white hair beaten flat against his skull.

'Jesus. Even if you don't wind up dead with your innards missing,' he said, as they followed the detective from the Kent police across the tarmac to the sea wall, 'it must be one hell of a come-down turning up on these shores when you're from somewhere hot like the bloody Congo.' He called after their guide. 'Rob, was it the Congo your victim was from or...?'

Rob looked back with watery eyes and a ruddy face that said even in his parka and beanie hat, he was as freezing as they were. 'Democratic Republic of. Not Congo on its own.'

'What's the difference?' van den Bergen asked George.

George cast her mind back to BBC news reports on world news that she had followed over the last few years. Articles she had read about the 'child witches' of Kinhasa. 'It's in turmoil,' she said. 'War between at least six countries – Rwanda, Angola, Uganda, Zimbabwe, Namibia – and fighting between factions within the Democratic Republic itself. Like the land that God forgot. Millions of kids have been killed. Young boys are made to fight by warlords. There's no infrastructure. The western world doesn't give a shit...oh, and it's one of the most dangerous places on earth to be a girl or a woman. Sexual violence is endemic.' She wished the Kentish detective would slow down so that she didn't have to jog. Would have liked the arsehole to turn around. Instead, she spoke to the back of his head and the fur on his hood.

'Rob, if the victim was naked, how do you know where he came from?' she asked.

Still facing straight ahead, he shouted over his shoulder. 'Tattoos and scarification on his back – specific to the area, our forensics guys reckon. Some tribal thing shows the victim's been a child soldier. He was only about nineteen.'

The detective came to an abrupt stop, backing away from the sea wall where an arc of spray shot some twenty feet or so into the air and cascaded down to the ground, drenching the blue and yellow chequered Kent Police Range Rover that had been parked too close to the edge.

'Mind out!' he said, ushering George and van den Bergen backwards. 'Can't believe that twat, Grayson, parked the sodding car there!'

George took in the backdrop to the drab scene. A roll on, roll off ferry was docked not far away. Behind them, heavy goods vehicles were parked diagonally, forming orderly chevrons on a large expanse of tarmac. Dated, low buildings housed the port terminal. In the distance, a colourful marina looked more picturesque and promising than Ramsgate had looked close-up when they had driven along the harbour road, past Victorian houses which were shabby and neglected.

'What a shit place to die,' she said.

Rob led them to where the brine of the sea had already washed away most of the white outline that had been sprayed on the ground, marking the spot where the body had been found.

'He didn't die here,' he said, staring dolefully at the smudged paint. He scratched beneath his beanie hat and sniffed his fingers. 'We've no idea how he got here.'

'What do you mean?' van den Bergen asked. 'Doesn't the port authority have cameras trained on this area.'

Rob nodded. 'Yeah. They do. But here's the thing.' He reached into the pocket of his parka and pulled out a cigarette packet. Looked inside. Seemed to think better of it and put it away again. 'Someone hacked the security software and erased the records from the day we found him.'

George exchanged a knowing look with van den Bergen.

'Same your end?' Rob asked, blowing on his reddened fingers.

Van den Bergen nodded. 'I've seen the photographs of your man and the forensics report. There's no doubt we're hunting the same killer, although in Amsterdam, he's also targeted women.'

'Could the victim have been a stowaway on one of those ferries?' George asked, pointing to the giant red and white tub onto which cars were driving in a sluggish trail. Bound for Ostend, no doubt.

Rob shrugged. 'Usually, when you get a guy comes into the country from some war-torn shithole, he's come in through Dover. Cargo ships dock from West Africa all the time there. Some of them are bona fide sailors. Some are trafficked slave labour.' He stamped his feet on the ground and slapped his hands on his arms. 'I don't know. He could have been an asylum seeker came in through another route and got on the wrong side of some two-bit gangster in the Big Smoke. Fellers like this get into trouble too easily. Especially young ones. They're vulnerable to crime.'

'And the other murders?' van den Bergen asked. 'You had two more disembowelled fishermen last month.'

The Kentish detective started to walk back towards the Range Rover, beckoning them to follow. 'Those poor sods were from Africa too. At first, we were convinced it was gangland activity. Eyes gouged out. Gutted, like you say.' He squinted and looked up at the gulls overhead that were buffeted on the stiff wind like kites. Crying out for better weather and perhaps a nicer view in that sorry, down-at-heel seaside town. 'But unlike this latest victim, their hearts were still in the right place. He he. If you get my meaning.'

His half-smile and attempt at a pun was met with a grimace from van den Bergen.

'And one of the victims – the older one of the two, who was reported to be about forty – still had his lungs,' Rob continued, the mirth now absent from his face. 'Pathologist said he had lung cancer – a tumour about the size of a golf ball, apparently, growing into the outer wall of the right side of his lung.'

'Lung cancer?' van den Bergen said, suddenly blanching. He grabbed George by her upper arm.

Feeling something was amiss, George looked at her friend. Took hold of his cold, cold hand. 'Are you okay?'

His lips were pale purple. He started to shake. Eyes glazed and staring. Breathing raggedly. 'I feel a bit dizzy. There's flashing lights. I—' He opened and closed his mouth. Gazed around him, appearing bewildered. A large, lost boy, all at sea. Held his other hand aloft to reveal white fingers. Started to shake. 'My fingers have gone numb, George.'

Rob unlocked the Range Rover. 'Come and sit in the car, mate,' he said, helping George to usher van den Bergen to the sea-drenched vehicle – no mean feat, given van den Bergen's size and the fact that his legs were starting to give way.

'I think I'm going to faint,' he said. Grabbing George by the arm, as he wedged himself onto the back seat of the Range Rover. Wide-eyed. Ashen-faced. 'Help me, George! I think I'm having a stroke or a brain haemorrhage.'

Palpitations made George's own breath come quick. *I'm going to lose him. He's going to go before I get a chance to tell him anything. All those words I rehearsed in my head, over and over.* 'Don't leave me, Paul! You're going to be fine. Keep breathing.'

Van den Bergen's skin was as cold and pale grey as marble. His lips barely moved; his voice hardly audible.

'George, I...'

At that moment, his eyes rolled back into his head.

CHAPTER 56

Soho, London, later

'Get into the fucking car, Giuseppe,' the short-arsed Italian said, pushing the barrel of that snub-nosed handgun into his back. 'You going for a little ride.'

'Luigi, mate,' Derek began, holding his quaking hands up. Where the hell was Sharon when you needed her?

'Mr frigging Gera, to you, *pigliainculo!*'

Eyes darting to and fro with tiny pupils said this loon was speeding like a choo-choo train, Derek assessed. He turned around slowly and looked down at the gun. Wondered if getting shot dead would actually hurt. Flick, flick to the left with the barrel, in the direction of some big, posh car or other. Not the four-wheel drive, this time. A Jag, maybe. Or one of those big Beemers. No, an Audi. Maybe. In any case, he was going to die in the back of a fucking nice car at the hands of Psycho di Roma, aka Mr Gera. Looked like a shiny-shoed accountant in a Crombie overcoat who had been shrunk on a fucking hot wash. Great. Would he get Harvey Keitel to come and clean up the mess, like Keitel did when John Travolta shot Marvin in the fucking face in *Pulp Fiction*? Is that how this was going to roll?

'Don't shoot me, Mr Gera,' Derek said, trying to connect with the loon. Trying to remember some Italian phrase from Nonna, although, given she'd left the old country before the war, she was about as Italian as Dolmio. A proverb sprang to mind. '*A chi dai il dito, si prende anche il braccio.*' Shit. What did that even mean?

'You want I take your arm as well as your finger?' Gera asked, grinning. 'Good. I like this idea.'

Fuck it if he hadn't landed himself straight in a damned Tarantino film. *Che cazzo.* Sharon had always said he was prize knob. *Check everything out*, he counselled himself. *Remember the details to tell the coppers. Black saloon. Check the registration plate on the car.* But Derek's brain was in overdrive, denying him the ability to absorb detail. And what did it matter anyhow, if he was being taken somewhere with this crazy bastard?

Sitting together on the back seat, Derek looked longingly through the tinted window at the club. His club. 'They're going to notice I'm gone,' he said, pointing, as one of the girls, still wearing her jeans and fun-fur civvies, pulled open the front door and disappeared inside. 'We open up in an hour. If you kill me, you're going to have Dermot Robinson on your case.'

Gera patted his hand. 'Dermot Robinson is no interest to me. Drive, Tony,' he told a brick shithouse at the wheel, who merely nodded in the rear view mirror.

Tony had the biggest head Derek had ever seen on a man. Tony's head was on steroids. The car pulled away.

'Where we going?' Derek asked, trying to take the lock off his phone. Maybe if he could ring Sharon and leave it ringing, they'd be able to track him with GPS or some shit. Find him before Gera got medieval on his arse.

'You're going to do a job for me,' Gera said, sniffing hard and wiping a dribble of clear snot on the silk handkerchief in the top pocket of his overcoat. Put his arm around Derek. Where was the gun? Still pointing at his ribs. 'My man, Rocco, he's busy in Germany. I am…How you say? Short-staffed. You are…How you say? My *puttana*. My beach.'

'Bitch.'

260

'*Chiudi il culo*, Giuseppe!' He pressed the barrel of the gun up against his lips. 'Shh! You do the job, I pay you a thousand pounds. You don't do the job, I think you know what will happen.'

Derek touched the bruising around his eyes. Still fresh. Still livid purple from the beating he had taken outside the farmhouse.

Gera threw his head back and laughed. 'Hey Tony,' he said to the driver. 'Giuseppe, here thinks I gonna beat him up if he fucks with me.'

Tony peered at Derek through the rear view mirror. Raised an eyebrow. 'You be fucking wishing at the end I'd beaten you up, mate.'

He hadn't intended to cry, of course. Men didn't cry. But Derek could not stem the salty flow from his tender, stinging eyes. He shook his head. Tried to speak clearly but could only stutter. 'I-j-just want to go h-home, Mr Gera. I ain't n-no gangster. I a-ain't cut out for this, man. Promise I w-won't tell no-one. Swear on m-my baby's life.'

'Ah, *si*. Tinesha, yes? *Bellissima*. Lovely girl. You must be very proud she's at university in Cardiff, no?'

His tears dried almost immediately. Derek felt the blood drain from his face, turning his lips to ice. In petrified silence, he stared at the Italian. 'What I got to do?'

CHAPTER 57

Ramsgate, later

In the semi-darkness of his hotel room, with the brown blackout curtains pulled – the only illumination coming from the bathroom light – van den Bergen wept.

'Come here to me, bwoy! Why you cry for?' George said in the same reassuring Jamaican patois Letitia had used on her when she had been a small child, waking from a bad dream. Rocking him back and forth on the bed, encircling him in her arms. Kissing his hair, so he'd know she was there for him and everything would be all right. Reassuring. 'You're fine. You've got to believe me. You've got to believe the doctors.'

'I'm not,' he said. 'I won't be.'

'Ah, gi mi sponge fi go dry up sea. Letitia used to say that to me too. You know what that means?'

He buried his head deeper into her chest.

'Means you're hard work, man. Come on, now. You've got to tell me what's going on.'

His lean body quaked against her chest as he sobbed silently. Presently, he spoke. 'I thought it was over,' he said. 'I've been waiting for death for so long.'

Holding his face between her hands, George looked directly

into his grey eyes. 'It was a panic attack, Paul. Not a stroke. Not a brain haemorrhage.'

'They don't know that,' he said, chest heaving unevenly.

She relinquished the grip on his face. Clasped his hands instead. 'They do,' she said. 'The CT scan was clear. Your blood tests were normal. Your ECG was normal. We spent three hours in A&E to be told you've got bloody anxiety. Come on, Paul. Tell me why.'

Van den Bergen blew his nose noisily on the tissues she handed to him. Downcast eyes focussed on her belly. 'I've been depressed for months.' He swallowed hard. 'Work. Tamara. But mainly, the anniversary of my dad's death...'

George took his chin between her finger and thumb. Made him look at her. 'That what set you off? The fact one of the victims had lung cancer?'

He nodded. Tears welled afresh and poured silently onto his cheeks, following the course of the grooves either side of his mouth. 'My dad was an arsehole but I loved him. I'm scared I'm going to turn into him. Every week, it's been getting worse.'

'When's the anniversary?'

'Today.'

George sucked her teeth. 'Why didn't you say?'

'Why would I? Who the hell wants to hear a middle-aged divorcé; a hypochondriac whingeing old bastard like me drone on about death? And spending night after night, unable to sleep and yet, barely being able to get out of bed in the morning when the alarm finally goes off. I'm just not myself. I've been doing mad things. I don't know...'

Running her fingertips over his knuckles, she clicked her tongue above the roof of her mouth. 'Did you get into a fight?'

He nodded.

'Is what Marie said true?'

In the dim light, he looked over towards the curtains. It was hard to see his expression clearly, but George felt sure it was one of weary resignation.

'Yes.'

'You beat up on a man in custody? Seriously?'

Nodded. His lip started to buckle out of shape. The sharp line of his jaw was suddenly uncertain. 'I'm a monster, George. A violent monster.' Those melancholy grey eyes met hers, holding her gaze steadily for a minute or more, as if he were challenging her to find the good in him.

How did she feel about his act of police brutality? Had it even been an uncharacteristic display, as she was inclined to believe? How much did she really know about this cop, twenty years her senior, who was addicted to prescription painkillers and whose self-esteem was clearly so low that he seemed deliberately to provoke everyone he met, apart from her, into disliking him intensely?

'Why did you do it?' she asked.

He didn't answer.

'You're not the type to go around, swinging punches for no reason. The guy must have provoked you in some way. Why, Paul?'

'He looked like Karelse. I don't know what came over me. Jealousy... I—'

Van den Bergen stared into her eyes, unmoving, unblinking. George leaned forwards and kissed him on the lips. His mouth was unyielding. His body, as still as stone, though a raised eyebrow betrayed his surprise. She kissed him again. This time, his lips parted. His eyes closed. He started to kiss her back, tenderly at first. Blood rushed in her ears and she was aware of her own pulse racing. Felt his eyelashes flutter against her cheek. Then, his tongue seeking out hers, hungrily, like a starving man enjoying his first meal in a long, long time. Her fingers found the buttons on his shirt. She started to undo them, touching the hairs that curled above his collar bone with inquisitive fingers. Probing the hard sheet of muscle that covered his chest and the ridges of his sternum. His hands slid down to caress the sides of her breasts.

Abruptly, he broke away. Panting. All trace of sadness in his face now gone.

'Why d'you stop?' She glanced down. Saw through his trousers that he was aroused. Felt the burn of anticipation between her own legs.

'Are you sure about this?' he asked.'Fuck, yes,' she said, throwing herself on top of him. Straddling his hips, feeling his hardness through her jeans. Pulling her T-shirt over her head and casting it onto the hotel room floor.

He reached up behind her and unfastened her bra. Ran his fingers along the contours of her full breasts. Stroked the dark brown skin of her nipples.

'Christ, you're beautiful,' he said.

She caressed the hair on his navel, flicking open the button of his trousers in one smooth manoeuvre. 'Get them off.'

With their clothes abandoned, as his long, practised fingers pleasured her, George appraised van den Bergen's wiry naked body between her legs. Broad shoulders and strong-looking athletic arms. Taut abdominal muscles. The grey-white body hair the only real sign of his age.

'You're a fine-looking man, Paul van den Bergen.' She was drunk on desire. 'I'm going to fucking ruin you.'

'Good. I'm going to make you come like you've never come before, Georgina McKenzie.'

CHAPTER 58

Soho, London, later

Groaning, Sharon tried again to pull a pint of bitter. Flicked the switch back and forth, but only honey-coloured froth came out of the tap.

'Derek!' she shouted through the cavernous club, empty but for a couple of girls doing their nails and drinking coffee in the back. 'I need you to change the barrel!'

No response. Sharon put the spent glass down and wiped her sticky hands on a bar towel.

'Where's that pain in the arse got to?' she asked her reflection in the mirrored wall that marked out her domain.

She adjusted her elaborate head attire until it sat perfectly balanced above her face. 'I'm a better artist than that Tracey Ermine with her skanky bed. Eat your heart out, skinny white gyal,' she told herself. Though, not yet made-up, she looked tired, she knew. 'Too much washing and ironing and cleaning for that lickle rarseclart, Patrice. Always bringing his dutty batty crease friends home, making a mess.' Checked out her new dress – a crossover leopard print number from Primark. Turn this way. Turn that way. Suck her belly in. Stick her chest out. Made her tits and bum look great. She slapped her own behind. 'Me gat plenty gravy on dem pork chop.' Laughed at the thought. A slick of lipstick and some eyeliner and she'd be fine.

'Derek!' she bellowed.

No Derek. She left her bar and ventured into the foyer.

The two girls who had been getting ready in the back came out of their dressing room, strutting past her in their heels towards one of the stages. A rangy tattooed blonde and a Chinese girl who had the tiny, muscular body of a ballet dancer. Ready to twist and gyrate the night away in underwear trimmed with feathers and spangles.

'All right, Shaz?' the Chinese girl asked.

'All right, Mae Ling? Cindy? You two seen Uncle Giuseppe on your travels?'

Mae Ling shrugged. Cindy shook her head. 'Nah. He was out front earlier with some short-arsed geezer in a fancy car. Nattering, like.'

Sharon frowned. 'Ta, girls,' she said.

Made her way down to the basement to check the barrel for herself. She hated the basement. It was creepy down there. Clickety clack in her Betty Boop heels on the old wooden stairs. Her feet were killing her. She needed to get those corns done. Only problem with carrying weight and doing a job that involved standing for hours was her knees and her feet were knackered.

In the shitty glare of the basement light, she looked around and found the empty bitter barrel. Unhooked it and got splattered by the remnants of booze still lurking in the pipes. Cursed several times. Located the new barrel. Tried to move it. It wouldn't budge, and her efforts were rewarded by a false nail flicking off and disappearing like a scuttling green cockroach behind the strong lager barrel.

'I'm gonna swing for you when I find you, Derek de Falco, you selfish dick. Leaving a woman to do all the dirty work, as usual.'

When the loud ring of a mobile phone broke the unsettling

silence down there, Sharon jumped. Dionne Warwick, asking if she knew the way to San Jose. Automatically patted herself down, though her own phone was upstairs by the ice bucket. Moving closer to where the song resonated from. She knew that naff ringtone anywhere. It was Derek's. She picked up the small white lozenge. Saw that there was an incoming call from Dermot Robinson. The Porn King.

'Hello, Mr Robinson,' Sharon said, holding Derek's greasy phone close to her ear but not against her skin. Dirty bugger never washed his hands enough. Thumb prints on the screen made her skin prickle with distaste. 'Sharon. Yes. Behind the bar. That's right. I'm good, thanks. No, I ain't seen him for about half an hour,' she told the Porn King, who sounded disgruntled that his minion had not picked up. 'Yeah, he was here when I arrived. No idea, love. Yes, this is his phone. He never normally goes nowhere without his phone, though. He can't be far. He'll turn up like a bad penny.' She affected a friendly laugh, though Derek's absence was anything but amusing. 'He always does.'

Back behind the bar, Sharon tried to work out the pin to unlock Derek's keypad and enter the unsavoury world of Uncle Giuseppe. Tried multiple combinations. Birthdays that might mean something. To no avail. Not even Tinesha's birthday yielded the phone's secrets. 'Bloody hell,' she said, flinging it down next to the till. 'I need our Patrice. I bet he'd be able to do it.'

Derek, chatting with a small man next to a flashy car. Derek, with no means of communication on him, doing a disappearing act during his shift. Derek, who had had whatever sense he still possessed almost entirely beaten out of him only days earlier by one of them big Italian geezers. Things didn't look promising. Sitting in her kitchen while she cleaned up his battered face, he had been petrified that the miniature Don Corleone of Soho would want him dead. Had Derek, a man prone to take the blind alleys in life, always the last to be in on the joke, always getting the wrong end of the shitty stick and managing to get himself beaten by it...had Derek Dickheaded de Falco finally been on the money?

Her frustration and anxiety mounted quickly until she was breathless and distracted. Couldn't get the bloody jammed optics working, now. Damn, damn, damn. When her own phone rang, she almost burst into tears. It was George, asking to swing by in the morning. Had the mystery Dutch policeman in tow.

"Course you can, darling.' Because she was Aunty Sharon and Aunty Sharon was a fixer of things, she was careful to keep the panic out of her voice. 'Didn't realise you was back in the country already. Amsterdam boring? You come over and see your Aunty Sharon. I'll bake.'

On the other end, an oddly breathless-sounding George let slip she was staying the night in Ramsgate. A man's voice in the background. Giggling and something that sounded like a slap. She didn't have time for the girl's frivolous bullshit. Not when Derek was missing.

'Look, I got to get off the line, babe,' she said. 'Derek's done one. He might be trying to get in touch.' She was about to switch her niece's voice off when something occurred to her. 'Oh, before you go, there's a certain someone been asking after you. Wanting face time, apparently. I've had text after text after text and I don't want no more messages cluttering up my inbox, yeah? So, if you're back in the country, if you want me to put my ear to the ground for gossip about some dead fellers, you gotta deal with this shit. D'you get me?'

On the other end of the phone, George went quiet. Asked who the persistent texter was.

'You ain't gonna like this,' Sharon said.

CHAPTER 59

Somewhere in Kent, an industrial estate, later

'Right, you know what to do?' Tony asked, looking over his shoulder.

Derek nodded, wishing he was anywhere but in the back of that bloody car. Actually, scrub that. He was just relieved that he wasn't dead, and that the pint-sized loon, Gera, had been dropped off at some big pile in Chislehurst.

'Well?' Tony glared at him. His head was so large; his brutish face so red and angry, Derek felt as though he were a small child getting a dressing down from a gargoyle or a demon or some biblical shit. 'Come on, Uncle fucking Giuseppe.'

'Okay, okay,' he said, scratching at the underside of his chin with a shaking hand. Looking out at the abandoned and seemingly derelict industrial estate. He had been made to wear a black hood over his head for a good twenty minutes or so, but he had seen through the fabric – not quite opaque – that they had travelled some way along the M20. Square, blue signs flashing by overhead. The white triangles of oast-house roofs in the distance. Maybe they were near the entrance to the Channel Tunnel. Maybe not. He couldn't be sure. 'So, I go in and I pick up a package and I bring it back out to the car and I put it in the boot.' It sounded

270

easy enough. 'Why don't Mr Gera have you doing this? Why does he want me involved?'

'I drive the car,' Tony said, gripping the steering wheel with a giant hand, encased in the largest leather glove Derek had seen. What kind of shop even made gloves that size? They were murderer's hands, of that, he was certain. 'That's my job. And I watch you to make sure you do your job.' Pointing at him with his other giant leathery hand. Reminded Derek of the gorillas he'd seen at the zoo as a kid. Big fucking hands, those silverback gorillas. 'Mr Gera's obviously training you up. We're like parts in an engine, right? All doing different bits. Your valves and your pistons and that. We all work to make the machine run smooth.'

Tony checked his watch. 'He's expecting you. Go on. Don't make no conversation. You ain't there to make fucking friends. Am I making myself clear?'

Shivering in his shirt, pointlessly wishing he'd had time to grab his coat and his phone, Derek got out of the car. Approached the industrial unit. Rusting corrugated iron shutters down over the door and a large opening at the front. Weeds growing up out of the cracked tarmac. Strappy twigs and shit growing out of the roof. As though nature was taking the place back.

He rapped on the shutters.

'Who is it?' came a man's voice from inside.

'Giuseppe,' Derek said, trying to sound confident but hearing a thin and weedy voice coming from his tight throat. 'Mr Gera sent me for the pick-up.'

The shutters on the door rolled up slowly. Derek stepped inside. He found himself in an empty space, lit overhead by fluorescent strip lighting. It looked as though it had once been a mechanic's body shop and was now maybe used to park cars away from prying eyes. There was a pronounced smell of diesel in the air and a black slick on the concrete floor that could have been oil, by the looks. Tyre tread marks were a dead giveaway.

The man that stood before him was nothing to look at. Reminded

271

Derek of an insurance clerk or a bank teller – slicked-back hair, mid thirties maybe, glasses – except he wore a white doctor's coat over a pair of jeans. The coat was stained with pale brown patches, as though it had been splattered with something dark that had failed to boil out on a bleach wash. Derek wrinkled his nose without being able to articulate why he found the man distasteful.

'I'm Giuseppe,' Derek said, holding out his hand.

'I know. You already said that,' the man said, keeping his own hands firmly in the pockets of his dirty white coat.

'What's your name, then?'

'Dr Fucking Doolittle.' The man gestured that Derek should follow through a red door to their right. 'Come on.'

Beyond the red door, a shabby corridor with a flickering overhead light and scuffed grey walls led to a row of Perspex door flaps. It smelled different here. A strong odour of alcohol stung in Derek's nostrils – but not the alcoholic smell of the club he was used to. It was the sort of smell he'd come across in hospitals when you had to rub your hands with that anti-bac shit every five minutes. But beyond that, there was a sickly, rotten whiff that caught the back of his throat. He'd once visited an abattoir to source cheap steak for the clubs. It had smelled similar there. Blood and shit and whatever else came out of a carcass. He looked again at Dr Doolittle's stained coat and shuddered.

On the other side of the heavy Perspex flaps, what he saw surprised him. It was a brightly lit space that looked like an operating theatre.

'Bloody hell,' Derek said, looking at all the monitors, the tangle of wires and peculiar equipment that surrounded a black vinyl bed in the centre of the room. 'When I thought I'd end up in hospital today, I didn't expect this. What you up to in here, mate? Bupa forgot to pay the rent?'

Tony's admonition that he should under no circumstances try to make conversation was long forgotten. The threat to Tinesha's wellbeing but a vague notion. Derek was fascinated.

272

Dr Doolittle handed him what appeared to be a large cool box. A biohazard label on the side of it said there was something ropey inside that Derek didn't really want to know about.

'Don't drop it,' Doolittle said. 'Precious cargo.'

But now, Derek wasn't paying attention. On the other side of this strange medical set-up, he spied yet another set of Perspex flaps that marked the threshold to somewhere else. Leaving Dr Doolittle holding the cool box, he strode past, pushing through the flaps. Gasped when he saw the unconscious girl shackled to a gurney. An operating gown hitched up around her belly, exposing her groin. Skin almost as pale as snow, her blood draining into a container below through a plastic tube that was plugged into the crook of her arm via a fat needle.

'Jesus!' he cried. 'What the fuck?!' This looked *all* wrong. Fear seeped into his body as though he had taken bad whizz. Dizziness, heart palpitating wildly, sweating freely all at once. Paranoid.

At his side, Dr Doolittle in his shitty white coat was grinning. Pulling the girl's gown down. Patting her hand, a smug little slicked-back haired shitbag.

'Our girl's got rare blood,' he said. 'Worth a lot of money to the right people.' Winked, as though Derek knew what the hell he was talking about. 'What's up with your face? You got paternal instincts?' He pointed to the girl. 'You can have a go if you like. I won't tell.' Started to laugh. 'She won't fucking tell, that's for sure.'

'I know her,' he said. Shit. He hadn't meant to say that. It had slipped out. He had to keep schtum.

'What do you mean, you know her?' Dr Doolittle said, still grinning, though the amusement was gone from his eyes.

Keep your mouth shut, Derek, he counselled himself. *That ain't your daughter lying there.* But it was as if, after all the grubby, clandestine transactions he had been a party to and profited from, and all the young girls of Tinesha's age and younger he had betrayed by allowing Gera to traffick them through the club, his

273

conscience finally spoke for him, forcing the truth out of his treacherous, lying mouth. 'She's a porn actress. Works for my boss.'

For God's sake! Why couldn't he have just kept that to himself? Honesty was overrated.

'Oh,' Dr Doolittle said hesitantly; eyeing him suspiciously. 'Well, I'm afraid this isn't going to go well for you, then.'

CHAPTER 60

Ramsgate, seafront B&B, 28 January

She was smiling. She was chatty. She was all, 'Morning, gorgeous. How are you feeling? Let's do it again before breakfast.' She was nothing short of wonderful. But as van den Bergen stood under a hot shower, washing the scent of his young lover from his tired body, he had never felt lower.

Rinsing the suds from under his foreskin, he considered the absence of moral rectitude in his having slept with somebody else's girlfriend, who was not only currently his employee – making their union an utter abuse of his power – but who was some twenty years his junior.

'Goddamn it!' He punched the tiled wall. Banged his head against his fist. 'What have I done? I'm such an idiot. I've ruined everything.'

'Are you all right?' George asked.

Through the steamy shower cubicle, he could see she was poking her head into the cramped hotel bathroom. Though they had spent the last twelve hours either making love or merely lying naked in each other's arms, talking, he felt suddenly exposed. He covered his penis with his hands.

'I'll be out in a minute,' he said.

Jesus. When he had already been a father at twenty-two, George would have been celebrating her second birthday. A toddler. A baby, really. It was preposterous. He looked down at the white hair on his chest and navel that ran all the way down to his saggy old bollocks. The skin around his knees starting to wrinkle. The firmness that his glutes had once enjoyed, now on the wane, giving way to a sorry, skinny pair of hairy buttocks that no beautiful young girl should ever see, let alone entertain as they bounced up and down between her firm, strong thighs.

His battered heart was heavy. His head sluggish. He felt as though he was maybe suffering from lead poisoning or something of that ilk. Wondered briefly if the water supply at work had been contaminated, perhaps by terrorists. It was always a possibility. He felt as woebegone as ever. And the spectre of his dead father seemed no less domineering in his mental landscape today, reminding him of his own mortality and fallibility, destroying any post-coital happiness he may have temporarily enjoyed overnight. He would have to let George down gently. It was for the best. He would only infect her life with sadness and discord and, ultimately, death.

Over breakfast, he had no appetite for the traditional English menu.

'Aren't you eating that sausage?' George asked, talking with her mouth full and already half way through her own enormous greasy feast. Notably, two fried eggs sat on their own on a side plate, which she ate with clean cutlery. She had given the cook specific instructions on how to prepare the eggs, although van den Bergen knew she could barely make a cup of coffee herself. On her main plate, she had made a dam for her beans using two fried potato croquets that she informed him were hash browns. The beans were not allowed to touch anything else. It took her five minutes to cut every piece of fat from her bacon rashers, which she put on a napkin. She rejected her fried tomato, explaining that it was sloppy, messy food and therefore not clean. But everything else on the table seemed to pass muster. 'This is glorious, man. I could eat a scabby horse after last night.' She grinned, radiant even with a piece of toast hanging out the corner of her mouth. 'We burned some calories, didn't we?'

He nodded. Wanted to stroke her face. Touch her hair. Settled for holding her left hand as she snatched up his uneaten sausage with her right. Bit into it.

'I can see you're not going to eat this and I don't mind having it because the beans ain't touching it. And you get top marks for following the bean etiquette. But you got to eat, Paul. You're too skinny at the moment, man. I mean, you're well fit for an old guy, but you know. You were lucky I didn't break you last night. So, you're going to need to keep your energy up if you're going to be with me because...' She started to whisper behind her hand in what was almost a childish cartoon gesture. He had rarely seen this playful, relaxed side to her. 'You give me the proper lady-horn. I'm so wet, I'm gonna need to be wearing incontinence knickers around you.'

Laughing loud enough to make the other diners look over to see what the commotion was about, she was giddy like a young schoolgirl.

Van den Bergen looked at her quizzically. 'If you're going to be with me?' he asked. 'What do you mean?'

Her incandescent expression of enthusiasm dimmed some-what. 'Our affair. We're lovers now, right? This wasn't just a booty call for me, Paul.' She drained her coffee cup. Clasped his hand again. Her skin was warm and soft. Beyond the smell of frying that permeated the hotel dining room, he could detect the residue of coconut shower gel coming from her arms. 'You know how I feel about you, don't you?'

'Yes.'

He nodded and made an effort to smile. Staring out the window, the squall of the grey-brown North Sea echoed the turmoil of conflicting emotions within him. His heart felt like it might quake and collapse under the strain. Did he love George?

277

She was looking at him for a response. Though she had not said the words outright – I love you – he knew she meant them and now she wanted him to reciprocate, he could see. Soulful brown eyes seeking the truth that lay behind the rationed, careful words of her older, clandestine paramour. Of course he loved her. He had fallen head over heels for this captivating, brilliant young woman pretty much as soon as they had met. She was his dahlia in full bloom. Perfect. Multi-faceted. Vibrant. But to harbour such desires for a girl who was old enough to be his daughter had felt wrong then, as it felt wrong now, even after their heady night of passion. Perhaps she had ruined him, after all.

'I'm not good enough for you,' he said, sipping hot coffee, watching a ferry chug slowly towards the horizon, growing smaller with every blink.

'Bullshit.' She slammed her coffee cup onto the saucer and wiped her mouth with the napkin. 'God, I've eaten too much now.' Unbuttoned her jeans. Puffed out her cheeks. Looked around the dated Victoriana dining room. 'This flowery wallpaper is hideous. Reminds me of my grandma's from when I was a kid. We've got to get out of here.' Checked her phone. Read a message, scrolling down on her screen with delicate fingers that had conquered every inch of van den Bergen within the last twelve hours, inside and out. 'London-bound, right? That Rob said the dead men may have been refugees that got into trouble with gangs. My Aunty Sharon is taking us to meet a woman who knows everything about everyone worth knowing anything about. She's an elder at one of the big gospel churches and works in an outreach centre for refugees.'

'There are eight or nine million people living in London,' van den Bergen said. 'What makes you think we can find out anything useful about three illegal immigrants?'

George winked. Stood up. Came round to his side of the table and kissed the top of his head. 'Wheels within wheels. Some things the police can't find out. But I can.'

Despite his best intentions, he found himself encircling her waist with his arms, pulling her to him. Stroking the contours of her womanly shape. She felt warm and reassuring, standing there. He knew the elderly diners were watching them; passing judgement on the nature of the relationship between this middle-aged white man and this young mixed race woman. But he didn't care. *You've cuckolded Karelse*, his conscience berated him. *Stop touching her. You must not kiss her. Do the honourable thing, for Christ's sake. Let her go.* But he found there in that dining room, drinking in the scent of her clean clothes and toiletries and her skin beneath them, he couldn't.

'What time's check-out?' he asked.

'Eleven,' she said.

'Then we've got forty minutes.'

CHAPTER 61

Somewhere in Kent, a field, later

Overhead the silver sky was punctuated by swathes of rain clouds, scudding by like hulking grey battleships on a drab sea. In his peripheral vision, Derek saw naked poplar trees bending in the wind, as though they were upturned brooms sweeping the heavens. He had never had such profound thoughts before. Maybe this was what actually happened before you died, rather than a mere replay of your life in your mind's eye.

What had his life even amounted to?

Sweet FA: a disastrous romance with Sharon Williams-May – the only woman he had ever really loved. A beautiful daughter. Yes, Tinesha was the sole good thing in his life and yet, even now, he had put her safety in jeopardy because of his greed.

How the hell had it come to this?

His parents had wanted him to join the Royal Air Force as a cadet. Instead, he had worked as a roadie for a soul band in the eighties, ending up working in shitty Soho bars and pubs once his back had gone, eventually landing a 'career' as the low-life manager of a titty bar. Now, he was lying with the sharp woody stalks of last year's wheat crop sticking into his back. In a field. In an area of outstanding natural beauty. In the middle of Kent. And the stalks weren't even the worst of it, because he couldn't feel them. He couldn't feel anything.

He was going to die.

Derek waited. Still watching the clouds. He hoped it wouldn't hurt more than the actual act of getting stabbed repeatedly and strangled.

He was definitely going to die, now.

It started to spit with rain; the kind that was so cold, it felt like needles puncturing your skin. Derek opened his mouth to let the moisture in, though just parting his lips drained him of all the energy he could muster. For another eon or possibly only a minute (for time runs differently in the shadow of death) he lay, motionless. Then, it occurred to him that could actually feel the rain. After a long while, or it could have been but moments, he realised that he was hurting all over. In fact, he was in agony.

'H.' He tried to make a sound but could only manage a shallow exhalation. The beginnings of a word. Did he imagine that he could open and close his right hand?

His throat was too dry. The sound would not come. Flickering movement in his fingers was not an indication that he was any less of a dead man than before the rain started to fall. But somehow, from a place within him that Derek de Falco had not hitherto been aware was there, he found a certain resolve. Courage, even. And he started to roll himself over.

This barren, frost-hard field in the rolling, bucolic Garden of England seemed to him a dream. A bad dream, with the whine of a high speed train a tantalisingly, potentially navigable distance away, carried to him on the wind. Eurostar, plummeting through the British countryside, carrying mainly business travellers and ordinary people celebrating big birthdays and milestone anniversaries from the cat-shit exoticism of Paris into the grubby bustle of London, with its Maccy D wrappers and ubiquitous Starbucks. Too skint to do the Orient Express, but a two-star mini-break, staying in the crappiest of the arrondissements, had done nicely. Every single one of those bastards was unaware that a middle-aged man in ripped, brown Farah slacks with one missing loafer and a blood-stained shirt lay dying some two hundred feet away.

The outlook was bleak to say the least. But somehow, Derek dragged his anaemic, plundered body a few metres. He had to get to a phone. Somehow attract attention to his plight and speak to Sharon. Tell the police everything he knew and all that had befallen him.

Dr Doolittle had turned out not to be a doctor at all. He was just some murderous little turd; a lowly pawn, mopping up blood and shit for an altogether more important piece on the chess board. Derek had asked too many questions and found himself checkmated, by means of what looked like a boning knife in the belly. And the shoulder. And the leg. And the chest. If his death – for he was certain he would die of exposure now, if nothing else – was written up in one of the red-top newspapers, they would definitely use the words, 'frenzied attack'.

Those hands that Tony the driver possessed, hidden inside the ridiculous leather gloves that had never in a month of Sundays come from a normal shop… Those hands had, indeed, turned out to be killer's hands, which had closed around his throat like unforgiving vices. Stabbed and strangled in a derelict industrial estate in the middle of nowhere. Nice move, Uncle Giuseppe. The girl on the gurney should count herself lucky. At least she was unconscious.

In the end, the only act of self-preservation available to Derek de Falco had been to play dead, which he had managed with sufficient aplomb as to have been driven out to this field and dumped.

In the sputtering imagination of a dying man, he saw his beautiful girl, Tinesha. Surely, if he did nothing else in this wasted life, he had to get to her. Had to warn her that she might be in danger because of her old dad's stupid, flapping mouth. Gleaned some strength from this need.

'Help!' he cried. Weak voice. Bruised, constricted throat.

Vomited with the effort. Had he been hit over the head as well? He hadn't the energy to lift his hand to check for blood on his scalp.

Just crawl, Derek, Sharon said. *You ain't nothing but a fucking cockroach anyways. So, do what you do best and crawl.* A hallucinatory hologram of Sharon, standing in that field of dead wheat stalks. Admonishing him, arms folded, though she was tucked up and hopefully safe in the club, grappling with empty barrels of bitter and disrespectful punters.

Perhaps he had advanced fifty feet. Perhaps five. It was hard to tell with the jaws of pain closing around him. Then, a dog barked in the distance and scampered closer, closer until it was sniffing this unexpected lump of meat in the field. Barking like a nutter. Deafening noise. It licked his wounds with a warm, wet tongue. Snuffling around his crotch. Cocking its leg and peeing on the gaping slash that formed a grim smile in his abdomen. Where was its owner?

A whistle some way off. The dog bounded away. Derek remained undiscovered.

In time, as the storm clouds rolled in, and the light began to fail in earnest, he made it, against every odd, to the train track. Now, somebody would definitely find him. People walked their dogs along train tracks, didn't they? And perhaps the Eurostar driver would see him in those powerful headlights. It was still light enough.

Telling Sharon would be the last thing he did. God was keeping him alive for this purpose and this purpose only, he realised. A sort of redemption.

Overhearing the conversation between Tony and Dr Doolittle, as they had driven him to the field, he now knew everything. The police in Britain were trying to solve the serial murder of illegal immigrants. The police in Holland were on the hunt for a surgeon with an interest in satanic ritual killing. Now he, Derek de Falco, knew the name of that perpetrator. His attackers had said it in

283

the car. He would remember it as long as there was breath in his body, so that he could tell it to Sharon. Then, he could die with a clear conscience.

But no ambling dog-walkers came. A magpie alighted on him and pecked at his leg, then flew off. Presently, the rumble in the earth beneath him said the train was coming, causing rabbits to scatter from their burrows beneath the tracks. Sound followed the reverberations, and finally the two pinpoints of strong light heralded the train's approach proper.

Stand up, Derek. Let the driver see you.

With the last of his breath, a blood-soaked Derek scrambled to his feet and waved his arms to and fro.

Please see me. Please stop.

The driver of the Eurostar, bound for St Pancras, did see what looked like a zombie, covered in blood, standing on the tracks, waving its arms. He balked. Sounded the horn. Slammed on the brakes. And came to a stop almost a quarter of a mile beyond the place where Derek had stood. Derek's body travelled on the front of the train, glued to it by forward momentum alone, for almost half of that distance before being flung like a savaged rabbit into the sidings. By the time the driver found him in the driving rain, he was conclusively, finally, very dead.

CHAPTER 62

Kent, on a train, then Amsterdam, mortuary, later

'This is the 11.05 Southeastern high-speed rail service from Ramsgate to St Pancras…' came the man's voice over the Tannoy. He spoke with an estuary twang that reminded George she was still far from the comfortable home turf of South East London, though they were, at least, on their way.

She stretched out and yawned. Scratched her crotch surreptitiously and readjusted the seam of her jeans. Sipped from the still-hot latte she had bought at the station. So far, so good.

Except the train slowed to a halt and it transpired that the man had not finished his announcement.

'Hello ladies and gentlemen. I'm sorry to announce that due to an earlier…er…fatality on the line involving the Eurostar, there will be a delay to this service. On behalf of Southeastern Rail, I'd like to—'

'Shit! Typical! The one time when we're over here together and we're on a bloody time limit!' George said, talking over the bad news. She turned to van den Bergen. Studied his face. 'You're quiet.'

His smile gave nothing away. 'Just tired.'

She could almost see turmoil like latent heat coming off his skin. Perhaps now was not the time to probe. He had seemed happy enough only half an hour ago when he had been inside her. George had her own demons to wrestle with – the most pressing of which was the spectre of a meet with Letitia the Dragon later that evening.

Letitia. With her fat neck and her 'Leroy this and Leroy that' and how it was all George's fault that Letitia had had to move to that shithole, three-bed box in Ashford, losing her family and her nice little fiddle at work. Letitia had a selective memory. She chose only to remember George as that grassing little cow who sold her mum up the fucking swanny. Convenient that Letitia forgot her own divisive role in all that had come to pass.

The train shunted forwards and began to pick up speed. On George's phone were three missed calls from Ad and a text, saying he would do anything to make her happy. This was the really onerous demon with which she must inevitably grapple, but he would keep for now.

She was just about to Google the woman Sharon was planning on introducing them to, when van den Bergen's phone rang.

He frowned at the screen. Looked askance at her. Answered, 'Van den Bergen. Speak!'

Though the phone was pressed to his ear, on the other end of the line, George could hear the high-pitched voice of a woman, clearly bawling him out.

'Marianne! Marianne, calm down!' he said, blinking rapidly. 'Take a deep breath. Tell me again. Slowly. Elvis and Leeuwenhoek are doing *what*?'

'They're arresting Strietman!' Marianne de Koninck said. 'For God's sake, van den Bergen. Call your dogs off. This is nonsense!'

On the other end of the phone, van den Bergen was explaining in a placatory tone that he had not ordered the arrest – in fact, that he had ordered the opposite; that he was sure it was some kind of mix-up.

She was tempted to cut him off in temper, but knew it was prudent to keep an ally on the line. But she wasn't really listening to the chief inspector's explanation. The scene before her was too absurd. The young detective Leeuwenhoek was reading Strietman his rights while Elvis, van den Bergen's normally unassuming sidekick, had *her* unassuming sidekick bent over the cadaver of an elderly man, who had died from suspected carbon monoxide poisoning.

'Jesus! You pair of baboons. You're contaminating this man's body!' she shouted at the two detectives, trying to pull Elvis off Strietman.

'Help me, Marianne!' Strietman said, panic in his eyes. 'Call the police!'

'We are the police,' Leeuwenhoek said. Smug prat was grinning. 'And as I said, just in case you missed it, I'm arresting you, Daan Strietman, for the murders of Magool Osman, Linda Lepiks and an as yet-unidentified man.'

Strietman wrestled in Elvis' grasp, like bait trying to wriggle free of the hook on the end of a fishing line. 'Then, I want a solicitor. Immediately!' Strietman looked pleadingly at Marianne. 'This is ridiculous. Please. You've got to get them to stop. Find me some legal representation, for Christ's sake!'

Marianne tugged at the sleeve of Elvis' leather jacket. Thought if she used his real name instead of the undignified moniker van den Bergen had saddled him with, he might pay her words heed. 'Leave him, Dirk! You know he can't possibly have murdered those people.' But her impassioned pleas seemed to hit the side of Elvis' hirsute face and slide off, unanswered.

She contemplated threatening the two policemen with the weight of the Ministry for Security and Justice. Although they were all governed from on high by the same authorities, when all was said and done, so that wouldn't work. Wondering how to play this, she scrutinised Strietman's unremarkable form, in his baggy scrubs and rubber shoes. Considered his soft-featured face and propensity to crack inappropriate jokes. How unlikely it appeared to be that this man who had worked under her for years would be a murderer. And yet, she realised she was making these assumptions of his innocence on the basis of what she knew of Strietman; the professional, easy-going colleague, whom she spent most of the working week with. But what was he like in his own time? How much did she really know about this man? Torn, she fell silent. Physically distanced herself from her number two, cutting van den Bergen off on the other end of her phone. Propping the worktop, wearing a concerned, disapproving expression but feeling like this was some sort of betrayal that she could not help but commit.

Eventually, when the handcuffs were securely fastened and Strietman's arms had been yanked up high against his back, Elvis looked her in the eye apologetically.

'It's out of my hands,' he said, his mouth arcing downwards with something that resembled regret, or at least uncertainty. 'We've got evidence linking him to another prime suspect and the Valeriusstraat crime scene. The errors in his autopsy look like an obstruction of justice. Hasselblad gave the order.'

'Van den Bergen said Valeriusstraat was a hoax!' Strietman yelled, twisting himself around to face his captor. 'Who the hell am I supposed to have been in cahoots with? I'm innocent!'

Leeuwenhoek unzipped his anorak. A florid rash spattered up his neck. His cheeks were shiny and red. Smiling like a Roman emperor about to lead a victory parade.

'Innocent? We know what you've done, you animal, and soon the whole world is going to know about you and your sidekick.'

CHAPTER 63

South East London, later

'When was the last time you went to church?' Dorothea Caines asked, occupying her plastic chair in the Kingdom of Heaven Church Community Hall in a way that said she ruled that draughty, damp space by divine right.

She was the sort of elder that made George itchy. A judgemental type in a home-sewn floral dress, full of nostalgic stories of the old country, as though she had personally stepped down the gangplank of the SS *Windrush*, along with her forefathers. Opining at every given opportunity in that loud, admonishing voice of hers, so that everyone could hear what she had to say; right along the Old Kent Road, from the fringes of Elephant to well beyond the boundaries of New Cross. She was always the woman the papers contacted for a sound-bite. Professionally mourning the loss of scores of young boys over the years, beaten/stabbed/shot on the streets of Peckham/Catford/Deptford and how it was the fault of the government/the police/the inequalities in society. Those boys, with their premature homecomings into the arms of sweet Jesus Christ the Saviour. She had a rousing way with words and put the pastor to shame, apparently. But Aunty Sharon had let slip that Dorothea Caines, possessor of the world's most outdated wet-look hair helmet, had been born in the Borough of

Lewisham in 1959 to borderline middle-class parents who were both medical professionals and was full of home-sewn legendary bullshit. Those stories weren't hers at all. And that dress was actually from Debenhams, not the product of her own industrious hands. Still, she was a font of wisdom, all right. Apparently.

'I don't go to church,' George said, absently watching swaggering teenaged boys, almost certainly excluded from school since they were here and not there, strutting around the hall in their baggy, low-rise trousers and Nikes. Carrying trays of fairy cakes and sandwiches for the old ladies in their Sunday best wigs and old men in button-down cardigans and tailored gabardine trousers. It was a heart-warming sight. The pensioners were sitting at long trestle tables, evidently having a fantastic time. It was somebody called Iris' eightieth birthday, judging by the cake. Maybe Dorothea Caines wasn't as bad as Aunty Sharon let on. 'Chief Inspector van den Bergen and I are here to find out about the deaths of these men.' She showed Dorothea the news clippings from weeks ago, where two African men had been found at the docks, and then, clippings from the subsequent discovery of the man in Ramsgate.

Tut. Tut. Tut. Dorothea Caines shook her head and sucked her teeth. Folded slender hands on her lap like a prim school teacher.

'You should give more thought to nurturing the spiritual side of you, young lady. Your Aunty Sharon, here, tells me you're quite a clever girl.'

'She is,' Sharon said, staring with unblinking eyes at van den Bergen's white hair, whilst gnawing at the icing on a fairy cake she had liberated from Iris' party buffet.

'But there ain't nobody cleverer than the Lord,' Dorothea said. 'He sees all. All.' She nodded slowly, as though she were imparting special wisdom.

George ran her fingers up and down the soft suede of her sheepskin coat, remembering tedious trips to church with Letitia, when she had been small. Having her hair brutally brushed out by Grandma beforehand and tied up into tight little bunches.

Always some face-wiping exercise involving spit and a hanky. Pure white knee socks that dug into the backs of her knees. Patent leather shoes that had no give to them. She had been forced to join in singing, though she couldn't hold a single note.

'Good. Good,' George said. 'Well, if the Lord sees all, can you ask him if he saw who killed these men?'

Aunty Sharon smirking behind her cake.

Pursed lips on Dorothea Caines, now. Not happy with the glib retort of this upstart seated before her. She looked down at the clippings. Shook her head. 'Nah.'

Van den Bergen, who looked ludicrously too long in the limb for those silly plastic chairs, leaned forwards. Clasped his hands together and peered at the elder over his glasses for some time before he spoke, as though choosing his words carefully. 'There's a possibility these men had been hiding in London before they were found dead,' he said, adding, 'Ma'am' as an afterthought.

'London's a big place,' Dorothea said.

'We need to catch this killer before he takes another member of your community.'

Dorothea looked at the clippings once more. 'If they're African immigrants, they ain't any members of *my* community,' she said. 'Maybe you wanna check the church down the way. Full of folks from Sierra Leone and that. They got their own way of doing things.'

Van den Bergen looked confused.

'Come on, Dot,' Aunty Sharon said, sweeping crumbs from her skirt onto the scarred parquet floor of the hall. 'I know there's gossip been going round about these dead fellers.'

'I can't tell you what I don't know.'

'How about I get my boss to make a charity donation for your thing?' Sharon examined her broken fingernail without looking up at Dorothea.

'Immoral earnings, Sharon. Why would I accept proceeds from Sodom and Gomorrah to do the Lord's work?'

'Because you're always on the tap, and my boss is worth a mint? I have the feeling he might find a couple of grand down one of the girl's thongs, if I ask him nicely. That might extend your outreach to some cake and sarnies that ain't actually stale. Know what I mean?'

Dorothea Caines closed her eyes in a begrudging show of consent. Turned to George, as though van den Bergen was not there. 'This all in strictest confidence, right? Nothing I tell you I'd put my name to.'

George nodded. It was like somebody had put fresh batteries into Dorothea Caines, then.

'Right, so, my Jeffrey done some legal work for a lad on Pepys Estate in Deptford, right? He specialises in immigration and criminal law, my Jeffrey.' The sudden animation in her stony face told George this woman liked nothing better than a good bit of gossip to go with the good Lord's gospel. 'So, this lad – I ain't naming names, but it was Slow Clyde Johnson, the one who got accused of ram-raiding B&Q with his mum's Nissan – this lad was saying there was these African guys ran away from a fishing trawler in Dover. They'd been abducted as slave labour, apparently, by some people traffickers in the DRC, right? Proper international intrigue. Came to the Pepys, thin like sticks and on their last legs. They'd been used as punch bags for a month or two, by the looks. And they was staying with some ropey Ghanaian pusher in one of the flats, there.' She was really getting into the swing, now. Folding her arms across her chest, squeezing minty words out in rapid succession like toothpaste from a tube. 'So, Slow Clyde is on probation for some other misdemeanour, like cussing a copper out or something. You know? And he's round the pusher's, buying a bag of weed and meets these fishermen. Tells them about my Jeffrey and how he can help them seek asylum and make it all legit. But it gets out, right? You know? And then, consequentially, these Italians are asking around for the boys. Some grassing rarseclart starts mouthing off for money. Next minute, there's

292

proper hot pursuit through the estate. Guns was fired, Lord protect us, although I couldn't say I seen it with my own eyes. Obviously, Deptford being outside my realm of influence and all. That's the last I heard of them, until we seen this in the papers.'

Van den Bergen cleared his throat. 'Did you not think to tell the police before, Mrs Caines?'

Dorothea looked him up and down. Laughed heartily. 'I do the Lord's work, here, Mr Dutch Thing. But *I* ain't ready to die on the cross for my sins.'

CHAPTER 64

Amsterdam, police headquarters holding cell, later

In his cell, Ahlers had been working hard. He ignored the commotion next door, when they brought somebody new in, although he could hear loud protestations from a man who, judging by his well-spoken voice, was not your average criminal. Perhaps under other circumstances, he would have stood by the door and tried to eavesdrop on the heated exchange between this new inmate and the detectives. But today, he was busy.

'Unless you give up the whereabouts of Noor's baby and your accomplices, Ruud, you're going away for a long time,' his solicitor had said, looking decidedly less slick than he had on previous visits. 'The Chinese girl with the ectopic pregnancy whom you performed an abortion on has died from MRSA. You're culpable for her death too. I don't think I could even get involuntary manslaughter for you.'

'I've told you,' Ruud had said, surreptitiously running his hands over his stomach; probing for signs that he had begun to shed weight with the appalling food they were giving him. He hadn't. 'If I give them the full story and rat out whom I've worked with, I'm dead anyway.'

Nothing had changed. As far as he knew, he was still prime

suspect for three, perhaps now four murders. Not good. It was fortuitous that the police seemed so preoccupied with this new inmate. And he hadn't seen the surly bastard of a giant for a couple of days. So, his handiwork in his cell had gone unnoticed.

Bit by bit, he had ripped his sheet into long strips, making cuts in the fabric initially by gnawing at the cotton using only his sharp incisors. His gums had now begun to bleed and were sore as hell. He had never paid much attention to the upkeep of his dental hygiene, it was true. But it had worked, at least, and his oral wellbeing was the last thing on his mind.

Knotting the pieces was easy. His father had been a keen sailor and had taught him the very strongest knots, which he had learned to tie with the dedication and precision of a small boy who admired his father more than any other human being on earth. The moot point was whether his home-made rope would take his weight.

'Only one way to try,' he said.

Fashioning the noose was tricky, with all those knotted sections, but he managed that too. Then, tying one end of the rope to the bars on the window, he moved the bed beneath the window itself. Put the noose around his neck. Got the tension just right. Time to jump.

Obviously, he cried a great deal, as he teetered on the edge of the bed. He didn't really want to bring his shoddy, sordid, insignificant life to an end like this at all. Though he grappled with the monster inside, who made him do the bad things, he had always been a survivor in the face of shocking odds. In fact, even despite his fall from grace, there was much about his life that he found great enjoyment in. But he appreciated that, although the monster could do time, Ruud Ahlers, the chubby doctor who felt remorse and whose good intentions underpinned some of the shittier things he had done, was not strong enough as a person to go to prison for even a year. And he would never, ever be safe from the Italians, The Duke and The Butcher. Their reach extended through thick prison walls, he knew.

No more internal debate. In many ways, as karmic payback for what he had done to all those vulnerable people, he deserved this. Yes. The monster had not won, after all.

'Get on with it, you fucking idiot,' he told himself.

Then, he jumped.

CHAPTER 65

Ashford, Kent, later

'So you think you can say jump and I say how high? Is that how you think this rolls?' Letitia said, stirring her Jack Daniel's and Coke too quickly so that droplets of drink flew onto the table, making George cringe.

She stared at her mother. Noticed how she had gone big like Aunty Sharon. Really big. Though she was still as glamorous as ever in the batwing sequinned number, with her face full of war paint and a caramel blonde weave that must have set her back hundreds. Fun-fur slung over the back of the chair. Ghettofabulous in The County Hotel. Ashford Wetherspoons' answer to Gloria Gaynor. She stuck out like a sore thumb topped by an impressive diamanté-studded nail extension.

'You were the one wanted to see me, remember?' George said, wondering how van den Bergen was doing in the nearby café. Wanting to wipe up the sticky Coke spillage.

'Yeah, but this ain't no time of day to be meeting and having a mother-daughter heart to heart,' she said, slurping her drink noisily through a straw. Fuchsia lipstick on the black plastic and her teeth. 'I'm on lates, innit? This my bedtime, nowadays. I got myself a career.'

Stifling the urge to throw the drink in Letitia's face, George shut her down with silence. Drank her coffee. Considered her words.

'What do you want, Letitia?'

'I don't want nothing off you, cheeky bitch.'

Oh, yes. Her mother was all feisty indignation now, with her pouting lips and head bobbing from side to side. Got her back up good and proper, though George felt certain there would be an ask for money somewhere along the line. Mum tax.

Call her bluff.

Rising out of her seat, George drained her coffee and set the cup back down – a metaphorical full stop to the proceedings. She knew this reluctant rendezvous had been a mistake.

'Sit down for Christ's sakes.'

'Since when did you tell me what to do?' George said. 'Unless you hadn't noticed, I'm a grown adult.'

Letitia sucked at her JD and Coke. 'You so fucking uptight, these days. That how living my sister working out for you? You found some sort of domestic bliss with your old Aunty Sharon cos she scrubs her floors more than I ever did? Nice. You must have been one of them alien kids swapped at birth, like a changing or something, cos I never understood how you ended up mine.'

'Changeling. It's a bloody changeling. And don't bring Aunty Sharon into this,' George said, looking down at this woman who had raised her. Once, she had sought comfort in those substantial arms. Luxuriated in the familiar motherly scent of rose water during the week or, at weekends, her market stall perfume. Like Calvin Klein's Eternity but not quite. Now Letitia just felt like a mother but not quite. 'Look, I've got a plane to catch. I'm living in Amsterdam at the moment. So, whatever you've got to say, spit it out or…or just stop wasting my time.'

'I'm getting married,' Letitia said. 'Me and Leroy. We getting married.'

George looked her mother in the eye but had been rendered speechless. Opened and closed her mouth. Mommie Dearest was going to be Mrs Leroy, enthusiastic step-mother to her two step-Leroys. Happy new families, where her old family had failed. George felt like a small girl, being pushed out of the number one spot, though she was now a woman. Realised she had jettisoned their relationship a long, long time ago. But as a child, she and Letitia had been a team of two. They had seen George's father only infrequently, when he was back in the country. Letitia had sheltered her small daughter from the slings and arrows of poverty and semi-abandonment. *Best Mum in the World* mug said it was so. Food on the table. Help with her homework. Pot plants on the kitchen windowsill. Even a garden, once they had moved from the high rise to the house. Sweet, before it had all turned sour and something had curdled within Letitia – coincidentally at the time George had started to blossom in her final years of junior school and the flower of Letitia's youth had begun to fade in earnest. Daddy Dearest, off the scene for good.

'Congratulations. I'm glad you've found happiness.' The words caught in George's throat.

'Ta.' Letitia drained her drink. 'Sharon says you still with that Dutch boy. How's that working out for you?'

George shrugged noncommittally.

Unexpectedly, Letitia reached out and squeezed her shoulder. 'You buy me another drink, I'll impart you with some motherly fucking wisdom, right?' She held her empty glass out.

Though it was freezing, they sat in the beer garden, smoking. Letitia looking like a giant mountain lion in her fun-fur, with that mane of hair. George, feeling old and grey. The wine helped a little. She could feel the tension seeping out of her shoulders.

Letitia the Dragon sucked hard on her cigarette. Breathed blue-yellow smoke out of her nostrils.

'I ain't never seen you looking so pissed off in years,' she told George.

'That's because you haven't seen me in years.'

'Save the attitude for someone who gives a shit. It's the boy. I can see it in your eyes.' She flicked her ash onto the ground. Tap, tap with shining nails too long and slender for her short, fat fingers.

Aligning her lighter perfectly with the edge of her cigarette packet, George scoffed. 'You think because you're getting married that you're suddenly qualified as an agony aunt, sniffing out the broken hearted so you can dispense advice like paracetamol? I am not gonna discuss my relationship with you.'

'Sharon told me you're having a thing on the side with that detective.'

'Fuck you.' George stared into her already depleted wine glass. Could feel the heat in her cheeks.

'Listen,' Letitia said, lighting a new cigarette off the glowing end of her spent one. 'Let me tell you a story about me and your father, right?' Moved a strand of blonde hair carefully out of her eye. 'I loved your dad in the beginning, yeah? Even though there wasn't no clouds bashing together or forked lightning or none of that shit. Me and him got it together one rainy Saturday, after a night at the Brixton Academy. Simple as. Nothing celestial. You know the story, don't you?'

George nodded.

'Anyway, I never thought it would amount to fuck all, him being a university dickhead and all. He was always meant to be just a one night stand. Except he wasn't. And then very quickly, you came along by accident. But you know, me and your dads weren't never gonna find happiness together, because we wasn't right for each other. We fought like cat and dog. The chemistry was all wrong. I ignored my gut feelings.' She chuckled and hugged her fun-fur tight around her. 'We fancied each other at first – man, he was fine looking. And he loved you. But he had a temper on him, the sulky bastard.'

George raised an eyebrow. '*He* had a temper on him?'

Letitia ignored her. 'We just couldn't get along, and this thing we'd committed to was tearing us both apart on the inside.

Splitting was the most sensible thing we ever did.' She looked wistfully up at the back wall of the pub. Her breath steamed on the cold air even without cigarette smoke in her lungs. 'Then, he fucks off and marries that tart from Spain, of course, and that's the last we seen of him.' She frowned. Cleared her throat and shook her head, as though trying to rid herself of painful memories. 'But still, I don't regret cutting him loose.' She grabbed George by the chin and made her meet her uncomfortably direct gaze. 'And you shouldn't neither with Dutch boy. If it ain't working, you ain't doing either of yous any favours. Life's too short, love. And you don't know what good things are round the corner. Especially not you, with your smart future all ahead of you.'

George wrenched her chin from Letitia's grip. Contemplated in silence what might lie just around the corner from her and Ad.

'I am proud, you know. I keep up with what you doing through your aunty.'

A tear forced its way out of George's left eye and began a slow, solitary journey down the side of her face. But she didn't want Letitia to see any emotion, so she acted like it wasn't there. Headed back inside. Busying her mother with movement and the transfer of her chattels from the weather-beaten beer garden table to a spot where they were now surrounded by pensioners coming in for an early dinner. Curry Club aficionados at The County Hotel.

'You finished?' George asked, once she was certain that her voice would be even and strong.

'I didn't think you'd want to come to the—'

'No. Don't bother inviting me. I can't afford an extra flight back at the moment.'

'Oh.' Letitia looked into her drink. Crestfallen.

Here it was. George could feel it coming.

'That's a shame. Cos what with the wedding plans and all costing so fucking much, I wondered if you could—'

'What? Lend you some cash?' She swallowed down, along with

301

the dregs of her warm chardonnay, memories of her time in prison, passing empty days in her ill-fitting tracksuit, listening to the anguished wailing of her fellow inmates while she curled up into a tight ball on her thin mattress in an empty, godforsaken cell; her time as one of the girls, running the gauntlet in hi-tops through the estate with the police on their heels. All of it down to Letitia. Selling her own daughter too cheaply, using Taiwanese handbags and her own freedom as the currency. Even after all these years, the skin was still raw beneath the barely formed scab. 'You don't fucking change,' she said.

Letitia opened her mouth to come back, no doubt, with some wise-ass remark. Paused abruptly, staring at something or somebody over George's shoulder. Several of the other drinkers in that hackneyed, homogenous pub interior were also staring.

Turning around, George saw van den Bergen, eye-catching at six feet five with that shock of white hair, stalking across the pub with an urgency that befitted the harried expression on his face.

'What's wrong?' she asked him.

He spoke rapidly in Dutch. 'We've got to go. Get on an earlier flight if we can.'

Letitia was out of her seat.

'Listen, Mr Jolly Green Giant, chatting foreign like I ain't even—'

'Shut it, Letitia,' George said. Grabbed van den Bergen's arm. 'What? What is it?'

He picked her coat off the back of her chair and held it in readiness for their departure. 'I got a call off Elvis. There's been another in Amsterdam. A child, this time.'

CHAPTER 66

Cambodia, 1992

The young prostitute looked terrified. Naked, bound and gagged, now, she wriggled in her seat. Making the muffled sounds of a desperate woman, scraping the chair along the bare floor as best she could. Though, should anyone in the neighbouring rooms be trying to eavesdrop, the sound would undoubtedly be camouflaged by the buzz of mopeds and bells ringing frantically, as men cycled their tuk-tuks on the bustling street below.

Wide-eyed, Veronica could see their captive was appealing to her, woman-to-woman, to be freed.

'Now, I'm going to stop, and I want to watch you strangle her,' Silas said, withdrawing his still-erect penis. He started to masturbate instead. Moved to the prostitute to caress the scarred stump of her right leg. Kicked her crude prosthetic limb out of the way.

'You want me to *what*? What the hell are you saying, Silas?' Veronica asked, rolling onto her back, panting. Beneath her, the grubby bed was damp with their sweat. Even with the shutters half closed, the humidity and heat were stifling. Flies throwing themselves against the badly distempered walls, believing that that way lay the sun. Above her, the ceiling fan made a half-hearted attempt at circulating the foetid air. 'It's too hot for this.' She wriggled around to change her orientation on the wet bed.

Tried to grab his elbow and pull him to her but he was beyond her reach. 'Just come back here and finish me off. Stop messing around.'

'I'm not messing around. I want you to choke the life out of her. Believe me, it's the best high you'll ever experience, my darling. I want to share it with you. Then, we're going to cut her up and dispose of her body. These whores are ten-a-penny. They have a dreadful, demeaning life. We'll be doing her and her family a favour. Sometimes you have to make sacrifices for the greater good.'

Veronica sat up abruptly. Staring at her lover in disbelief. Had Papa been right about him?

'I don't want you seeing him any more,' Papa had said. Stern in his white coat. Addressing her at his Harley Street practice between appointments with rich old hags to discuss how he was going to fix up their pendulous breasts or administer a discreet nip and tuck to their collapsing faces. Dismissive, as usual. Immediately turning his attention to a small oil painting that he had been taking out of its packaging. A little treat for his office wall from Bonhams, no doubt. Keeping Mama's legacy alive. What a fucking joke.

'I'm not a child any more,' Veronica had said, digging her nails into the gold leaf on the visitor's chair. Spattering her nappa Ralph Laurens with gold dust. 'I can make my own choices. I love Silas.' Why had she even been sitting there, making excuses to this disengaged automaton?

'Veronica, he's not for you. He's too old. He's not in our league.'

'But he's good enough to work with you, right? You're such a hypocrite, Dad.'

'He worked *for* me. Don't call me Dad.' Her father, Papa Alpha, donned his glasses and looked down his nose at her.

'Or what? What the hell can you do about it, if I call you Dad or keep seeing Silas?'

'I can stop your allowance.'

He had had a point, the old man. Life without the allowance would be intolerable. The trust fund Mama had set up for her was pitiful. At twenty-one, she had inherited a shitty Chevvy and a cramped, tumbledown shack in the Hamptons that was no more than 2000 square feet. The bulk of the money and property had become the sole preserve of her father. Other than what he deigned to give her as an allowance, she wouldn't get a bean out of the old bastard until he died. And that was providing he didn't hook up with some Hollywood starlet in the interim and leave it all to her or some new-age, third-eye bullshit factory in the Hills.

'Okay! Okay!' she had said. Holding up her hands in surrender. 'I'll let him down gently.'

He had given the command and had expected her to obey. Of course, she hadn't. She had exited his consultation rooms with her flight ticket in her handbag. Had the driver take her straight to Heathrow, where she had met up with Silas under the departures board, Cambodia-bound. A passionate kiss bonding them in their worthy subterfuge.

At the other end, she had been surprised by the primitive feel of the place. Even when she had taken herself off to explore what Papa had stipulated as no-go neighbourhoods in New York, she had never seen such dereliction before as in Phnom Penh. Fat black electrical cables strung from one side of the street to another between crumbling 60s low-rise blocks, like a giant, intricate cat's cradle. A child dressed in filthy rags, squatting in the street and defecating into open drains. Makeshift food stalls with colourful awnings that said this was a ghost city only just being reclaimed. The place had an honesty to it.

When they had made for the train, bound for the spot where the charity was currently clearing mines, Silas had put his arm around her.

'What do you think, my love?' he had asked, kissing her forehead. Leading her along the tracks, overgrown with grass. Pushing the peasants out of the way as they tried to hawk food on platters they were carrying on their heads to the passengers. Helping her onto the packed train, along with the small suitcase that they were sharing.

Though she was wilting from the combination of jetlag and intense heat, she was intoxicated. The sunshine seemed stronger here. She was fascinated by the sound of people talking animatedly in a language that was completely foreign to her. Could smell their poverty and the vitality that came with it, pungent on the air. So different from the over-indulged westerners her parents mixed with – sickly sweet, white patricians, poisoning everything around them with their own narcotic-fed malignancies. 'It's amazing. This is the real world. I can't believe it, Silas. I feel free.' She pointed to the Cambodian men who were perched on the top of the carriages. 'I want to go on the roof!'

Silas smiled and shook his head. 'Too dangerous for you, my princess.'

'You're so thoughtful,' she had said, marvelling that she had found an all-consuming love like this – his was a beautiful, illuminating soul in a world of sham and material misery.

On the journey, he had talked animatedly about his work, assisting the emergency medical teams near the border, who operated on the victims of landmines.

'You must try to be brave when you see them,' he had said, steadying her when the train jolted over intersection points. 'There are thousands of them. Mostly men, but women and children too.' Feverish, as he described their injuries to her. 'Some of them have no legs at all. Some have lost arms. They get about on crutches or little carts with wheels. Last time I was over here, I saw people begging on the streets of Phnom Penh. They only had torsos, some of them. It's dreadful.' He had a tear in his eye, but there was something behind the show of sadness that bordered on excitement and fascination. Veronica knew enough by now of her lover's sexual proclivities to know that his interest in amputees went beyond the realm of the medical. Still, turning a blind eye to the quirks of this exceptional man was the least she could do. He felt like something so much better than family.

She looked out at the sweltering green tangle as the train carved its way through jungle, over rickety bridges that traversed ravines and across the flats of swamp-like rice paddies. Cambodia was the polar opposite to New York or London or Berlin. It was beautiful and dreadful all at once.

During their journey, he explained how the Vietnamese military had used the landmines to push the Khmer Rouge over the border into Thailand, and how the mines ran as a lethal barrier along the entire length of the border.

She had worked as a nurse, there. Smelling and touching for the first time in her life the filth and stink of ordinary people. Watching Silas administer forgetful anaesthetic to the injured, who writhed in agony, carried by relatives onto the operating table. The surgeons' nimble fingers cut and sutured with great skill. Talking French or English or German. All European doctors, earning the shine on their halo before disappearing off back to their own promised lands of private practice and an excellent pension scheme. Veronica felt, as a novelty, a certain reverential regard for her father, who performed the odd ground-breaking cosmetic procedure for the truly needy and disfigured, in amongst the arse-lifts and lipo for the narcissists of Knightsbridge and the Upper East Side who refused to accept the inevitability of decay.

It had been their second week in the small, makeshift hospital. The sun had still been strong and the heat had bounced off the dirt. Strolling back to their humble, bombed-out accommodation, arm-in-arm, they had walked through a thicket. Some fifty metres ahead, a woman had carried a fat bag of clothing on her head. A T-shirt hanging out of the load was a giveaway. Washing day.

'Let's get a shower and then take an early dinner,' Silas had said. 'I quite fancy sitting out front with a beer or two.'

'Sounds good,' Veronica had said, patting his arm.

'And I've got something for you. A gift.' From his shorts pocket, he took out a small package wrapped in Cambodian newspaper. Covered in the elegant scrolling calligraphy of Khmer.

'For me?' Veronica had smiled. Started to unwrap the gift. It was a clay figurine. Local art, showing a female figure, missing her arms. It was underwhelming. 'That's very thoughtful. Thanks.'

'I'm going to buy some new pieces for my collection, while we're here,' he had said. 'The Cambodians show exquisite skill in their clay work. We should visit a workshop when we get a day off.'

'I'm not sure—'

The explosion had knocked her to the ground. Before she had fallen, she was aware of a cloud of red mist colouring the space where the woman with the bag of washing had been standing. Her ears ringing with tinnitus. Some way off, the woman had screamed. Babygros and underpants hanging from the trees. Dazed, Veronica had noticed Silas was no longer by her side. Had he been injured?

She looked up to see that he had run to the woman's aid. Caught up with him, to find him kneeling next to the dying woman, masturbating. An unsettling light in his glazed eyes. A faraway look that she had sensed was focussed on something in the past.

'Silas! For fuck's sake. Help her!'

And now, back in the sweat-drenched stink of Phnom Penh, in the privacy of their concrete 'hotel', which was no more than a squalid tumbledown shell, whose original inhabitants may or may not have been buried alive in Pol Pot's Killing Fields, Veronica was faced with a dilemma.

'Come on,' Silas said, ferociously tugging on his erection. Breathing the stench from the diesel-powered generators and putrefying vegetable waste strewn along the street below in and out and in and out through flaring nostrils. 'Squeeze her neck. It will be easy for a strong girl like you. Put her out of her misery.'

'And what if I don't?' she asked.

'You will,' he said. 'You love me.'

'I won't. I can't,' she said. 'Just let her go. She doesn't even understand a word you've been saying. All she knows is you're some kinked john.'

Silas continued to masturbate, slowing down, now. Savouring the prostitute's anguish, perhaps.

'Silas, you're acting crazy. Stop.'

When Silas Holm put his hands around the neck of the young girl he had paid for pleasure by the hour; when he had choked the life from her twitching body, Veronica wondered in earnest if Papa had been more intuitive than she had hitherto given him credit for. When Silas had thrown the dead prostitute into the dumpster at the back of the hotel under cover of darkness, Veronica wondered if she would be next.

CHAPTER 67

Amsterdam, mortuary, 29 January

'This is the worst thing I've seen in years,' Marianne de Koninck said, looking dolefully at the girl on her slab. A blind, blonde angel, probably fair of face when whole, with the red and white of her ribs peeled back like ghastly wings put there by the devil himself. 'The poor little mite can't be more than eleven or twelve. Look what the beast has done to her. I know she's been treated in exactly the same way as the other victims, but...' She shook her head. Exhaled sharply and clicked off her voice recorder.

Van den Bergen hugged himself tight. Ran his hand over his stubble and closed his eyes. Perhaps this was it. The end of the road for him as a policeman. It was a hateful job he did, year in, year out, though by God, he did it well. But he was no longer sure he could find the light in amongst so much darkness. It was just overpowering.

'Somehow it seems worse this time,' he said. 'Right?'

Until now, he had been averting his gaze from the child's body. Staring at some of the surgical equipment. The tiles on the floor. Anything but the girl's remains. He turned to George, who was sitting in silence on the other side of the mortuary. 'What sort of monster does this to a child, George? Tell us.'

But George appeared to be crying. Rigid in her chair, her stillness punctuated only by intermittent heaving, as she sobbed noiselessly. Van den Bergen felt an incredibly strong urge to walk over to her. Put his hand on her shoulder. Show her he cared and that he would make it all better. But he couldn't. It was impossible to make her unsee what she had seen. He had failed to protect her. And he knew, if he embraced George and Marianne saw the close physical rapport that they shared, the pathologist would realise that they had become more than just colleagues.

His musings were interrupted by a familiar face, beaming at him from the threshold of the mortuary entrance.

'Sabine! Come in! Come in!' Marianne beckoned her friend inside. She turned to van den Bergen. 'Given the fact we're dealing with a child victim, I wanted to get Sabine in again to give the girl the once-over. What she doesn't know about the physiology of children, isn't worth knowing.' Turned to George. 'Have you met Dr Schalks?'

George had folded her arms high on her chest. Sat bolt upright in her chair. 'All right, Sabrina? Your reputation precedes you,' she said, sounding as though the words were sticking just a little in her throat. Notably, George did not offer the newcomer more than a nod in greeting. And he guessed she had deliberately called her by the wrong name.

Van den Bergen sat on his hands to disguise the fact that he was squirming in the presence of his young lover and the attractive, middle-aged paediatrician who had recently engaged him in several bouts of professional flirtation. Hadn't she showed up at reception for him, bearing a tray of cakes? He had told George and the others that a grateful mugging victim had left them for the team. Hadn't she called and invited him to her fundraising gala dinner in aid of the hospital she was building in Kosovo? He had opted to make a donation of fifty euros to the cause instead. It was all he could afford – on every level.

After donning protective clothing, Sabine proceeded to examine the girl's corpse. Van den Bergen couldn't help but be impressed by her cool demeanour. Really professional. Tears standing in her eyes at the end, though.

'Where was the girl found?' she asked.

'On Middenweg. In a little thicket of trees,' van den Bergen said. 'Right by the New East Arboretum. It's a very public place. Lots of traffic. Right on a tram route. I have no idea how our murderer came to dump her body there without being seen.'

He recapped all that he and George had discovered so far.

Sabine raised an eyebrow. Looked alarmed. 'People trafficking? England as well? Hasselblad told me you're looking for a serial killer with an interest in paedophilia.' Turned to Marianne. 'And I thought you said, Daan Strietman—'

A tight-lipped Marianne nodded, not bothering to conceal her displeasure. 'I've got five bodies in the fridges still need autopsies performing on them. My number two gets arrested in the middle of bloody flu season on trumped-up charges.'

A certain ingrained loyalty resonated within van den Bergen. Though privately he had nothing but disdain for Hasselblad, he would not publicly undermine the authority of his superior. 'Only time will tell if they're bona fide charges or not, Marianne. I'll be looking into it now I'm back. We can't rule out the possibility Strietman is involved somehow if it's a trafficking ring,' he said. 'Especially since he's been linked to the Valeriusstraat builder. I have questions that still need answers, as far as that mattress goes. How did it get there? Whose blood is on it? And I want to know why the forensics report on Linda Lepiks' place has conveniently gone astray. Let's not jump to any conclusions, shall we?'

Sabine finished examining the girl. Hooked her hair behind her ears, as she scanned Marianne's preliminary report. Tutted. 'This girl's been raped repeatedly – by several different men. I've seen this level of abuse before in living victims, of course. But all those missing organs… Maybe it *is* ritual killing by a member or members of a paedophile ring. It's not unheard of.'

'Haven't you been listening?' George said. 'This is about trafficked people. Trafficked organs.'

Sabine folded her arms and stood a little straighter. 'I think it's *wholly* plausible that ritual satanic—'

'Violent sex offenders and serial murderers often dress their brutality up as something to do with satanic worship,' George said, raising her voice. 'But the ritual side is almost always superficial and for dramatic effect.' She blinked repeatedly at the paediatrician.

'What do you know?' Sabine asked. 'I thought you were an assistant.'

Narrowed eyes said George was disgruntled. 'Oh, I know, all right. This is a complex case. The backdrop to these murders is almost certainly gangland trafficking. But the killer himself – recruited for his surgical abilities, in all likelihood – is a different kettle of fish. He's shown escalating sadistic behaviour. Taking more of the organs with each victim we find. The term for it is conducting "in vivo trials". Maybe now, he's perfected his technique. But what's he doing it for really? Business…or pleasure?'

Sabine turned away from George back to the dead girl. 'The contents of her stomach – still in situ, thankfully – have not been digested yet.'

Marianne nodded. 'Yep. Pitta bread, lamb meat, salad. She'd had a kebab shortly before death.'

'Exactly,' Sabine said, snapping her fingers and pointing. 'Perhaps she'd been brought in on a flight from Turkey.'

'Bullshit!' George shouted, causing everyone to turn to see what had caused such an impassioned response.

She wheeled her typing chair rapidly from side to side. From the left to the right to the left to the right. Playing with some forceps. Open, shut. Open, shut.

'I'm sorry?' Sabine said.

George glanced over at the girl's body. 'You can buy a kebab on any street in Amsterdam. Why the fuck would this girl necessarily have come from Turkey? She's white, for a start. Lily-white. So, unless she's an abducted holidaymaker from Bodrum – and

I doubt that, since it's off season and school term time – then she's got to be local, or at least, northern European. Anyway, a flight from Turkey takes hours. She'd have digested food during that time, right? And I never went on a plane that served up a nice kebab as your in-flight meal. Have you?'

'Georgina's got a point,' van den Bergen said, moving discreetly over to her chair and holding the back so she was forced to stop fidgeting. Placed a reassuring hand on her shoulder, to show he was on her side. 'I'll get my team to look into missing persons in the Benelux countries, France, Germany. Maybe Europol knows something. Dead porn stars and immigrant fishermen are one thing, but the murder of a European child who has been abducted, forced into sexual slavery and eventually used as part of a supply chain for black market organs suddenly takes this to a different league. That's the stuff of international news headlines.'

'We're looking for a sociopath,' George said, though it seemed only van den Bergen was now listening, as Sabine engaged in an entirely different, altogether personal conversation with Marianne about her failed love life. She shouted over their chatter. 'A sophisticated, skilled individual who likes to kill and has no conscience whatsoever.'

A rogue tear rolled down George's cheek. While the other women weren't looking, gossiping away as though they were on a nice coffee break at a seminar, rather than talking in the presence of a murdered child, van den Bergen put his hand on her shoulder. 'I'm sorry you have to see this. I forget you're—'

She took his hand into hers surreptitiously. He felt he could almost see the essence of her being in those sorrowful, passionate, dangerous eyes.

'It's fine. This is what I do, now. I realise it's going to take years to really harden to it though. The things that killers do...'

He chuckled and withdrew his hand. 'Oh, you never harden to it. Not if you have a soul.'

CHAPTER 68

South East London, mortuary, later

The doors to the lift opened. Sharon stepped out gingerly into the dark corridor. Noticed the shiny, navy-blue linoleum floor, wondering how they got it so sparkling. One of those buffer machines, most likely. Funny the things you thought of when there was crap all over the fan and your heart was teetering on the brink.

'You okay?' the copper asked.

He had a kind face. She was normally distrustful of his ilk, but given the circumstances, his bulk was somehow comforting. Those Ds were always built like brick shithouses – as had been the uniforms who had shown up on her doorstep. All hissing walkie talkies and big hats and Kevlar vests. It was like fucking RoboCop at your door. Hope the neighbours couldn't see. Except, bugger the neighbours, because something had gone wrong, obviously. Bad news, always, when a squad car rolled up outside your house, and the coppers' mugs were respectful and solemn like they were at church.

'My Patrice been in trouble?' she'd asked, barely able to breathe her way through the fear that seemed to crush the air from her lungs. 'You come about my son? Cos he's a good boy, you know.'

'No. Nothing like that, Ms Williams-May. Can we come in?'

When they had told her, the tears took a good twenty minutes and a sweet cup of tea to appear. She felt she had to conjure the memory of Derek and instruct her heart to break. Detached from the announcement. Shock, they called it. How could she break the news to her baby girl, if it did turn out to be her dad?

'How comes you're sure it's him?'

'We found a wallet on the deceased,' the lady copper had said. 'But we'll need you to ID him. If it is Derek de Falco, you're down as his next of kin.'

Now, the end was near, and now she faced the final curtain. Derek had always said he wanted a Frank sonata at his funeral. Maybe the poor bastard's wish was going to come true. Half of Soho and Bermondsey, sitting in a cold hall at the crem or lining the pews in The Most Holy Trinity RC Church or wherever it was he got sent as a kid. Floral tributes making everyone sneeze. Readings and a world of hypocritical shit. She would have to arrange it all. Jesus. She could barely put one foot in front of another, but the moment of truth had come.

Followed the policeman to the viewing room or whatever they called it. There was a body under a white sheet. She could already tell it was him from the size. Grief struck her down and her heart was no longer teetering. Worse, when she saw his battered grey face.

'Stupid fucker, Derek de Falco!'

She hadn't expected her sorrow to be tinged with anger. Hot tears pouring onto her décolletage, wishing Letitia was there to hug her and tell her it was gonna be all right, like she had when Mum had gone for the belt.

She turned to the D. Hiccoughing through her words. 'You need to line me up with an interview with your boss, right? My Derek – he was in some deep shit, man. And it's got him killed. I ain't scared of grassing no more. Not if you can guarantee me protection like yous did with my niece.'

'What do you mean, Sharon?' the detective said, taking out his notepad and pen.

'I know some stuff you're gonna want to hear.'

CHAPTER 69

Amsterdam, later

'Do you think we'll track her down?' George asked Marie, peering up at the faceless office block on Weerdestein, uncomfortably eating messy falafel in the pool car.

'Maybe,' Marie said. 'It's nice to get out, though.' She spoke whilst crunching crisps, spraying the dash with globs of white pulp. Oblivious to George wincing beside her. 'After a morning of trawling through the crap on Strietman's laptop, I was glad of a change of scenery.'

'What do you mean?' George marvelled at how Marie was utterly oblivious to her own spit-mess.

'Kinky photos of men in body bags. Like, necrophilia porn.' Marie laughed and blushed through to the roots of her red hair. 'I mean, it makes sense, when you consider the job he does, but I've known Daan Strietman for years.' She looked directly at George. A shard of crisp clinging to the down above her top lip. 'I'd never have had him down as a pervert. Never. He's a total dick, but not perv material.'

'Shows how much you can ever know about a colleague,' George said, thinking about van den Bergen's unexpected sense of adventure and athleticism in the bedroom. *Not here. Not now, George. Put that shit out of your mind.* She peered up at the office block.

'I'm a bit disappointed. I thought they'd know Magool personally.'

'The Emancipation Servicepoint just deal with offering financial guidance to women,' Marie said, rustling the crisp packet. 'Older women, at that.' Trying to get the dregs out. Pouring them in her mouth directly from the bag, so that crumbs fell onto her top, which she brushed all over her knees, the car and George.

George dumped her half-eaten falafel dramatically onto the dashboard. 'Can you watch what you're doing, for Christ's sake? I didn't come out to get a shower in your chewed-up lunch.'

Marie screwed up her crisp packet and threw it in the back of the car. Defiant. Unapologetic. 'Oh, and you're not stinking out the car with the smell of bloody garlic and onions?'

Stalemate. George could see arguing was pointless.

'Forget it,' she said. 'So, what have we pieced together? Magool went to the Emancipation Servicepoint place, asking for advice on how to make money and how to set up a bank account. Right? But you've got to be twenty-five at least to qualify for the organisation's services, so they put her in touch with IFTIN.'

'Yes. The Somali women's thing on Mercatorplein,' Marie said, reading her notes. 'And all they could give us was an address of another asylum seeker who went looking for support around the same time as Magool. We're going round in circles a bit. Could be a dead end.'

'We won't know until we try,' George said, wiping her fingers with an anti-bacterial wipe and buckling up.

'So, I come back to find Ahlers in hospital, Strietman and Buczkowski are both in the cells and the forensics from Linda Lepiks' flat missing?' van den Bergen shouted, his irritation fighting its way up and out through the numbing fuzz of codeine. 'I go away for two days – not twenty-two, but *two* days, for God's sake – with my phone switched on.'

Elvis cleared his throat. 'Actually, boss. I tried to get hold of you sooner, but your phone kept going to voicemail for most of the time you were there. I wondered if something bad had gone down. You know…? On a personal level.'

Van den Bergen tried to disguise being wrong-footed by Elvis' perspicacity by thumping his chest, as he did when he had crippling stomach acid. 'Bloody English food. Plays havoc with—'

'Strietman's guilty as hell,' Kees said. 'Has Marie told you about the gay snuff on his hard drive?'

'No, actually, Detective Leeuwenhoek. I've been too busy attending the post mortem of a child and meeting a paediatrician who is coming in to advise you all on paedophile rings, so I suggest you cultivate a little tact and good manners. And she comes from a world where they dress like real professionals. So, it might help if you actually took off that grubby old anorak.'

Kees was sitting astride his chair. Cocky. Van den Bergen felt instinctively that in his absence, this borrowed detective had been engaging in some very successful arse-kissing with Hasselblad. Time to let a little air out of the puffed-up idiot.

'Marianne de Koninck personally wants your head on a platter if it turns out you're wrong,' he told the gap-toothed, irritating shit. 'Did you even check first to see if he has an alibi? Or have you lot just conspired behind my back to ridicule this department and my good name as rapidly and thoroughly as possible?'

The reddening in Kees' face was revealing. 'Strietman says he has a cast iron alibi but won't tell me what it is. I like to think I inherited my dad's legendary Leeuwenhoek bullshit-detector, and I'd say he's like a dirty stall in a dairy farm.'

Elvis turned to Kees. 'Kees, mate. They don't have bulls on dairy farms,' he said. 'Cows are female. You know that, right?'

'Stud farm, you remedial idiot,' van den Bergen said. 'Strietman won't give his alibi up, eh?'

An image of George, naked, luxuriating post-coitally in their hotel bed, popped unbidden into his mind. He batted it away.

There were some alibis a man simply couldn't confess to. He turned to Elvis.

'What did you find at his apartment?'

'Ah, well,' Elvis said, tugging at a stray hair in his otherwise perfectly sculpted quiff. 'That's the most interesting part...'

CHAPTER 70

Amsterdam, Nieuw West area, then, police headquarters, later

'What do you want?' the girl asked, speaking through the letterbox.

'We're police. Come on! Open up,' Marie said, flashing her ID through the gap.

'No,' said the girl. 'I am alone. That is maybe counterfeit.'

'It's not fake.'

George crouched so that she was level with the letterbox. Got a clear view of the girl. She was about seventeen, dark-skinned like Magool, wearing a yellow hijab trimmed with a floral pattern. Trepidation in her eyes. Though her Dutch was good, even if the woman at IFTIN had not already told George this girl was a Somali, her accent would have betrayed her as a recent immigrant. Plus, the Slotervaart Overtoomse Veld block of flats that the apartment was in, and the Nieuw West area in general, were the sort of grim places only recent arrivals in the country and the very poor would want to live in. 1960s concrete, medium to high rises. Grey, brightened here and there with almost arbitrary splashes of green that the council had seen fit to provide, when the area had been planned as overspill from the city. Panels of colour, where blocks had been given a facelift by some hip and trendy architect or other who didn't have to live there. Hardly any different from the sort of area George had grown up in on the other side of the North Sea. Except this place was actually clean.

'Please. We want to talk to you about Magool Osman,' George said. Looking directly into the girl's eyes. Trying to convey her sincerity.

The flap to the letterbox clattered shut. Clicking, clacking as locks were undone. The door opened abruptly. 'Magool?' the girl asked. Alarm clearly visible in the way her hand and lips trembled. The girl looked furtively onto the landing. Beckoned them in.

The interior of the apartment was sparsely furnished. A couple of threadbare Tree of Life rugs. A smoked glass coffee table and battered tan leatherette sofa that looked as though it might convert into some kind of double bed arrangement. Smears on the windows said they hadn't been cleaned in years. Mattresses stacked against the living room wall – one, two, three, four… seven, George counted. Smelled of a strange mixture of cooking, sweat and fresh washing.

'Please, sit down!' the girl offered them a seat on basic, collapsible wooden chairs that had been hanging on nails on the wall.

'How many people live here?' Marie asked, pen at the ready.

'There are ten of us. But please, to keep your voice down. A couple of the women are sleeping. They are working nights.'

The girl explained that her name was Amaal Samatar, also from Mogadishu, and that she had been sent to the Kakuma refugee camp in northwestern Kenya, whereupon a trip to Nairobi to visit relatives had seen her threatened with deportation to Mogadishu. Though her aunt had been herded onto a plane and shipped back to Somalia under spurious grounds that her refugee-status document was not in order, Amaal had managed to gain the support of the United Nations Refugee Agency and had boarded a flight to the Netherlands.

'So, you've been here how long?' Marie asked.

Amaal shrugged. 'Nearly two years. Something like that.'

'And how did you meet Magool?'

Amaal scratched beneath her headscarf and clutched her cardigan shut over her floor-length dress. 'What has happened to her? Is she okay?'

'How did you meet Magool?' Marie asked again.

George nodded at the girl. Encouraging her to speak.

'We were both at Katwijk together,' she said. 'Both young and without parents or chaperones. I am remembering her when she arrived. They are putting her in the room next to mine. She was in a mess.'

'What happened then?' George asked. 'How did you come to be here?'

'I am wanting to learn while my asylum application goes through,' Amaal said. 'I study science and Dutch at college.' She smiled only very slightly, as if she daren't allow herself more than a glimmer of relief, George thought. 'They are letting me rent this place with some of the other women under the self-care agreement.'

'Some!' Marie scoffed, eyeing the mattresses.

'We cannot afford bigger apartment.'

'And when was the last time you saw Magool?' George asked.

Frowning momentarily, Amaal said, 'Two weeks ago or more. She went out to work and is not coming back. I am wondering if I will get the police showing up at the door.'

'Wait a minute,' Marie said, tugging at the pearl in her ear. Starting to grin like a suspicious hyena, sensing a kill was nearby. 'Are you telling me Magool lived here?'

Amaal stared blankly at the detective. '*Lived?* So, something is wrong with her!'

George reached out and grabbed Amaal's hand. 'Look. She's dead. I'm so sorry.'

As Marie turned to George, her shoulders seemed to stiffen. 'That's not how we break that kind of news. You're not following protocol.'

'Fuck protocol,' George said. 'You're stringing her along. It's not right.' She turned back to Amaal. 'Magool was murdered. Brutally. We need to know everything you can tell us about her life. Where she worked. Who she hung out with. What happened to her baby. If you help us, we might be able to find her killer.'

Crumpled up on the makeshift chair, suddenly looking like a lost child swathed in too much fabric, Amaal started to weep. Wiping her face on her pretty headscarf, the pink floral border turning a deeper hue with hot tears, until George produced a clean tissue from her coat pocket.

'She is always going out at night,' Amaal began, haltingly. 'She says she works as a cleaner in offices. One job as a waitress. She is sending money home to her relatives, she told me one time. But she does not ever speak of her family. Except her brother. She says her little brother was adopted by a rich white family and is living in Italy. To be honest, I do not know any of her friends. She has very western tastes. Not an observant Muslim like me and some of the other women here. She goes to nightclubs. Drinks alcohol. Mixes with men.'

'What men?' Marie asked.

'I do not know.' Amaal shrugged. 'I am never meeting any of them, but people in the Somali community gossip about her a bit. They say she is loose-moraled. *Haram.*'

'Did she say if she had a boyfriend?' George asked.

A shake of the head. More tears.

'And the baby?'

'She is going out one morning, when she was heavily pregnant and was coming back in a taxi. No baby.' Amaal blew her nose and sat up straighter. Wiped her eyes. Looked resolutely at George. 'She has said she had the baby adopted because she needs the money and cannot offer the baby a respectable Halal life. But she says one day, when she is older and has her own place and a good job, she is hoping, *Insha'Allah*, to use some of the money she is earning to buy the baby back.'

Her breathing was uneven. Her expression utterly sorrowful and bewildered. She rose from her chair, disappeared into the kitchen and returned with a grey, lockable cash tin.

'Magool asks me to look after this when she is out. I hide it from the other women because three of them are thieves from Tanzania.' She unlocked the tin and revealed roll after roll of money inside, all high euro denominations. 'This is her money for her family and the baby.'

'Jesus!' Marie said, unfolding one of the rolls and flicking through the notes. 'There must be twenty thousand or more in there. Maybe thirty.'

George whistled low. Turned to Amaal. 'You're a good, honest friend, Amaal, to hide this cash for her. And you're doing really well,' George said. 'I hope one day, we can give this money to Magool's son or daughter. Now, we know the doctor who delivered the baby, but do you know who bought it? Did Magool ever tell you that?'

Amaal looked suddenly uncertain. Narrowed her eyes. Clicked her tongue against the roof of her mouth. Then, finally, nodded.

'Who the hell is Daan Strietman?' van den Bergen asked. Swaying slightly now the codeine had taken hold. Staring down at the folder full of provocative and highly sexualised images of children.

'Who knows, boss?' Elvis said, taking photos of the books on the bookshelf in Strietman's little office.

Van den Bergen sat heavily in Strietman's desk chair. A leather affair that was a damn sight better than his at the office. He adjusted the height so that his legs were no longer bunched up near his ears. Banged his knees on the too-low desk. Caught his large foot in the tangle of cables that were left behind now Marie had taken the pathologist's laptop.

'Fucking dwarves!'

'Boss?'

'Nothing.' He placed the folder back onto the desk, feeling

slightly nauseous. Hoping those photos had been photoshopped in some way to *look* like children performing lewd acts. 'I don't know how Marie ploughs through this kind of crap all day.' Took his glasses off, letting them hang on their chain. Steepled his fingers in contemplation. Staring out at the attractive Old South apartments opposite. 'Tell me what you think, Elvis,' he said. 'Regardless of what Kamphuis' lackey keeps dripping into your ear.'

Elvis perched on the edge of the desk and glanced up at the proliferation of Scandi-noir whodunits, real-life-crime tomes, written by jazzy-sounding American criminologists, and non-fiction books about cultures that practised voodoo. These constituted about seventy percent of the literature on Strietman's bookshelves. The other thirty percent seemed to be medical text-books and the occasional fantasy or sci-fi box set. Tolkien. George R. R. Martin. Frank Herbert. He sighed.

'I don't know, boss.' He counted his observations on his fingers. 'There's a connection to Buczkowski, who's got mental health problems and a shady past. This place is only three streets away from Valeriusstraat. How the hell does he afford a pad like this, unless he's on the take from a job he does on the side? Forensics pays okay, but not *that* well for someone in his thirties! And Strietman can't give us – or *won't* give us – alibis for the nights that any of those murders took place. He's got the surgical skills. He's into dead men and kids, sexually. And he seems to have vanished some of the Lepiks forensics info.' He turned to van den Bergen and sniffed. 'Buczkowski's DNA is all over the Valeriusstraat hoax scene. How can they not be our prime suspects?'

'But has he been to England?'

Elvis scratched at his sideburns and smiled wryly. 'Would you believe it? Yes! He went to some medical conference recently. The timing fits with your Ramsgate man.'

Nodding thoughtfully, van den Bergen slid his glasses back on and looked at the photograph of a naked little girl. 'Jesus. This is a potential PR disaster for the Dutch authorities.' He rubbed his face with his broad palms. 'Let's get that paediatrician in tomorrow for her thoughts. I don't care what she's doing. I want her input first thing. It looks like Leeuwenhoek Junior has found us our murderers. Shit.'

CHAPTER 71

Amsterdam, Ad's apartment, then NOS TV studios, then police headquarters, 30 January

'What's wrong?' Ad asked, biting into his toast. Chewing noisily.

George had only recently noticed that he chewed like the goats at the urban farm Letitia used to take her to. Grinding his food methodically between those big white molars of his. He had good teeth. Good skin. Lovely soft dark hair. A decent brain. A well-meaning soul. Why the hell wasn't he enough? Why was she such a philandering shitbag?

'Wrong? What do you mean?' she asked, spooning the bran flakes carefully into her mouth.

Ad reached out and put his hand on top of hers. 'You seemed down before, but you're a million miles away since you got back from England. Did everything go okay? Did something happen between you and that grumpy old fart?'

Could he hear that her heart was banging against the inside of her chest? Could he see the sweat beading on her top lip? Feel it emerge hot, wet and shameful from her palms?

'Happen? What do you mean?' She giggled nervously. 'Nothing happened.' Withdrew her hand and stood too quickly. Rush of blood to the head. Bowl, flung into the sink with a clatter.

Tell him, you coward! her conscience yelled. *Just finish this. It's over. It's run its course. You're not happy. He's not happy. You love him but not in the right way. Let him go. You're not a twenty-year-old undergrad, impressed by his accent any more. He's suffocating you. You want to be with Paul.*

Glaring through the window at the car park below, George wished she could blame someone else for this mess she had got herself into; blame something else – hell, if she could blame the neighbours' cars, she would.

She was going to do it. Fess up. Come clean. Thought about the lies Letitia told. The lies her father had told. Lies were cankerous. *If you can tell it how it is in your working life, you can sodding well do it in your personal life too. You deserve that much.*

But the tendency towards petty dishonesty ran thickly through George's veins, it would seem. Bonded the basic decency that formed the very core of her being with corrupt genetic material from her deceitful parents. Polluted her, so that in the matter of her sexual transgression in Ramsgate, she could not tell the truth. At best, she could continue to keep quiet, letting the blissful memory of van den Bergen making her body sing, fester instead of blossom.

'I'm going to work.'

She kissed Ad half-heartedly on the forehead, pulled on her coat and left.

Wobbling along the canals precariously on a bicycle van den Bergen had lent to her, built and adjusted to suit a man who had legs that reached up to her chest, George heard her phone ringing inside her coat pocket. She ignored it. Then it pinged three times in succession. The call was almost certainly from Ad. One ping would be voicemail. But what were the texts or emails about?

As she pedalled her way towards the police station, she checked her watch. Already sweaty despite the freezing drizzle and mist.

Too early for work, because she had made the fast getaway from Ad. The timorous sun had only been up an hour and showed no signs of clawing its way through the dense, low-hanging cloud. It even smelled foggy.

On Nassaukade, she juddered to a halt. Barely able to operate the back-step brakes on the bicycle. Threw herself sideways, praying she would land upright on her left foot. Her crotch was sore where the saddle and its owner had been digging in. She smiled mischievously at the thought. Then felt immediately guilty. Flung the bike against the wall. Sat down on the stone steps to one of the beautiful old apartment blocks and lit a cigarette.

Gazing at the bobbing row-boats that were tethered to the canal wall on the opposite side was a soothing enterprise. The water was wide here, though not wide enough to remind her of the Thames back home, and the area too built up to be the picturesque Cam, with its Cambridge colleges and the backs, transcending any shitty East Anglian weather with their sheer medieval beauty. Still, this Amsterdam had not lost its charm for her.

'Now, who's trying to get hold of me this early in the morning, then?' she said, dragging on her clandestine cigarette.

She took out her phone and read a text from Sally Wright. Full of righteous indignation as had recently been the case? No. The words rang with alarm.

```
Have done some digging into how Silas
Holm came to send you a letter. He has
had a visit from someone purporting to
be a doctor…
```

But the phone was ringing shrilly, now. Distracting her as she read. Who on earth used the word 'purporting' in a bloody text, anyway? Before the screen was dominated by the incoming caller, she registered the additional words:

```
Be on your guard.
```

and:

```
Highly irregular breach of security.
```

Shit. Needed to answer the call. It was Aunty Sharon. Family first.

'All right, Aunty Shaz,' she said. 'What's eating you?'

'So, the music comes on,' the Dutch Broadcast Foundation – NOS TV – producer said. A young man with a receding hairline and too-tight jeans. Bouncing with energy; possibly pharmaceutically powered. 'I give the countdown and the fingers, like I explained.' He mimed three, two, one with his hand, chopping the air. Pointed to the presenter. A smartly dressed woman in her thirties, wearing the heaviest makeup van den Bergen had ever seen. 'She reads the autocue and introduces you.'

The female presenter smiled benignly. Patted her hair. 'I'm going to ask you the questions you went through with the production assistant. Okay?' Pressed her earpiece and looked away, as though she were listening to an internal voice from the other dimension.

'Okay.' Van den Bergen could feel the sweat rolling freely down his back. He wondered if damp patches would be visible to the viewing public. Perhaps he was going to be sick. He felt dizzy as hell. Maybe it was his labyrinthitis playing up. Where was Jan de Hoop? Who was this young woman in her sharp suit? Did it even matter? Where were his codeine tabs? He fingered the blister pack in his trouser pocket. Wished George were there. Why had he been so quick to send her calls to voicemail?

'Chief Inspector?' the producer asked.

'I'm fine.'

Van den Bergen sipped from his glass of water, light-headed. All eyes in the gaudy NOS studio boring into him. The camera men. The interviewer. The producer. Assistants. A sinister-looking group of other TV execs, nodding knowingly at one another and whispering who knew what. The first press conference had been stressful enough. But at least it had been on familiar turf at the police station. With these cameras on him, however, he would have to address the nation. And there was talk of this being streamed through the BBC too. He hadn't even had his third cup of coffee.

The programme's bleeping, ephemeral theme music began. To his right sat Hasselblad. Shining like the fairy on top of the Christmas tree in his ceremonial uniform. Frog-eyes bulging with delight under the harsh limelight.

'Don't fuck it up, van den Bergen. The Queen's watching you,' he said. Helpful fat bastard.

Well, if he failed to get his words out on air, he was sure Hasselblad would waste no time in stepping in.

Three, two, one. Go.

'Is it true that the Netherlands police has arrested not one, but two prime suspects, with a further man in detention, suspected of being a part of an international trafficking ring?'

Stammering his way through the first few seconds, van den Bergen found the words came more easily if he thought about the victims. Especially the unidentified little girl. He confirmed the arrests of Daan Strietman and Iwan Buczkowski.

'So, you're confident you've found your killers?' the news presenter asked.

When he couldn't bring himself to answer, imagined Marianne de Koninck and the forensics community screaming abuse at the TV, Hasselblad interrupted.

'Absolutely,' he said. 'As far as I'm concerned, it's another triumph for the Netherlands police. Our streets are safe again, thanks to my team's hard work. Case closed.'

As soon as they were off air, van den Bergen bolted for the toilets and threw up. He sat on the toilet cubicle floor, spitting into the bowl, the neck of his shirt open and his tie hanging loose. At that moment, all he wanted to do was call George and hear her reassuring voice. *Weak, weak man.* He dialled her number and found she was engaged. Took an unexpected, incoming call from Tamara.

'Darling. What's wrong?' he asked, leaning against the sink, now. Splashing water on his mouth with his free hand.

'Hi Dad! Me and Willem just watched you on the TV. You were great!'

The fact that she actually squealed with approval made him feel just a little better. Without pause, she rattled on about Numb-nuts' most recent gig, which had been packed with fifteen students and six friends. Eulogised about a new coffee machine they had bought. Their arrangements for something or other, which he didn't catch, as he was blowing his nose loudly. Commented that he sounded breathless and should see a doctor.

'That's where I'm going next,' he said, checking his watch.

'Now, don't forget the sixteenth, will you?' Her voice was lovely. Squeaky and feminine. She didn't sound much different to how she had sounded as a little girl. She had inherited her mother's dainty vocal chords, except Andrea had eventually sounded like a squawking vulture as she circled her ex-husband's carrion, picking off what was left to share with that incredible turd, Groenewalt.

'What's happening on the sixteenth?'

'Seriously?' The loveliness had disappeared from Tamara's voice.

'Oh, the wedding. Right. Right.'

As van den Bergen walked out to the car, he said *sixteenth, sixteenth, sixteenth* over and over in his head. *Wedding. Don't forget the bloody wedding. Get a new shirt. In fact, get a new suit.* Unlocked his car. Wanted to take George as his date, but wondered if that was appropriate, seeing as she was not far off Tamara's age. One in the eye for Andrea, though. Except he was going to set

333

George straight and put their relationship back on a strictly professional footing, because he was a man of honour. Not a cradle-snatching pervert. Who else to ask? Maybe Sabine Schalks...

In a neglected corner of his consciousness, as he folded himself into the Mercedes, he was dimly aware that somebody was watching him.

'Let me see him!' Marianne de Koninck said, thumping Elvis' desk hard.

She could see she had startled him. He blanched and moved his chair several inches away from her.

'It's not a drop-in centre, Marianne,' he said, fixing his gaze on the pea-green coat she had hastily thrown over her scrubs. 'You can't just show up and demand a visit, I'm afraid. He's being transferred out on remand later today, pending trial. Anyway, shouldn't you be at work?'

Irritated, she wanted to ask this impertinent arse of a man-boy – too reminiscent of Jasper, given his youth – who the fuck he thought he was? What did he know of a boss' loyalty to their team? What did he know of the important service they provided for the dead, who could no longer speak for themselves? 'You've never even been inside my mortuary, *Elvis*. You were too much of a wimp to get your Hep B jab, so don't you come over all concerned about my work.' She felt a degree of satisfaction when his eye started to twitch. 'And it's Dr. de Koninck to you. That's my employee you've got in your cell. I want to talk to him. I want to check he's okay.'

She stifled a yawn. Feeling raw after a sleepless night, weighing up what she knew about Daan Strietman against the accusations levelled at him. Battling instincts: defend or repel. By the morning, she had decided she was not the kind of disloyal person to distance herself from the accused and hope her shine did not rub off as a result of him losing his. Here she was. Seeking the truth. Giving

Strietman the chance to explain himself to her. If van den Bergen's gatekeeper would let her get that far.

'Please, Dirk,' she said, purposefully softening. 'We're all on the same team. Van den Bergen would let me, if he was here. But you're in charge right now. You call the shots.'

He sat a little more upright in his chair. The suggestion of a smile on his lips. Picked up the phone. 'I'll have them bring him to one of the interview rooms.'

Men were so predictable.

She hardly recognised Strietman when she saw him. His usual effervescence was gone. Grey-faced and dark under his eyes. Looking shabby in clothes he had been wearing clearly too long. He smiled at her, though it was a clear veneer of optimism, given the claustrophobic room they were in, with a uniform standing in the corner and furniture bolted to the floor.

'You came! How are the stiffs? Are they missing me?'

'Jesus, Daan! You look a mess. I can't believe this. What the hell is going on? Why won't you give them an alibi? What's the connection between you and the Pole?'

Strietman examined his fingernails – usually spotless, now a line of black grime under them.

'I can't. It's personal.'

'What's so terrible you're willing to sacrifice your freedom to keep quiet? There's a rumour going round they've found child pornography at your apartment.'

Strietman swallowed hard. Tears welled in his eyes and spilled onto his cheeks.

CHAPTER 72

Amsterdam, police headquarters, later

'Yes, yes,' Sabine Schalks said, examining Strietman's lurid photographs of naked children with Marie. 'These are definitely the sorts of images paedophiles share with one another over the internet.' She crossed her long legs and hooked her hair behind her ear. 'But these have a certain arty quality to them you don't normally see, and there are no adults in the frame. Undeniably evidence of abuse, though. See the bruising on the children's arms and thighs?'

Marie nodded. 'I thought I'd run it by you for a second opinion. They're not as hardcore as some of the images I normally come across. Not as alarming as the adult necro-porn he's got on his hard drive.' Pointed to Sabine's earrings. 'I love your pearls.'

Sabine smiled. Touched her ears. Blushed. 'Thank you. I wish I had your lovely red hair.' She laughed. It was a girlish laugh like the happy trill of a song bird.

In the corner of the team meeting room, slouching in her chair, George made a retching noise.

The paediatrician spun around quickly. 'I'm sorry?' Her smile was warm and guileless. 'What was that?'

Hoisting herself out of her seat and marching over to Marie's pinboard, George appraised the photos of the victims. Cards bearing facts written in black felt tip pen. A timeline, created with drawing pins and string. Looked at the sightless face of the dead little girl, since identified, thanks to the joys of Europol, as missing twelve-year-old Ewa Silbert from just outside Hamburg. This was so much bigger than a Satanist builder and a pathologist, executing a murderous spree that had been planned during the fitting of the pathologist's new Poggenpohl kitchen.

She turned to the two women to offer some kind of input on the use of child pornography by convicted paedophiles, but Marie and Sabine were talking about sculpture.

'Oh, I *love* Henry Moore's treatment of the human form!' Sabine said.

'He was always my favourite at school,' Marie said. 'We went on this art trip to England, once, and there's these three figures in…where was it?' Marie was grinning. Engaged. Full of it. Since when was Marie a fan of sculpture? And her hair wasn't red that day. It was brown with grease from not having been washed for at least a fortnight. 'Battersea Park! They were ace.'

'Have you seen his Madonna and child in St Paul's cathedral?' Sabine asked.

'I have! It was *amazing*.'

George had heard enough. 'Sabine, why are you here, if we've got the killers incarcerated?' she asked.

Then, without having to hear some disingenuous answer, she realised. In fact, she'd known it all along. Sabine Schalks was there for Paul van den Bergen.

'Chief Inspector van den Bergen's not here. You can't see him,' the uniformed policewoman on the front desk said. Hatchet-faced and unyielding.

Ad ground his teeth together. Balled his fists. Hot and cold at the same time. Vaguely aware that he must look a lunatic wearing only a T-shirt and jeans, when it was minus one outside. Goosebumps on his arms. Fire in his belly.

'Well, I want to see Georgina McKenzie and I know *she's* here! It's urgent.'

'Sir, I suggest you calm down and take a seat. I'll phone up.'

Throwing himself onto a chair, sandwiched between a woman who stank of stale cigarettes and whisky and a sharp-suited man clutching a fat briefcase, Ad considered what he had found. Went over the chain of events in his mind's eye.

When George had left early for work, he had enjoyed a blinding moment of epiphany. Their relationship was in trouble. And if he was to win back George's affections properly, he knew he must make more of an effort. Resolved to get the place neat and clean by George's standards before lectures. Tidying up the mess that Jasper had left in the living room. Exasperated on her behalf. Beer cans on every surface. A full ashtray. Empty crisp packets on coffee table. Cup rings and crumbs. Men's magazines left lying around – well thumbed, clinging onto germs from their readers, which he knew made George uncomfortable. No wonder she was fed up, staying here with two ball-scratching morons. He had been remiss as a thoughtful boyfriend.

Once he had deemed the living room and kitchen satisfactory, he had turned to their bedroom. A quick half hour should do it and he still wouldn't be late for his lecture. He would make the bed and unpack her suitcase from her trip to Ramsgate. Put a wash on. Poor George hadn't even had the time to do that much.

One by one, he had removed the stale garments from the case. Spent underwear. A damp towel – stolen from the hotel, by the looks. He tutted and chuckled. A black top that smelled of curry. That was when he saw the small, square object, shining in the bottom of the case. Torn foil of some sort. He picked it up, curious. All at once, he knew exactly what had come to pass in that hotel in Ramsgate.

Seething, now, he checked his watch. Where was she? He wanted to ask the woman on the desk again but felt intimidated by her uniform that somehow made her seem larger. Was still debating whether he would get into trouble for nagging, when he noticed the tall, stately figure entering the building, bearing

ID; loping quickly across the reception area with some swagger.

'You bastard!' Ad shouted. Up and out of his chair now. Not caring if they arrested him. 'You fucked my girlfriend, you dishonourable old shithouse.' Threw a punch that landed on van den Bergen's jaw.

Though he expected the chief inspector to pulverise him, van den Bergen merely pinioned Ad's arms to his sides and shouted, 'What are you talking about, Karelse?' Red in the face. From shame or the punch?

'Stop bluffing! I found the empty condom packet!'

When she saw them both arguing like that, in the foyer in front of everyone, George instinctively wanted to flee back upstairs. Pretend she had never witnessed the confrontation.

Ad caught sight of her. 'Bitch!' he shouted. Spat in her direction.

She gasped. Pushed aside the uniformed officers who had run to van den Bergen's aid.

'What did you fucking call me?' she said, hand on hip. 'Did you just spit at me, Adrianus Karelse?'

Though he was caught in van den Bergen's grip, his mouth and vitriol reigned freely. 'You've been sleeping with the boss, eh? Smart move, George. I'm no longer of use to you any more, am I? Can't help your precious career.'

His eyes were wild. She had never seen him incensed like this. Hadn't realised he had it in him. Had she made him like this? Then she remembered back to the beginning, when they had fought. Recriminations about her having hidden her past. Passive aggressive arsehole. Yes, he had always had this in him.

'Go home, Karelse,' van den Bergen said. Calm. Soothing voice, as though he were trying to charm a threatened cobra back into its basket.

'Do you love him?' Ad asked.

It was too much. George turned and fled back upstairs. As she ran, she heard Ad still shouting behind her. 'I can change! I can be more like him.'

My God! she thought. *He hasn't even got the spine to dump me, even though I deserve it. I just can't face him.*

For the next hour, her phone rang incessantly. She switched it off. Was forced to watch that sycophantic, upper-class Barbie cooing at van den Bergen. Nursing his bruised jaw where Ad had walloped him. Holding court, with Elvis, Marie, Kees and van den Bergen entranced; hanging on her every word. Made even worse, when de Koninck dropped by after she'd seen Strietman and was all, 'Oh fancy seeing you here!' like it was some fucking coffee morning at the Women's Institute or some school reunion shit.

Twelve o'clock. Her stomach already growling, George pulled van den Bergen aside. 'Can we go for a sandwich and talk?' she asked.

'I can't,' he said. Looking down at his feet. Looking out of the window. Anywhere but at her. 'I'm taking Sabine to lunch. I think you need to go home and sort things out with Karelse.'

'Oh. Is that how this is?' She felt at that moment like he had taken the pen from the breast pocket of his shirt and jabbed her repeatedly in her heart with its tip.

Finally, his grey eyes met hers and she could see what lay behind them.

'I care very deeply about you, George.'

'But… Where's the but?'

'There's no but.'

'There's always a but.'

'But we can't be lovers.'

'There we go! I knew it.' Hastily, she wiped away the tear that betrayed her anguish.

'I was taking advantage of you.'

'You love me.' She held his chin gently. Tried to pull him towards her for a kiss. Didn't care who the hell might be passing in the hall. 'We're dead right together.'

340

He pulled away. Pushed her hand back down, though he caressed her knuckles as he did so. 'I'm sorry.'

'Well, fuck you too!'

Collecting her things. Snatching her bag. Not even taking time to put on her coat or say goodbye, she fled the station. On the street, she dialled Aunty Sharon. Pick-up after ten.

'What is it, love?'

'I'm coming home.'

CHAPTER 73

Amsterdam, hospital, 31 January

Ruud Ahlers was suddenly aware that a terrible, repetitive noise was encroaching on his sleep. Beep, beep, beep without respite. Intolerable. He had been dreaming about being whipped by Katja. It had been a deeply satisfying corner of his mind to inhabit after what seemed to be an eon spent in the dark. Katja in hotpants and thigh-length boots. Not just a whip, but that cat-o-nine-tails that really bit into your skin. There had been a nice steak in the dream too. And a single malt. Lovely. But all of that was punctuated by the infernal beeping. What was it?

'Ruud, darling. Can you hear me? It's Katja! Wake up, honey.'

The Pole's voice. Was she talking to him in the dream or was this some sort of stage of wakefulness?

'His eyelashes are moving,' Katja said. Somewhere on his right.

'Nurse!' Another voice. That of a man. 'I think he's waking up.'

Some kind of alarm went off. Bing, bing. Beep, beep, beep. Hiss. Hiss. It was like a synthetic orchestra, clanging away inside his head. His throbbing head. Presently, he realised his throat was on fire. Tried to swallow but there was something constricting his throat. An unyielding object. Choking. He started to thrash his hands around, as he struggled with his spit. Drowning in his own saliva, unable to bypass the thing in his oesophagus.

Opened his eyes. Bleary. Bright lights and machinery. Digital displays and the smell of rotting tulips in a vase of furred water. Something partially obscuring his face. What was it? A mask. An oxygen mask. He grabbed at the regalia and tugged it away from his face.

'Calm down, Dr Ahlers,' a nurse said, leaning over him. 'We'll look after you. Don't touch your breathing apparatus, now.'

How the hell had he got here? Clearly he was in hospital. His burning neck brought the memory back in high resolution. Standing on his bed in that ghastly cell. Home-made noose around his neck. He had jumped.

But not died. Christ. How did he feel about that? Disappointed? No. Bloody elated! He was alive.

'I'm alive!' he tried to shout, although the tube in his throat prevented the sounds from coming out as more than a gurgle.

'He's going to make it!' Katja standing over him. Red curls, framing her face like the halo of a fallen angel. Tears leaking from her eyes in ghoulish black streaks of eyeliner and mascara. A clockwork orange ticking timebomb, as Ahlers remembered why he had attempted suicide. The Gera brothers. The Duke. The Butcher. Shit. He was done for. Or was he?

He must have passed some kind of test. The gods had seen fit to spare his life. They had a different fate in store for him than an eternity spent crawling through the cleansing fire of the underworld, never to return to the sunlight above. Now, a new challenge faced him, where he must repay their mercy in whatever currency they deemed fit. His story had taken on mythological qualities. He was Jason, seeking the golden fleece; Theseus, slaying the Minotaur. Beautifully fitting.

To his left, he spied one of the detectives. The one with the quiff whom they called Elvis. That was it. He knew what form the repayment would take.

Mustering all the energy he had, he ripped the tube out of his throat.

'I'll tell you,' he croaked. 'Cut me a deal and I'll tell you the lot.'

But his words were little more than gurgle as blood bubbled inside his oesophagus.

'Oh my God! He's spitting blood. Get the doctor!' Katja started to scream.

CHAPTER 74

Amsterdam, police headquarters

'How can you let your freedom slip through your fingers?' van den Bergen asked Strietman.

Silence. Strietman sat in his chair. Hands in his lap. Eyes cast downwards but seemingly looking at nothing. More dishevelled than ever.

'Marianne is absolutely certain you're innocent,' he said, opening the folder of photographs. Laying five out, one by one. A girl of about five. A boy of about eleven. Another boy of roughly seven. A girl with a boy, possibly pre-pubescent. A boy, no more than three. 'She thinks there's more than meets the eye to all this.' He tapped the photographs with a long finger. Wanted to slap Strietman's face. Force him to make eye contact. 'You're refusing to give these so called "cast iron alibis". You've turned away your defence lawyer. What the fuck is wrong with you?'

Silence. The glimmer of a tear in Strietman's eye.

'Buczkowski won't speak either.' Van den Bergen leaned over the table so that he was encroaching on the pathologist's space. 'Hasselblad will see your heads roll for this, loose ends or no loose ends. He'll find a way of making it stick, you know. He's all about the stats and the glory. But I'm not Hasselblad. And I'm not so sure. I have to be certain before I take your scalp. Do you understand me, Daan?'

Tight-lipped silence. He wished he could have discussed this with George before she had stormed out. She had said the killer was a narcissist. Before him, he saw only a broken man.

How would George have approached Strietman? She would say that things are not always as they seem. She would look into the whys. *Why did Strietman have an interest in dead men in body bags and children?* But van den Bergen acknowledged he was no psychologist. His brain functioned in a different way. He was a man who put complex jigsaw puzzles together, working on the picture he could see, not on the underlying structure that was hidden from view. *Think more like George. Why is Strietman concealing his alibi? Is it that he doesn't want to incriminate someone or is he ashamed of having met someone in particular? Come on, van den Bergen. What guilty secret would have made you clam up at Strietman's age?*

Sketching a picture of a reclining George from memory, as he and Strietman both sat facing each other in a stale interview room in complete silence, van den Bergen remembered how he had kept news of his paintings being exhibited in small galleries from his father. He had never introduced his father to any of his arty friends, for fear of the ridicule that would come from such candour.

Dead men. Abused children.

'Do you come from a religious background, Daan?' he asked, observing the pathologist from beneath sharp hooded eyes.

Strietman looked up. 'Yes, actually,' he said. 'My parents used to be members of the Church of the Latter Day Saints. The congregation near The Hague. Why?'

'Used to be?'

'They were asked to leave.'

Van den Bergen felt instinctively like he had just removed the lid off the can of worms. Wriggling out. Headed for the floor. Strietman's forehead was shining with sweat.

'Oh. How come?'

Silence. How would George play this?

'You know,' van den Bergen said, shuffling in his seat. Attempting to cross his legs in a manner that said casual and open to idle chat. 'My own father was a religious man. A Calvinist. And terribly right wing. Believed men were men, and women should be grateful. That kind of bullshit.'

Wiping his eyes on his sleeve, Strietman cocked his head sideways, as though he were at least open to listening.

'I was an artist. Still am, really, though only in an amateur sense.'

'You sketch very well,' Strietman said, nodding towards the picture of George on the notepaper.

'Hmn. I could never talk to my old dad about my art. He thought I was a pansy and one of life's losers. Never passed up a chance to belittle me.'

More nodding. A half-smile in sympathy, by the looks.

'What's your father like, Daan? I bet he's a hard-line old bastard if he's in some strange religious sect.'

'Oh, he's made my life a misery over the years.'

Hands unfolded on the table top. But Strietman's eyes put van den Bergen in mind of a crystal blue lake that turns to the colour of sludge when heavy clouds roll in at speed. He sensed great sorrow in the pathologist.

'Is that so?' he said. 'Strietman, were you with another man the nights of the murders? Is that why you won't give us your alibis?'

'I-I don't know what you're talking about.' Fear in those eyes, now. Hands folded again. White knuckles.

'What on earth are you ashamed of, Strietman? Being gay in Amsterdam of all places. Are you *mad*? This city is the spiritual bloody home of gays.'

Strietman stood abruptly. 'How dare you!'

'Did your father abuse you? Is that what these horrible photos are about? Or would you rather keep schtum, and we brand you a paedophile? Do you know what they do to paedophiles in prison?'

Slumping back into his chair, Strietman began to weep openly. 'You don't understand! You have no idea of the pain!'

'Who were you with on the night of the murders, Strietman? Who are you hiding? Someone else who has a problem being open about their sexuality? Are the paedo photos for his benefit?'

'No! No! No!' Strietman yelled. Spittle flying from his mouth in anger. His face flushed red. Drumming the table with his fists.

'You're going to go to prison, and your father's going to have a field day, Strietman. Do you want to give the old bastard the satisfaction? You're scared to fall short in his bigoted, child-abusing eyes, and that's why you'll continue to pay for his violence instead of him. Are you happy to let us all think you and your mystery lover rape children? Because that's the kind of stereo-typical prejudice about gay men that went out of fashion in—'

'We don't! I don't. It's all lies. I'm writing memoirs about my experiences. About child abuse. That's why I've got the pictures. It's research, you smug, judgemental bastard. I can show you the file on a USB stick. I didn't want to share it.'

Van den Bergen's heart beat fast and strong. He felt alive. The air in that room didn't seem so stale or oppressive any more. 'So, what is the identity of this lover you're protecting? If he gives a fig about you, he's hardly going to want you to take the rap for serial murder, is he?'

Strietman clenched his fists and rubbed his eyes. 'Buczkowski!' he shouted. 'We've been having an affair since he fitted my damn kitchen. He didn't want his girl to know. He's a practising Catholic and feels he owes the church for saving him from bad habits. And I've got a thing for pictures of dead men in body bags. There. Skeletons all out of the closet, you bully.'

Van den Bergen grinned broadly, visualising in his mind's eye Kees Leeuwenhoek, his Jedi master, Kamphuis, and that pushy, ambitious prick, Hasselblad, all swinging from the gallows when the media got wind of this witch hunt.

'Just clarify for the tape, Daan,' he said, pointing to the microphone. 'Did you kill Magool Noor, Linda Lepiks, an unidentified Filipino man, Ewa Silbert and three unidentified African men in Britain?'

'No. I bloody well did not and neither did Iwan Buczkowski. We went out to dinner, went clubbing and spent the night together on all of those dates you've been haranguing me about. We've got witnesses. There. I've said it. Happy now?'

'Very. Thank you.' Banged his chest. 'I think you've just cured my stomach acid.'

CHAPTER 75

South East London, 14 February

'The car's waiting for you, Ms Williams-May,' the man from the funeral place said. All dressed in black, looking like an emissary of Death himself.

Aunty Sharon nodded. Lifting her sunglasses just enough to dab her eyes with a large man's hanky. Poignantly embroidered with a blue D. Collecting her handbag from the worktop. Peering inside, though it wasn't clear she was actually looking for anything. George felt sure she was just going through the motions. Keep busy. Keep it together. By her side, Tinesha and Patrice clung to one another. Weeping openly, the poor bastards. Fat tears rolling down Tinesha's cheeks. Reluctant moisture brimming in Patrice's eyes – still bereft, though Derek had not been his father.

Leaning against the fridge, Letitia stood with Leroy. Arm in arm, with her flashy ring glinting under the shitty hundred-watt light, as though this were the time and the place to flaunt her romantic success.

'You looking well smart, love,' she said, straightening Leroy's tie, though it didn't need to be straightened. Reaching up on tippy toes to kiss his chin, almost taking his eye out with her down-market department store fascinator. All petrol-coloured feathers and something akin to close-weave chicken wire. Looked like she'd mugged a cockerel.

Leroy on the other hand looked uncomfortable in his suit. A plain, ageing man with cropped hair and a double chin. Dry skin around his mouth where he had shaven and acne on his neck.

'You suit that hundred-percent silk tie and matching hanky I got you.'

'Yes, love.'

'Lilac's your colour. Goes with your skin, innit?' Letitia looked over at her sister, who was pulling a thin black veil over her face. 'Shame you not got a fella to help you through this, Shaz. I'd lend you mine, but this fine brother's taken, I'm afraid.'

George sucked her teeth dramatically. 'You're a fucking piece of work, do you know that? You really think this is the time or place to pull that sibling rivalry bullshit, when they're all grieving? Why have you got to be such a bi—'

Aunty Sharon grabbed George's arm. 'Leave it, darling. Let's go. Derek's waiting.'

Uniformed police stood on the steps of the church. Legs akimbo. Kevlar vests bulking them up. Menacing. Two German shepherds obediently watching at their masters' sides, smelling fear in the mourners. Reminding those who filed in wearing suits they might have purchased only for court appearances and funerals, that they had come to say goodbye to a murdered man. Little Derek de Falco, who had tried to run with the big boys and got left for dust to dust. Protecting their witness, Aunty Sharon, who might never have been more susceptible to Mr Gera's unsubtle art of persuasion to shut her fucking fat black mouth, should he show up in person to pay his disrespect.

George had been careful to modify her appearance. It wouldn't do to provoke déjà vu in the wrong people.

Inside the church, though her feet were warm in her incongruous winter boots, the rest of her shivered in her best dress, normally worn with heels to formal dinners at college, where she would sit making the sort of chit-chat only academics made, dining on salmon en croute, prepared en masse, rehydrated to eating-point thanks to sauvignon blanc in copious quantities. Those were happy occasions for George. Derek's funeral was not.

Strippers in their daytime clothes lined the pews, there. Dermot Robinson, looking sombre near the front in a double-breasted black overcoat. Thin black tie. Row after row, filled with wailing women of Italian descent, dressed in black, all mourning the loss of their cousin/brother/uncle/great uncle/second cousin, twice removed/something or other by marriage. Elaborate floral displays packed into every nook. Blood red roses spelled 'Derek'. Crysanths in white paid tribute to 'DAD'. Lilies from the relatives who had made a bob in the restaurant trade. Got themselves a bit of class. Unlike the girls from Skin Licks, who had clubbed together to get their Uncle Giuseppe a teddy fashioned from carnations, wrapped in purple ribbon. There was barely room for the priest to stand in his pulpit. Late-comers, genuflecting before the crucifix that hung over the altar; a forlorn-looking Jesus, clearly unhappy with the thorns and the nails and the general ennui that came with simply hanging there, dying painfully to save a bunch of ingrates who wouldn't know a moral existence if it came up and slapped them in the face with five thousand wet kippers.

Poor tragic Jesus, George thought, presiding over a travesty of biblical proportions. Looked down at the ornate silver coffin beneath his bleeding feet. Filled with Derek, whose body the police had finally agreed to release, now that the post mortem had been performed. Poor broken, dead Derek. Kept fresh for two weeks in an industrial fridge, so the police could make sense of his multiple injuries, concluding that he had been stabbed to death in a frenzied manner and strangled, before being hit by Eurostar, effectively affording Derek three modes of violent death in one – a hellish unholy trinity. Kept fresh, so that he could be interred in the good South East London soil inside his hideously expensive casket; bid *arrivederci* by his hundreds of friends and relatives to the off-key performance of 'Ave Maria' and 'My Way' by a semi-famous Bermondsey club singer, who was wearing an evening dress with the BHS label showing at the back. Kept fresh, while George returned from the other side of the North Sea, where she had left Ad sobbing beneath the departures board in Schiphol, promising her they could patch things up and that he would overlook her transgressions. Poor, forgiving Ad. How like Jesus he was. And how like Judas van den Bergen had turned out to be.

'Dearly beloved, we are gathered here to mourn the passing of Paul van den Bergen from the life of Georgina McKenzie. Though they were soul mates for some four years, spending long hours together, engaging in the intimacies of portraiture, gardening, failure to cook anything edible and crime-solving, the illegitimate consummation of their relationship displeased the Father, the Son and the Holy Spirit. A fiery throng of vengeful angels did cast Georgina into purgatory, where she has been tormented by the sight of her one-time friend consorting and cavorting *in flagrante delicto* with a long-limbed succubus of patrician origin.'

'I didn't realise you even liked Derek,' Letitia said, shoving several screwed-up pieces of toilet roll into George's hand. 'Why you so broken hearted for?'

'Fuck off, Letitia,' George whispered loudly, blowing the hair from the auburn wig she was wearing out of her stinging eyes. She stared in disgust at the toilet roll. Threw it back into her mother's lap.

'I didn't blow my nose on it, you cheeky cow,' Letitia said. 'It's clean.'

'Nothing that comes from you is clean.' She winced and rubbed her hands on the skirt of her dress. Wiped her tears on the back of her arm. 'And I don't expect you to understand empathy.'

George put her arm protectively around Tinesha, who flanked Aunty Sharon on one side. Patrice attempting badly the stiff upper lip of a solid young bruv on the other. Being a rock for his women folk, where Derek de Falco, his errant, weedy not-even-really-stepfather, had let them down.

'Let it out, Tin,' George told her cousin. 'It's okay.'

Bawling, bereft Tinesha was almost certainly, like George, weeping for the things she had thought she deserved but which had been cruelly snatched away from her, though they had only ever, at best, dangled tantalisingly, just out of reach.

'Let us pray,' the priest commanded his flock.

But the mournful Our Father murmurings of the lapsed-Catholics and non-believers in that congregation may never have reached God's ears. Despite the police presence outside, there was a commotion at the back of the church. The creak and boom of the door. Slamming open and shut. Screaming. Turning around to see some black boy in a hoodie, running down the aisle. A gun in his hand. Scanning the congregation for someone. Police too slow to let the dogs off their leashes. Made it to the front row, where he stood, momentarily nonplussed. Wide-eyed and panting. Waving the gun to and fro between Sharon and Letitia.

Sharon screaming uncontrollably. Tinesha shrieking. Letitia open-mouthed.

'Which one of yous is Sharon?'

'I ain't no fat-arsed fucking Sharon,' Letitia said. 'Little dick-head.'

'Police! Drop the weapon.' The men in black, advancing slowly.

In the sliver of a second before the boy pulled the trigger, George saw the muscles in his index finger tighten. Watched, as his nostrils flared. Biting his lip in concentration. Turning the gun to the side, like he was some badass, riding shotgun in an outlandish Compton drive-by, instead of being a kid who had been bunged a ton or maybe even a monkey by Luigi Gera to ice Derek's loud-mouthed, sort-of widow. *Brap, brap. You is dead, yeah?*

Without any of the consideration she might give the situation if she had more time, George grabbed the underside of the pew and high-kicked the boy's hand. Caught him squarely with the steel toecap of her boot. But the gun went off.

CHAPTER 76

Amsterdam, hospital, later

Marie glanced into the side-room where Ahlers was recovering. Van den Bergen was seated on one side of the bed, finally taking Ahlers' statement. Elvis, on the other with the recording equipment. She could hear the boss' rich, deep voice even through the glass. She had been listening to the interview as it had unfolded.

'So, you were approached by a consortium of traffickers, after your public fall from grace.'

'Yes. That's right. The go-between was an Italian man. But he wasn't the big cheese. He made it clear from the outset that he worked for someone higher up the food chain.'

Ahlers' croaky voice. Propped in bed, looking pale and as though he might have lost a good half stone over the last fortnight, thanks to his new diet of slops.

'Can you give me the big cheese's name?'

'No way.'

'Do you know it?'

'Yes. But I'm not about to blab that.'

Then, Elvis' voice. Thin and stringy. Irritated. 'For Christ's sake, Ahlers! You promised you would tell us everything in return for protection. And need I remind you we're talking about a drastically reduced sentence in a *minimum* security facility? Stick to your side of the bargain, will you?'

But van den Bergen had continued undeterred. 'Can you give me the name of the Italian, then?'

'No.'

'Why not?' Elvis asked.

'Is it Luigi Gera?' van den Bergen said.

Ahlers had been shaking his head a little too energetically for a man who was recovering from having had an oesophageal stent inserted into his throat. 'How do you know Gera?'

Van den Bergen had crossed his long legs and treated Ahlers to one of his grim, downturned smiles. 'Perhaps you're not the only one who's had enough of being the fall-guy for this network of scumbags.'

Marie had known, of course, that van den Bergen had been referring to McKenzie's aunt, over in London – a barmaid in a strip club, no less – who had been sitting on information about people traffickers that, had she spoken up sooner, could have saved the life of her ex-lover – the manager of said titty bar. What a classy family that McKenzie was from. No wonder she was so uptight about cleanliness. It must have been difficult coming from the upper echelons of British society and having to mingle with the unwashed, clog-wearing Dutch proletariat.

Van den Bergen speaking again: 'We believe Gera and his men are near the top of this trafficking ring and that the murderer – yes, we know it's not you, so stop gargling spit and making like you're going to asphyxiate – is another surgeon.' He leaned forward, his triangular nose almost touching that of the Ahlers. 'Do you know who the surgeon is?'

No answer. Rapid, noisy breathing and more gurgling. Marie thought Ahlers sounded like her mother's blocked waste disposal unit. A frustrated sigh from Elvis.

'Okay, who bought the baby from Magool? I want a name.'

Ahlers spoke. But Marie failed to hear the name. The biggest, baddest looking beast of a man she had ever seen loomed into view at the end of the corridor. Clutching a gun. A long, thin silencer on the end. Moving quickly towards her. Twenty paces. Ten. Five. She did not even have time to draw her own service weapon. A blow against her temple with the butt of the weapon sent her reeling to the ground. Instantly dizzy and vomiting over her hands as she tried to push herself back up.

Dimly, she saw the man enter Ahlers' room. Point the gun, as van den Bergen fumbled to draw his Walther P5. Elvis frozen in shock. Blip, blip, blip. Three muffled shots fired. Men down?

'Help!' Marie shouted. 'Help me! Kees!'

The man with the gun emerged from the room. Stopped by her head. Huge feet in smart leather shoes. She hadn't the energy to look up at him.

'Keep your mouth shut, *puttana*,' he said, before he kicked her sharply in the face.

CHAPTER 77

Soho, London, later

'What do you mean, you want to work?' Dermot Robinson asked, sipping brandy at the bar of his club. Packed with de Falcos and the gritterati of Bermondsey, tonight, laughing and knocking back Jägerbombs behind a cordon for VIPs. A rare visit from the Porn King himself, but seeing as it was Derek's wake…

'Just give me the fucking mop and bucket, Mr Robinson,' George said, pulling the irritating wig from her head. Unleashing her own hair beneath, which she had pinned into a tight bun. 'Please.'

'You're shaking, love. Have a drink instead. Comfort your poor aunty.' He snapped his fingers at the barman, brought in for the evening from one of the other clubs to give Sharon a night in which to drink to the memory of her ex. 'Give her a sherry or something, Al.'

'I don't want a sherry,' George said, dragging on her e-cigarette with trembling hands. 'Thanks. But no thanks. I need to clean. You said you'd keep my job open for me.'

'I lied. We got a replacement. You've been gone too long.'

'Just for tonight. I need something to do with my hands. You know? It's all got too much.' Would a man like Dermot Robinson understand her need to wrestle order from chaos by means of limescale-removing bathroom cleaner and anti-bacterial surface spray?

'What's too much? Some black kid shooting the head off a giant flower teddy bear at a funeral? Or you been doing more of that porn studying over there?'

He laughed into his glass. Looked up at the dancers on the stage, naked but for the tiniest of thongs, winding their lithe bodies around the brass pole. His girls. His stage. His pole. Covered in weeks' worth of neglected sticky finger marks, George could see.

'You're going to rot your brain, girl,' he said. 'Take it from one who knows.'

'I've been working with the Dutch police on serial murders. Remember I called your PA, Marge, to see if she'd heard of Linda Lepiks?'

He nodded. His mood suddenly sombre. 'One of my actresses has been missing for over a month. Then, Derek gets killed and I find out the scheming fuckwit has been letting some wops from Rome pimp out their underage whores in here.' He poked the bar emphatically. '*My* fucking club, part of *my* empire that I built in *my* name with *my* sweat and tears. I wanna find my missing girl. If them wops took her, I want them dead. While that girl was working for me, she was my property. Know what I mean?'

And there it was. Ownership. Like her ex-teen-squeeze, Danny. Like his small-time-henchman-turned-big-time-psychopath, Jez. Like Ad. Like her old Dutch tutor, that manipulative sex-pest, Fennemans. Men, claiming ownership over women's bodies. Nothing like the man she loved – van den Bergen – who steadfastly refused to accept even temporary tenure of hers.

'You think your mates in the police can find my girl?' he asked, eyeing George's heavy boots.

'Give me the mop and bucket and I'll see what I can do,' she said.

He nodded. 'What exactly you got on your feet? Thought you

girls all wore fuck-me shoes with a nice dress. What you call them, then?'

'Don't fuck me shoes.'

In the course of the evening, mopping around the feet of the mourners who now didn't look too mournful at all with a few inside them, George found herself getting more and more irritated by her situation. She hated walking away from unfinished business and she knew that was exactly what she had done in coming home. Derek's funeral had just been a cover for the deep, deep hurt of having that stupid, lanky old sod reject her, choosing Dr Lovely Legs, Friend to the Dying Children, instead. Hiding in her cupboard, surreptitiously smoking a real cigarette, blowing her exhaled smoke out through the old Vent-Axia fan that sucked the vapours of evil from the club and spat them into a back alley somewhere off Peter Street, she checked her phone. Her in-box was at capacity, piled high like an EU sugar mountain with sickly sweet texts from Ad. Swimming in acidic emails from Sally, like an *appellation d'origine* non-*contrôlée* wine-lake, demanding she make contact. Nothing from van den Bergen. Typical. But here was one from Marie.

```
Hit-man took out Ahlers this morning and
wounded Kees. I got assaulted — fractured
cheekbone. VdB told me to warn you to keep
a look out for unfriendly Italian faces.
Murderers are not Strietman & Buczkowski.
Marie.
```

George emerged from the cupboard, still smoking. Scanned the room too quickly in panic. Scanned it again and again like an unreadable bar code. They were *all* unfriendly Italian faces. The extended de Falco clan had split to sit one side of the VIP area, whilst a gathering of two – Aunty Sharon and Letitia – sat the other. Was a murderer among them?

Cleaning would not expunge this fear so easily, now. Ahlers was dead. A man she had broken bread with was dead. A sleazy arsehole, an abuser of the vulnerable, but a friend of Katja nonetheless. He had welcomed her into his home, perhaps with the intention to fuck her but apparently not with the intention to murder her. And he had been whacked. Like a two-bit informant in a gangster film.

There was safety in numbers. She made a beeline for Letitia's chicken hat.

'Where's your fiancé?' George asked her mother, swigging from Sharon's glass of rum. 'He jilted you the minute he got a whiff of an altar?'

Letitia was all folded arms and heaving breasts. 'Think you some fucking comedian? He took Tinesha and Patrice home, *actually*,' she said. 'Cos my Leroy is well caring.'

'This ain't no place for children,' Aunty Sharon slurred. 'Not my children, anyways.' She hiccoughed and downed her drink. Foisted the glass into George's bleach-dry hands. Gave her a twenty. 'Get another round. One for yourself. Come and sit with your Aunty Shaz, love.' Slapped the banquette affectionately. Knocked her hat to the floor but seemed not to notice.

George returned from the thronging bar, her small hands struggling to encase three potent drinks. Downed a large gin and tonic quickly, sucked up through a straw. Gasping as sharp bubbles pushed their way out of her nostrils. Alcohol on an empty stomach. Instant hit. At Aunty Sharon's behest, chased it down with another. Then a glass of wine.

Letitia eyed George critically through false lashes. Sipping her Tia Maria and green BOLS. 'Where you been the last couple of hours?' Sniffed the air near her. With those incongruous caramel blonde tresses that hung like doggy ears either side of her head, she put George in mind of a beagle trying to pick up the scent of the fox's lair. 'You ain't been fucking cleaning, have you? In a posh dress?'

'What's it to you?' George stared absently at the dancers, wondering what it was about sex workers that had particularly appealed to the murderer. Perhaps he came into regular contact with working girls and porn stars. Used their services. Perhaps the killer was here right now. Had a Skin Flicks actress not gone missing? Scanned the drunken, leering faces in the packed club. Most of the women from the funeral had gone now. Mainly men; their tongues hanging out at flesh they hadn't seen that firm and blemish-free for decades. Felt suddenly uncomfortable as though she were being watched. 'I needed to do a shift, anyway. All this flying back and forth… Paying towards rooms in three different places. I'm potless.'

'Better ways to earn money if you're skint,' Letitia said. 'You, of all people, should know that. Or you grown a conscience nowadays?'

'Stick it up your arse, Letitia.'

'Bet you could earn ten times what you get, cleaning other people's shit up, by dancing.' Winking. Nodding towards a Chinese girl who had just enclosed her thighs around the top of a pole and was now corkscrewing slowly down to the ground. Straight, black hair sweeping the floor.

'What the fuck would I want to take my clothes off for?' George asked, palpably drunk. The room spinning. Her head pounding with the beat of the dance music.

'You scared the punters wouldn't pay to watch you dance?' Gave her daughter the once-over. 'Actually, I don't think they would. You far too fucking frumpy. I seen them posh white women dressing like you in Waitrose one time. Bet they got some pig ugly, raggedy old undies on under them pensioner clothes. Bet you do too.'

Without fully understanding why she did it, but feeling that festering resentment and the compulsion to shock her mother might underpin her actions, George lifted her dress over her head and strutted unevenly in her underwear and boots to the stage.

'Come back!' her mother yelled. 'I didn't mean it. Get back here, girl! You making a fucking spectacle of yourself!'

George offered her the finger.

Jeering and applause from strangers.

Go on, you pissed-up cow. Show us your tits. Get them off.

As she spun herself drunkenly around the pole, gyrating in non-matching underwear – budget black pants from M&S paired with an expensive red Triumph Amourette bra – she caught sight of someone besides her mother, Aunty Sharon and Dermot Robinson, all staring at her with horrified expressions. A familiar face attached to an unfamiliar body. Blinked. Gone. She must have imagined it. Now, there were men trying to stuff ten-pound notes into her knickers and Letitia was trying to throw her coat around her. Shouting in patois that she should be ashamed of herself, and had she not been brought up to know better?

'No. I dragged myself up, remember?' she answered, barely registering the slap across her cheek.

She threw her dress back on. Marched up the stairs, too drunk to feel the bite of the chill night air as she fell through the door onto the street. Hugged her coat tightly around her, trying to make out the time on the face of her watch. Shouldn't have had that extra glass of wine. Idiot. Tubes and trains still running, hopefully, though she couldn't remember what day it was. Stumbling along.

On the train back to Catford, she felt eyes on her. Young lads staring at her wig, worn askew. When they got off, she still had that feeling of being the focus of someone's attention. Too tired to scrutinise the other passengers thoroughly. She kept losing the thread of her thoughts, the posters on the train riding up the walls and down the walls.

Then, off at her stop. Doors bleeping as they started to close. Someone had got off behind her, jamming their body into the doors at the last minute; forcing them to open again. Bleeping. The train moved off, but she heard footsteps behind her. But nobody in her peripheral vision.

It must have been late, because the streets were graveyard-deserted. Not even a fox. Lights out in all the houses. Frost, settling in jagged patterns on car windscreens. Then, footsteps quickening behind her. A tall figure.

George spun around just in time to see the shining blade of the scalpel catch the light from the streetlamp. Blinding her momentarily. She only glimpsed her attacker – wearing a surgical cap and mask. A hand jabbing down towards her neck. She screamed.

CHAPTER 78

Laren, the Netherlands, 15 February

Lying in a strange bed, in a strange home, waiting for the return of a new lover whom he didn't love. It was a peculiar experience, van den Bergen thought. The last time he had done something so decadent and foolish, he had been a young man, dating Andrea. Except he hadn't been burdened by guilt back then. Now, old enough to know better, he was thinking of George whilst luxuriating in Sabine Schalks' Egyptian cotton bedding. Trying to focus on the quiet, elegant ambience of her country house in Laren, which had been a relatively short drive southeast of Amsterdam.

As if her Koninginneweg house hadn't been grand enough.

'You've got to go *right* now?' he had asked the previous afternoon, watching Sabine dress hastily, spraying perfume in the air above her. Masking the fact that she had not even taken the time to shower the scent of him off her body. 'Seems a little sudden.'

'Yes. Sorry. I must, must, must be in London by this evening. Business. But you can stay until you're ready to go.'

'Why did you invite me over if you knew you've got a flight to catch?'

'Spontaneity,' she had said. Throwing clothes into a case. 'Aren't you glad I did?' Blew him a kiss.

He picked up his watch from her nightstand. Checked the time. Three o'clock. Hasselblad would haul him over the coals for going AWOL in a time of crisis. 'Give me five minutes. I'll be dressed and out of here.' He had thrown the duvet aside to reveal his nakedness.

Shaking her head. Hastily putting in her earrings. 'If I don't go now, I'll not get a flight. Some things won't wait, I'm afraid.' Zipping her small case closed. 'Now, make sure you lock up this place properly when you go,' Slipping on her high heels, though she hardly needed the extra height. It was the first time he had not needed to stoop to speak to a woman. 'Especially after the shenanigans with the building site at the back, I've got to be really on the ball about security.'

Van den Bergen cast a glance at the window that faced onto the enclosed courtyard gardens below. Smiled.

'What were the odds of Marianne's expert paediatrician living in the very house that backs onto the Valeriusstraat building site?' He laughed at the curious irony.

'It was obviously fate,' Sabine said, grabbing his hand, gathering up her leather skirt and thrusting his fingers into the warm wetness inside her knickers. 'There. A little something to remember me by while I'm gone. Dior couldn't bottle that.'

Van den Bergen withdrew his hand. Found himself blushing like a schoolboy.

'Are you marking your territory?' he asked. 'I thought only men did that.'

She smirked and winked. 'I call it Eau de Sabine. Anyway, listen! I'll meet you at the Laren house. Three locks. Easy enough. Let yourself in. Get the open fire going. I'll be back before you know it.'

She had leaned in for a kiss that promised more. Her hair fell onto his face. He drank in the smell of her expensive perfume. But her lips were harder than George's; her tongue more probing and aggressive. She was a beautiful woman by any standards. And yet, he found her slightly intimidating, despite the fact that they had just made love. Well, less making love – something he had definitely done with George – more, had enjoyed surprisingly perfunctory but adequate afternoon-sex. Still, two different lovers in the same month after years of romantic drought was nothing short of a miracle. On paper, he was a stud. In reality, he was nothing but a love rat, betraying his own heart, as well as his friend. His head was in bits. George had not lied when she had mischievously promised she would ruin him.

Sabine had tossed the keys to him. 'Catch!'

'I can't just turn up to another man's house and make myself at home,' he had said, swinging his long legs over the side of the bed.

'It's not another man's house, Paul. It's my house. And sure you can. Be my guest. You won't be pestered by nosey neighbours. There's never anyone around anyway. You've got the keycode for the gates and the alarm. Relax! Enjoy it. Get the bed warm for me.'

Laren. The sort of neighbourhood and home that had no place even on the periphery of van den Bergen's conscious mind or memory. Somewhere between a traditional Dutch country house on steroids and a Beverley Hills mansion. Who knew Sabine was so wealthy?

He stared at the beamed ceiling in that house, now, and tried to imagine what kind of a man Thomas Schalks must have been. Incredibly rich, if nothing else. Even the dust motes that drifted in the air here looked like slivers of platinum, falling to the ground like munificence from the warming sunlight. At home, in his place, they just looked like dust. Bits of dead skin and minute dirty particles that drifted in from the diesel-stink of the roads outside. Not here. Here, it was silent but for the sounds of nature. Birds on the wing, excited by the promise of spring in the burgeoning buds of deciduous trees. The wind rustling in the evergreen holly and specimen pines in the garden. Smelled of fresh grass and wealth.

How odd it must have been to be left a widow at forty, in possession of your spouse's massive family fortune. And now, he, Paul van den Bergen, was apparently dating this merry widow. Laughing out loud at the very thought, he rolled over and hugged the plump pillow. Thought of George's pillowy bosom. The feel of her curvaceous, womanly shape in his arms. He held the pillow tight and clenched his eyes shut, as the pain crowded out the superficial euphoria of his artificial high. Sabine was not George. She would never be George. He had known that even before she had kissed him.

Why had he allowed himself to be seduced so easily?

'Poor you,' she had said. 'Come back to mine,' she had suggested. 'You're shaking. You need a drink!' she had observed.

And he had succumbed to the novel oblivion that four brandies on an empty stomach and easy sex with a thoughtful and admirable woman had afforded him. A panacea to the most dreadful turn of events and the ensuing unbearable anguish.

'I've fucked up, Sabine,' he had said, sipping the Hennessey she had pushed into his hand. Standing by the fireplace in her grand Koninginneweg living room. Gazing at the quaint African figurines on her mantel. Large-breasted fertility figures, by the looks, with no arms or legs. 'Ahlers is dead. I almost got two young people killed. One's in hospital with a hole in his shoulder! A couple of inches in another direction and it could have been curtains. This is all down to me.'

'How can it be? Some things, you just can't control,' she had said. Thawing him with a warm smile and a friendly caress on his brow.

He thought of the lonely ache that George's absence had left in his heart. 'It's not just that. I've blown it with someone I care for very deeply.'

'Your English assistant?'

Sabine had been a good listener, nodding sympathetically as he had confided how he admired George's intellect. Related a deliberately abridged tale of how, despite the close friendship they developed over time, he had pushed George away with harsh words. All the way back to London. He was careful not to mention that he was head over heels in love with her, of course – even more so, since they had both finally given in to a mutual attraction more compelling than anything he had ever before considered possible. There was definitely no need for Sabine to know that.

'Well, if she'd drop the case and walk out on you like some tantrum-throwing toddler, she's probably not worth worrying about,' Sabine had said. 'Sounds like you misplaced your loyalties.'

'Oh, she won't drop the case,' van den Bergen said. 'I know George. She'll be in the UK, mulling things over. Looking into the Ramsgate killings. Last time we hit a bump in the road, she consulted the serial killer, Silas Holm, for advice, would you believe it? And got the information she needed, too! She's resourceful all—'

Sabine had taken his glass from him and kissed him confidently, interrupting his eulogy.

He had pulled away in stunned silence. Still continuing to berate himself as though the kiss had not happened; as though his brain had not registered the paediatrician's advance.

'I'm a failure.'

'You're far from a failure, Paul.'

Sabine Schalks had said the right thing to him at just the right time. Touched him in a vulnerable place. And he had fallen at her size 42 feet; uncharacteristically sharing intimacy with her that felt unearned by her, unburdening himself to her about George, letting slip that Ahlers had given him the name of the woman who had bought Magool's baby only moments before he had been executed. How out of sorts he was.

And yet, here he lay now in an antique bed that might have cost almost as much as his own apartment, in a house worth millions. Downstairs, he thought he heard the front door slam. Sabine must have returned. Another clandestine night of indulgence planned – uninterrupted this time, with any luck. Not a single soul knew his whereabouts or with whom he was consorting, except for the lovely Sabine herself.

When she did not appear in the bedroom, he pulled on her robe that hung on the back of the en suite door and went downstairs.

Finding nobody in the house, he felt a sense of unease.

'Sabine?' Nothing. 'Sabine, is that you?' Not a sound.

He padded from room to room, until he reached a workshop or studio of some description. It was messy, unlike the rest of the place. Pots on shelves. A potter's wheel. Here must have been the place where Sabine practised her sculpture. In one corner of the large space stood what appeared to be a kiln – almost industrial in size. Curious, he approached it. Opened the heavy door. Balked when he saw the kiln's charred contents.

'Jesus Christ!' he said.

'Not Jesus Christ,' came Sabine's voice behind him. 'But not far off it.'

CHAPTER 79

Cambridge, St John's College, later

'Christ on a bike, Georgina McKenzie!' Sally Wright snapped. 'You've got some brass neck, coming back here, after nothing but radio silence. How dare you go over my head! Who the hell do you think you are?'

Standing by the oriel window in her office, into the senior tutor's face were etched deep lines, accentuated now by the level of ferocity in her intent. Mouth, pruned with dissatisfaction, dragging hard on a cigarette. Her blunt fringe hanging too high on her forehead to obscure wiry grey eyebrows angled upwards in almost cartoon-like rage.

George gripped the sofa's arms.

'I can explain,' she said. But she started to shake violently. Body twitching as though she had been possessed by the devil. 'Oh, I feel weird.'

Cigarette still in mouth, Sally ran over to her. Put her arms around her.

'Dear God! What's going on with you? Don't you dare have a fit on me!' she said, dropping ash onto the threadbare red Persian rug that covered the floor boards.

George relished the warmth of her body. Drank in the familiar nicotine and coffee smell of the woman who had not given her

372

life but had given her much more than that: she had given her a future.

'It's a-adrenalin,' she stammered. 'My brain's about to b-blow a g-gasket. You wouldn't believe what happened to me last n-night.'

Sally threw an old tartan blanket around George. Strutted to her tea urn. Steam rising from water near boiling point, spitting all over her hands from the unruly tap. 'Bastard thing!' She sucked her scalded skin. Gave George some weak tea in a chipped china cup. Produced a hip flask from her battered briefcase. Tipped amber liquid into the tea. 'Hot toddy. Cure for all ills,' she said, winking.

'Thanks,' George said, eyeing the cup in disgust. 'But I can't drink out of that cup. It's chipped. I can't…'

Backing away, Sally glowered at her. Jabbing in her direction with her almost-spent cigarette to emphasise every syllable she spoke. 'You broke every rule in the book, young lady. You defy my authority. You make a mockery of protocol. I expressly told you not to go to Amsterdam. I told you, it would end in disaster. And here you are, turning your nose up at my fucking hot toddy!'

She stubbed out her cigarette in a large, dirty cut-glass ashtray on an aspidistra stand by the window. Lit another. Tossed one to George who lit up willingly.

'The least you owe me is an apology.'

George exhaled blue smoke in two billowing jet-streams from her nostrils. Afterburners of indignation. Considered Sally's demand. Cheeky old bag, pushing her around; browbeating her into deference like she was some wayward charge, rather than a capable woman, all grown-up now. 'No. No way am I saying sorry for something I don't regret. You, of all people, should respect my right to autonomy. *My* life. *My* choices. *My* risk. I ain't no wet-behind-the-ears undergrad, now.'

Sally perched on the edge of her desk. Narrowed her eyes, hard and unforgiving behind those cat's-eye glasses. 'Oh. You don't regret almost having your head blown off by some two-bit hoodie in a church?'

'You know about that?' George clutched the blanket close. Defensive. Feeling like Sally's remark was somehow meant as ridicule. Belittling her stab at independence as haphazard at best, downright dangerous at worst. 'How?'

'Van den Bergen. He emailed me soon after you stormed out on him. Warning me that you might be in danger. That the murderer had not yet been caught, despite news reports to the contrary. And news must travel fast on the police grapevine, because there was a missive from him regarding the church shooting sitting in my in-box this morning.'

Under scrutiny in that enclosed space, George felt like she was in the claustrophobic tunnel of an all-seeing MRI scanner. Sally's eyes, stripping away the layers of artifice to find the truth of George's secrets laid bare beneath. Was there any limit to the things Sally Wright could gather intelligence on? Did she know about what had happened in that hotel room in Ramsgate with that treacherous, gorgeous disappointment, van den Bergen?

'You two have got no right, chatting shit about me behind my back,' George said. 'Making decisions about my life. *My life.*' Prodding herself in the chest. Quaking for a different reason, now. 'Not your fucking life, Sally. Not van den Bergen's life. I went to Amsterdam because you were keeping me here like it was an open bloody prison. I came back because *my family* needed me. *My family*, Sally. *Flesh and blood.*'

George felt like a fire had been sparked within her. She might scorch all in her path; spitting highly flammable vitriol at this woman who saw herself as her surrogate mother. Except George had fed at the breast of Letitia the Dragon.

Letitia, who had unexpectedly come thundering up that deserted Catford road behind George's attacker, wielding a discarded exhaust pipe she must have found in amongst the trash that grows like strange and wonderful weeds by the railway stations of South East London.

'I'm gonna kill you, bastard!' she had shouted. 'That's my

fucking daughter.' Murder in her voice. Aunty Sharon steps behind. Tottering down the road to help, though it was Letitia who had sprinted after the tall attacker in her bare feet. Fast for a fat woman.

George had been lying on her back: a dying cockroach in somebody's front garden. Thought she was about to be gutted by some six-foot-tall masked wraith bearing a scalpel. Instead, watching the counter attack unfold in what seemed like slo-mo. Straight out of a ninja film, man.

The exhaust pipe had whistled impressively through the air before it had connected with the head of George's assailant. Hit home with a clunk. Hadn't knocked him out but another swipe square across the shoulder blades had spooked him enough to make him flee.

'Yeah, go on, you piece of shit!' Letitia screaming in her bare feet. The figure, rapidly diminishing as he made his getaway. 'Come back, and I'll fucking finish the job. I ain't scared of you, motherfucking rapist cunt.' A good fourteen stones of motherly rage, shaking a balled fist in the air. Hair extensions still hanging perfectly in place, though there would be no dawn chorus issuing forth from the cockerel hat now that it had lost its strut.

Lights on inside the house. Twitching curtains revealed an old black man in his pyjamas, looking out. Fearful of whatever over-sized cats might be on the prowl, using his tiny garden as their litter tray. Surprised when he saw Letitia the Dragon dragging George up from the bed of crushed hyacinths by her underarms, as though she was an oversized baby. Breathing brandy, whisky, Tia Maria fumes all over her. Aunty Sharon, screaming *Call the cops!* Stumbling around, still pissed on rum n Ting. If someone had flicked a match into life, all three of them would have gone up like plum puddings.

Rescued from certain death by the one person she had never thought would come to her aid. Maybe blood was thicker than water, after all. 'Family,' she said once more, under her breath.

A tendon in Sally's lean, smoker's face was twitching. Stinging from the slight.

'Van den Bergen cares about you, young lady,' she said. Arms folded. Legs folded. Emotional origami, trapping the hurt inside. 'I care about you. We may not be blood relatives, but it takes more to bind people together than the chance provision of DNA. And those bonds such as we share are not easily undone.'

George could feel an apology trying to force its way out. Swallowed it back – a concession she was not prepared to make. Stubborn. She got that from Letitia too. The bond of shared DNA was perhaps stronger than Sally or George had hitherto appreciated.

Change the subject.

'Listen, I don't want to get into all this blame-apportioning bullshit,' George said. 'I thought I had a right to get out of the country for a bit. You didn't. I'm back now. So, let's agree to differ and move on.'

'Is that an apology?'

Damn it! The woman's like a dog with a bone. This is power play for her. Don't rise to it.

'What's the score with Silas Holm and that letter? You said he'd been visited by some doctor called…' She frowned. Started to scroll back through old emails on her phone. 'What was it?'

'A South African woman called Roni de Zwarte.' Sally looked down at the chipped red nail varnish on her nails. Matched her oversized plastic beads. 'When I spoke to security at Broadmoor, she was the only unusual visitor he had received. There was no other way the letter could have got out.'

Roni de Zwarte. George held her breath. Pulse, pounding in her ears. Not only déjà vu, but also déjà entendu. A familiar name she could see written in the font of her texts in her mind's eye. She surreptitiously brought to life the screen on her phone, careful not to let Sally see. Another leaked text Marie had sent her, keeping her posted on the case.

```
Ahlers gave name of woman who adopted
Magool's baby before he was killed.
Doctor called Roni de Zwarte.
```

Though Marie's words resounded in her head at a deafening volume, Sally was oblivious to the connection that George had just made. She continued to talk. Hands clasped behind her back. More relaxed, now. Gazing out of her window once again at the fast-moving clouds that streaked across a bleak, East Anglian sky. Winter still teasing the tips of those medieval spires with ice and a wind that bit.

'Holm is allowed contact with several non-staff, including you. Although believe me, madam, now you're back, I shall be calling to have your clearance revoked. I don't deal in idle threats.' She turned around. Almost pierced George with her pointed glare. Menace in those nicotine-stained jagged teeth, like a vengeful piranha. 'You can find yourself another study subject and think about what you could have done differently.'

George stared at her in sullen silence, mentally tipping the hot toddy that had now gone stone cold all over her horrible severe hairdo. *Fuck off, surrogate mummy, with your saggy, barren tits.*

'Anyhow, they allowed this Dr de Zwarte access,' Sally continued, shaking her head. 'All her credentials seemed intact. They even had clearance documents logged on their computer system, which flummoxed the head of security in retrospect. When I call, I'll see if there's any more news.'

So, Sally hadn't yet made the call to Broadmoor. Which meant George still had clearance to visit Silas Holm. With so many questions that demanded answers, she knew exactly where she was headed next. She would worry about breaking all the rules another day.

CHAPTER 80

Laren, the Netherlands, 16 February

Inside the windowless place – a panic room of sorts, given the unyielding metal shutters, separating him from the rest of the house, and the CCTV monitoring equipment in there – van den Bergen had stopped struggling against his bonds. He had long since tipped over the chair that Sabine had strapped him into, bashing his head; maybe dislocating his shoulder as he had hit the deck. The pain was intense. Had thought it unbearable, though as time had crawled by he had had no choice but to bear it. Sleep would not take him. Fainting at will was not possible. By now, he was subdued. No more muffled screams, because no one was coming. No more attempts at escape, because she had known what she was doing when she had tied him up and strapped his mouth shut.

He was going to die. Might as well do it with some dignity.

Minutes or hours or days earlier – it was hard to tell in that windowless place – he had wept at the thought that he would end up like the thing in the kiln. An effigy of a man, split into pieces. Head. Torso. Limbs. Too realistic to be sculpture and yet, apparently, cast in clay.

'What is it?' he had asked Sabine. Already jumpy, given she had appeared with hardly any warning like some menacing apparition. 'It's my husband,' she had said. A glint of something deadly in her eyes.

'What do you mean?' he had asked. Not registering the shining thing in her hand. Idiot. If only he had trusted his instincts – the sense of unease that had brought him downstairs in the first place.

She was fast. She was strong. She was tall enough to grab him from behind with ease, holding a scalpel to his throat. He could barely breathe. The blade dug in; stung as blood seeped forth, warm and wet on his fingers as he tried to loosen her grip.

She spoke, close to his ear with that murderous mouth he had kissed just over twenty-four hours earlier. Hot breath on his cold, goose-pimpled skin, making the hairs on the back of his neck stand involuntarily. 'When I killed him, I made a cast of his body parts before I cooked them to ashes in my kiln. Then, I used the cast to immortalise him in terracotta. I think it has artistic merit, don't you? Like a funerary mask.'

Van den Bergen had wept. Considered throwing her off. But he knew that her blade, already millimetres into his skin, would slice through sinew and muscle to cut his jugular and carotid artery, meeting no more resistance than a steak knife through *stamppot*. He had seen what she had done to the others.

'Please, Sabine. Let me go.'

Hot tears rolling down to the cut on his neck. Stinging, where the salt met the blood. He thought of his father. Dead in the hospice. Mouth slightly open. At first, the nurses hadn't come when he had pressed the alarm button. He had held a mirror to the old man's mouth to see if his breath still left vapour on the glass. Felt suddenly so alone when the mirror had remained clear. Had wept like a little lost boy for all the harsh words said and the times when he had looked up to and loved that broken body, suffocated and raddled by the big C until the life of Matthijs van den Bergen was no more. So lonely, then, even though Tamara had been just outside the room. Tamara, whose wedding it was tomorrow.

'My daughter's getting married tomorrow afternoon! Please, Sabine. I beg of you. Don't do this. There must be another way.'

'Get in here!' Sabine had started to drag him backwards towards a door he had not noticed before. The grim sculpture of her dead husband taunting him in the corner of his eye, as he tried to catch a glimpse of where he was being taken. The windowless room. This panic room. How apt.

She had made him sit on the chair. He should have reacted. Should have resisted. But the ten codeine he had taken that day had rendered him weak, sluggish, slow. Strapping the tape around his body, pinning him to the chair. Was this how she had despatched her other victims? Had they started down the road to hell, duct taped to a chair in a glorified cupboard meant to preserve life, not aid and abet the snuffing out of it?

'You sit still until I come for you. Right?'

Now he realised why the sex had felt like a mechanical enterprise instead of a passionate encounter. Looking properly into those eyes, he could see no soul in this woman. Whatever humanity she had once possessed had gone.

'Don't try anything stupid, Paul. I need you...unblemished.' Long, cold fingers stroking the stubble on his chin, like a caress from the legs of a venomous spider. Blowing a kiss that may as well have been from a hissing cobra. A praying mantis ready to consume her mate.

She stood back, scrutinising his bonds. Considering him like she might appraise a life-sized sculpture in a gallery. Nodding at her handiwork.

'You're in good shape,' she said. 'A little thin, but otherwise fit. You're going to save a *lot* of lives.' Smiling. Clasping her hands together demurely, head cocked to the side. A homicidal Florence Nightingale.

How could it be? A woman who healed the sick; a woman who specialised in the medical care of children; a killer who cut the organs out of the vulnerable for resale, clearly enthusiastic about the prospect of destroying life. Even if he had been able to speak, van den Bergen had neither the vocabulary nor the understanding to articulate the bewilderment he felt.

Tamara would walk down the aisle tomorrow, believing that her selfish shit of a father had not cared enough even to show up to her wedding to Numb-nuts. Elvis and Marie, his ersatz children, would believe he had abandoned them to navigate the stormy high seas of the Netherlands police force without a captain at the helm of their sinking ship. George…he had pushed beautiful George away, though he loved her with such ferocity, thinking dating this upper-class ghoul was somehow a better choice for everyone concerned. Now he was going to die alone, no longer able to tell the people he loved that he loved them.

> *Like father, like son, like unholy spirit.*
> *Our Father, whose head be severed,*
> *Gallows be thy fate.*
> *Though Armageddon come,*
> *Thy will be undone*
> *In hell, for there is no heaven.*
> *Nobody to deliver him from evil.*

Neither dozing nor fully awake, lying on the floor, now, focusing on the parallel lines of the shutter, his heart quailed when the metal leaves clanked into life and started to rise. The door on the other side opened. There were Sabine's feet in the sort of surgeon's rubber shoes Marianne de Koninck wore.

'It's time, Paul.'

CHAPTER 81

Broadmoor Psychiatric Hospital, later

'I wondered how long it would take you to come,' Silas Holm said.

A smile playing on his chapped lips. Steadily gazing into George's eyes until she felt like she was being undressed by him. Her instinct was to look away but she willed herself to hold that gaze defiantly.

'Where did you get my address in Amsterdam from, Silas?' she asked. Sitting back in her chair, now with legs astride. One hand on her hip. Showing this cheeky arsehole that he couldn't spook her so easily.

Silas put those immaculately manicured hands behind his head and grinned. Yellowing teeth that made the hairs stand up on her arms. When he raised his head to contemplate the ceiling, she saw the length of his neck exposed. Pale skin with salt and pepper stubble coming through. His top had ridden up to reveal greying navel hair. Involuntarily, she thought of van den Bergen's naked body, taut and muscled beneath her. Hip-bones jutting. A chevron of grey hair lighting the way down to his groin. Sudden, unwanted images in her head of her and Silas Holm. Those perfect hands of his, gripping her by the hair; holding her in place. *Jesus! No!*

The mind played some terrible tricks.

She felt a pulse of anger flicker through her. Lunged forwards and slammed her palms on the table, though she realised too late he would now probably get a glimpse of her collar bone and chest.

'Who gave you that Amsterdam address?'

Silas' voice was so quiet, she had to strain to hear him even in that otherwise silent room. 'Did you read my letter, dear Georgina?'

Cat and mouse. Okay. If that's the way he wanted to play it. 'Maybe I did. Maybe I tore it up.'

'Ah, that would be such a travesty if you had,' he said. Turned to Graham, who sat at his side, giant arms folded. 'I sent Georgina here a lovely letter all about my formative years.' Turned back to George, locking onto her eyes once more. Mischief in his.

'We are sorry, Ms McKenzie,' Graham said. 'You should never have got that letter. We have looked into it. It was a terrible breach of security and we are still not certain how it happened.'

'Roni de Zwarte,' George said, simply. She had expected to see a glimmer of apprehension in Silas' eyes, but if anything the almost palpable mischief became more intense. What the hell was he up to?

'Ah, Dr de Zwarte,' he said, breathing in through his nose, as though he had detected an appetising smell on the air. Licked his lips. A wet, red tongue darting out. Revolting. Seductive.

'I know she bought a baby on the black market from one of the victims. How come you know her, Silas? What is Roni de Zwarte to you? Why have you got her posting love letters to me?'

'Oh, Georgina. So little self-esteem in some ways and such arrogance in others. It's as if you're two different people entirely.' A big yellow-toothed grin.

George shuffled uncomfortably in her chair. Noticed a loose thread in the inside seam of her jeans. Felt moisture emerge abruptly from her palms and upper lip.

Silas could see it, she was sure. 'That was not a love letter, my dear.' He reached beneath the table. Scratching something. Hopefully his leg. 'They were reminiscences I wanted to share with you. A pondering on the nature of why we become the people we become.' He steepled those beautiful fingers together with precision and elegance. 'You come here to study the nature of desire, do you not? You ask me questions about my taste in pornography. Tell me, Georgina, how do we come to fetishise certain things? Certain objects. Attributes in people. Hair, for example. Shoes. Or amputated limbs.'

The air particles between them were charged; negatively, positively, sexually. George opened and closed her mouth, wondering if his questions were meant as rhetorical. Wishing those unbidden images would dissipate. Silas sat perfectly still. Pursed his lips. Awaiting an answer, clearly. So, she wracked her brains for an answer.

'We form libidinal attachments to people…sometimes objects too,' she said. 'In childhood. We bond. Stimulants we're exposed to regularly…how something looks, how it smells. Touch and taste too. They become sexualised, maybe because they're important. A significant occurrence makes them special, triggers arousal.' She was busking.

Silas Holm nodded. 'Yes. So, what did you deduce from my letter?'

George remembered the implausibly neat hand on the watermarked paper. Tales of abuse from a Nazi-war-hero-turned-POW. Silas, a child who was desperate to please his hostile, distant amputee father. 'That your fetish is rooted in your relationship with your father. That your thirst for violence against women stems from a disruptive childhood, where your father beat up on your mother regularly and made her out to be a whore. You wanted his approval and eventually went to the extreme of having your leg chopped off to be just like Daddy.'

Clapping, now. 'Yes!' Silas beamed at her. Nodded at Graham,

384

as if to pull him into this celebration of George's insightful analysis. 'She's got it! Well done, Georgina. You really have put your finger on it. Now, have you heard of the artist, Frida Kahlo?'

'Yes. What's she got to do with it?'

'A turning point in Kahlo's life was a terrible bus crash. Covered in strange gold dust another passenger had been carrying, she lay dying on that bus in immense pain. Scroll forward some years, and she paints herself with wounds to her neck, death hanging over her, gold often featuring in her painterly palette. She was profoundly affected by this tragedy. It made her the artist we all know. What was your Frida Kahlo moment, Georgina? I know mine. What is our murderer's Frida Kahlo moment?'

George felt like she was being played. 'Hang on a fucking minute, Professor Freud.' Noticed a face at the door trying to catch Graham's attention. Instincts screaming that Sally had sussed her. Phoned through to get her permissions revoked. Yes. The woman at the door was frowning at her. Opening the door.

'Can I have a word, Graham?' A thick-set female officer from security. Stony expression indicated she meant business. Keys swinging at her side. Handcuffs and a baton. The trappings of authority. Hands like a man.

Would Graham give George the few seconds she needed on her own with Silas? Could she risk even a fleeting moment, sitting within reaching distance of that serial murderer of women? A man who could choke the life out of her with those delicate-looking fingers. Hunger in Silas Holm's ice-blue eyes. She could see that much. His chapped lips parted as his breath also became rapid in anticipation.

George held her breath. Her pulse thumping in her ears. Graham rose from the table. Backed up several feet, though he didn't leave the room. The security guard, whispering in his ear, checking George through narrowed eyes. Flint-faced cow. Now or never.

She propelled herself across the table and grabbed Silas' hands.

He reached out for her, as though he'd been expecting the contact. Those murderer's hands were warm and soft but not clammy. He stroked her knuckles. The image of dismembered women she had seen in case notes. Blood everywhere. Lifeless eyes. But George kept holding him.

'You know who the killer is, don't you?' she asked him. 'You know who butchered those people and scooped them clean.'

Nodding. He knew all right. Smiling. 'An empty vessel makes the most noise, Georgina. What do those bodies tell you? What is the nature of your murderer's fetish?'

Graham and the security guard turned to them both. Poised to break them apart like ill-fated lovers. 'Let go of his hands, Ms McKenzie. Get off her, Dr Holm! Hands behind your back. Back in your seat!'

The baton was out. The cuffs were hanging at the end of the security woman's hand in readiness. Yanking Silas' right arm away and up between his shoulder blades. It must have hurt like hell, but he didn't even wince. Still looking at George, his eyes softer now. Playful and warm.

'Roni de Zwarte,' George said. 'Is she linked to the killer? Find her, find him, right?'

Silas Holm winked. 'Clever, clever Georgina. Just one step away from illumination. Be careful to take that step in the *right* direction.' He was bent over the table now, as the security officer cuffed him. Dragged him into an upright position. 'Or you might be too late...'

Graham took hold of Silas and started to march him towards the door. 'I'm sorry, Ms McKenzie. You're going to have to leave.'

'Too late for what?' George shouted.

CHAPTER 82

A secret location near Laren, later

Sabine checked the clock. Watched the second hand and counted backwards as the anaesthetic kicked in. Ten, nine, eight. Van den Bergen was out cold at seven. Now, he was hers. She looked down at his long, wiry body. In such excellent shape for a man of his age, despite the white hair. Regarded his penis, lying hapless and flaccid between his thighs, though it had been a thing of majestic proportions two nights ago. And he had known what to do with it. The last time she had enjoyed a man like that...well, she hadn't enjoyed sex with a man in many a year. Van den Bergen had been considerate and artful. Like Lepiks, it was almost a shame to use him. But he knew too much and The Duke was waiting for a new organ delivery.

'Supply and demand, Paul,' she said.

The chief inspector's face was unrecognisable, contorted as it was by the intubation up his nose, the mask over his mouth, the tube down his throat. Never mind. On with business.

As a general surgeon who had retrained as a paediatrician, after years spent patching people up in the war-torn dustbowls of the world, Sabine tackled even the steepest of learning curves with enthusiasm. She had perfected the art of pulmonary artery catheterisation by now. Administered a cocktail of hormones and steroids to halt complications in their tracks. Check his oxygen levels and his body temperature. As soon as she started to remove the major organs, his brain would die and that was where the real challenge lay. That's where it all went to pieces quickly, without aggressive donor management. Cardiovascular collapse. Diabetes insipidus. Hyperchloraemic acidosis. Hadn't she screwed up little Noor's heart by being taken unawares by the catecholamine storm? She tutted, remembering the panic. A wasted major organ. Eventually, she had got it right but not without failure first. Still, setting up and managing your own intensive care unit with zero support staff was a tall order. And she had been relatively new to this donor harvesting gig when she had killed Noor. General surgery did not prepare a doctor for this specialist activity. Paediatrics certainly didn't.

The first few experiments had ended up having to be incinerated in her kiln. Very messy. She had scattered the ashes in the garden onto her rose bed, but really, although the garden was big, she didn't need *that* much bloody ash. The gardener had started to ask questions. But there was no way she was going to start digging shallow graves for the redundant cadavers in quiet corners of farms or woodland. She was certainly as strong as any man. Hadn't she dragged that mattress through the loose panel in the fence of her Koninginneweg house to the building site and up the staircase to the attic? But she was no gravedigger! It had therefore been a wise move to start leaving the bodies for the police to find.

She started to sing 'Message in a Bottle' by The Police. Vaguely reminded of her childhood nights in that apartment in Manhattan – stifling and sweaty in summer, freezing in winter – where there had been such lavish parties. *Block it out. Ding dong, the bitch is dead.*

Busying herself with ventilation management, now, to ensure van den Bergen's lungs were kept in good shape. Ah, she felt satisfied in her work. She was good at this now. Prepared to administer methylprednisolone to reduce the cytokine release before harvesting his liver.

Now, this would all have to be very quick if she were to retrieve as many of van den Bergen's organs as possible successfully. Scalpel at the ready. All the tools to hand. She clicked on her stereo; echoing and metallic, the music bounced off the unadorned walls of the industrial facility she rented, using a manufacturer of pickles and preserves as a front.

What a coincidence! The Police CD had still been in the machine. Sending an SOS that would sadly not reach the world.

'Ready to die, Paul?'

CHAPTER 83

Stansted airport, Essex, later

'Fuck it!' George grimaced at her phone. No bars. She had been cut off in the midst of a call to Marie. Van den Bergen had apparently not showed at his own daughter's wedding.

Enshrouded by darkness, the lights in the train carriage sputtered. Then, came back on. Harsh yellow, reflecting her in the black of the window as they slowed to a crawl in the tunnel.

'Come on!' she said, checking her watch. Rechecking.

Would she make that flight she had booked so hastily on a maxed-out credit card? Still not there. Feeling dizzy at the thought. They would be telling passengers to *go to gate* on the overhead displays by now. Shit.

The train shot out of the tunnel. Her phone started to ring. Aretha Franklin exclaiming that he made her feel like a natural woman. Except that meant it was Ad. And he no longer did.

'Why the hell have you been ignoring my calls, George?' he said. 'I've been trying to get hold of you. Sharon said you were attacked after the funeral. Are you okay? Why wouldn't you call and tell me? I've been worried sick!'

She glanced round at the other passengers, wondering if they knew she was being dressed down by the boyfriend she had been skipping out on. 'I'm coming back. All right? I meant to ring you.

I did. Honestly. I'll come over to yours but I need to go straight out again. I've got something I need to do.'

'George, this is ridiculous,' he said. 'The last time we had this distance between us…do you remember? It was just before I was abducted by the Firestarter and shot by that dick with plucked eyebrows. But we got past that didn't we?'

Pulling into Stansted, George pulled her hastily packed bag from the overhead luggage rack. The Firestarter. Something was tugging urgently at the back of her mind. The beginnings of an idea. Mr Flaming Hot Coals had had several monikers, forged using adaptations of his real name and wordplay.

'Look, we really need to talk,' Ad said, unaware that George's synapses were whirring and flashing into life like overloaded circuitry.

Roni de Zwarte. What are the possible permutations of that name? Roni. Short for Ronald. Ronald fucking McDonald. Not McDonalds. A woman's name. Veronica. De Zwarte…

'Oh, and I might need to borrow your car,' she told Ad absently.

Cut him off. Checking the time. If she ran, she'd make the gate. As long as there wasn't a queue at the check-in desk. Brain ticking over. Thrumming, in fact, like the engine of an Aston Martin. George pushed to the front of the queue amid protest and tutting. Flashed the police station ID van den Bergen had given her. Kept her finger over the words 'assistant' and 'temporary'.

'The gate has closed for your flight, I'm afraid,' the girl said. Thick orange foundation and immaculately scraped-back hair. Red lippy on her teeth. Coffee breath said she hadn't eaten all day.

Tapping on the shoulder.

'Young lady. You may not just push in.'

George saw red. Turned round to find a smartly dressed white man of about fifty glowering at her. Incensed that his patience had been short-changed by a black girl in shabby student clothes, bumping him down a place. George waved her ID in his face like a gun.

'Police, arsehole. Button it and back off!'

Turned back to the check-in girl, who was fingering her walkie talkie as though she hadn't yet decided whether to help George or call security.

Heart pounding. Thoughts still cascading into a pool of possible scenarios, which she took out and dried off, one by one. De Zwarte meant black. Negro. Schwartz in German. Veronica Black?

'Sorry, Miss McKenzie.' Looking down at the ID and her passport. 'Like I said. The gate's closed. Take-off in fifteen minutes. You'll have to go back to the desk and rebook your flight, I'm afraid.'

Twinkly-eyed fucking check-in girl. I would like to deck your idiotic orange face with a well placed bunch of fives. The next flight's not for hours. Van den Bergen is going to end up unzipped like the others.

A flash of the teeth. A demure expression. Van den Bergen wouldn't thank her if she got herself arrested and his kidneys ended up in a cool box, bound for the highest bidder on whatever version of eBay it was that international criminal networks used. 'Please. It's an emergency, miss. Police business. I *have* to get that flight. There are lives at stake.' Bordering on flirtatious. Everybody liked to be flirted with. 'I love your eyes, by the way. What colour would you say they are? Green? Pearl blue?'

'I'll radio through.'

Last passenger on. Angry faces because she had delayed take-off by ten minutes. Seatbelts on. She had only minutes before she would have to switch her phone to safety-mode. Started to Google.

Veronica Black. Some large-chested porn starlet, by the looks. An author with four stars on Goodreads. Nope. Neither women were Roni de Zwarte. Veronica Negro. Following on Twitter. A housewife from Spain maybe. Not Roni de Zwarte. Veronica Schwartz. Google threw up so many, with different versions of the spelling. Some with a T. Some without.

'Madam, would you mind turning off your phone?' the air stewardess asked.

George looked up. 'Sure. Sorry.'

The plane started to gather speed. Hurtling down the runway. She wondered if van den Bergen was safe. No way on God's earth would he have missed his daughter's wedding. Had always eulogised about her. *Tamara inherited the best of me and her mother, thank God. Tamara is so clever. Tamara deserves better than that workshy soap-dodger, Numb-nuts.*

Up, up and away. East Anglia fell away below her and, within minutes, they were above the sea. Her ears popped. Seatbelt signs off. She could use the in-flight internet, as long as she paid with her credit card first, of course.

Veronica Schwartz. Several pages bore no fruit, though she didn't know for sure what she was looking for. Then, just as she feared she would have to abandon the search, she came upon an archive piece from an old society magazine. *Miss Manhattan.*

City mourns Heidi Schwartz, first lady of modern art.

The death of a socialite, 1989. Retrospective photographs of a thin, flamboyant woman. Always with a young, exotic-looking man of dubious sexual orientation on her arm. Except in a family shot, linking arms with her young daughter on one side. Tall, grumpy-looking father on the other. The leathery kind that had spent too much time on sun-beds and supplemented the shortcomings of his dick with a hairweave. But it was the daughter that caught George's eye. Long legs. Hair like a horse that screamed good breeding and money. A chubbier face back then. Miserable as hell, under close scrutiny, despite the fixed smile. Downcast expression otherwise. Dead behind the eyes. George knew about family love. George knew about family loathing. Everything about the photo screamed false, false, false.

She Googled Heidi Schwartz. Found another archived obit from a glossy.

Daughter, Veronica, tried to save Heidi's life.

A failed bone-marrow donation that had hastened her own leukaemia-stricken mother's death. There was the Frida Kahlo moment of Veronica Sabine Schwartz – a patrician heiress, internationally set to jet off to London, where she would work through her bereavement whilst studying medical science at UCL.

So what did *Veronica Schwartz, medic* throw up?

Schwartz helps landmine victims in Cambodia.

'Oh, my days!' George shouted, squinting at a photo of selfless Veronica in her scrubs, standing outside a medical tent, rigged with a jungle backdrop, holding the hand of a smiling one-legged Cambodian boy. At her side was a young and remarkably handsome Silas Holm – trim under the scrubs, full head of short, dark hair, a tan, clean white teeth. Two whole legs. 'Now this makes sense! Silas, you dark horse.'

'Are you okay, miss?' the elderly man at George's side asked.

'Just eat your fucking peanuts and mind your own, mate,' she said, engrossed.

Google revealed more, three search engine pages in – *Schwartz heiress marries South African doctor, Thomas Schalks* – though George didn't need to read the accompanying words. The bride's face in the photograph was enough. It hadn't changed, though the teen glower and chubbiness had gone from it. The dead eyes had grown more lifeless still. High cheekbones, the hair and the turned-up nose remained the same.

'You murderous, stuck-up, man-stealing bitch. You're gonna rue the day you tried to fuck with George McKenzie.'

CHAPTER 84

Amsterdam, then Laren, later

'Give me the bloody key, Ad!' George said, dumping her small carry-on case in the hallway. Ignoring Jasper who was standing in the doorway to the living room, waving.

'What? This?' Ad said. Dangling it before her. Closing his fingers around it. Gone, like some cheap magician's trick at a children's party.

'Please!' Looking at his hand only. Avoiding meeting that probing gaze of his. She knew he was trying to spy the truth behind her own eyes. But this was not the time for honesty.

'You're going to him, aren't you? Van den Bergen. You want to borrow my car so you can drive to his and spend the night with him?'

'It's a matter of life and death.' She jumped up to grab the key out of Ad's hand, but he held it easily out of her reach. He was just too tall.

'You're on a provisional licence!' he said.

'I can drive fine.' She pushed past him. Grabbed her full can of hairspray from the bathroom. Shoved it in her deep coat pocket. Had noticed Jasper's car keys on the kitchen table as she had walked past the doorway. Made for her quarry, swiping them lightning quick with a pickpocket's hands. Neither man noticing. 'Suit your fucking self, Ad,' she said, heading out the door. 'If van den Bergen dies, it's on you, honey. I've got places to be.'

Tears welling in her eyes as she made for the car park. Wiped them away angrily. Held the fob out, pressing the button to see which car unlocked. When a white BMW Z4 blipped at her, she allowed herself a smile. Ad, hammering his palms against the living room window upstairs. Shouting something at her. Jasper out the corner of her eye, sprinting across the car park.

She got in. Fired up the roadster. Backed into the car behind with a jolt. The sound of shattered glass hitting the tarmac. An alarm crying out. Whoops. Jasper almost upon her now, wearing a look of pure horror. Mouthing 'No' as if in slow motion, while she stole his baby.

'Too late, motherfucker.' She kangarooed out of the car park, almost mowing down the car's owner as she went.

What Ad hadn't realised was that George had stolen enough cars in her time to know how to drive. Within minutes she had mastered the car's gears and brought the snarling engine to heel beneath her booted foot. Ignoring the ringing phone. Chewing up the motorway, topping a hundred mph, to the Laren address Marianne de Koninck had offered up over the phone, knowing Marie and Elvis were on their way to Koninginneweg. One of them had to be on the money.

'Jesus,' she said, parking some way along from the country house. Headlights snuffed out. Looking up at the high walls and tall metal gates. CCTV cameras directed at the surrounding curtilage. 'It's Fort Knox.'

Darkness had fallen in earnest. Good. Though it was remote, there was always the chance a nosey neighbour would witness her intrusion and raise the alarm. She had some climbing to do. George left the heavy bulk of her sheepskin on the passenger seat. Pulled her black hood over her hair. Shoved the tin of hairspray in the pouch at the front of the hoodie. Big bunch of keys from her places back home within reach in her jeans pocket, along with her lighter. Breath coming short.

'Let's do this.'

Brisk walking to the perimeter wall, George prayed silently to a god she didn't believe in that there would be no dogs. Grabbed a sturdy ivy climber and shinned up it to the top, dropping into a deep border on the other side. Her fall had been cushioned by something prickly that almost refused to release her from its grip. Holly. But she was barely aware of the burning scratches. Her mind was on van den Bergen only.

Crunching on the gravel drive was unavoidable. No lights came on. The huge house with all its gabled windows upstairs and leaded lights downstairs was in complete darkness. No cars out front but deep grooves in the gravel, made by a vehicle with a long wheel base.

Something was off about the place.

Walking round the far side of the house. The security light clicking on was the only source of illumination. At a set of single-glazed French doors, George selected her skeleton key from her bunch of keys. Gained entry easily and silenced the alarm after four goes on the keypad, trying out various significant dates Marie had texted to her. In the end, it was the death date of Sabine's mother, Heidi, that had worked: 0307.

As she padded noiselessly through the house with the stealth of a panther, she realised nobody was home. When she switched on the light to the panic room, she knew van den Bergen had been there. A roll of duct tape sitting on a console that held three computer keypads. A used syringe next to it. On the floor, an overturned chair with traces of the sticky silver tape still on it. A small pool of blood on the carpet. And there was the real giveaway: van den Bergen's glasses. The chain that he wore around his neck broken. The lenses smashed where they had been trodden underfoot perhaps during a struggle.

George felt her phone vibrate in her pocket. Read a text from Marie.

He's not at Valeriusstraat.

Wracking her brains, she considered what she would do if she were a surgeon, harvesting the organs of abducted victims in secret. She would need somewhere quiet. An operating theatre where no prying eyes would reach.

'Try the garage,' she whispered, remembering how Ad had been held captive in the garage of a country house. Hooked up to a drip for days, awaiting his turn as the Firestarter's next human bomb in a cardboard box.

She found the door through the utility room. Could this be where van den Bergen lay, at the mercy of a psychopathic surgeon? Adrenalin coursing through her veins, she shook as she took out the can of hairspray. Held it in her left hand as she opened it with the right. But there was only darkness on the other side of that door. Breathing out heavily with relief, she switched on the light. A large black Lexus, the red light of its immobiliser flashing lazily on and off. So, something else had made those deep indentations in the gravel outside. A van.

'But if he's not here, where the hell is he?' George said, scanning the contents of the garage, as she combed her brain for salient thought. Time was running out. In the corner of the garage, next to the draining board of a sink, she spotted an old filing cabinet. Broke into it with practised ease. Started to rifle through the folders until she found what she was looking for.

'Bingo!' It was the lease on an industrial unit, some five miles away.

CHAPTER 85

A secret location near Laren, later

'What do you mean, I'm not delivering my side of the bargain?' Veronica had screamed down the phone. 'I've got the chief inspector heading up the investigation on my operating table right this minute. If it wasn't for constant interruption by that jumped-up little prick, Gera— Who the fuck does he think he is to talk to me like that, by the way?'

The Duke went quiet on the other end of the phone. 'Have you finished?' he had asked.

She had been seething at his arrogance. *Have you finished?* As though she were still a child to be silenced. Gagged by her mother's ridicule. Censored by her father's disapproval. *Have you finished?*

'No. And if you don't like hearing what I've got to say, find yourself another stooge who'll keep you in black market organs and stolen babies.'

His voice had been placatory on the other end. 'There's no need to be like that, Roni. Nobody could replace you.' Beautifully spoken English that got her every time. Reminded her of Silas in the beginning, except this was a real alpha male.

Outside, she heard a car pull up. Held her breath. Looked down at the sleeping van den Bergen. Still intact, but fully prepped for surgery. Not long now.

'I've got a surprise,' he said down the phone.

'I think there's someone here.'

'I know there's someone there.'

The visitor had a key. Footsteps in the reception area. She held the scalpel high ready to strike.

'Guess who!' on the other side of the door. That English accent. Public-school breeding.

She breathed a sigh of relief. It was him.

'You bastard! I thought it might have been the police.'

They kissed passionately, as she dragged him inside by the collar of his cashmere coat. He eyed the tall chief inspector on the table.

'That's van den Bergen?' he asked, staring at the policeman's penis. 'He's thinner than I expected.'

The Duke had grabbed Sabine from behind and slid his hand into her loose-fitting green trousers. Smelled of L'Egoiste after-shave and cigars. 'Gera and his boys have got to lie low. I've come instead.'

Veronica had laughed. Turned around and started to undo his belt; unzipping his trousers. 'As if you'd run your own errands. Admit it. You missed me.' Encased his erect penis in her latex-gloved hand and started to masturbate him slowly.

He had produced a baggie of white powder from the breast pocket of his suit jacket. Waved it in the air. 'Can't hurt to mix a little pleasure with business.' Looked over at van den Bergen. 'He can wait a while, can't he?'

It had never been her intention to get waylaid like this, but she was already so wired at the prospect of opening van den Bergen up. The temptation of doing a little marching powder and letting The Duke fuck her hard up against the wall had been too great to resist. Though he was a good four inches shorter than she, his muscular legs were strong enough to bear her weight. And she was lithe enough to wrap her long legs around him; her arousal intensified at the sight of van den Bergen, out for the count on the operating table. Yet, time was ticking by. She didn't want to have the chief inspector under for too long, lest it put an unnecessary strain on his heart.

The Duke had come too early with a grunt. Withdrew. Let her legs fall to the ground and yanked up his trousers quickly.

'You selfish jerk,' she had said. 'What about me?'

He laughed, revealing the diamond stud in his tooth that was totally at odds with his upper-class persona. Good boy gone bad. Took out a gun from his coat pocket. A long-barrelled AMT Hardballer. Pointed it at her vagina. 'This is always hard,' he said.

'That loaded?' She had bitten her lip and narrowed her eyes at him. Thrilled by the prospect of something new. A risk. An erotic gesture masquerading as an act of violence.

Backing to the operating table, she had pushed van den Bergen's legs out of the way; opened her own to receive the cold barrel of the gun.

'Oh, you're a very naughty girl, Roni.'

'I've always been one to break the rules.'

Sore but satisfied now, enjoying the prospect of having an appreciative audience for a change during the harvest, instead of being on her own or having that seedy little lowlife who masqueraded as her assistant in Kent, she turned her attention back to van den Bergen.

'I'm going to perform what's called a midline laparotomy now,' she told The Duke. 'Know what that is? That's where I cut him open from his ninth thoracic vertebra down to his umbilicus. Then I cut from his umbilicus to his pubic symphysis. Hold your nose. It always stinks to high heaven. And no passing out!'

She pressed the number 22 scalpel into van den Bergen's skin and began to cut.

CHAPTER 86

A secret location near Laren, moments later, then, the Laren house

Killing the lights of the Z4, George coasted into the industrial estate using momentum, rather than gas. Wanting to make as little noise as possible. Apprehension was lodged high in her throat, a precarious stopper holding all the grief inside at the prospect of being too late to save her friend; her lover. Images of van den Bergen opened up and emptied out like the other victims flickered in her imagination like an uncensored, unwanted slide show of the macabre. His expressive grey eyes, so large and full of melancholy or else mischief, packed in ice inside a cool box.

George admonished herself for allowing such notions into her head.

'Can that crap, you wimp. Paul needs you to be strong. You can take this stuck-up streak of piss.' Psyching herself up for a confrontation with a killer who was a good seven or eight inches taller than her. But she had stood up to the Firestarter, hadn't she? And if Sabine *had* been her backstreet attacker in London, she had been made short shrift of by none other than Letitia. 'I ain't so fucking vulnerable, Veronica Schwartz or whatever your name is. I come from a long line of ferocious bitches.' Puffing air hard out of her cheeks. Checking she had her discreet makeshift weapons on her person.

This Veronica hadn't come from the street. This Veronica had never had to defend herself in a women's prison full of desperate inmates. This Veronica had never peddled drugs in a high rise and got up after a kicking, giving back as good as she got. George did. George had. George always would.

'Time to teach you a lesson in manners, man-tiefing bastard.'

The van came into view as George rounded the corner in an otherwise deserted industrial estate. These places all look the same, wherever they may be in the world, George knew. Hastily built breeze-block units with brick fascias. Steel shutters on the plate glass shop fronts and doors at night. No security roaming this one, though George didn't give a shit. She had the law on her side and van den Bergen's life to fight for.

He's still alive. I know it. But what if I'm too late? What do your guts tell you, George? They tell you he's still breathing.

A long-wheel-based Mercedes Sprinter. Shaft of light shining beneath the largest of the shutters. Shutter up over the door. But what was this? As she crept forwards, George spotted something unanticipated. Plumes of smoke rising on the far side of the van. Making as little noise as possible, she slid up to the vehicle and peered beneath the undercarriage. Spotted a pair of men's shoes and trouser legs. The wheels of a car, out of sight where she crouched. The distinctive fat, white *B* in the middle of shining alloys. A Bentley. She held her breath, close enough to be heard by the man, should he have been paying attention to the noises in that deserted place.

No way in through the front door. Retreating with feather-light steps, she ebbed into the shadows until she was able to walk without fear of discovery. Round the back. There was always a loading bay. Wasn't there? Time running out. But here was the back of the unit, she was sure. A harsh white beacon slicing upwards through the black night sky from the skylight in the roof. She flattened herself against the wall. Security light clicking on at her approach. With crab-like movements, edged sideways. Tried the door. Locked. Produced her skeleton key but the lock was too sophisticated. Shit!

George looked up at the shaft of light emanating from inside. *Only one way in. No time for vertigo, now.*

Clambering onto an industrial-sized dumper that stood against the wall, outside the unit, she started to hoist herself up the drainpipe. Biceps screaming in complaint. *Get up that fucking pipe, woman. Don't look down!* Heart beating so hard, she wondered if the smoking man at the front would hear it.

Crawling along the roof. Would it even take her weight? Pigeon guano squelching beneath her hands and knees. She gagged. Swallowed down the urge to vomit. The light coming closer, closer, now. Clenching her teeth, as though that would make her quieter. Slipping around. She was too high up. How the hell could she even get into the unit? *You're a fucking idiot, McKenzie. You haven't thought this through.*

Then, she peered into the skylight. Saw the scene below.

Van den Bergen almost unrecognisable with tubes going in; tubes coming out. Machinery all around him, filtering, aspirating, monitoring him. A livid, blood red line down his middle. Veronica in green scrubs, bent over his abdomen. Busy about her victim. Opening the line wider, wider. Cutting. Slicing.

George clawed at the Perspex. *No. No.* Mouthing the words. Tears forcing their way out of her eyes and onto her cheeks. Watching this monster thrust her hands in van den Bergen's stomach.

Suddenly she was gripped in the jaws of anger. A rabid dog savaging its prey. It shook George about. And her trepidation was punctured. And her sadness flung aside. George was consumed whole. Only naked fury remained.

On that slanting Perspex roof, she stood, jumped. Veronica Schwartz peered up, askance, trying to spy what caused the din. Jumped again. Creaking plastic, weakening screws.

George crashed through the skylight, yelling as she fell. A battle-cry. No time to die. Landing some twenty feet below on the table that held an array of shining surgical tools. Buckling beneath her, but breaking her fall.

'You!' Schwartz said in English, quick to slash with the scalpel.

But George was quicker still. Prepared. Adrenalin pumping. Feeling no pain. Out with the can of hairspray in her right hand. Lighter in the left. Old dogs had taught her some novel tricks. She sprayed the choking lacquer stink into Schwartz's eyes. Flicked her lighter into life. A budget drug-store flame-thrower.

Schwartz clasped her gloves to her face, screaming. Stumbling backwards, taking the drip stands with her in a tangle of tubing and rubber shoes. Clattering to the concrete ground. Ripping the cannula out of van den Bergen's motionless arm. A glint of something silver in George's peripheral vision.

The surgeon steadied herself. Deadly focus in eyes that stared out of a bloody, scorched face. She snatched up a long-nosed silver pistol that had been lying on a chair. Waving it at George, now.

'Put the hairspray down, Georgina!' she said. Ice cold voice. Seemed not to feel the agony of having been burned. Gesticulating towards the chair where the gun had been. 'Go on!'

Stalemate. George stood, holding the spray and lighter in front of her. Unflinching. Trying to take in the surreal scene before making a decision. In addition to the medical equipment, and van den Bergen, split open like an edamame bean on the operating table, George noticed a steel trestle table, on top of which was a small empty plastic bag, a rolled-up fifty-euro note and a credit card. She caught the scent on the air. Above the pungent stench of alcohol, blood and shit, she could smell something else. Sex.

Schwartz and the man outside. Partying inside, while van den Bergen lay prepped for death. The surgeon was high. Her reactions would be skewed. Good.

Towering above her, Schwartz clicked the safety off the gun.

'I said, put down the spray, you black midget.'

George sucked her teeth, long and low; raising an eyebrow like this standoff was child's play, though her head was swimming and her heart thundered inside her chest at a hundred and eighty bpm. 'Fuck you, chicken tits. Put the gun down or I'll torch you again. Your kind crisps up real nice like a suckling pig.'

Schwartz' scorched face became a sinister mask of hatred. She pointed the gun at George's heart. Pulled the trigger. The gun went off.

The full metal jacket bullet punched into George. Sent her careening backwards into the table that held the coke paraphernalia. The aerosol can uselessly bursting into a cloud of Albert Heijn's super-hold above her head. Tinnitus buzzing in her ears from the deafening thunderclap that ricocheted off the breeze block walls. Agony all at once, she dropped the spray and lighter. Gasped, clutching her chest. Blood oozing warm between her fingers.

'No signs of life, here,' Elvis said. 'Any texts from George?'

Marie looked down at her phone. 'No reception. Damn.'

They trudged around to the back of the seemingly empty country house. Peering into blackness through locked doors and windows. Scenarios where she would have to explain her father's death to the newly married Tamara played out in Marie's mind, until her phone suddenly vibrated in her pocket. She took it out, lighting up the screen – the only illumination in that dark place apart from Elvis' torch. A text, sent by George ten minutes earlier. It had only just reached her phone. Two bars.

```
VdB being held in industrial unit north
of Laren. Need backup. Come asap
```

She showed it to Elvis. 'No address,' she said. One bar.

'Get onto Google maps. Better pray that wi-fi connection holds up,' he said, just as the last bar of reception disappeared.

CHAPTER 87

A secret location near Laren, later

Standing over her, Schwartz smiled. 'I told you I'd shoot.'

George started to shake. Feeling the energy drain from her like a wounded character in *Grand Theft Auto*. But the bullet seemed to have missed her heart. Maybe. She was still breathing, wasn't she? Just. Grey-faced, she was sure. Everything prickling, as though the world was about to fade from view. Willed herself to stay. *Get up. Get on your feet, girl.*

Vaguely aware that a door had slammed shut somewhere within the unit.

'Roni! What the fuck—? My God! What happened to your face?'

A man's voice behind her, now. Sounded alarmed. Speaking English like a toff. George, back on her knees, craned her neck to see the newcomer. A finely dressed middle-aged man who looked like a hedge fund manager, but for the diamond in his tooth and the milky white stain on the crotch of his dark grey gabardine trousers. Stockily built. Shorn dirty blond hair. Scalp shining pinkish under the bright lights.

He swiftly made for George, grabbing her from behind in a headlock.

'Let me go!' she cried weakly.

407

Hand over her mouth, holding her in a vice-like grip. His fingers reeked of cigarettes and pussy.

'This is the snooping little cow I tried to finish off in London,' Schwartz said. Putting the gun down onto the operating table, beside the sleeping form of van den Bergen. Dabbing at her livid, shining face with some kind of surgical wipe. She kicked George in the stomach with a foot the size of a man's. '*Untermensch*. You're scum.'

Holding steady, though the kick winded her and made the blood seep faster from her wound, George resolved to show no fear. No weakness. No pain. Fixed her adversary with a stare that could strip the flesh from those elongated aristocratic bones. *I am not going to die here. And neither is van den Bergen. Not at the hands of this child-murdering skank.*

The Englishman dragged George to her feet. One of her arms was pinioned by him across her chest, stemming the flow of blood from the gunshot wound. But her other; her right arm hung loose. *Big mistake, dickhead.*

Surreptitiously, she reached into her jeans pocket. Arranged her keys into a makeshift knuckleduster – one key between each finger. Had to be quick. Right arm flung upwards, praying her fist would make contact with the Englishman's face. The jagged keys found their mark. Soft tissue yielded.

The man screamed. Dropped to his knees. Mortise key in the eye. Blood rolling down his cheek, dripping onto his crisp clothes. A scene from a horror movie.

'Give me my fucking keys back, man!' George pulled the knuckleduster free with a revolting squelch. Punched him again as hard as she could. Again.

He clasped his hands to his face, still screaming. 'Kill her, Roni! End the bitch.'

George kicked him in the neck with her steel toecap. He fell silent and still.

Schwartz lunged for the gun by van den Bergen's head. Shot

at George again. Missed, plugging the concrete floor, throwing up a residue puff of grey. Held the long pistol in front of her. Arm wavering. Those things weighed a ton.

But George had run out of tricks. She knew she was bleeding to death. On the operating table, van den Bergen was every colour apart from good. Blue around his lips, his earlobes. His fingertips purple. The chasm down his middle had filled with blood that was so rich, it was almost black. How long did he have? His heartbeat was frenetic, coming through on the monitor in a flurry of beeps. The alarm going off. Oxygen monitor clipped to his finger, protesting that his brain was dying.

'Save him!' George yelled at Schwartz. 'Save Paul, and kill me. Take my organs.'

Her strength was failing her in earnest. Her hoodie drenched in a circle of warm blood, rapidly turning cold. Skids of red on the floor, where she had trodden a path that led to her own demise. But George was aware of several things. The Englishman was either dead or out cold. A persistent, wailing sound broke through above the beeping of those infernal monitors. If she could distract Schwartz even momentarily, she might take this killer down with her.

The chair. First thing inmates went for when a riot broke out. Whatever furniture ain't nailed down.

'The cops are coming,' George said, peering hopefully over Schwartz' shoulder.

It was a childish trick, but Schwartz was high. Fell for it. Turned momentarily.

George snatched up the chair and used whatever strength she had left in her broken body to bring it crashing down on her opponent's outstretched hands. The gun flew from Schwartz' grip, sliding across the floor to the opposite side of the room. Raised the chair again. Smashed it against Schwartz' singed head. Wood, splintered into pieces. Schwartz' eyes rolled to reveal the whites. She slumped towards the floor, falling against the rubber mattress of the operating table. Grabbing on. Glazed expression. She was fading. But George took no chances. She picked up a large shard of corrugated Perspex from the shattered skylight and drove it into the surgeon's shoulder, pinning her to the operating table.

Van den Bergen's heart monitor flat-lined. But it was too late for George to do anything. She had blacked out.

CHAPTER 88

Amsterdam, hospital, 18 February

'There she is!' Marie said, smiling.

George opened her eyes blearily. Focussed on the large yellow-headed spot on Marie's chin. Jesus. Is this what being alive held in store for her? She closed her eyes again, but remembered van den Bergen. Lids shot open.

'Where's Paul? Is he—?'

'He's in intensive care,' Elvis said, standing just beyond Marie.

Tears welled in George's eyes. 'But he was blue! He was dying. Will he live? Will he be…all right?' Looking hopefully at Marie. Reaching out to take her hand and thinking better of it. Putting her hand beneath the thin hospital blanket.

Marie chewed her bottom lip. 'It's touch and go. He's got a perforated bowel. Schwartz was coked off her head. She cut too deep. It's developed into peritonitis. They've got him on strong antibiotics but—'

George felt tears stab at the backs of her eyes. 'Tell me he's not going to die. Tell me I didn't kill him.'

Elvis shook his head. 'You didn't kill him, George. None of this is down to you. Don't blame yourself.' He put his hand on her good shoulder. 'If it wasn't for you jumping through that skylight, he'd definitely be dead.'

Looking into Marie's eyes for the truth, George blinked aside hot tears. 'Brain damage? There were alarms going off.'

Marie examined her fingernails. Eyes glassy but no tears came. 'Look, the boss is in a coma. They don't know if he's going to wake up. And if he wakes up, it's too early to tell what state he'll be in.'

'The main thing is, they've done an MRI scan on his brain and it seems okay,' Elvis said. 'And no vital organs were damaged. When he comes round...' he glared at Marie, who only fleetingly made eye contact with him and then sniffed dismissively '...there's every likelihood he'll be back at work in no time, driving us all mental and moaning about his prostate gland.'

George chuckled, though her heart was breaking. *Stop this crap, you self-indulgent, spoiled little cow. You're awake. You will live. He's in a coma. He may not live. You should have been quicker. You should have fought harder for him. You could have stayed in Amsterdam and been there to defend him. You're a failure of the worst, most treacherous kind and you don't deserve to feel hurt.*

At that moment, though he had never asked for her forgiveness, she forgave van den Bergen. He had rejected her passionate love in favour of meaningless sex with a murderous psychopath with legs. But that was fine. Her feelings were irrelevant. All she wanted was for her friend – her beloved idiot, stubborn, prescription painkiller junkie of a friend – to recover. No doubt, his reasoning for favouring Sabine Schalks had been sound and had come from a good place. *Can this nonsense 'til later. Don't let them see.*

'What happened after I passed out?'

George tried to sit up in bed, the bullet wound beneath the bandages stinging. She clasped her hand to her chest but her movements were hampered. Realised she was hooked up to a drip. Stared in horror at the needle in her arm. Thought briefly about MRSA and how dirty hospitals could be. Said nothing.

Marie poured George a glass of water from a plastic jug. 'We arrived on the scene, expecting a shoot-out, but when we got there, everyone was unconscious. Schwartz was pinned to the boss' operating table by a splinter of Perspex. You were out cold. The boss was technically dead.'

'I did mouth to mouth,' Elvis said. 'Until the ambulances arrived, that is. We'd phoned for backup and paramedics on the way from the Laren house. They came really quickly.'

George examined the plastic cup Marie had given her. Lip marks on the plastic. Not hers. Marie's fingerprints on the side. 'I'm not thirsty thanks.'

'Don't be an idiot,' Marie said. 'You've been given a few bags of blood and some saline but the doc said you're still dehydrated as hell.'

Rolling her eyes, George took a sip of the iced water. Half expected it to come pouring through the hole in her chest.

'That bullet missed your heart by about six millimetres,' Elvis said, grinning. 'That earns you legend status at the station.'

'Hang on.' George cocked her head to the side, mentally reversing over Marie's words. 'Where was the man? The English guy I stabbed in the eye with my keys? I thought I'd broken his neck.'

The two detectives turned to one another. Shook their heads. Looked quizzically at George.

'There was nobody else at the scene apart from you, the boss and Schwartz,' Elvis said.

'The gun! The gun!'

'No trace of a gun. We've got the bullet they pulled out of your body. But nobody's found the weapon yet.'

George groaned. 'Shit. There was this guy – with a diamond in his tooth. Upper-class Brit, by the sounds. Drove a Bentley. He'd been screwing with Schwartz. You could smell it. She must have got high with him. There was a credit card on the side. Coke.'

Marie shook her head.

413

'He was definitely there, that guy. Well-dressed. Sharp suit. A smart coat. The works. I took him for a player in this organ-trafficking ring.' She tutted. Thumped the bed. 'And he's gone?'

'Leave it to forensics, George,' Marie said. 'De Koninck's all over the place with Strietman.'

George frowned. Sipped her water. 'I thought Strietman was banged up. The kiddy pictures. He's a paedo, right?'

'Turns out he's been studying at night for a psychology quali-fication. He'd been writing some semi-autobiographical thesis about child abuse,' Elvis said. 'Used the pictures for that. His tutor verified his claims.'

'That Kees screwed up big time,' George said. 'How is he?'

Marie gave a wry smile. 'He caught one in the shoulder. Got discharged yesterday. He's going to be back at the station next week, smarming up to Kamphuis with his arm in a sling.'

'More like his ass in a sling,' Elvis said. 'Strietman's suing.'

'Thought Kees was your big pal,' Marie said.

Elvis merely blushed and scratched at his sideburns.

'But what's happened with that lanky witch, Schwartz?'

Fingering the bruise on her forehead, Marie smiled. 'They stitched her up and threw her back in our direction. We've got her banged up where she belongs. She's pleading diminished mental capacity.'

'No way will a judge fall for that,' George said, thinking about the complex web of deceit and criminality that underpinned the murders.

'They might, if we can't prove the links to organised crime,' Marie said. 'I'm close to pinpointing the hacker who wiped the Port Authority and pathology records. The missing forensics report on Linda Lepiks' place showed up just before you caught your flight back to the Netherlands. The guys at the government data centre found it on a backup server. Fluids on Lepiks' sheets prove she had slept with another woman the night she was murdered – I'm putting my money on Schwartz – and I think this hacker's on somebody's payroll. If we can find the hacker and find the guy who took out Ahlers and—'

'Where's Magool's baby?' George asked.

Marie shook her head. 'We still don't know. There are piles of records at Schwartz' Laren house, hidden under floorboards in her office. It's going to take weeks to unravel. Problem is, we need someone to testify to her being a calculated murderer. Seems she kept up an immaculate front at work and in her social life. Her lawyer might try to go for schizophrenia or multiple personality thingy or something. I don't know all the terminology.'

George closed her eyes and saw a man in scrubs, standing in the Cambodian jungle. Tanned and pearly-toothed, with close cropped hair. A once-handsome man who had won the Evelyn Baker Medal from the Association of Anaesthetists. A man with an axe to grind as much as wield.

'I don't know if it would be admissible in court, but... Leave it with me,' she said.

CHAPTER 89

Broadmoor Psychiatric Hospital, later

'So melancholy,' he said, quietly to the pencil drawing of Linda Lepiks. 'So beautiful.' Mimed the intricate moves with those perfect fingers of his along the edge of the desk.

In his room, Silas Holm was listening to the soaring, searing piece of music that was 'The Heart Asks Pleasure First' by Michael Nyman. Arpeggios of painful longing and desire, which had been performed with surprising finesse by Holly Hunter on a beach in *The Piano*. Later, Silas had taught himself to play it, though his musical accomplishments were nothing to write home about. It had always been a favourite of his when he and Veronica had been in love, when he and Veronica had argued and eventually when he and Veronica had split because of her persistent infidelity with the South African pig.

He had discovered her treachery the very night he had proposed to her. A helicopter ride to view the romantic majesty of Mount Kilimanjaro. Down on one knee – still in possession of both legs, then. He couldn't have planned it better. And yet, she had turned him down.

I want to be free, she had said. *I've met someone new. It's over.*

How could she have thought she could ever start fresh with another man and another name? Unlearn what he had taught her: that taking a life offered the most narcotic high imaginable, and that to kill and kill again wiped away the anger and hurt in almost palpable increments? Every ending, the promise of a new beginning.

She thought she had bought her freedom and safe departure from him by agreeing to take his leg.

Veronica Sabine Schwartz. The woman he had worshipped so fervently. The woman he had been spurned by. The woman he had vowed to have his revenge upon. This music, so inextricably linked to his memories of her, was as much a soundtrack to love as it was to misery. Today, it was a soundtrack to triumph.

He picked up his pen and wrote in a hand so neat, so controlled, it looked almost like the work of a word-processor.

Dear Georgina,

I cannot be certain this letter will ever reach you, but I wanted to say thank you. Thank you for engaging so willingly in my little game. Thank you for indulging me and reminding me what it is to flirt with a woman like a man, not a murderer. Thank you for helping me to bring things full circle – I hear through the grapevine that you followed the noise made by those empty vessels right back to someone I once loved but who betrayed me. Treachery is perhaps the hardest thing to forgive. It makes easy victims of us all.

Revenge is a dish best served cold, however, and you have been instrumental in mine being frosted with dazzling ice crystals akin to diamonds.

I look forward to our next tryst, Georgina.

All my love

Silas

Silas took his pen, replaced the lid and scratched at his stump, smiling all the while. Now, he could lay the ghost of his broken heart to rest.

He looked at a dog-eared copy of Shakespeare's *Taming of the Shrew* which lay on his desk. Like Petruchio, he had sought to tame his Katherina. In simpler times, he might have brought this wayward lover to heel by encasing her head in a Scold's bridle. He could have killed her! But Silas had succeeded in punishing his once beloved Roni with something so much worse than public ridicule or the physical restriction of her freedom or even death. The cracked ribs of her very own victims trapped Veronica, instead of an unforgiving iron cage. Georgina McKenzie was the spike in the tongue which had finally silenced her. Now, exchanging the metaphorical bars of a bridle for the very real bars of a prison cell. *Adieu*, Frau Doktor Schwartz.

CHAPTER 90

Amsterdam, hospital, later

'You're not supposed to get out of bed,' the nurse told George. 'Miss McKenzie, please get back into bed. Doctor's orders.'

Clutching the tight, itchy bandaging around her chest, propping herself with the drip stand, George glared at the nurse. A woman with big, mottled red arms who had seen too many chocolate thank-yous from her patients. 'You can't tell me what to do,' she said. 'I'm going to see my friend. Chief Inspector van den Bergen. He's in intensive care.'

She slid her bare feet into her boots, only now aware that her back was entirely exposed to the world in this ugly sack of an operating gown.

'Where's my pyjamas?' she asked the nurse.

Folded arms and downturned thin lips said nursey was not impressed. 'You haven't got any pyjamas. Your own clothes were soaked in blood. Haven't you got family who can bring you something in?'

Thinking about Letitia and Aunty Sharon on the other side of the North Sea prickled more than the wound. Would Ad even show? He had every right not to.

'That's all right,' she told the nurse. 'People want to see my

419

arse, they can have a good look. My pleasure. It's my only redeeming feature.'

Garnering alarmed glances from visitors, doctors, auxiliary staff as she shuffled, semi-clad in boots and an ill-fitting operating gown, George wheeled her drip all the way to intensive care.

'Are you family?' the male nurse asked through the intercom. She felt a camera on her somewhere.

'Yes,' she said. 'I'm his...'

But she hadn't needed to clarify her status. The locked door clicked, offering her entry to this inner sanctum for the desperately ill. There, in a ward containing four men, she saw van den Bergen. White hair, plastered to his head. Cocooned by tubes and IV lines. Topped off by an oxygen mask. At his side, a young woman sat, dabbing at her eyes. A shining yellow-gold band on her wedding finger. Long-limbed and dark-haired. Hooded, grey eyes beneath brows that looked like they had been overplucked. She was almost the image of her father.

'Tamara?' George asked.

Tamara looked up at her. Those eyes were bloodshot. Mournful. A window to a sensitive soul, as were van den Bergen's. 'I told them you could come in,' she said.

She stood and grabbed George into a bear hug. Though agony lanced through her, George did not seek to push her away. She instinctively liked this girl.

'How is he?' she asked, accepting the blanket that the nurse brought her to cover her semi-nakedness. Seated herself gingerly next to van den Bergen in that place where machines hissed and bleeped as they sustained fragile life.

'Responding to the antibiotics, thankfully.' Tamara blew her nose. The same sharp, triangular nose as her father. Turned to George. 'I didn't want to believe he'd ditched me on my wedding day. Dad's a good man. But he forgets. Gets obsessed and ends up in this little bubble. He makes bad decisions.' She reached over and took her father's hand into hers. Stroked the dried blood that had turned to

420

black powder. 'You know he's been in love with you for years?'

The directness of the revelation took George by surprise. She clasped the blanket close. Imagined van den Bergen in bed with Schwartz. Doing the things that lovers do, as they had. Only days before. It stung worse than her injuries. She thought about Letitia's cruelty and neglect. Danny's manipulation. Jez's violence. So many arseholes. And yet, van den Bergen had to be the exception, didn't he?

'I don't think he loves me. But I don't care. I just want him to pull through.'

Unexpectedly, Tamara let go of her father's hand and took hold of George's instead. 'He needs his girls to believe in him. You can believe in him, right?'

The cynic in George saw this offering of solidarity from a stranger as off key. But then she registered the glassy film of sorrow on Tamara's grey eyes, and recognised the loneliness of an only child. Perhaps Tamara needed the comfort of knowing there was someone else rooting for her dad. She opted to squeeze her hand, though it was unpleasantly clammy. 'Yes. Definitely. He's the most stubborn arsehole I've ever met. He's going to make it, without a doubt.'

She stood. Leaned over and kissed van den Bergen's forehead. His skin smelled of medicinal alcohol and unwashed hair.

'No kissing!' the nurse said. Stern-faced and disapproving. 'This is a clean ward. Keep your germs to yourself.'

'Too late,' George said. Her heart was buckling. She knew it could be the last time she saw her beloved friend alive. The nurse could go and fuck himself.

Feeling guilty that she was somehow upstaging Tamara's grief – as though van den Bergen's daughter had more of a legitimate claim to sorrow than his sometime lover – George took her leave. She saved her selfish tears until she was outside the intensive care unit. Then, let her own torment out. Imagining holding van den Bergen's broken body close to her, as she had during their time in Ramsgate. So much was still to pray for, and George was not a praying woman.

CHAPTER 91

Soho, London, later

'On your knees, you fucking spaghetti-guzzling scum,' Dermot Robinson said. His voice had a deathly calm to it. Venom distilled into those over-enunciated consonants.

Before him, two of the three Italians were trying to front it out, like they had some fucking mafia code of honour to uphold. Keeping their bruised and bleeding heads held high, though the pride should have been tortured out of them by now. Amazing what you could do in a sex dungeon, when you had all kinds of clamps, vices and spiked equipment to hand. They were strung up by manacles, attached to the basement wall by long, thick chains. Harsh lights recently used for filming, making them squint and sweat. Let them feel it was an interrogation. Nowhere to go but to the other side.

But the short one was still full of it. '*Vaffanculo!* You don't get to speak to us like that,' he said.

Dermot swiped him across the face with the riding crop he had dipped in vinegar for a little extra sting. 'Shut your fucking trap, you borlotti bean bastard. You're on *my* turf now. You came into *my* clubs. Creaming off *my* profit margin. Damaging *my* reputation. Murdered *my* manager and *my* actress.' He paced theatrically up and down in the dungeon.

It would have been easier just to have these two spivs whacked

422

somewhere further afield. Technically, he was shitting on his own doorstep. But there had been little time to react, once he'd got the call from Sharon.

She'd sounded like she had the winning lottery ticket. Nothing like a woman scorned. 'I'm telling you, Mr R. I'd recognise them anywhere. Swear to God. The Stockpot on Old Compton Street. I'm having a nice lunch with my sister, yeah? And them bastards walk in. Ordering stuff. Sitting around, eating like they ain't even got a care, when they know Soho's yours. Them murdering wankers got more front than Margate.'

When de Falco had been found dead; once the police had found Dermot's girl in that derelict industrial unit in Kent, lying abused and abandoned in her own filth to die; once rumours of some Mr Gera had started to spread like dry rot in the woodwork, he'd called the fixer. Agreed a price straight away. Put word out: anyone with information on those cunts, leading to their capture and execution, gets a reward. The fee for the fixer would be money well spent, of course. Professionals cost. The ten thousand reward was just a necessary tax on top of that.

And now, here they were. The Italians. On the trusty dungeon set used in many a BDSM flick. His bitches.

'What you did amounts to a serious attempt to fuck me in the arse,' he told them. Raising his voice, now. Spit flying everywhere. 'Nobody fucks with Dermot Robinson. I do the fucking around here.' He could feel his blood pressure rising. Marge would be on his case about that.

Dermot gave the sign to the big ugly bastard in his pay. The Porn King of Soho could not show weakness before his enemies. Didn't want his other subjects getting any big ideas. But the Porn King didn't wish to get his hands dirty either. He was strictly legit. Let the fixer fix it.

With a whistle, the fixer swung a baseball bat through the air. Once. Twice. Knocking the Italians to their knees. Blood spattering from the backs of their heads.

'Better. You're Catholic boys, aren't you?' Dermot said. 'Just like me. Now how's about you tell me who you work for? Think of it as your last confessional.' He patted the tripod that held the bright lights. 'That's not electricity, fellers. It's the heavenly light of the almighty. Speak up!' He cupped his hand to his ear.

The Italians had fallen to the floor, groaning. Dermot walked over to Gera and put his large foot on the man's cheek. Gera looked up at him with dazed eyes.

'I know you're just the rubbing rags. Who's the big wheel?'

Silence. *Niente.* These two-bit thugs weren't going to speak, even after the torture and the prospect of death looming over them. Fucking waste of time.

He turned to the fixer. 'Put a couple of bullets in them. Leave them somewhere where they'll be found. But not on my patch. Right?'

Walking up the stairs with the gunshots ringing in his ears, he dialled George's number. A long, foreign ringtone. Funny. He'd only seen her at de Falco's funeral the other day.

When she picked up, she sounded rough.

'Hello, love. Tell your aunty it's all sorted,' he said. 'She'll know what I mean. Listen, I'm calling about a special cleaning job I've got for you on one of my film sets. I'll pay you double.'

'Sorry, Mr Robinson,' she said. He liked the way she was so respectful. That was a girl who would go far. 'I can't. I'm not... er. There's someone coming.' A change in her voice that sounded like dread. 'I've got to go.'

Realising word would get out that her aunty had given up the whereabouts of the Italians, he was just about to warn her to watch her back when she cut him off.

CHAPTER 92

Berlin, Germany, 23 February

The maid made to slam the heavy door to the Charlottenburg villa, but Elvis shoved his shoe in the way, scuppering her attempt to shut them out.

'I told you, sir' she said in halting English. 'You cannot come in.' Wiping a hand covered in orange food mess on her otherwise spotless, starched apron. 'I am very busy.'

Marie stepped forward, thinking there might be some way of connecting with this woman. Perhaps she was frightened and alone. Berlin was hardly a crime-free city, and the rich were always targets for burglars, con artists and even kidnappers. She showed her ID again. 'I promise we're legitimate. Police from the Netherlands. See? We just want to talk about a missing child.'

There had been no paperwork in the Laren house files, showing the final destination of Magool's baby. Not in the filing cabinet in the garage. Not under the floorboards of Schwartz's office. In the recesses of Marie's orderly mind, she realised that if there were meticulous records available, showing everything from the payments to Erik at Rotterdam Port Authority for hacking-services-rendered, to invoices for medical advice to Skin Flicks and Scream Screen Productions, to an audit trail that tracked the purchase and sale of scores of harvested organs and fifteen newborn babies – all the children of cash-strapped illegal immigrant girls, who had succumbed to Ahlers' collusive offer of a discreet and safe delivery – it stood to reason that there would be paperwork on Magool's baby. Didn't it?

It was only after a twelve-hour shift, sifting through the files, that she had come across old deeds of sale for a villa in an expensive part of Berlin. 1970s. Registered to Schwartz' father, though the father had been dead for more than a decade. No deed of transfer to darling Veronica, Herr Doktor Schwartz' legatee. Strange. Who lived there?

Visiting the house had been Elvis' idea. The department was in such disarray with van den Bergen out of action and Hasselblad under investigation for sanctioning the arrest of Strietman, there was nobody around to protest if he and Marie were to slope off on a little unscheduled jaunt to Berlin. A snooping exercise, more on a whim than a bona fide hunch.

Now, they had flown for just over an hour, using departmental funds that had not been signed off, to stare at the unflinching, unfriendly face of a maid through a six-inch crack in the door.

'You could get into a lot of trouble if you don't speak to us,' Marie said. Wondered if the woman, who looked of Middle-Eastern descent, was legal. Perhaps she could threaten her with deportation. Any kind of manipulation would feel like a cheap trick, but Marie owed this to the boss; to the victims of whatever traffickers Schwartz had been working for; especially to Magool. 'We'll have to bring the Berlin police, madam. *Die Berliner Polizei. Verstehen Sie das?* Understand?'

Apparently, she understood.

The interior of the house was immaculate. Antiques. Persian rugs. Chandeliers. Modern art on the walls. But it had the air of a mausoleum about it. It smelled like it had not been renovated in twenty years or more. The place was a memorial to a time gone by – left unchanged by its owner and occupier, who was ostensibly the very dead Herr Dr Schwartz.

'What is your name, madam?' Elvis asked the maid.

'Hilal.' Her back was turned. She was leading them through to the kitchen, perhaps.

Walking down the hallway, open doors gave glimpses of sumptuous, dated salons beyond. Tall windows ushering light in. It was breathtaking and suffocating. A Miss Havisham of a house, Marie mused. But one of the doors was shut. She heard banging beyond it. Loud, adult voices talking to one another in a childish manner.

Marie's pulse thundered. Instincts screaming that closed doors signified secrets beyond. How to play it? If she asked to gain entry to the room, she was sure the maid would refuse. Banging. Still banging within. But not the sound of a workman. The sound of metal on plastic.

As Elvis followed close behind the maid, she hung back. Grasped the brass knob of the door, heart thudding. Breaking and entering of a sort. Sod it. Made as little noise as possible.

Inside the room there was a giant, flat screen television, attached to the wall – some kids' channel blaring out *Sesame Street*, overdubbed in German. Big Bird having a conversation with Oscar the Grouch in his trash can. In that room, the floor was carpeted with toys. Big ones. Small ones. Of every description. No expense spared. And there, strapped into a high chair, laughing hysterically at the Grouch, plastered in what seemed to be pasta and tomato sauce, bashing his spoon noisily onto the plastic tray, was a tiny boy. He couldn't have been more than eighteen months old. Two at a push. Turned to look quizzically at Marie. Big brown eyes and thick black lashes. Delicate-featured and dark-skinned. He was the living image of his dead mother, Magool.

427

CHAPTER 93

Amsterdam, hospital, later

'I wondered when you'd turn up,' George said, slipping her phone onto the nightstand. 'Took your time.'

Ad standing over her. Clutching a bunch of ugly orange chrysanthemums and dyed blue daisies in his mouth. At a time of the year where ranunculus and tulips were in season, he had chosen those. Typical. In his hands, he carried a cardboard box. Perhaps he had brought clothes. Good.

'Thanks for the flowers,' she said, pointing to a vase on the windowsill. 'They're lovely.'

He looked tense. Something around the eyes. They lacked the usual warmth. Was he still pissed off at her for stealing Jasper's car? Surely he'd read her text about the attempted murder of van den Bergen. That had to count for something in the way of an excuse.

Calm down. He's brought you the flowers. It must all be cool.

But she knew it wasn't cool at all. George had slept with van den Bergen. And it hadn't just been a furtive fumble between friends that she had instantly regretted – a heat-of-the-moment thing. She had planned for it; had meant every touch, every kiss. Every time van den Bergen had made her come, she had relished it deeply. Diving headlong into the sea of desire, guilt had been

428

a storm cloud hanging over a distant island on the horizon. She had resolved to worry about it another day.

Today that day had come. She had broken the trust between her and Ad. Deep within her lurked the conviction that she had fallen out of love with him. That she needed to end it not just because of her infidelity, but because it was no longer what she wanted.

'Is Jasper still sore over the car?' she asked.

Ad perched on the end of her bed. Hadn't taken his reefer jacket off. Cardboard box on the floor by his feet. Looked pale and pinched, as though he were sickening for something. 'What do you think?'

'The police's insurance will cover it. He'll get it repaired. Tell him I'm massively sorry.'

He nodded in silence.

'George, we need to talk,' Ad said. Haltingly. Hesitantly. Biting his lip, which was almost devoid of colour.

No kiss. No niceties. No, 'How are you doing?' Just a shit bunch of flowers, a face like the proverbial smacked arse and now this. He was going to tell her off.

She could feel a lecture coming her way. She hated lectures. Maybe she wasn't strong enough to end it yet, after all. At that moment, she just fancied a hug and a little unconditional love. She swallowed hard.

'Oh yeah? Sounds ominous.' Smiling. Treating him to that grin he always said was alluring.

He picked up the box. Set it on his knees. Opened the flaps. Sighed at the sight of the contents.

'What's up?' she asked, wincing as she tried to lean forward and see the cause of this dejected demeanour. Was he still sore about van den Bergen? He had said he'd forgiven her. 'You got me some clothes, before I freeze to death?

Fixing her with those soft brown eyes, now so hard. Disappointment that ran deep, leaching the happiness that had once come easily to him. 'All your things from my place. Everything's in this box. I can't take it any more, George.'

'But—'

'It's over.'

CHAPTER 94

Amsterdam, women's prison, 28 February

In the dismal, cramped isolation of solitary confinement, where she had been put for her own safety, Veronica thought about the forthcoming trial. She knew she would be branded a crime against nature. A killer of the vulnerable. A seller of babies.

Maybe she was.

She had failed to save Mama's life all those years ago. Her donated bone marrow had been inadequate, heightening Mama's pain; speeding her demise. All she had ever wanted was to win her love. To save her. To reverse time.

Giving a second chance to the sick and needy was the closest she could come to bringing Mama back. Selling the organs of those who didn't count to those who were too desperate to wait their turn in agony. Selling babies to people who wanted nothing more than to lavish love on a child. It meant, at least, there would be fewer children like her in the world.

Unwanted. Unappreciated. Just like her.

Bitch. She had never really wanted to save Mama. How she'd loved to have sliced open that evil snake with her scalpel and ripped out that ice cold heart. Fuck you, Mama. Fuck all those beatings you dished up over the years and the toxic torment that rolled off your forked tongue so easily. And fuck you, Papa. The dirt-poor boy-made-good who despised the great unwashed, once his surgically lifted butt was sitting pretty on top of Mama's money mountain. He had given as much of a shit about his own daughter as he did about the needy and vulnerable. And now, his daughter was so much like him. And yet, so different.

The love. The hate. The anger. They effervesced inside her. A confused, tormented mess. Only acts of simultaneous violence and nurture seemed to calm the storm. This was what her parents had turned her into. This was what Silas had made her.

Curled up into the foetal position on her narrow cot, Veronica thought about her lot. Wept openly. Sobbing for the first time in years; perhaps since childhood. She had tried to right the wrongs done to her by being the best mother she could to little Silas. The moment she had seen Magool's beautiful boy, she had known she would not part with him. He was so tiny. So perfect. So pure. And yet, motherhood had not come naturally to her, as she had hoped it would. Though she had lavished material things on her son, though he had the motherly bosom of Hilal to cleave to, she had felt the same strange detachment from the child perhaps as her father had from her. Now, she would never see beautiful little Silas again. He would be fostered out and then put up for adoption. Ripped from her life, as he had been ripped from his mother's belly in return for a couple of thousand euros.

She had nothing left, now. Silas, *the son*, was gone. Her liberty would be taken away. Everyone would forget that she had lived her life as a pillar of the community and a physician of repute. All that would be left would be filthy newsprint, where the ink would never wash off, branding her as nothing more than a psychopathic serial murderer.

She still clutched the letter that the English criminologist had brought her in prison. A prune-faced woman with ugly spectacles called Dr Sally Wright. Connected in some way to that beastly midget, Georgina McKenzie. Who the fuck was Dr Sally Wright, with her nicotine-stained teeth and her bad breath, to bring her mail from Silas, *the man*? A man she had been so intimately entangled with, that she had finally agreed to take his leg as payment for her freedom. Now, here was a strange woman in ugly glasses, brandishing the envelope like a bribe, as she asked if she, the great Frau Doktor Veronica Schwartz, would consent to becoming a research subject once the trial was over? Unbelievable!

At first mention of Silas' name, her heart had leaped, she admitted. The thought that he had been thinking about her during her predicament was cheering. Gave her hope. But then, she read the letter. It wasn't even addressed to her! It was a photocopy of an outpouring he had written to that slut, McKenzie. An accusation of treachery. Talk of bringing things full circle. She felt like she had been little more than a pawn in the chess game that was Silas Holm's miserable, corrupt, stunted life. The love she had been denied by her parents had left an aching, gaping chasm inside her. He had always known that. She had thought Silas Holm's love would fill that hole. He had *promised* her it would, and it hadn't. Now, he talked of her victims as empty vessels. But it was he who had stripped her clean. She was the empty vessel now.

Checkmate, you bastard. Checkmate.

CHAPTER 95

Amsterdam, the Cracked Pot Coffee Shop, then, the hospital, later

'It's so spartan,' Sally said, peering into the kitchenette, which had been emptied out of George's bits and scrubbed until it was clinically clean. 'How have you managed, living here?' She wrinkled her nose at the sun-bleached, old-fashioned curtains.

'I lived here for a full year, remember?' George said, zipping up the suitcase that lay on the bed, stripped of its bedding. 'It's fine. It's just been a temporary measure since me and Ad...'

She sighed. Felt a pang of regret in her heart. It was the end of a long, hard journey. The end of the road for so many things. And here she was. In a bedsit above the Cracked Pot Coffee Shop. Back to the beginning.

'Check that view, though,' she said, advancing to the window and peering out so that Sally could not see her tears. 'I always loved those rooftops.'

She felt Sally's hand on her shoulder. Her bony fingers massaging her through her jumper as a gesture of solidarity.

'Got a ciggy?' George asked, sniffing. Wiping her eyes furtively. Staring into the spring sunshine, hoping Sally wouldn't judge her.

They lit up together and hung out of the open window, blowing their smoke into the crisp morning sunshine. Watching the flow

434

of tourists beneath them, filing to and fro alongside the canal. Prostitutes perched on their bar stools in the red-lit booths opposite. Bored-looking women who switched on their dazzling smiles like UV lights every time a man walked past, snatching a glance at this forbidden fruit.

'I love this crazy place,' George said. 'Pity I have to leave. But I've nothing to stay for, now.'

'I'm so sorry,' Sally said, flicking her ash into the moss-blocked gutter. 'You've been through so much. For all you're an utter pain in the arse, dear, you've been fiendishly brave. It must be very hard.'

Tears started to trickle in determined rivulets down the sides of George's face. She could feel her mouth buckle. Felt embarrassed by the show of weakness. Wiped hard at the snot with her sleeve, as though she resented it. Not caring about the mess. She mustn't cry.

'I wanted to stay. Until they decide to switch the machines off. But Tamara won't let them. It could go on indefinitely.'

Sally inhaled deeply. Toyed with her red beads, as though she was saying a rosary silently to herself. 'Poor, poor man.'

George's bullet wound ached. Pricking inside her chest. She felt guilty and resentful that she should still be standing, while van den Bergen lay in his impenetrable dreamworld. She hoped that his dreams were, at least, good ones.

'Come on,' Sally said, checking her watch. 'We'll miss our flight.'

Taking her leave from Jan, Katja and Inneke, George promised to visit. There would always be a piece of her in this building, after all. On the journey to Schiphol airport, she wondered if her heart would ever mend. At the check-in desk, she felt certain she would never laugh again. That she would carry the heavy millstone of her misery for the rest of her life.

And then, her phone rang. It was Tamara. Crying almost to the point of being unintelligible.

'Oh, George. I'm so sorry. You've got to come to the hospital straight away. It's Dad.'

Leaving Sally standing with their baggage, George ran straight back to the train station. Headed for the hospital. No time to spare. Tamara hadn't elaborated, but George was certain from the tears that they were switching her friend's life support off. It would be her last chance to say goodbye. She couldn't bear it, but she would regret it for the rest of her life if she didn't see that misanthropic, cantankerous, wonderful fool one last time.

Running down corridors, through automatic doors. She had to get to him. Had to see this through.

Hesitated at the entrance to intensive care. *Fuck it. Do this.* She rubbed alcohol gel into her hands and pushed her way inside. There, in the middle bed, was van den Bergen. Still wires going in. Wires coming out of his skin. But no mask over his face. They had already stopped his oxygen. No Tamara. Only an austere-looking doctor in a three piece suit, reading the clipboard from the end of his bed.

George threw herself into the seat at the side of van den Bergen. Her face, cold with fear. His large hand in her small hand, fever-ishly warm.

'Oh, Paul,' she said. 'Don't leave me, you big lanky arsehole.' Her voice wavered, burdened by the grief of letting go. 'Please God, don't let this be the end.'

And though the doctor was standing there, perhaps judging her frailty, eavesdropping on her supplication to a God she had long since parted company with, George wept openly. She wanted to be punished. She deserved to suffer. She had walked this man whom she loved so dearly straight into the valley of the shadow of death. And she had left him there. Alone.

Now, George offered her tears heaven-wards as a show of remorse. Willing her rotten, broken heart to stop beating. An eye for an eye. Perhaps, then, a life for a life. Praying that her star-crossed lover would wake, for never was a story more of woe, than this of Juliet and her ageing Romeo.

Wishing she had never ruined this man.

Wishing he had more to show from half a lifetime lived hard than shattered dreams and a dying body.

Wishing she had never broken the rules.

Acknowledgements

The response to *The Girl Who Wouldn't Die* has been wonderful. When the e-book hit the virtual shelves in April 2015, I had no idea that George McKenzie's and Paul van den Bergen's adventures would be so popular with readers and critically so well-received, let alone that they would go on to win a Dead Good Reader Award and feature in Amazon's top 100 bestseller list for weeks! So I'd like to take this opportunity to thank the readers, my friends, my fellow crime authors, supporters in the children's writing world – especially Carnegie Medal Winner, Tanya Landman, who let me take her name in vain - the tremendous book-bloggers, reviewers – a special thanks to Euro-noir critic, Barry Forshaw, who provided me with a glowing quote for my debut at short notice - and members of book clubs – particularly THE Book Club on Facebook - who have all got behind both George and me.

While I was in the midst of debut-launch mayhem, however, I was penning *The Girl Who Broke the Rules*. The book is a complex one and wouldn't have come together without the help of the following people:

Christian, Natalie, Adam and my Mum, who put up with my glazed looks, as I ruminated over plot, tricky extended metaphors and dialogue. They listened to my constant noise about rankings, reviews and deadlines. My mother-in-law, Svea, who has been a fabulous advocate of my writing amongst the seriously savvy Scandi ladies. Thanks always to you all!

My agent, Caspian Dennis at Abner Stein, who has provided cast-iron professional support and a great deal of pastoral care and friendship at a very difficult time in my life. Special thanks to him and to his brilliant Abner Stein team.

My Avon publisher, Eli Dryden who has got behind me and the series. I'm hugely grateful for her belief in me, so thanks! Thanks too to Helen Huthwaite, who was my interim editor, and to my new editor, Kate Ellis for managing the launch of this second novel. The Avon backroom staff members who do marketing and computing acts of strange genius are fab, as is the Lightbrigade PR gang, and though she's jumped ship, that Katy Loftus did a cracking job on editing *The Girl Who Broke the Rules*, so thanks to those wonderful folks too.

Kirstine Szifris at Cambridge University's Institute of Criminology and Dr. Hannah Quirk at Manchester University's School of Law, who gave me all the wonderful details I needed to bring George to life as a criminologist. Thanks, you fab women! And a big ta to my mate, Dr. Martin Pool who put me in touch with Hannah.

Dr. Zoe Adams-Strump for shooting the breeze with me over all sorts of medical matters, for trying to arrange a viewing of an autopsy and for giving me the confidence to stick with my idea for an endocrinology sub-plot – not everyone's idea of scintillating, maybe, but that's how I roll. Thanks, Zoe! You're a brill neighbour. One day I *will* get to observe that post-mortem!

To my word-posse, Steph Williams, Wendy Storer, Ann Giles and The Cockblankets (you know who you are) – thanks for keeping my head reasonably straight! And finally, a big whoop for Helen Smith who masterminded the BritCrime festival, of which I am immensely proud to have been a part.

Enjoyed *The Girl Who* series? Get your hands on the fifth gripping thriller in the George McKenzie series.

Available now.

How far would you go to protect your empire?

A heart-stopping read with a gritty edge, perfect for fans of
Martina Cole and Kimberley Chambers.